Praise for *New York Times* bestselling author B.J. Daniels

"Daniels is truly an expert at Western romantic suspense."

—*RT Book Reviews* on *Atonement*

"B.J. Daniels is a sharpshooter; her books hit the target every time."

—#1 *New York Times* bestselling author Linda Lael Miller

"Daniels is a perennial favorite on the romantic suspense front, and I might go as far as to label her the cowboy whisperer."

—*BookPage*

Praise for author Nicole Helm

"An intimate, rewarding romance with a hot hero whose emotional growth is as sexy as his moves in the bedroom."

—*Kirkus Reviews* on *Want You More*

"Nicole Helm has done a great job of writing three-dimensional characters... A super beginning to this series. I look forward to the next book in the series, *Wyoming Cowboy Protection*."

—*Harlequin Junkie* on *Wyoming Cowboy Justice*

UNDER THREAT

NEW YORK TIMES BESTSELLING AUTHOR

B.J. DANIELS

Previously published as *Steel Resolve*
and *Stone Cold Texas Ranger*

Recycling programs for this product may not exist in your area.

ISBN-13: 978-1-335-40637-8

Under Threat
First published as Steel Resolve in 2019.
This edition published in 2021.
Copyright © 2019 by Barbara Heinlein

Stone Cold Texas Ranger
First published in 2016. This edition published in 2021.
Copyright © 2016 by Nicole Helm

This edition published by arrangement with Harlequin Books S.A.

For questions and comments about the quality of this book, please contact us at CustomerService@Harlequin.com.

Harlequin Enterprises ULC
22 Adelaide St. West, 40th Floor
Toronto, Ontario M5H 4E3, Canada
www.Harlequin.com

Printed in U.S.A.

CONTENTS

B.J. Daniels is a *New York Times* and *USA TODAY* bestselling author. She wrote her first book after a career as an award-winning newspaper journalist and author of thirty-seven published short stories. She lives in Montana with her husband, Parker, and three springer spaniels. When not writing, she quilts, boats and plays tennis. Contact her at bjdaniels.com, on Facebook or on Twitter, @bjdanielsauthor.

Books by B.J. Daniels

Harlequin Intrigue

Whitehorse, Montana: The Clementine Sisters

Hard Rustler
Rogue Gunslinger
Rugged Defender

The Montana Cahills

Cowboy's Redemption

HQN

Sterling's Montana

Stroke of Luck
Luck of the Draw

The Montana Cahills

Renegade's Pride
Outlaw's Honor
Hero's Return
Rancher's Dream

Visit the Author Profile page at Harlequin.com for more titles.

STEEL
RESOLVE

B.J. Daniels

This one is for Terry Scones,
who always brightens my day. I laugh when
I recall a quilt shop hop we made across Montana.
She was the navigator when my GPS system
tried to send us through a barn.

Chapter 1

The moment Fiona found the letter in the bottom of Chase's sock drawer, she knew it was bad news. Fear squeezed the breath from her as her heart beat so hard against her rib cage that she thought she would pass out. Grabbing the bureau for support, she told herself it might not be what she thought it was.

But the envelope was a pale lavender, and the handwriting was distinctly female. Worse, Chase had kept the letter a secret. Why else would it be hidden under his socks? He hadn't wanted her to see it because it was from that other woman.

Now she wished she hadn't been snooping around. She'd let herself into his house with the extra key she'd had made. She'd felt him pulling away from her the past few weeks. Having been here so many times before, she was determined that this one wasn't going to break her heart. Nor was she going to let another woman take him from her. That's why she had to find out why he hadn't called, why he wasn't returning her messages, why he was avoiding her.

They'd had fun the night they were together. She'd felt as if they had something special, although she knew the next morning that he was feeling guilty. He'd said he didn't want to lead her on. He'd told her that there was some woman back home he was still in love with. He'd said their night together was a mistake. But he was wrong, and she was determined to convince him of it.

What made it so hard was that Chase was a genuinely nice guy. You didn't let a man like that get away. The other woman had. Fiona wasn't going to make that mistake even though he'd been trying to push her away since that night. But he had no idea how determined she could be, determined enough for both of them that this wasn't over by a long shot.

It wasn't the first time she'd let herself into his apartment when he was at work. The other time, he'd caught her and she'd had to make up some story about the building manager letting her in so she could look for her lost earring.

She'd snooped around his house the first night they'd met—the same night she'd found his extra apartment key and had taken it to have her own key made in case she ever needed to come back when Chase wasn't home.

The letter hadn't been in his sock drawer that time.

That meant he'd received it since then. Hadn't she known he was hiding something from her? Why else would he put this letter in a drawer instead of leaving it out along with the bills he'd casually dropped on the table by the front door?

Because the letter was important to him, which meant that she had no choice but to read it.

Her heart compressed into a hard knot as she carefully lifted out the envelope. The handwriting made her pulse begin to roar in her ears. The woman's handwriting was very neat, very precise. She hated her immediately. The return address confirmed it. The letter was from the woman back in Montana that Chase had told her he was still in love with.

Mary Cardwell Savage, the woman who'd broken Chase's heart and one of the reasons that the cowboy had ended up in Arizona. Her friend Patty told her all about him. Chase worked for her husband, Rick. That's how she and Chase had met, at a party at their house.

What struck her now was the date on the postmark. Her vision blurred for a moment. *Two weeks ago?* Anger flared inside her again. That was right after their night together. About the same time that he'd gotten busy and didn't have time, he said, to date or even talk. What had this woman said in her letter? Whatever it was, Fiona knew it was the cause of the problem with her and Chase.

Her fingers trembled as she carefully opened the envelope flap and slipped out the folded sheet of pale lavender paper. The color alone made her sick to her stomach. She sniffed it, half expecting to smell the woman's perfume.

There was only a faint scent, just enough to be disturbing. She listened for a moment, afraid Chase might come home early and catch her again. He'd been angry the last time. He would be even more furious if he caught her reading the letter he'd obviously hidden from her.

Unfolding the sheet of paper she tried to brace herself. She felt as if her entire future hung on what was inside this envelope.

Her throat closed as she read the words, devouring them as quickly as her gaze could take them in. After only a few sentences, she let her gaze drop to the bottom line, her heart dropping with it: *I'll always love you, Mary.*

This was the woman Chase said he was still in love with. She'd broken up with him and now she wanted him back? Who did this Mary Savage of Big Sky, Montana, think she was? Fury churned inside Fiona as she quickly read all the way through the letter, the words breaking her heart and filling her with an all-consuming rage.

Mary Savage had apparently pretended that she was only writing to Chase to let him know that some friend of his mother's had dropped by with a package for him. If he confirmed his address, she'd be happy to send the package if he was interested.

But after that, the letter had gotten personal. Fiona stared at the words, fury warring with heartbreaking pain. The package was clearly only a ruse for the rest of the letter, which was a sickening attempt to lure him back. This woman was still in love with Chase. It made her sick to read the words that were such an obvious effort to remind him of their love, first love, and all that included. This woman had history with Chase. She missed him and regretted the way they'd left things. The woman had even included her phone number. In case he'd forgotten it?

Had Chase called her? The thought sent a wave of nausea through her, followed quickly by growing vehemence. She couldn't believe this. *This woman was not taking Chase away from her!* She wouldn't allow it. She and Chase had only gotten started, but Fiona knew that he was perfect for her and she for him. If anyone could help him get over this other woman, it was her. Chase was hers now. She would just have to make him see that.

Fiona tried to calm herself. The worst thing she could do was to confront Chase and demand to know why he had kept this from her. She didn't need him to remind her that they didn't have "that kind" of relationship as he had the other times. Not to mention how strained things had been between them lately. She'd felt him pulling away and had called and stopped by at every opportunity, afraid she was losing him.

And now she knew why. If the woman had been in Arizona, she would have gone to her house and— Deep breaths, she told herself. She had to calm down. She had to remember what had happened the last time. She'd almost ended up in jail.

Taking deep breaths, she reminded herself that this woman was no threat. Mary Cardwell Savage wasn't in Arizona. She lived in Montana, hundreds of miles away.

But that argument did nothing to relieve her wrath or her growing apprehension. Chase hadn't just kept the letter. He'd *hidden* it. His little *secret*. And worse, he was avoiding her, trying to give her the brush-off. She felt herself hyperventilating.

She knew she had to stop this. She thought of how good things had been between her and Chase that first night. The cowboy was so incredibly sexy, and he'd remarked how lovely she looked in her tailored suit and heels. He'd complimented her long blond hair as he unpinned it and let it fall around her shoulders. When he'd looked into her green eyes, she hadn't needed him to tell her that he loved her. She had seen it.

The memory made her smile. And he'd enjoyed what she had waiting for him underneath that suit—just as she knew he would. They'd both been a little drunk that night. She'd had to make all the moves, but she hadn't minded.

Not that she would ever admit it to him, but she'd set her sights on him the moment she'd seen him at the party. There was something about him that had drawn her. A vulnerability she recognized. He'd been hurt before. So had she, too many times to count. She'd told herself that the handsome cowboy didn't know just how perfect he was, perfect for her.

Fiona hadn't exactly thrown herself at him. She'd just been determined to make him forget that other woman by making herself indispensable. She'd brought over dinner the next night. He'd been too polite to turn her away. She'd come up with things they could do together: baseball games, picnics, movies. But the harder she'd tried, the more he'd made excuses for why he couldn't go with her.

She stared down at the letter still in her hands, wanting to rip it to shreds, to tear this woman's eyes out, to—

Suddenly she froze. Was that the door of the apartment opening? It was. Just as she'd feared, Chase had come home early.

At the sound of the door closing and locking, she hurriedly refolded the letter, slipped it back into the envelope and shoved it under his socks. She was trapped. There was no way to get out of the apartment without him seeing her. He was going to be upset with her. But the one thing she couldn't let Chase know was that she'd found and read the letter. She couldn't give him an excuse to break things off indefinitely, even though she knew he'd been trying to do just that for the past couple of weeks—ever since he'd gotten that letter.

She hurried to the bedroom door, but hesitated. Maybe she should get naked and let him find her lying on his bed. She wasn't sure she could pull that off right now. Standing there, she tried to swallow back the anger, the hurt, the fear. She couldn't let him know what she was feeling—let alone how desperate she felt. But as she heard him coming up the stairs, she had a terrifying thought.

What if she'd put the letter back in the drawer wrong? Had she seen the woman's handwriting on the envelope? Wasn't that why she'd felt such a jolt? Or was it just seeing the pale lavender paper of the envelope in his sock drawer that had made her realize what it was?

She couldn't remember.

But would Chase remember how he'd left it and know that she'd seen it? Know that if she'd found it, she would read it?

She glanced back and saw that she hadn't closed the top dresser drawer all the way. Hurrying back over to it, she shut the drawer as quietly as possible and was about to turn when she heard him in the doorway.

"Fiona? What the hell?" He looked startled at first when he saw her, and then shock quickly turned to anger.

She could see that she'd scared him. He'd scared her too. Her heart was a drum in her chest. She was clearly rattled. She could feel the fine mist of perspiration on her upper lip. With one look, he would know something was wrong.

But how could she not be upset? The man she'd planned to marry had kept a letter from his ex a secret from her. Worse, the woman he'd been pining over when Fiona had met him was still in love with him—and now he knew it. Hiding the letter proved that he was at least thinking about Mary Cardwell Savage.

"What are you doing here?" Chase demanded, glancing around as if the answer was in the room. "How the hell did you get in *this* time?"

She tried to cover, letting out an embarrassed laugh. "You startled me. I was looking for my favorite lipstick. I thought I might have left it here."

He shook his head, raking a hand through his hair. "You have to stop this. I told you last time. Fiona—" His blue gaze swept past her to light on the chest of drawers.

Any question as to how he felt about the letter was quickly answered by his protective glance toward the top bureau drawer and the letter from his first love, the young woman who'd broken his tender heart, the woman he was still in love with.

Her own heart broke, shattering like a glass thrown against a wall. She wanted to kill Mary Cardwell Savage.

"Your lipstick?" He shook his head. "Again, how did you get in here?"

"You forgot to lock your door. I came by hoping to catch your building manager so he could let me in again—"

"Fiona, stop lying. I talked to him after the last time. He didn't let you in." The big cowboy held out his hand. "Give it to me."

She pretended not to know what he was talking about, blinking her big green eyes at him in the best innocent look she could muster. She couldn't lose this man. She wouldn't. She did the only thing she could. She reached into her pocket and pulled out the key. "I can explain."

"No need," he said as he took the key.

She felt real tears of remorse fill her eyes. But she saw that he was no longer affected by her tears. She stepped to him to put her arms around his neck and pulled him down for a kiss. Maybe if she could draw him toward the bed…

"Fiona, stop." He grabbed her wrists and pulled them from around his neck. *"Stop!"*

She stared at him, feeling the happy life she'd planned crumbling under her feet.

He groaned and shook his head. "You need to leave."

"Sure," she said and, trying to get control of her emotions, started to step past him. "Just let me look in one more place for my lipstick. I know I had it—"

"No," he said, blocking her way. "Your lipstick isn't here and we both know it. Just like your phone wasn't here the last time you stopped by. This has to stop. I don't want to see you again."

"You don't mean that." Her voice broke. "Is this about the letter from that bitch who dumped you?"

His gaze shot to the bureau again. She watched his expression change from frustrated to furious. "You've been going through my things?"

"I told you, I was looking for my lipstick. I'm sorry I found the letter. You hadn't called, and I thought maybe it was because of the letter."

He sighed, and when he spoke it was as if he was talking to a small unruly child. "Fiona, I told you from the first night we met that I wasn't ready for another relationship. You caught me at a weak moment, otherwise nothing would have happened between the two of us. I'd had too much to drink, and my boss's wife insisted that I let you drive me back to my apartment." He groaned. "I'm not trying to make excuses for what happened. We are both adults. But I was honest with you." He looked pained, his blue eyes dark. "I'm sorry if you thought that that night was more than it was. But now you have to leave and not come back."

"We can't be over! You have to give me another chance." She'd heard the words before from other men, more times than she wanted to remember. "I'm sorry. I was wrong to come here when you weren't home. I won't do anything like this again. I promise."

"Stop!" he snapped. "You're not listening. Look," he said, lowering his voice. "You might as well know that I'm leaving at the end of the week. My job here is over."

"Leaving?" This couldn't be happening. "Where are you going?" she cried, and felt her eyes widen in alarm. "You're going back to Montana. *Back to her.* Mary Cardwell Savage." She spit out the words as if they were stones that had been lodged in her throat.

He shook his head. "I told you the night we met that there was no chance of me falling for another woman because I was still in love with someone else."

She sneered at him. "She broke your heart. She'll do it again. Don't let her. She's nobody." She took a step toward him. "I can make you happy if you'll just give me a chance."

"Fiona, please go before either of us says something we'll regret," Chase said in a tone she'd never heard from him before. He was shutting her out. For good.

If he would only let her kiss him... She reached for

him, thinking she could make him remember what they had together, but he pushed her back.

"Don't." He was shaking his head, looking at her as if horrified by her. There was anguish in his gaze. But there was also pity and disgust. That too she'd seen before. She felt a dark shell close around her heart.

"You'll be sorry," she said, feeling crushed but at the same time infused with a cold, murderous fury.

"I should have never have let this happen," Chase was saying. "This is all my fault. I'm so sorry."

Oh, he didn't know sorry, but he would soon enough. He would rue this day. And if he thought he'd seen the last of her, he was in for a surprise. That Montana hayseed would have Chase over her dead body.

Chapter 2

"I feel terrible that I didn't warn you about Fiona," his boss said on Chase's last day of work. Rick had insisted on buying him a beer after quitting time.

Now in the cool dark of the bar, Chase looked at the man and said, "So she's done this before?"

Rick sighed. "She gets attached if a man pays any attention to her in the least and can't let go, but don't worry, she'll meet some other guy and get crazy over him. It's a pattern with her. She and my wife went to high school together. Patty feels sorry for her and keeps hoping she'll meet someone and settle down."

Chase shook his head, remembering his first impression of the woman. Fiona had seemed so together, so…normal. She sold real estate, dressed like a polished professional and acted like one. She'd come up to him at a barbecue at Rick's house. Chase hadn't wanted to go, but his boss had insisted, saying it would do him good to get out more.

He'd just lost his mother. His mother, Muriel, had been sick for some time. It was one of the reasons he'd come to Arizona in the first place. The other was that he knew he could find work here as a carpenter. Muriel had made him promise that when she died, he would take her ashes back to Montana. He'd been with her at the end, hoping that she would finally tell him the one thing she'd kept from him all these years. But she hadn't. She'd taken her secret to the grave and left him with more questions than answers—and an urn full of her ashes.

"You need to get out occasionally," Rick had said when Chase left work to go pick up the urn from the mortuary. It was in a velvet bag. He'd stuffed it behind the seat of his pickup on the way to the barbecue.

"All you do is work, then hide out in your apartment not to be seen again until you do the same thing the next day," Rick had argued. "You might just have fun and I cook damned good barbecue. Come on, it's just a few friends."

He'd gone, planning not to stay longer than it took to drink a couple of beers and have some barbecued ribs. He'd been on his second beer when he'd seen her. Fiona stood out among the working-class men and women at the party because she'd come straight from her job at a local real estate company.

She wore high heels that made her long legs look even longer. Her curvaceous body was molded into a dark suit with a white blouse and gold jewelry. Her long blond hair was pulled up, accentuating her tanned throat against the white of her blouse.

He'd become intensely aware of how long it had been since he'd felt anything but anguish over his breakup with Mary and his mother's sickness, and the secret that she'd taken with her.

"Fiona Barkley," she'd said, extending her hand.

Her hand had been cool and dry, her grip strong. "Chase Steele."

She'd chuckled, her green eyes sparking with humor. "For real? A cowboy named Chase Steele?"

"My father was an extra in a bunch of Western movies," he lied since he had no idea who his father had been.

She cocked a brow at him. "Really?"

He shook his head. "I grew up on a ranch in Montana." He shrugged. "Cowboying is in my blood."

Fiona had taken his almost empty beer can from him and handed him her untouched drink. "Try that. I can tell that you need it." The drink had been strong and buzzed through his bloodstream.

Normally she wasn't the type of woman he gravitated toward. But she was so different from Mary, and it had been so long since he'd even thought about another woman. The party atmosphere, the urn behind his pickup seat and the drinks Fiona kept plying him with added to his what-the-hell attitude that night.

"How long have you two been dating?" Rick asked now in the cool dark of the bar.

"We never dated. I told her that first night that I was in love with someone else. But I made the mistake of sleeping with her. Sleeping with anyone given the way I feel about the woman back home was a mistake."

"So you told Fiona there was another woman." His boss groaned. "That explains a lot. Fiona now sees it as a competition between her and the other woman. She won't give up. She hates losing. It's what makes her such a great Realtor."

"Well, it's all moot now since I'm leaving for Montana."

Rick didn't look convinced that it would be that easy. "Does she know?"

He nodded.

"Well, hopefully you'll get out of town without any trouble."

"Thanks a lot."

"Sorry, but according to Patty, when Fiona feels the man pulling away… Well, it makes her a little…crazy."

Chase shook his head. "This just keeps getting better and better." He picked up his beer, drained it and got to his feet. "I'm going home to pack. The sooner I get out of town the better."

"I wish I could talk you out of leaving," Rick said. "You're one of the best finish carpenters I've had in a long time. I hope you're not leaving because of Fiona. Seriously, she'll latch on to someone else. I wouldn't worry about it. It's just Fiona being Fiona. Unless you're going back to this woman you're in love with?"

He laughed. "If only it were that easy. She's the one who broke it off with me." He liked Rick. But the man hadn't warned him about Fiona, and if Rick mentioned to Patty who mentioned to Fiona… He knew he was being overly cautious. Fiona wouldn't follow him all the way to Montana. She had a job, a condo, a life here. But still, he found himself saying, "Not sure what I'm doing. Might stop off in Colorado for a while."

"Well, good luck. And again, sorry about Fiona."

As he left the bar, he thought about Mary and the letter he'd hidden in his sock drawer with her phone number. He'd thought about calling her to let her know he was headed home. He was also curious about the package she'd said a friend of his mother had left for him.

Since getting the letter, he'd thought about calling dozens of times. But what he had to say, he couldn't in a phone call. He had to see Mary. Now that he was leaving, he couldn't wait to hit the road.

Mary Cardwell Savage reined in her horse to look out at the canyon below her. The Gallatin River wound through rugged cliffs and stands of pines, the water running clear over the colored rocks as pale green aspen leaves winked from the shore. Beyond the river and the trees, she could make out the resort town that had sprouted up across the canyon. She breathed in the cool air rich with the scent of pine and the crisp cool air rising off the water.

Big Sky, Montana, had changed so much in her lifetime and even more in her mother's. Dana Cardwell Savage had seen the real changes after the ski resort had been built at the foot of Lone Peak. Big Sky had gone from a ranching community to a resort area, and finally to a town with a whole lot of housing developments and businesses rising to the community's growing needs.

The growth had meant more work for her father, Marshal Hud Savage. He'd been threatening to retire since he said he no longer recognized the canyon community anymore. More deputies had to be hired each year because the area was experiencing more crime.

Just the thought of the newest deputy who'd been hired made her smile a little. Dillon Ramsey was the kind of man a woman noticed—even one who had given her heart away when she was fifteen and had never gotten it back.

Dillon, with his dark wavy hair and midnight black eyes, had asked her out, and she'd said she'd think about it. If her best friend Kara had been around, she would have thought Mary had lost her mind. Anyone who saw Dillon knew two things about him. He was a hunk, and he was dangerous to the local female population.

Since telling him she'd think about it, she had been mentally kicking herself. Had she really been sitting around waiting to hear from Chase? What was wrong with her? It had been weeks. When she'd broken it off and sent him packing, she hadn't been sitting around moping over him. Not really. She'd been busy starting a career, making a life for herself. So what had made her write that stupid letter?

Wasn't it obvious that if he'd gotten her letter, he should have called by now? Since the letter hadn't come back, she had to assume that it had arrived just fine. The fact that he hadn't called or written her back meant that he wasn't interested. He also must not be interested in the package his mother's friend had left for him either. It was high time to forget about that cowboy, and why not do it with Dillon Ramsey?

Because she couldn't quit thinking about Chase and hadn't been able to since she'd first laid eyes on him when they were both fifteen. They'd been inseparable all through high school and college. Four years ago he'd told her he was going to have to leave. They'd both been twenty-four, too young to settle down, according to her father and Chase had agreed. He needed to go find himself since not knowing who his father was still haunted him.

It had broken her heart when he'd left her—and Montana. She'd dated little after he left town. Mostly because she'd found herself comparing the men she had dated to Chase. At least with Dillon, she sensed a wild, dangerousness in him that appealed to her right now.

Her father hadn't liked hearing that Dillon had asked her out. "I wish you'd reconsider," he'd said when she'd stopped by Cardwell Ranch where she'd grown up. She'd bought her own place in Meadow Village closer to the center of town, and made the first floor into her office. On the third floor was her apartment where she lived. The second floor had been made into one-bedroom apartments that she rented.

But she still spent a lot of time on the ranch because that's where her heart was—her family, her horses and her love for the land. She hadn't even gone far away to college—just forty miles to Montana State University in Bozeman. She couldn't be far from Cardwell Ranch and couldn't imagine that she ever would. She was her mother's daughter, she thought. Cardwell Ranch was her legacy.

Dana Cardwell had fought for this ranch years ago when her brothers and sister had wanted to sell it and split the money after their mother died. Dana couldn't bear to part with the family ranch. Fortunately, her grandmother, Mary Cardwell, had left Dana the ranch in her last will, knowing Dana would keep the place in the family always.

Ranching had been in her grandmother's blood, the woman Mary had been named after. Just as it was in Dana's and now Mary's. Chase hadn't understood why she couldn't walk away from this legacy that the women in her family had fought so hard for.

But while her mother was a hands-on ranch woman, Mary liked working behind the scenes. She'd taken over the accounting part of running the ranch so her mother could enjoy what she loved—being on the back of a horse.

"What is wrong with Dillon Ramsey?" Dana Cardwell Savage had asked her husband after Mary had told them that the deputy had asked her out.

"He's new and, if you must know, there's something troublesome about him that I haven't been able to put my finger on yet," Hud had said.

Mary had laughed. She knew exactly what bothered her father about Dillon—the same thing that attracted her to the young cocky deputy. If she couldn't have Chase, then why not take a walk on the wild side for once?

She had just finished unsaddling her horse and was headed for the main house when her cell phone rang, startling her. Her pulse jumped. She dug the phone out and looked at the screen, her heart in her throat. It was a long-distance number and not one she recognized. Chase?

Sure took him long enough to finally call, she thought, and instantly found herself making excuses for him. Maybe he was working away from cell phone coverage. It happened all the time in Montana. Why not in Arizona? Or maybe her letter had to chase him down, and he'd just now gotten it and called the moment he read it.

It rang a second time. She swallowed the lump in her throat. She couldn't believe how nervous she was. Silly goose, she thought. It's probably not Chase at all but some telemarketer calling to try to sell her something.

She answered on the third ring. "Hello?" Her voice cracked.

Silence, then a female voice. "Mary Cardwell Savage?" The voice was hard and crisp like a fall apple, the words bitten off.

"Yes?" she asked, disappointed. She'd gotten her hopes up that it was Chase, with whatever excuse he had for not calling sooner. It wouldn't matter as long as he'd called to say that he felt the same way she did and always had. But she'd been right. It was just some telemarketer. "I'm sorry, but whatever you're selling, I'm not inter—"

"I read your letter you sent Chase."

Her breath caught as her heart missed a beat. She told herself that she'd heard wrong. "I beg your pardon?"

"Leave my fiancé alone. Don't write him. Don't call him. Just leave him the hell alone."

She tried to swallow around the bitter taste in her mouth. "Who is this?" Her voice sounded breathy with fear.

"The woman who's going to marry Chase Steele. If you ever contact him again—"

Mary disconnected, her fingers trembling as she dropped the phone into her jacket pocket as if it had scorched her skin. The woman's harsh low voice was still in her ears, furious and threatening. Whoever she was, she'd read the letter. No wonder Chase hadn't written or called. But why hadn't he? Had he shown the letter to his fiancée? Torn it up? Kept it so she found it? Did it matter? His fiancée had read the letter and was furious, and Mary couldn't blame her.

She buried her face in her hands. Chase had gone off to find himself. Apparently he'd succeeded in finding a fiancée as well. Tears burned her eyes. Chase was engaged and getting married. Could she be a bigger fool?

Chase had moved on, and he hadn't even had the guts to call and tell her.

Angrily, Mary wiped at her tears as she recalled the woman's words and the anger she'd heard in them. She shuddered, regretting more than ever that stupid letter she'd written. The heat of humiliation and mortification burned her cheeks. If only she hadn't poured her heart out to him. If only she had just written him about the package and left it at that. If only…

Unfortunately, she'd been feeling nostalgic the night she wrote that letter. Her mare was about to give birth so she was staying the night at the ranch in her old room. She'd come in from the barn late that night, and had seen the package she'd promised to let Chase know about. Not far into the letter, she'd become sad and regretful. Filled with memories of the two of them growing up together on the ranch from the age of fifteen, she'd decide to call him only to find that his number was no longer in service. Then she'd tried to find him on social media. No luck. It was as if he'd dropped off the face of the earth. Had something happened to him?

Worried, she'd gone online and found an address for him but no phone number. In retrospect, she should never have written the letter—not in the mood she'd been in. What she hated most since he hadn't answered her letter or called, was that she had written how much she missed him and how she'd never gotten over him and how she regretted their breakup.

She'd stuffed the letter into the envelope addressed to him and, wiping her tears, had left it on her desk in her old room at the ranch as she climbed into bed. The next morning before daylight her mother had called up to her room to say that the mare had gone into labor.

Forgetting all about the letter, she'd been so excited about the new foal that she'd put everything else out of her mind. By the time she remembered the letter, it was gone. Her aunt Stacy had seen it, put a stamp on the envelope and mailed it for her.

At first, Mary had been in a panic, expecting Chase to call as soon as he received the letter. She'd played the conversation in her head every way she thought possible, all but one of them humiliating. As days passed, she'd still held out hope. Now after more than two weeks and that horrible phone call, she knew it was really over and she had to accept it.

Still her heart ached. Chase had been her first love. Did anyone ever get over their first love? He had obviously moved on. Mary took another deep breath and tried to put it out of her mind. She loved summer here in the canyon. The temperature was perfect—never too cold or too hot. A warm breeze swayed the pine boughs and keeled over the tall grass in the pasture nearby. Closer a horse whinnied from the corral next to the barn as a hawk made a slow lazy circle in the clear blue overhead.

Days like this she couldn't imagine living anywhere else. She took another deep breath. She needed to get back to her office. She had work to do. Along with doing the ranch books for Cardwell Ranch, she had taken on work from other ranches in the canyon and built a lucrative business.

She would get over Chase or die trying, she told herself. As she straightened her back, her tears dried, and she walked toward her SUV. She'd give Deputy Dillon Ramsey a call. It was time she moved on. Like falling off a horse, she was ready to saddle up again. Forgetting Chase wouldn't be easy, but if anyone could help the process, she figured Dillon Ramsey was the man to do it.

Chapter 3

Chase was carrying the last of his things out to his pickup when he saw Fiona drive up. He swore under his breath. He'd hoped to leave without a scene. Actually, he'd been surprised that she hadn't come by sooner. As she was friends with Rick's wife, Patty, Chase was pretty sure she had intel into how the packing and leaving had been going.

He braced himself as he walked to his pickup and put the final box into the back. He heard Fiona get out of her car and walk toward him. He figured it could go several ways. She would try seduction or tears or raging fury, or a combination of all three.

Hands deep in the pockets of her jacket as she approached, she gave him a shy smile. It was that smile that had appealed to him that first night. He'd been vulnerable, and he suspected she'd known it. Did she think that smile would work again?

He felt guilty for even thinking that she was so calculating and yet he'd seen the way she'd worked him. "Fiona, I don't want any trouble."

"Trouble?" She chuckled. "I heard you were moving out today. I only wanted to come say goodbye."

Chase wished that was the extent of it, but he'd come to know her better than that. "I think we covered goodbye the last time we saw each other."

She ignored that. "I know you're still angry with me—"

"Fiona—"

Tears welled in her green eyes as if she could call them up at a moment's notice. "Chase, at least give me a hug goodbye. Please." Before he could move, she closed the distance between them. As she did, her hands came out of her jacket pockets. The blade of the knife in her right hand caught the light as she started to put her arms around his neck.

As he jerked back, he grabbed her wrist. "What the—" He cursed as he tightened his grip on her wrist holding the knife. She was stronger than she looked. She struggled to stab him as she screamed obscenities at him.

The look in her eyes was almost more frightening than the knife clutched in her fist. He twisted her wrist until she cried out and dropped the weapon. The moment it hit the ground, he let go of her, realizing he was hurting her.

She dived for the knife, but he kicked it away, chasing after it before she could pick it up again. She leaped at him, pounding on his back as she tried to drag him to the ground.

He threw her off. She stumbled and fell to the grass

and began to cry hysterically. He stared down at her. Had she really tried to kill him?

"Don't! Don't kill me!" she screamed, raising her hands as if she thought he was going to stab her. He'd forgotten that he'd picked up the knife, but he wasn't threatening her with it.

He didn't understand what was going on until he realized they were no longer alone. Fiona had an audience. Some of the apartment tenants had come out. One of them, an elderly woman, was fumbling with her phone as if to call the cops.

"Everything is all right," he quickly told the woman.

The older woman looked from Fiona to him and back. Her gaze caught on the knife he was holding at his side.

"There is no reason to call the police," Chase said calmly as he walked to the trash cans lined up along the street, opened one and dropped the knife into the bottom.

"That's my best knife!" Fiona yelled. "You owe me for that."

He saw that the tenant was now staring at Fiona, who was brushing off her jeans as she got to her feet.

"What are you staring at, you old crone? Go back inside before I take that phone away from you and stick it up your—"

"Fiona," Chase said as the woman hurriedly turned and rushed back inside. He shook his head as he gave Fiona a wide berth as he headed toward his apartment to lock up. "Go home before the police come."

"She won't call. She knows I'll come back here if she does."

He hoped Fiona was right about the woman not making the call. Otherwise, he'd be held up making a statement to the police—that's if he didn't end up behind bars. He didn't doubt that Fiona would lie through her teeth about the incident.

"She won't make you happy," Fiona screamed after him as he opened the door to his apartment, keeping an eye on her the whole time. The last thing he wanted was her getting inside. If she didn't have another weapon, he had no doubt she'd find one.

Stopping in the doorway, he looked back at her. Her makeup had run along with her nose. She hadn't bothered to wipe either. She looked small, and for a moment his heart went out to her. What had happened to that professional, together woman he'd met at the party?

"You need to get help, Fi."

She scoffed at that. "You're the one who needs help, Chase."

He stepped inside, closed and locked the door, before sliding the dead bolt. Who's to say she didn't have a half dozen spare keys made. She'd lied about the building manager opening the door for her. She'd lied about a lot of things. He had no idea who Fiona Barkley was. But soon she would be nothing more than a bad memory, he told himself as he finished checking to make sure he hadn't left anything. When he looked out, he saw her drive away.

Only then did he pick up his duffel bag, lock the apartment door behind him and head for his truck, anxious to get on the road to Montana. But as he neared his pickup, he saw what Fiona had left him. On the driver's-side window scrawled crudely in lipstick were the words *You'll regret it.*

That was certainly true. He regretted it already. He

wondered what would happen to her and feared for the next man who caught her eye. Maybe the next man would handle it better, he told himself.

Tossing his duffel bag onto the passenger seat, he pulled an old rag from under the seat and wiped off what he could of the lipstick. Then, climbing into this truck, he pointed it toward Montana and Mary, putting Fiona out of his mind.

There were days when Dana felt all sixty-two of her years. Often when she looked at her twenty-eight-year-old daughter, Mary, she wondered where the years had gone. She felt as if she'd merely blinked and her baby girl had grown into a woman.

Being her first and only daughter, Mary had a special place in her heart. So when Mary hurt, Dana did too. Ever since Chase and Mary had broken up and he'd left town, her daughter had been heartsick, and Dana had had no idea how to help her.

She knew that kind of pain. Hud had broken her heart years ago when they'd disagreed and he'd taken off. But he'd come back, and their love had overcome all the obstacles that had been thrown at them since. She'd hoped that Mary throwing herself into her accounting business would help. But as successful as Mary now was with her business, the building she'd bought, the apartments she'd remodeled and rented, there was a hole in her life—and her heart. A mother could see it.

"Sis, have you heard a word I've said?"

Dana looked from the window where she'd been watching Mary unsaddling her horse to where her brother sat at the kitchen table across from her. "Sorry. Did you just say *cattle thieves*?"

Jordan shook his head at her and smiled. There'd been a time when she and her brother had been at odds over the ranch. Fortunately, those days were long behind them. He'd often said that the smartest thing he'd ever done was to come back here, make peace and help Dana run Cardwell Ranch. She couldn't agree more.

"We lost another three head. Hud blames paleo diets," Jordan said, and picked up one of the chocolate chip cookies Dana had baked that morning.

"How many does this make?" she asked.

"There's at least a dozen gone," her brother said.

She looked to her husband who sat at the head of the table and had also been watching Mary out the window. Hud reached for another cookie. He came home every day for lunch and had for years. Today she'd made sandwiches and baked his favorite cookies.

"They're hitting at night, opening a gate, cutting out only a few at a time and herding them to the road where they have a truck waiting," the marshal said. "They never hit in the same part of any ranch twice, so unless we can predict where they're going to show up next... We aren't the only ones who've had losses."

"We could hire men to ride the fences at night," Jordan said.

"I'll put a deputy or two on the back roads for a couple of nights and see what we come up with," Hud said and, pushing away his plate and getting to his feet, shot Dana a questioning look.

Jordan, apparently recognizing the gesture, also got to his feet and excused himself. As he left, Hud said, "I know something is bothering you, and it isn't rustlers."

She smiled up at him. He knew her so well, her lover, her husband, her best friend. "It's Mary. Stacy told me earlier that she mailed a letter from Mary to Chase a few weeks ago. Mary hasn't heard back."

Hud groaned. "You have any idea what was in the letter?"

"No, but since she's been moping around I'd say she is still obviously in love with him." She shrugged. "I don't think she's ever gotten over him."

Her husband shook his head. "Why didn't we have all boys?"

"Our sons will fall in love one day and will probably have their heartbreaks as well." She had the feeling that Hud hadn't heard the latest. "She's going out with Deputy Dillon Ramsey tonight."

Hud swore and raked a hand through his graying hair. "I shouldn't have mentioned that there was something about him that made me nervous."

She laughed. "If you're that worried about him, then why don't you talk to her?"

Her husband shot her a look that said he knew their stubborn daughter only too well. "Tell her not to do something and damned if she isn't even more bound and determined to do it."

Like he had to tell her that. Mary was just like her mother and grandmother. "It's just a date," Dana said, hoping there wasn't anything to worry about.

Hud grumbled under his breath as he reached for his Stetson. "I have to get back to work." His look softened. "You think she's all right?"

Dana wished she knew. "She will be, given time. I think she needs to get some closure from Chase. His not answering her letter could be what she needed to move on."

"I hope not with Dillon Ramsey."

"Seriously, what is it about him that worries you?" Dana asked.

He frowned. "I can't put my finger on it. I hired him as a favor to his uncle down in Wyoming. Dillon's cocky and opinionated."

Dana laughed. "I used to know a deputy like that."

Hud grinned. "Point taken. He's also still green."

"I don't think that's the part that caught Mary's attention."

Her husband groaned. "I'd like to see her with someone with both feet firmly planted on the ground."

"You mean someone who isn't in law enforcement. Chase Steele wasn't."

"I liked him well enough," Hud said grudgingly. "But he hadn't sowed his wild oats yet. They were both too young, and he needed to get out of here and get some maturity under his belt, so to speak."

"She wanted him to stay and fight for her. Sound familiar?"

Hud's smile was sad. "Sometimes a man has to go out into the world, grow up, figure some things out." He reached for her hand. "That's what I did when I left. It made me realize what I wanted. You."

She stepped into his arms, leaning into his strength, thankful for the years they'd had together raising a family on this ranch. "Mary's strong."

"Like her mother."

"She'll be all right," Dana said, hoping it was true.

Chase was determined to drive as far as he could the first day, needing to put miles behind him. He thought of Fiona and felt sick to his stomach. He kept going over it in his head, trying to understand if he'd done anything to lead her on beyond that one night. He was clear with her that he was not in the market for anything serious. His biggest mistake though was allowing himself a moment of weakness when he'd let himself be seduced.

But before that he'd explained to her that he was in love with someone else. She said she didn't care. That she wasn't looking for a relationship. She'd said that she needed him that night because she'd had a bad day.

Had he really fallen for that? He had. And when she became obsessed, he'd been shocked and felt sorry for her. Maybe he shouldn't have.

He felt awful, and not even the miles he put behind him made him feel better. He wished he'd never left Montana, but at the time, leaving seemed the only thing to do. He'd worked his way south, taking carpenter jobs, having no idea where he was headed.

When he'd gotten the call from his mother to say she was dying and that she'd needed to see him, he'd quit his job, packed up and headed for Quartsite, Arizona, in hopes that his mother would finally give him the name.

Chase had never known who his father was. It was a secret his mother refused to reveal for reasons of her own. Once in Arizona, though, he'd realized that she planned to take that secret to her grave. On her death bed, she'd begged him to do one thing for her. Would he take her ashes back to Montana and scatter them in the Gallatin Canyon near Big Sky?

"That's where I met your father," she said, her voice weak. "He was the love of my life."

She hadn't given him a name, but at least he knew now that the man had lived in Big Sky at the time of Chase's conception. It wasn't much, but it was better than nothing.

* * *

He was in the middle of nowhere just outside of Searchlight, Nevada, when smoke began to boil out from under the pickup's hood. He started to pull over when the engine made a loud sound and stopped dead. As he rolled to stop, his first thought was: could Fiona have done something to his pickup before he left?

Anger filled him to overflowing. But it was another emotion that scared him. He had a sudden awful feeling that something terrible was going to happen to Mary if he didn't get to Montana. Soon. The feeling was so strong that he thought about leaving his pickup beside the road and thumbing a ride the rest of the way.

Chase tried to tamp down the feeling, telling himself that it was because of Fiona and what she'd done before he'd left when she'd tried to kill him, not to mention what she'd done to his pickup. The engine was shot. He'd have to get a new one and that was going to take a while.

That bad feeling though wouldn't go away. After he called for a tow truck, he dialed the Jensen Ranch, the closest ranch to Mary's. He figured if anyone would know how Mary was doing, it would be Beth Anne Jensen. She answered on the third ring. "It's Chase." He heard the immediate change in her voice and realized she was probably the wrong person to call, but it was too late. Beth Anne had liked him a little too much when he'd worked for her family and it had caused a problem between him and Mary.

"Hey Chase. Are you back in town?"

"No, I was just calling to check on Mary. I was worried about her. I figured you'd know how she's doing. Is everything all right with her?"

Beth Anne's tone changed from sugar to vinegar. "As far as I know everything is just great with her. Is that all you wanted to know?"

This was definitely a mistake. "How are you?"

"I opened my own flower shop. I've been dating a rodeo cowboy. I'm just fine, as if you care." She sighed. "So if you're still hung up on Mary, why haven't you come back?"

Stubbornness. Stupidity. Pride. A combination of all three. "I just had a sudden bad feeling that she might be in trouble."

Beth Anne laughed. "Could be, now that you mention it. My brother saw her earlier out with some young deputy. Apparently, she's dating him."

"Sounds like she's doing fine then. Thanks. You take care." He swore as he disconnected and put his worry about Mary out of his mind. She should be plenty safe dating a deputy, right? He gave his front tire a kick, then paced as he waited for the tow truck.

It had taken hours before the tow truck had arrived. By then the auto shop was closed. He'd registered at a motel, taken a hot shower and sprawled on the bed, furious with Fiona, but even more so with himself.

He'd known he had a serious problem when he'd seen the smoke roiling out from under the hood. When the engine seized up, he'd known it was blown before he'd climbed out and lifted the hood.

At first, he couldn't understand what had happened. The pickup wasn't brand-new, but it had been in good shape. The first thing he'd checked was the oil. That's when he'd smelled it. Bleach.

The realization had come in a flash. He'd thrown a

container of bleach away in his garbage just that morning, along with some other household cleaners that he didn't want to carry all the way back to Montana. He'd seen the bleach bottle when he'd tossed Fiona's knife into one of the trash cans at the curb.

Now, lying on the bed in the motel, Chase swore. He'd left Fiona out there alone with his pickup. He'd thought the only mischief she'd gotten up to was writing on his pickup window with lipstick. He'd underestimated her, and now it was going to cost him dearly. He'd have to have a new engine put in the truck, and that was going to take both money and time.

Three days later, while waiting in Henderson, Nevada for his new engine to be installed, he called Rick.

"Hey, Chase, great to hear from you. How far did you make it? I thought you might have decided to drive straight through all night."

"I broke down near Searchlight."

"Really? Is it serious?"

"I'm afraid so. The engine blew. I suspect Fiona put bleach in the oil."

Rick let out a curse. "That would seize up the engine."

"That's exactly what it did."

"Oh, man I am so sorry. Listen, I am beginning to feel like this is all my fault. Is there anything I can do? Where are you now? I could drive up there, maybe bring one of the big trailers. We could haul your pickup back down here. I know a mechanic—"

"I appreciate it, but I'm getting it fixed here in Henderson. That's not why I called."

"It's funny you should call," Rick said. "I was about

to call you, but I kept putting it off hoping to have better news."

His heart began to pound. "What's wrong?"

His former boss let out a dry chuckle. "We're still friends, right?"

"Right. I forgave you for Fiona if that's what you're worried about."

"You might change your mind after you hear what I have to tell you," Rick said. "I didn't want you to hear this on the news." He felt his stomach drop as he waited for the bad news. "Fiona apparently hasn't been at work since before you left. Patty went over to her place. Her car was gone and there was no sign of her. But she'd called Patty the night you left from a bar and was pretty wasted and incoherent. When Patty wasn't able to reach her in the days that followed, she finally went over to her condo. It appeared she hadn't been back for a few days." Chase swore. She wouldn't hurt herself, would she? She'd said he would regret it. He felt a sliver of fear race up his spine. As delusional as the woman was—

Rick cleared his voice. "This morning a fisherman found her car in the Colorado River."

His breath caught in his throat. "Is she…?"

"They're dragging the river for her body, but it's hard to say how far her body might have gone downstream. The river was running pretty high after the big thunderstorm they had up in the mountains a few days ago."

Chase raked a hand through his hair as he paced the floor of his motel room as he'd been doing for days now. "She threatened to do all kinds of things, but I never thought she'd do something like this."

"Before you jump to conclusions, the police think it could have been an accident. Fiona was caught on video leaving the club that night and appeared to be quite inebriated," Rick said. "Look, this isn't your fault. I debated even telling you. Fiona was irrational. My wife said she's feared that the woman's been headed for a violent end for a long time, you know?"

He nodded to himself as he stopped to look out the motel room window at the heat waves rising off desert floor and yearned for Montana. "Still I hate to think she might have done this on purpose because of me."

"She wasn't right in the head. Anyway, it was probably an accident. I'm sorry to call with this kind of news, but I thought you'd want to know. Once your pickup's fixed you'll be heading out and putting all of this behind you. Still thinking about going to Colorado? You know I'd love to have you back."

No reason not to tell him now. "I'm headed home as soon as the pickup's fixed, but thanks again for the offer."

"Home to Montana? You really never got over this woman, huh."

"No, I never did." He realized that when he thought of home, it was Mary he thought of. Her and the Gallatin Canyon. "It's where I grew up. Where I first fell in love."

"Well, I wish you luck. I hope it goes well."

"Thanks. If you hear anything else about Fiona—"

"I'll keep it to myself."

"No, call me. I really didn't know the woman. But I care about what happened to her." He thought of the first night he'd seen her, all dressed up in that dark suit and looking so strong and capable. And the other times when she'd stopped by his apartment looking as if she'd just come home from spring break and acting the part.

"It was like she was always changing before my eyes. I never knew who she was. I'm not sure she did."

He and Rick said goodbye again. Disconnecting, he pocketed his phone. He couldn't help wondering about Fiona's last moments underwater inside her car. Did she know how to swim? He had no idea. Was it too deep for her to reach the surface? Or had she been swept away?

Chase felt sad, but he knew there was no way he could have helped her. She wanted a man committed to her, and she deserved it. But as he'd told her that first night, he wasn't that man.

If only he had known how broken and damaged she was. He would have given her a wide berth. He should have anyway, and now he blamed himself for his moment of weakness. That night he'd needed someone, but that someone had been Mary, not a woman he didn't know. Not Fiona.

"I'm so sorry," he whispered. "I'm so sorry." He hoped that maybe now Fiona would finally be at peace.

Looking toward the wide-open horizon, he turned his thoughts to Mary. He couldn't wait to look into her beautiful blue eyes and tell her that he'd never stopped loving her. That thought made him even more anxious. He couldn't wait to get home.

Dillon walked her to her door and waited while Mary pulled out her keys.

"I had a wonderful time," he said as he leaned casually against the side of her building as if waiting to see if she was going to invite him up. Clouds scudded past the full moon to disappear over the mountaintops surrounding the canyon. The cool night air smelled of pine and clear blue trout stream water. This part of Montana was a little bit of Heaven, her mother was fond of saying. Mary agreed.

She'd left a light on in her apartment on the top floor. It glowed a warm inviting golden hue.

"I had fun too," she said, and considered asking him up to see the view from what she jokingly called her penthouse. The balcony off the back would be especially nice tonight. But her tongue seemed tied, and suddenly she felt tired and close to tears.

"I should go," Dillon said, his gaze locking with hers. He seemed about to take a step back, but changed his mind and leaned toward her. His hand cupped her jaw as he kissed her. Chastely at first, then with more ardor, gently drawing her to him. The kiss took her by surprise. Their first date he hadn't even tried.

His tongue probed her mouth for a moment before he ended the kiss as abruptly as it had begun. Stepping back, he seemed to study her in the moonlight for a moment before he said, "I really do have to go. Maybe we could do something this weekend if you aren't busy?"

She nodded dumbly. She and Dillon were close to the same age, both adults. She'd expected him to kiss her on their first date. So her surprise tonight had nothing to do with him kissing her, she thought as she entered her building, locking the door behind her and hurrying up to her apartment.

It had everything to do with the kiss.

Mary unlocked her apartment door with trembling fingers, stepped in and locked it behind her. She leaned against the door, hot tears filling her eyes as she told herself she shouldn't be disappointed. But she was.

The kiss had been fine, as far as kisses went. But even when Dillon had deepened the kiss, she had felt nothing but emptiness. The memory made her feel sick. Would she always compare every kiss with Chase's? Would every man she met come up lacking?

She didn't bother to turn on a lamp as she tossed her purse down and headed toward her bedroom, furious with herself. And even more furious with Chase. He'd left her and Montana as if what they had together meant nothing to him. Clearly it didn't. That's why he'd gotten engaged and wasn't man enough to call her himself and tell her.

Still mentally kicking herself for writing that letter to him, she changed into her favorite T-shirt and went into the bathroom to brush her teeth. Her image in the mirror startled her. She was no longer that young girl that Chase had fallen in love with. She was a woman in her own right. She dried her tears, the crying replaced with angry determination. If that was the way Chase wanted to be, then it was fine with her.

Her cell phone rang, startling her. She hurried to it, and for just a moment she thought it was going to be Chase. Her heart had soared, then come crashing down. Chase had moved on. When was she going to accept that?

"I couldn't quit thinking about you after I left," Dillon said. "I was wondering if you'd like to go to the movies tomorrow night?"

She didn't hesitate. "I'd love to." Maybe she just hadn't been ready for his kiss. Maybe next time...

"Great," Dillon said. "I'll pick you up at 5:30 if that's all right. We can grab something to eat before we go to the theater."

"Sounds perfect." If Chase could see her now, she thought as she hung up. Dillon was handsome, but less rugged looking than Chase. Taller though by a good inch or two, and he wanted to go out with her.

She disconnected, determined to put Chase Steele behind her. He had moved on and now she was too. Next time, she would invite Dillon up to her apartment. But even as she thought it, she imagined Chase and the woman he was engaged to. While she was busy comparing every man she met to him, he'd found someone and fallen in love. It made her question if what she and Chase once had was really that unique and special. Just because it had been for her...

Mary willed herself not to think about him. She touched her tongue to her lower lip. Dillon had made her laugh, and he'd certainly been attentive. While the kiss hadn't spurred a reaction in her, she was willing to give it another chance.

Her father didn't trust the man, so didn't that mean that there was more to Dillon than met the eye? Chase had always been a little wild growing up. Her father had been worried about her relationship with him. Maybe there was some wildness in Dillon that would make him more interesting.

As she fell asleep though, her thoughts returned to Chase until her heart was aching and tears were leaking onto her pillow.

Chapter 4

"How was your date?"

Mary looked up the next morning to find her mother standing in the doorway of her office holding two cups of coffee from the shop across the street. "Tell me that's an ultimate caramel frappaccino."

Dana laughed. "Do you mean layers of whipped cream infused with rich coffee, white chocolate and dark caramel? Each layer sitting on a dollop of dark caramel sauce?"

"Apparently I've mentioned why I love it," she said, smiling at her mother as Dana handed her the cup. She breathed in the sweet scent for a moment before she licked some of the whipped cream off the top. "I hope you got one of these for yourself."

"Not likely," her mother said as she sat down across the desk from her. "The calories alone scared me off.

Anyway, you know I prefer my coffee to actually taste like coffee. That's why I drink it black."

Mary grimaced and shook her head, always amazed how much she looked like her mother but the similarities seemed to have stopped there. What they shared was their love of Montana and determination to keep Cardwell Ranch for future generations. At least for the ones who wanted to stay here. Her three brothers had left quickly enough, thrown to the far winds. She wondered about her own children—when she had them one day with the man she eventually married. Would they feel wanderlust like Chase had? She knew she wouldn't be able to make them stay nearby any more than she had him.

She took a sip of her coffee, hating that she'd let her thoughts wander down that particular path.

"I'm trying to tell if the date went well or not," her mother said, studying her openly. "When I walked in, I thought it had, but now you're frowning. Is your coffee all right?"

Mary replaced her frown with a smile as she turned her attention to her mother and away from Chase. "My coffee is amazing. Thank you so much. It was just what I needed. Normally I try to get over to Lone Peak Perk when it opens, but this morning I was anxious to get to work. I wish they delivered."

Her mother gave her a pointed look. "Are you purposely avoiding talking about your date, because I'm more interested in it than your coffee habit."

Laughing, she said, "The date was fine. Good. Fun, actually. We're going out again tonight."

Her mother raised a brow. "Again already? So he was a perfect gentleman?" Her mother took a sip of her coffee as if pretending she wasn't stepping over a line.

"You're welcome to tell Dad that he was," she said with a twinkle in her eye.

"Mary!" They both laughed. "So you like him?"

Mary nodded. *Like* was exactly the right word. She had hoped to feel more.

"You are impossible. You're determined to make me drag everything out of you, aren't you?"

"Not everything," she said coyly. Her mother seemed to like this game they played. Mostly Dana seemed relieved that Mary was moving on after Chase. She didn't like to see her daughter unhappy, Mary thought. It was time to quit moping over Chase, and they both knew it.

"So how did we do?" Deputy Dillon Ramsey asked his friend as he closed the cabin door and headed for the refrigerator for a beer as if he lived there.

"Picked up another three head of prime beef," Grady Birch said, and quickly added, "They were patrolling the fences last night just like you said they would be. Smart to hit a ranch on the other side of the river. We got in and out. No sweat."

"It's nice that I know where the deputies will be watching." Dillon grinned as he popped the top on his beer can and took a long swig.

"Trouble is, I heard around town that ranchers are going to start riding their fences. Word's out."

Dillon swore. "It was such easy pickings for a while." He plopped down in one of the worn chairs in Grady's cabin, feeling more at home in this ratty-ass place than in his nice apartment in Big Sky. "So we'll cool it until the heat dies down."

"Back to easy pickings, how did your date go?"

He grinned. "A couple more dates and I'll have her eating out of my hand."

Grady looked worried. "You're playing with fire, you know. The marshal's daughter?" His friend shook his head. "You sure this game you're playing is worth it?"

Dillon laughed. "To be able to drive out to the Cardwell Ranch, sit on that big porch of theirs and drink the marshal's beer right under his nose? You damn betcha it's worth it."

"Maybe I don't understand the end game," Grady suggested.

"I need this job until I can get enough money together to go somewhere warm, sit in the shade and drink fancy drinks with umbrellas in them for the rest of my life. I have plans for my future and they don't include a woman, especially Mary Savage. But in the meantime…" He smiled and took a slug of his beer. "She ain't half bad to look at. For her age, I get the feeling that she hasn't had much experience. I'd be happy to teach her a few things."

"Well, it still seems dangerous dating his daughter," Grady said. "Unless you're not telling me the truth and you're serious about her."

"I'm only serious about keeping the marshal from being suspicious of me. I told you, he almost caught me that one night after we hit the Cardwell Ranch. I had to do some fast talking, but I think I convinced him that I was patrolling the area on my night off."

"And dating his daughter will make him less suspicious of you?"

"It will give him something else to worry about," Dillon said with a grin. He knew he'd gotten the job only because of his uncle. He'd gone into law enforcement at his uncle's encouragement. Also, he'd seen it as a get-out-of-jail-free card. No one would suspect a cop, right?

Unfortunately, his uncle had been more than suspicious about what Dillon had been doing to make some extra money. So it had come down to him leaving Wyoming to take the deputy job in the Gallatin Canyon of Montana.

"Mary Savage is a good-looking woman, no doubt about that," Grady said as he got up to get them more beer.

Dillon watched him with narrowed eyes. "Don't get any ideas. I've been priming this pump for a while now. And believe me, with your record, you wouldn't want Marshal Hud Savage looking too closely at *you*. That's one reason we can't be seen together. As far as anyone knows, you and I aren't even friends."

Marshal Hud Savage had been waiting patiently for the call since Deputy Dillon Ramsey had gone off duty. Still, when his phone rang, it made him jump. It wasn't like him to be nervous. Then again, this was about his daughter. He had every right given his feelings about Dillon Ramsey.

He picked up the phone, glad to hear the voice of Hayes Cardwell, Dana's cousin, on the other end of the line. It was nice to have several private investigators in the family. "Well?"

"You were right. He headed out of town the moment he changed out of his uniform," Hayes said. "He went to a cabin back in the hills outside Gallatin Gateway. You're probably more interested in who is renting the cabin than who owns it. Ever heard of a man named Grady Birch?"

The name didn't ring any bells. "Who is he?"

"He has an interesting rap sheet that includes theft and assault. He's done his share of cattle rustling."

"And Dillon went straight there."

"He did. In fact, he's still inside. I'm watching the place from down the road with binoculars."

"So it's away from other houses," Hud said. "Any chance there's a truck around with a large horse trailer?"

"The kind that could be used to steal cattle?"

"Exactly," the marshal said.

"There's an old one parked out back. If they both leave, I might get a chance to have a look inside."

"I doubt they're going to leave together," Hud said. "Thanks for doing this but I can take it from here."

"No problem. What's family for?"

"I'll expect a bill for your time," the marshal said. "Or I'll tell Dana on you."

Hayes laughed. "Don't want *her* mad at me."

"No one does. Also," Hud added, "let's keep this just between the two of us for now." He disconnected and called up Grady Birch's rap sheet. Hayes was right. Grady was trouble. So why wasn't he surprised that his new deputy was hanging out with a man like that?

He'd known it the moment he laid eyes on the handsome lawman. Actually, he'd suspected there would be a problem when Dillon's uncle called, asking for the favor. He'd wanted to turn the man down, but the uncle was a good cop who Hud had worked with on a case down in Jackson, Wyoming.

Hud rubbed a hand over his face. Dillon was everything he'd suspected he was, and now he was dating

Mary. He swore. What was he going to do about it? In the first place, he had no proof. Yet. So warning Mary about him would be a waste of breath even if she *didn't* find something romantic about dating an outlaw. Some people still saw cattle rustling as part of an Old West tradition. Also, his daughter was too old to demand that she stop seeing Dillon.

No, he was going to have to handle this very delicately, and delicate wasn't in his repertoire. That didn't leave him many options. Catching Dillon red-handed wouldn't be easy because the deputy wasn't stupid. Arresting him without enough evidence to put him away was also a bad move.

Hud knew he had to bide his time. He told himself that maybe he'd get lucky, and Dillon or Grady would make a mistake. He just hoped it was soon, before Mary got any more involved with the man.

Chase finally got the call. His pickup engine was in and he could come by this afternoon to pick it up. He hadn't talked to Rick in a few days and feeling at loose ends, pulled out his cell phone and made the call, dreading the news. Rick answered on the second ring.

"Has there been any word on Fiona?" The silence on the other end of the line stretched out long enough that Chase knew what was coming.

"They gave up the search. The general consensus is that her body washed downstream and will be found once the water goes down more."

"I'm sorry to hear that. I'm sure Patty is upset."

"She is," Rick said. "She felt sorry for Fiona. That's why she didn't cut ties with her after high school. Patty's over at Fiona's condo now cleaning it out since she has no next of kin. She found out from a bank statement that Fiona had drained her bank account almost a week ago. Took all of it in cash. Who knows what she did with that much money. Hell, it could be in the river with her. Patty's going to try to organize some kind of service for her."

"She doesn't have any family?"

"I guess I didn't tell you. Her whole family died in a fire when Fiona was eleven. She would have perished with her parents and three older stepbrothers, but she'd stayed over at a friend's house that night."

"Oh man. That could explain a lot," he said more to himself. "I wish I'd known all of this. Maybe I could have handled things better."

"Trust me, it would take a psychiatrist years to sort that woman out. So stop blaming yourself. I'm the one who should have warned you. But it's over now."

The fact that he felt relieved made him feel even more guilty as he promised to stay in touch and hung up.

Chapter 5

"Just fill out this application and leave it," the barista said as she dropped the form on the table in front of the dark-haired woman with the pixie haircut and the kind of cute Southern accent and lisp because of the gap between her front teeth.

She'd introduced herself as Lucy Carson, as if Christy was supposed to recognize the name.

"You're sure there's no chance of an opening soon?" Lucy Carson asked now before glancing at her name tag and adding, "Christy."

Christy shook her head. "Like I said. I just got hired, so I really doubt there will be anything for the rest of the season unless someone quits and that's unlikely. Jobs aren't that easy to find in Big Sky. Your application will be on file with dozens of others, so if I were you, I'd keep looking."

She didn't mean to sound cruel or dismissive, but she'd told the woman there weren't any openings. Still, the woman had insisted on filling out an application. If she wanted to waste her time, then Christy wasn't going to stop her. She just thought it was stupid.

From behind the counter, she watched how neatly Lucy Carson filled in each blank space. Was it stubbornness or arrogance? The lady acted as if she thought the manager would let someone go to hire *her*. That sounded like arrogance to Christy.

"What about a place to live nearby?" the woman asked, looking up from the application.

Christy laughed. "You'll have even worse luck finding an apartment. I've been waiting for months to get into the one across the street, and it's just a small bedroom."

Lucy glanced in the direction she pointed. "There's rentals over there?"

"There *was*. I got the last one. I'm moving in tomorrow." This Lucy was starting to get on her nerves. She found herself wishing that some customers would come in just so she had something to do. Usually she loved the slow afternoons when she could look at magazines and do absolutely nothing, even though she was supposed to be cleaning on her downtime.

The woman studied her for a moment, then smiled and resumed filling out the application.

"You should go down to Bozeman," Christy told her. "More opportunities in a college town than here in the canyon." Jobs weren't easy to get in Big Sky especially during the busy times, summer, and winter. Not just that, this job didn't even pay that well. Too many young people would work for nothing just to get to spend their free time up on the mountain biking and kayaking in the summer, skiing and snowboarding in the winter.

The woman finished and brought her application over to the counter. Christy glanced at the name. "Is Lucy short for something?" she asked.

"My mother was a huge fan of *I Love Lucy* reruns."

She looked at the application, almost feeling sorry for the young woman. According to this, she had a lot of experience as a barista but then so did a whole lot of other people. "I see you didn't put down an address." She looked up at the woman who gave her a bright smile.

"Remember, I'm still looking for a place to stay, but once I start working I'm sure an apartment will open up."

Christy couldn't help but chuckle under her breath at the woman's naive optimism. "Most everyone who works in Big Sky ends up commuting at least forty miles a day. There just aren't any cheap rentals for minimum wage workers even if you should luck out and get a job."

Lucy smiled. "I'm not worried. Things just tend to work out for me. I'm lucky that way."

Whatever, Christy thought. "I'll give your application to Andrea but like I said, we don't have any openings."

"Not yet anyway," Lucy said. "So where do you go to have fun on a Saturday night?"

"Charley's if you like country. Otherwise—"

"I'm betting you like country music," Lucy said. "Your car with the George Strait bumper sticker gives you away."

"My car?" Christy frowned.

"Isn't that your SUV parked across the street?"

She looked out the window and laughed. "Not hardly. Mine is that little blue beat-up sedan with all the stuff in the back since I can't move into my apartment until tomorrow. I've been waiting for weeks, staying with my mother down in Bozeman and driving back and forth when I can't find someone to stay with here. Do you have any family you could stay with?"

Lucy shook her head. "No family. Just me. Maybe I'll check out Charley's tonight." She smiled her gap-toothed smile. "Hopefully I'll get lucky and some hand-some cowboy will take me home with him. Or maybe it's not that kind of place."

"No, it is. There'll be cowboys and ski bums."

"I might see you there then?" Lucy said. "Don't worry. I won't intrude if you've found your own cow-boy. I'm guessing there's one you're planning to meet tonight."

Christy felt herself flush. "Not exactly. I'm just hop-ing he'll be there."

Lucy laughed. "Hoping to get lucky, huh? Well, thanks again for your help." She left smiling, making Christy shake her head as she tossed Lucy's application on the desk in Andrea's office. She'd ended up almost liking the woman. Now if she could just get through the rest of the day. She was excited about tonight at Charley's. She did feel lucky. She had a job, an apartment to move into tomorrow and with even more luck, she would be going home with the man she had a crush on. Otherwise, she would be sleeping in her car on top of all her belongings.

Tomorrow though, she'd be moving into the apart-ment across the street that Mary Savage owned. How handy was that since she could sleep late and still get to work on time with her job just across the street?

* * *

Lucy Carson was also looking at the small apartment house across the street from Lone Peak Perk as she walked to her car. She had her heart set on a job at the coffee shop and an apartment across the street in Mary Cardwell Savage's building. Not that she always got what she set her heart on, she thought bitterly, but she would make this happen, whatever she had to do.

As she climbed into her new car, she breathed in the scent of soft leather. She really did like the smell of a new car. Her other one was at the bottom of the Colorado River—or at least it had been until a few weeks ago when it was discovered.

Her disappearing act had gone awry when she'd tried to get out of the car and couldn't before it plummeted toward the river that night. By the time she reached the bank way downriver, she'd wished she'd come up with a better plan. She'd almost died and she wanted to live. More than wanted to live. She'd wanted to kill someone. Especially the person responsible for making her have to go to such extremes: Chase Steele. As she'd sat on that riverbank in the dark, she knew exactly what she had to do. Fortunately, when she'd tried to bail out of the car, she'd grabbed her purse. She'd almost forgotten the money. Her plan really would have gone badly if she'd lost all this money. With it, she could do anything she wanted.

But as close a call as it had been, everything had worked out better than even she'd planned. The authorities thought she was dead, her body rotting downriver. Fiona Barkley was dead. She was free of her. Now she could become anyone she chose.

Since then she'd had to make a few changes, including her name. But she'd never liked the name Fiona anyway. She much preferred Lucy Carson. Getting an ID in that name had been easier than she imagined. It had been harder to give up her long blond hair. But the pixie cut, the dark brown contacts and the brunette hair color transformed her into a woman not even she recognized. She thought she looked good—just not so good that Chase would recognize her.

Her resulting car wreck had pretty much taken care of her change in appearance as well. She had unsnapped her seat belt to make her leap from the car before it hit the water. Had she not been drunk and partway out of the car, she wouldn't have smashed her face, broken her nose and knocked out her front teeth.

As it turned out, that too proved to be a stroke of luck. She'd lost weight because it had hurt to eat. When she looked in the mirror now, she felt she was too skinny, but she knew once she was happy again, she'd put some pounds back on. She still had curves. She always had.

It was her face that had changed the most. Her nose had healed but it had a slight lean to it. She liked the imperfection. Just as she liked the gap between her two new front teeth. It had taken going to a dentist in Mexico to get a rush job. She liked the gap. It had even changed the way she talked giving her a little lisp. She'd been able to pick up her former Southern accent without any trouble since it was the way she'd talked before college. It was enough of a change in her appearance and voice that she knew she could get away with it—as long as she never got too close to Chase.

In the meantime, she couldn't wait to meet Mary Cardwell Savage.

* * *

Mary stood across the street from Lone Peak Perk thinking about her date last night with Dillon. She'd seen the slim, dark-haired woman come out of the coffee shop and get into a gray SUV, but her mind had been elsewhere. As the SUV pulled away, she turned from the window, angry with herself.

She was still holding out hope that Chase would contact her. The very thought made her want to shake herself. It had been weeks. If he was going to answer, he would have a long time ago. So why did she keep thinking she'd hear from him? Hadn't his fiancée told him that she'd called? Maybe he thought that was sufficient. Not the man she'd known, she thought.

And that was what kept nagging at her. She'd known Chase since he was fifteen. He'd come to work for the Jensen Ranch next door. Mary's mom had pretty much adopted him after finding out the reason he'd been sent to live in the canyon was because his mother couldn't take care of him. Muriel was going through cancer treatment. He'd been honorable even at a young age. He wasn't the kind of man not to call and tell her about a fiancée.

So his not calling or writing felt…wrong. And it left her with nagging questions.

That was only part of the problem and she knew it. She'd hoped that Dillon Ramsey would take her mind off Chase. They'd been dating regularly, and most of the time she enjoyed herself. They'd kissed a few times but that was all. He hadn't even made a pass at her. She couldn't imagine what it was about Dillon that had worried her father. At one point, she'd wondered if her father the marshal had warned him to behave with her.

The thought made her cringe. He wouldn't do that, would he?

She'd asked Dillon last night how he liked working for her dad.

"I like it. He's an okay dude," he'd answered.

She'd laughed. No one called her father a dude.

Now, she had to admit that Dillon was a disappointment. Which made her question what it was she was looking for in a man. A sense of adventure along with a sense of humor. Dillon didn't seem to have either.

Was that why she felt so restless? She looked around her apartment, which she'd furnished with things she loved from the turquoise couch to the weathered log end tables and bright flowered rug. But the spectacular view was the best part. The famous Lone Peak, often snow-capped, was framed in her living room window. The mountain looked especially beautiful in the moonlight.

Which made her think of Chase and how much she would have liked to stand on her back deck in the moonlight and kiss him—instead of Dillon. She groaned, remembering her hesitation again last night to invite Dillon up to her apartment. He'd been hinting that he really wanted to see it. She could tell last night that he'd been hurt and a little angry that she hadn't invited him up.

Standing here in the life she'd built, all she could think about was what Chase's opinion would be of it. Would he be proud of her accomplishments? Would he regret ever leaving her?

She shook him from her head and hurried back downstairs. She still had work to do, and all she was doing right now was giving herself a headache.

* * *

By the next morning, news of the hit and run death of Christy Shores had spread through most of Big Sky and the canyon.

As Marshal Hud Savage walked into Charley's, the last place Christy Shores had been seen alive, he saw the bartender from last night wasn't alone.

"Mike French, bartender, right?" Hud asked the younger of the two men standing nervously behind the bar. Twentysomething, Mike looked like a lot of the young people in Big Sky from his athletic build to the T-shirt and shorts over long underwear and sandals.

If Hud had to guess, he'd say Mike had at least one degree in something practical like engineering, but had gotten hooked on a lifestyle of snowboarding in the winter and mountain biking or kayaking in the summer. Which explained the bartending job.

He considered the handsome young man's deep tan from spending more hours outside than bartending. It made him wonder why a man like that had never appealed to his only daughter.

He suspected Mary was too much of a cowgirl to fall for a ski bum. Instead, she was now dating his deputy, Dillon Ramsey. That thought made his stomach roil, considering what he suspected about the man.

The bartender stepped forward to shake his hand. "Bill said you had some questions about Christy?"

Hud nodded and looked to the bar owner, Bill Benson, before he turned back to Mike. "I understand she was one of the last people to leave the bar last night?"

Mike nodded as Hud pulled out his notebook and pen. "I was just about to lock up when she came out of the women's bathroom. She looked like she'd been crying. I hadn't realized she was in there since I had already locked the front door." He shot a guilty look at his boss. "I usually check to make sure everyone was gone, but last night…"

"What was different about last night?" Hud asked.

Mike shifted on his feet. "A fight had broken out earlier between a couple of guys." He shot another look at Bill and added, "Christy had gotten into the middle of it. Not sure what it was about. After I broke it up, I didn't see her. I thought she'd left."

"Christy's blood alcohol was three times the legal limit," Hud said.

Again Mike shot a look at his boss before holding up his hands and quickly defending himself. "I cut her off before the fight because she'd been hitting the booze pretty hard. But that doesn't mean she quit drinking. The place was packed last night. All I know is that I didn't serve her after that."

Hud glanced toward the front door. "Her car is still parked outside. You didn't happen to take her keys, did you?"

The young man grimaced. "I asked for her keys, but she swore to me that she was walking home." He shrugged. "I guess that part was true."

Hud had Christy's car keys in a plastic evidence bag in his patrol SUV. The keys had been found near her body next to the road after she was apparently struck by a vehicle and knocked into the ditch.

"I'm going to need the names of the two men who were involved in the fight," he said. He wrote them down, hiding his surprise when he wrote Grady Birch, but Chet Jensen was no surprise. Chet seemed to think of the local jail as his home away from home. "What about friends, girlfriends, anyone Christy was close to."

Mike shook his head. "She hadn't been working at Lone Peak Perk very long. I'm not sure she'd made any friends yet. When she came into the bar, she was always alone. I think someone said that she was driving back and forth for work from Bozeman where she was living with her mom."

"Did she always leave alone?" he asked.

With a shake of his head, the bartender said, "No." He motioned toward the names he'd given the marshal. "It was usually with one or the other of those two."

Hud thanked Mike and went outside to the car. He'd already run the plates. The vehicle was registered to Christy Shores. Bill came out and drove off, followed by Mike who hopped on his mountain bike.

Christy's older model sedan wasn't locked Hud noted as he pulled on latex gloves and tried the driver's-side door. It swung open with a groan. He looked inside. Neatness apparently wasn't one of the young woman's traits. The back seat was stuffed full of clothing and boxes. He'd been told that she was planning to move into an apartment on the second floor of Mary's building today. The front floorboard on the passenger side was knee-deep in fast-food wrappers and Lone Peak Perk go cups.

He leaned in and took a whiff, picking up the stale scent of cigarettes and alcohol. All his instincts told him that after the apparent night Christy'd had, she would have driven home drunk rather than walk.

On impulse, he slid behind the wheel, inserted the key and turned it. There was only a click. He tried again. Same dull click. Reaching for the hood release, he pulled it and then climbed out to take a look at the engine, suspecting an old battery.

But he was in for a surprise. The battery appeared to be new. The reason the car hadn't started was because someone had purposely disabled it. He could see fresh screwdriver marks on the top of the battery.

Hud suspected that whoever had tampered with her battery was the same person who had wanted Christy to take off walking down this road late last night.

When Mary walked across the street to the Lone Peak Perk the next morning, she was surprised to find her favorite coffee shop closed. There was a sign on the door announcing that there'd been a death.

She wondered who had died as she retraced her footsteps to climb into her pickup and head for the ranch. Cardwell Ranch was a half mile from Meadow Village on the opposite side of the Gallatin River. She always loved this drive because even though short, the landscape changed so drastically.

Mary left behind housing and business developments, traffic and noise. As she turned off Highway 191 onto the private bridge that crossed the river to the ranch the roar of the flowing river drowned out the busy resort town. Towering pines met her on the other side. She wound back into the mountains through them before the land opened again for her first glimpse that day of the ranch buildings.

Behind the huge barn and corrals, the mountains rose all the way to Montana's Big Sky. She breathed it all in, always a little awed each time she saw it, knowing what it took to hang on to a ranch through hard times. Behind the barn and corrals were a series of small guest cabins set back against the mountainside. Her aunt Stacy lived in the larger one, the roof barely visible behind the dark green of the pines.

At the Y in the road, she turned left instead of continuing back into the mountains to where her Uncle Jordan and his wife, Liza, lived. The two-story log and stone ranch house where she'd been raised came into view moments later, the brick-red metal roof gleaming in the morning sun.

There were several vehicles parked out front, her father's patrol SUV one of them. When she pushed open the front door, she could hear the roar of voices coming from the kitchen and smiled. This had been the sound she'd come downstairs to every morning for years growing up here.

Mary knew how much her mother loved a full house. It had been hard on her when all of her children had grown up and moved out. But there were still plenty of relatives around. Mary had seven uncles and as many aunts, along with a few cousins who still lived in the area.

As she entered the kitchen, she saw that there was the usual group of family, friends and ranch hands sitting around the huge kitchen table. This morning was no exception. Her uncle Jordan signaled that it was time to get to work, giving her a peck on her cheek as he rose and headed out the door, a half dozen ranch hands following him like baby ducks.

Mary said hello to her aunt Stacy and kissed her mother on the cheek before going to the cupboard to pull down a mug and fill it with coffee. There was always a pot going at Cardwell Ranch. The kitchen had quieted down with Jordan and the ranch hands gone. Leaning against the kitchen counter, she asked, "So what's going on?" She saw her mother glance down the table at the marshal.

"Some poor young woman was run down in Meadow Village last night," Dana said, getting up from the table as the timer went off on the oven. "It was a hit and run," she added, shaking her head as if in disbelief.

Mary moved out of the way as her mother grabbed a hot pad and pulled a second batch of homemade cinnamon rolls from the oven.

"You might have known her," her mother said. "She worked at that coffee shop you like."

"Lone Peak Perk?" she asked in surprise as she took a vacated seat. "I stopped by there this morning and it was closed. There was a note on the door saying there'd been a death, but I never dreamed it was anything like that. What was the woman's name?"

"Christy Shores," her father said from the head of the large kitchen table.

"Christy." She felt sick to her stomach as she called up an image of the small fair-haired young woman. Tears filled her eyes. "Oh, no. I knew her."

"Honey, are you all right?" her mother asked.

"Christy was going to move into the apartment I had available today. She'd only been working at the coffee shop for a few weeks. I can't believe she's dead. A hit and run?" she asked her father.

He nodded and glanced at his watch. "The coroner should have something more for me by now," he said, getting to his feet.

"Do you have any idea who did it?" she asked her father.

Hud shook his head. "Not yet. Unfortunately, it happened after the bars closed, and she was apparently alone walking along the side of the road dressed in all black. It's possible that the driver didn't see her."

"But whoever hit her would have known that he or she struck something," Dana said.

"Could have thought it was a deer, and that's why the person didn't stop," Hud said. "It's possible."

"And then the driver didn't stop to see what it was? Probably drunk and didn't want to deal with the marshal," Aunt Stacy mocked. "I've heard he's a real—"

"I'd watch yourself," her father said, but smiled as he took his Stetson off the hook on the wall, kissed his wife and left.

Mary took a sip of her coffee, her hands trembling as she brought the mug to her lips. It always shocked her, death and violence. She'd never understood how her father could handle his job the way he did. While there wasn't a lot of crime in the canyon, there was always something. She remembered growing up, overhearing about murders but only occasionally. Now there'd been a hit and run. Poor Christy. She'd been so excited about renting Mary's apartment, which was so close to her work. It would save her the commute from her mother's house in Bozeman, she'd said.

As the patrol SUV left, another vehicle pulled in. "Well, I wonder who that is?" she heard her mother say as she shifted in her seat to peer out the window.

Mary did the same thing, blinking in the bright morning sun at the pickup that had pulled up in front of the house almost before the dust had settled from her father leaving.

She stared as the driver's-side door opened and Chase Steele stepped out of the vehicle.

Chapter 6

"It's Chase," Mary said as if she couldn't believe it. For weeks she had dreamed of him suddenly showing up at her door. She shot a look at her mother.

"Do you need my help?" Dana asked. "If you aren't ready to talk to him, I could tell him this isn't a good time."

She shook her head and turned back to watch Chase stretch as if it had been a long drive. He looked around for a moment, his gaze softening as he took in the ranch as though, like her, he still had special memories of the place. He appeared taller, more solid, she thought as she watched him head for the front porch. Was he remembering how it was with the two of them before he left?

"I can't imagine what he's doing here," Mary said, voicing her surprise along with her worry.

Her mother gave her a pitying look. "He's here to see you."

"But why?"

"Maybe because of the letter you sent," Dana suggested.

She couldn't believe how nervous she was. This was Chase. She'd known him since they were teens. Her heart bumped against her ribs as she heard him knock. "He could have just called."

"Maybe what he has to say needs to be said in person."

That thought scared her more than she wanted to admit. She hadn't told her mother about the call from Chase's fiancée. She'd been too embarrassed. It was enough that her aunt Stacy had told her mother about the letter she'd sent him.

"Do you want me to get that?" her mother asked when he knocked. "Or maybe you would like to answer it and let him tell you why he's here."

Another knock at the door finally made her move. Mind racing, she hurried to the door. Chase. After all this time. She had no idea what she was going to say. Worse, what *he* would say.

As she opened the door, she glanced past him to his pickup. At least he was alone. He hadn't brought the woman who'd called her, his fiancée who could by now be his wife.

"Mary."

The sound of his voice made her shift her gaze back to the handsome cowboy standing in her doorway. Her heart did a roller-coaster loop in her chest, taking all her air with it. He'd only gotten more handsome. The sleeves on the Western shirt he wore were rolled up to expose muscled tanned arms. The shirt stretched over his broad shoulders. He looked as solid as one of the large pines that stood sentinel on the mountainside over-looking the ranch.

He was staring at her as well. He seemed to catch himself and quickly removed his Stetson and smiled. "Gosh dang, you look good."

She couldn't help but smile. He'd picked up the expression "gosh dang" from her father after Hud had caught Chase cussing a blue streak at fifteen out by their barn. The words went straight to her heart, but when she opened her mouth, she said, "What are you doing here?"

"I had to see you." He glanced past her. "I'm sorry it took me so long. My pickup broke down and… Could we talk?"

She was still standing in the doorway. She thought of her mother in the next room. "Why don't we walk down to the creek?"

"Sure," he said, and stepped back to let her lead the way.

Neither of them spoke until they reached the edge of the creek. Mary stopped in the shade of the pines. Sunlight fingered warmth through the boughs, making the rippling clear water sparkle. She breathed in the sweet familiar scents, and felt as if she needed to pinch herself. Chase.

She was struck with how different Chase looked. Stubble darkened his chiseled jawline. He was definitely taller, broader across the shoulders. There were faint lines around his blue eyes as he squinted toward the house before settling his gaze on her.

She felt heat rush to her center. The cowboy standing in front of her set off all kinds of desires with only a look. And yet after all this time, did she know this man? He'd come back. But that didn't mean that he'd come back to *her*.

"I got your letter," he said as he took off his Stetson to turn the brim nervously in his fingers.

"You didn't call or write back," she said, wondering when he was going to get to the news about the fiancée.

His gaze locked with hers. "I'm sorry but what I wanted to say, I couldn't say over the phone let alone in a letter."

Her heart pounded as she thought, *Here it comes*.

There was pain in his gaze. "I've missed you so much. I know you never understood why I had to leave. I'm not sure I understood it myself. I had to go. Just as I had to come back. I'm so sorry I hurt you." His blue-eyed gaze locked with hers. "I love you. I never stopped loving you."

She stared at him. Wasn't this exactly what she'd dreamed of him saying to her before she'd gotten the call from his fiancée? Except in the dream she would have been in his arms by now.

"What about your fiancée, Chase?"

"*Fiancée?* What would make you think—"

"She called me after I sent the letter."

He stared at her for a moment before swearing under his breath. "You talked to a woman who said she was my fiancée?"

She nodded and crossed her arms protectively across her chest, her heart pounding like a drum beneath her ribs. "Wasn't she?"

He shook his head. "Look, I was never engaged, far from it. But there was this woman." He saw her expression. "It wasn't what you think."

"I think you were involved with her."

He closed his eyes and groaned again. When he opened them, he settled those blue eyes on her. "It was one night after a party at my boss's place. It was a barbecue that I didn't even want to go to and wish I hadn't. I'd had too much to drink." He shook his head. "After that she would break into my apartment and leave me presents, go through my things, ambush me when I came home. She found your letter, but I never dreamed that she'd call you." He raked a hand through his hair and looked down. "I'm so sorry. Fiona was…delusional. She was like this with anyone who showed her any attention, but I didn't know that. I told her that night I was in love with someone else." His gaze came up to meet hers. "You. But I didn't come here to talk about her."

Fiona? Of course he had dated while he was gone. So why did hearing him say the woman's name feel as if he'd ripped out another piece of her heart? She felt sick to her stomach. "Why *did* you come here?"

"That's what I've been trying to tell you. I hated the way we left things too," Chase said. "Mary, I love you. That's why I came back. Tell me that you'll give us another chance."

"Excuse me."

They both turned to see a man silhouetted against the skyline behind them. Mary blinked as she recognized the form. "Dillon?"

Chase's gaze sharpened. "Dillon?" he asked under his breath.

"What are you doing here?" she asked, and then realized that she'd agreed to a lunch date she'd completely forgotten about because of Chase's surprising return.

"Lunch. I know I'm early, but I thought we'd go on a hike and then have lunch at one of the cafés up at the mountain resort," he said as he came partway down the slope to the creek and into the shelter of the pines. "More fun than eating at a restaurant in the village." He shrugged. "When your pickup wasn't at your office, I figured you'd be here." Dillon's gaze narrowed. "Why do I feel like I'm interrupting something?"

"Because you are," Chase said, and looked to Mary. "A friend of yours?"

"Mary and I are dating," Dillon said before she could speak. "I'm Deputy Dillon Ramsey."

"The deputy, huh," Chase said, clearly unimpressed.

Dillon seemed to grind his teeth for a moment before saying, "And you are..."

"Chase Steele, Mary's..." His gaze shifted to her.

"Chase and I grew up together here in the canyon," she said quickly as she saw the two posturing as if this might end with them exchanging blows before thrashing in the mud next to the creek as they tried to kill each other. "I didn't know Chase was...in town."

"Passing through?" Dillon asked pointedly.

Chase grinned. "Sorry, but I'm here to stay. I'm not going anywhere." He said that last part to her.

His blue eyes held hers, making her squirm for no reason she could think of, which annoyed her. It wasn't like she was caught cheating on him. Far from it since he had apparently recently dated someone named Fiona.

"If you're through here," Dillon said to her, "we should get going before it gets too hot."

"Don't let me stop you," Chase said, his penetrating gaze on her. "But we aren't finished."

"You are now," Dillon said, reaching for Mary's hand as if to pull her back up the slope away from the creek.

Chase stepped between them. "Don't go grabbing

her like you're going to drag her away. If she wants to go with you, she can go under her own steam."

Dillon took a step toward Chase. "Stop," Mary cried, sure that the two were going to get physical at any moment. She looked at Chase, still shocked by his return as well as his declaration of love. "I'll talk to you later."

He smiled again then, the smile that she'd fallen in love with at a very young age. "Count on it." He stepped back and tipped his Stetson to her, then to Dillon. "I'll be around." In a few long-legged strides, he climbed the slope away from the creek.

"You coming?" Dillon asked, sounding irritated.

She sighed and started up the slope away from the creek. As they topped the hill, she saw Chase had gone to the house and was now visiting with her mother on the front porch. She could hear laughter and felt Dillon's angry reaction to Chase and her mother appearing so friendly.

He seemed to be gritting his teeth as he asked, "What's his story, anyway? He's obviously more than a friend," Dillon said as he opened the passenger-side door of his pickup and glared in Chase and Dana's direction.

"I told you, we grew up together," she said as she slid in and he slammed the door.

Dillon joined her. He seemed out of breath. For a moment he just sat there before he turned toward her. "You were lovers." It wasn't a question.

"We were high school and college sweethearts," she said.

"He's still in love with you." He was looking at Chase and her mother on the porch.

She groaned inwardly and said nothing. Of course with Chase showing up it was only a matter of time before he and Dillon crossed paths in a place as small as Big Sky. But why today of all days?

"He acts like he owns you." Dillon still hadn't reached to start the truck. Nor did he look at her. "Did he think he could come back and take up where the two of you left off?"

She'd thought the same thing, but she found herself wanting to defend Chase. "We have a history—"

He swung his head toward her, his eyes narrow and hard. "Are you getting back together?"

For a moment she was too taken aback to speak. "I didn't even know he was back in town until a few minutes ago. I was as surprised as you were, but I don't like your tone. What I decide to do is really none of your business." Out of the corner of her eye, she saw Chase hug her mother, then head for his pickup.

"Is that right?" Dillon demanded. "Good to know where I stand."

"You know, I'm no longer in the mood for a hike or lunch," she said, and reached for the door handle as Chase headed out of the ranch.

Dillon grabbed her arm, his fingers biting into her tender flesh. "He comes back and you dump me?"

"Let go of me." She said it quietly, but firmly.

He quickly released her. "Sorry. I hope I didn't— It's just that I thought you and I... And then seeing him and hearing him tell you that he was still in love with you." He shook his head, the look on his face making her weaken.

"Look, I told you. It came as a shock for me too," she said. "I don't know what I'm going to do. I'm sorry if you feel—"

"Like I was just a stand-in until your old boyfriend got back?"

"That isn't what you were."

"No?" His voice softened. "Good, because I'm not ready to turn you over to him." As he said the words, he trailed his fingers from her bare shoulder slowly down to her wrist. Her skin rippled with goose bumps and she shivered. "I still want to see that penthouse view. Can I call you later?"

She felt confused. But she knew that she wasn't in any frame of mind to make a decision about Dillon right now. She felt herself nod. "We'll talk then," she said, and climbed out of the pickup, closing the door behind her. Still rattled by everything that had happened, she stood watching him drive away, as tears burned her eyes. Chase had come back. Chase still loved her.

But there was the threatening woman who'd called her saying she was his fiancée. Fiona. And no doubt others. And there was Dillon. Chase had no right to come back here and make any demands on her. He'd let her go for weeks without a word after he'd gotten the letter.

Chase and Dillon had immediately disliked each other, which Mary knew shouldn't have surprised her. Dillon's reaction threw her the most. Did he really have feelings for her? She felt as if it was too early. They barely knew each other. Was it just a male thing?

Still, it worried her. The two men were bound to run into each other again. Next time she might not be around to keep them from trying to kill each other.

* * *

Chase mentally kicked himself. He should have called, should have written. But even as he thought it, he knew he'd had to do this in person. If it hadn't been for Fiona and her dirty tricks… He shook his head. He was to blame for that too and he knew it.

Well, he was here now and damned if he was going to let some deputy steal the woman he loved, had always loved.

He let out a long breath as he drove toward the ranch where he would be working until he started his carpenter job. All the way to Montana he'd been so sure that by now he'd be holding Mary in his arms.

He should have known better. He'd hurt her. Had he really thought she'd still be waiting around for him? He thought of all the things he'd planned to tell her—before that deputy had interrupted them.

Assuring himself that he'd get another chance and soon, he smiled to himself. Mary was even more beautiful than she'd been when he left. But now there was a confidence about her. She'd come into her own. He felt a swell of pride. He'd never doubted that the woman could do anything she set her mind to.

Now all he had to do was convince her that this cowboy was worth giving a second chance.

Hud read through the coroner's report a second time, then set it aside. Prints were still being lifted from Christy Shore's car, but the area around the battery where someone had disabled the engine had been wiped clean. Fibers had been found from what appeared to be a paper towel on the battery.

There was no doubt in his mind that Christy's death had been premeditated. Someone had tampered with her battery, needing her to walk home that night so she could be run down. Which meant that the killer must have been waiting outside the bar. Just her luck that she had stayed so late that there was no one around to give her a ride somewhere.

The killer wanted him to believe the hit and run had been an accident. He'd already heard rumors that she'd been hit by a motor home of some tourist passing through. He knew better. This was a homicide, and he'd bet his tin star that the killer was local and not just passing through.

Picking up his notebook, he shoved back his chair and stood. It was time to talk to the two men who'd fought over Christy earlier in the night. Only one name had surprised him—Grady Birch, Deputy Dillon Ramsey's friend—because the name had just come up in his cattle rustling investigation.

He decided to start with Grady, pay him a surprise visit, see how that went before he talked to the other man, Chet Jensen, the son of a neighboring rancher who'd been in trouble most of his life.

But when he reached the rented cabin outside Gallatin Gateway, Grady was nowhere around. Hud glanced in the windows but it was hard to tell if the man had skipped town or not.

Mary joined her mother in a rocking chair on the front porch after Chase and Dillon had left. Dana had joked about feeling old lately, and had said maybe she was ready for a rocking chair. Mary had laughed.

But as she sat down in a chair next to her, she felt as if it was the first time she'd looked at her mother in a very long time. Dana had aged. She had wrinkles around her eyes and mouth, her hair was now more salt than pepper and there was a tiredness she'd seldom seen in her mother's bearing.

"Are you all right?" her mother asked her, stealing the exact words Mary had been about to say to her. Dana perked up a little when she smiled and reached over to take her daughter's hand.

"I saw you visiting with Chase," Mary said.

Her mother nodded. "It was good to see him. He left you his phone number." With her free hand she reached into her pocket and brought out a folded piece of notepaper and gave it to her.

She glanced at the number written on it below Chase's name. Seeing that there was nothing else, she tucked it into her pocket. "What did he tell you?"

"We only talked about the ranch, how much the town has grown, just that sort of thing."

"He says he came back because he loves me, never stopped loving me. But I never told you this…" She hesitated. There was little she kept from her mother. "I got a call from a woman who claimed to be his fiancée. She warned me about contacting him again."

Dana's eyes widened. "This woman threatened you?"

"Chase says it was a delusional woman he made the mistake of spending one night with. Fiona." Even saying the name hurt.

"I see. Well, now you know the truth."

Did she? "I haven't forgotten why we broke up." She'd caught Chase kissing Beth Anne Jensen. He'd sworn it was the first and only time, and that he hadn't initiated it. That he'd been caught off guard. She'd known Beth Anne had had a crush on Chase for years.

But instinctively she'd also known that her parents

were right. She and Chase had been too young to be as serious as they'd been, especially since they'd never dated anyone else but each other. "You try to lasso him and tie him down now, and you'll regret it," her father had said. "If this love of yours is real, he'll come back."

She'd heard her parents love story since she was a child. Her father had left and broken her mother's heart. He'd come back though and won her heart all over again. "But what if he isn't you, Dad? What if he doesn't come back?"

"Then it wasn't meant to be, sweetheart, and there is nothing you can do about that."

"Will you call him?" her mother asked now.

"I feel like I need a little space without seeing either Dillon or Chase," she said. "I still love Chase, but I'm not sure I still know him."

"It might take some time."

"I guess we'll see if he sticks around long enough to find out." She pushed to her feet. "I need to get to my office."

"I'm glad he came back," her mother said. "I always liked Chase."

Mary smiled. "Me too."

But as she drove back to her office, she knew she wouldn't be able to work, not with everything on her mind. As she pulled into her parking spot next to her building, she changed her mind and left again to drive up into the mountains. She parked at the trailhead for one of her favorite trails and got out. Maybe she'd take a walk.

Hours later, ending up high on a mountain where she could see both the Gallatin Canyon and Madison Valley on the other side, she had to smile. She was tired, sweaty and dusty, and it was the best she'd felt all day.

The hike had cleared her mind some. She turned back toward the trailhead as the sun dipped low, ignoring calls on her cell phone from both men.

Down the street from Mary's building, Lucy studied herself in the rearview mirror of her SUV, surprised that she now actually thought of herself as Lucy. It was her new look and her ability to become someone else. It had started in junior high when she'd been asked to audition for a part in a play.

She'd only done it for extra credit since she'd been failing science. Once she'd read the part though, she'd felt herself become that character, taking on the role, complete with the accent. She'd been good, so good that she'd hardly had to try out in high school to get the leading roles.

Now as she waited, she felt antsy. Mary had come home and then left again without even getting out of her car. Lucy had been so sure that Chase would have made it to Montana by now. Waiting for him, she'd had too much time to think. What if she was wrong? What if he hadn't been hightailing it back here to his sweet little cowgirl?

What if he'd left Arizona, then changed his mind, realizing that what he had with her was more powerful than some old feelings for Mary Cardwell Savage? What if he'd gone back for her only to find out that she'd drowned and that everyone was waiting for some poor soul to find her body along the edge of the river downstream?

The thought made her heart pound. Until she remembered what she'd done to his pickup engine. Who knew where he'd broken down and how long it would take for him to get the engine fixed. If it was fixable.

No, he'd made it clear that he didn't want her. Which meant he would show up here in Big Sky. She just had to be patient and not do anything stupid.

She'd realized that she should approach this the same way she'd gone after prospective buyers in real estate. The first step was to find out what she was up against. Lucy smiled. She would get to know her enemy. She would find her weakness. She already had a plan to gain Mary's trust.

Not that she was getting overconfident. Just as important was anticipating any problems—including getting caught. With each step toward her goal, she needed to consider every contingency.

Some precautions were just common sense. She'd purchased a burner phone. She hadn't told anyone she'd known that she was alive, not even Patty. She hadn't left a paper trail. Taking all her money out of the bank before what the authorities thought was an attempted suicide had been brilliant. Just as was wearing gloves when she tampered with Christy Shores' battery.

It had been pure hell living with three older stepbrothers. But they'd taught her a lot about cars, getting even and never leaving any evidence behind. She'd used everything they'd taught her the night she burned down her stepfather's house—with her stepfather, mother and stepbrothers inside.

But sometimes she got overzealous. Maybe she'd gone too far when she'd put the bleach into Chase's engine oil. She'd considered loosening the nuts on his tires, but she hadn't wanted him to die. *Not yet.* And definitely not where she wouldn't be there.

But what if he couldn't make it to Montana now? Shouldn't he have been here by now? If he was coming. She was beginning to worry a little when she saw him. As if she'd conjured him up, he drove past where she was parked to stop in front of Mary's building. Lucy watched him park and jump out. Her heart began to pound as he strode purposely toward Mary's building to knock on the door.

Her stomach curdled as she watched him try to see into the windows before he stepped back to stare up at the top floor. "Sorry, your little cowgirl isn't home," she said under her breath. There were no lights on nor was Mary's pickup where she always parked it. But it was clear that Chase was looking for her. What would he do when he found her? Profess his undying love? As jealousy's sharp teeth took a bite out of her, she was tempted to end this now.

She'd picked up a weapon at a gun show on her way to Big Sky. All she had to do was reach under her seat, take out the loaded handgun, get out and walk over to him. He wouldn't recognize her. Not at first.

He would though when she showed him the gun she would have had hidden behind her back. "This is just a little something from Fiona." She smiled as she imagined the bullet sinking into his black heart.

But what fun would that be? Her plan was to make him suffer. The best way to do that was through his precious Mary. She'd promised herself she wouldn't deviate from the plan. No more acting on impulse. This time, she wouldn't make the same mistakes she'd made in the past.

As she watched Chase climb back into his pickup and drive away, she was trembling with anticipation at just the thought of what she had in store for the cowboy and his cowgirl.

Chapter 7

The next morning, Mary saw that Lone Peak Perk was open again. Just the thought of one of her ultimate caramel frappaccinos made her realize it was exactly what she needed right now.

Stepping through the door, she breathed in the rich scent of coffee and felt at home. The thought made her smile. She would be in a fog all day if she didn't have her coffee and after the restless night she'd had...

As she moved to the counter, she saw that there was a new young woman working. Had they already replaced Christy? The woman's dark hair was styled in a pixie cut that seemed to accent her dark eyes. She wore a temporary name tag that had LUCY printed neatly on it.

"So what can I get you?" Lucy asked with a slight lisp and a Southern accent as she flashed Mary a wide gap-toothed smile.

"One of your ultimate caramel frappaccinos to go."

The young woman laughed. "That one's my favorite."

"I was so sorry to hear about Christy," Mary said.

"I didn't really know her." Lucy stopped what she was doing for a moment to look over her shoulder at her. "I was shocked when I realized that Christy was the one who took my application. She was nice. I couldn't believe it when I got the call. I hate that her bad luck led to my good luck. My application was on the top of the pile."

"What brought you to Big Sky?" Mary asked, seeing that she'd made the young woman uncomfortable.

"Wanderlust. I had a job waiting for me in Spokane, but I found exactly what I was looking for right here in Big Sky, Montana. Is this the most beautiful place you've ever seen?"

Mary had to smile. "I've always thought so. Where are you from? I detect an accent."

Lucy laughed. "Texas. I can't seem to overcome my roots."

"I'd keep it if I were you."

"You think?" the woman asked as she set down the go cup on the counter in front of her.

Mary nodded. "I do. I hope you enjoy it here."

"Thanks. I know I will."

Chase was relieved when he got the call from Mary. He'd had a lot of time to think, and he didn't want to spend any more time away from her. He'd gone over to her place last night in the hopes that they could talk. But she hadn't been home. Was she out with the deputy? The thought made him crazy.

But he had only himself to blame. He'd broken her

heart when he'd left Montana. Even now though, he knew that he'd had to go. He was definitely too young for marriage back then.

But he'd grown up in the years he'd been gone. He'd learned a trade he loved. He'd seen some of the world. He wasn't the kid Mary used to hang out with. He'd known for some time what he wanted. It wasn't until he'd gotten her letter that he'd realized there was still hope. He'd been afraid that Mary had moved on a long time ago. But like him, she hadn't found anyone who tempted her into a relationship. That was until the deputy came along.

"I'm sorry about the other day, surprising you like that. You were right. I should have called."

"That's behind us," she said in a tone that let him know there was a lot more than a simple phone call to be overcome between them. He'd hurt her. Had he really thought she'd forgive him that quickly? "Just understand, I wrote that letter to tell you about the package that came for you. The rest of it was just me caught in a weak moment."

"I didn't think you had weak moments," he joked.

"Chase—"

"All I'm asking is for a chance to prove myself to you." Silence. "There's something I didn't tell you. My mother contacted me. She'd been sick off and on for years, in and out of remission. This time she was dying and wanted to see me. That's why I went to Arizona. She recently died."

"Oh, Chase, I'm so sorry. I hadn't heard."

"She asked me to bring her ashes back here. To Big Sky." He could almost hear Mary's hesitation.

"Did she…?"

"Tell me who my father was? No. I was with her the night she died. She took it to her grave."

"I'm so sorry." Mary knew how not knowing had haunted him his whole life. It was a mystery, one that had weighed him down. He wanted to know who he was, who he came from, why his mother refused to tell him. Was his father that bad? He'd known there was much more to the story, and it was a story he needed to hear.

"She did tell me one thing. She'd met the man who fathered me here in Big Sky. It's why she wanted her ashes brought back here."

"But that's all you know."

"For now. Listen—"

"I called about the package," Mary said quickly. "If your mother met your father here, well that would explain why a woman saying she was once your mother's friend left you the package. If you'd like to stop by my office to pick it up—"

"I can't come by before tomorrow. I'm working on the Jensen Ranch to earn some extra money. I had pickup trouble on the way back to town. But I was hoping we could go out—"

"I need time. Also I'm really busy."

"Is this about that deputy?" he asked, then mentally kicked himself.

"I'm not seeing Dillon right now either, not that it is any of your business. You don't get to just come back and—"

"Whoa, you're right. Sorry. I'll back off. Just know that I'm here and that I'm not going anywhere. I want you back, Mary. I've never stopped loving you and never will."

* * *

As if Mary could forget that Chase was back in town. After the phone call, she threw herself into her work, determined not to think about the handsome cowboy who'd stolen her heart years ago. Dillon kept leaving her messages. She texted him that she had a lot of work to do, and would get back to him in a day or two.

That night, she lay in bed, thinking about Chase, her heart aching. He'd hurt her, and angry, she'd broken up with him only to have him leave. She'd lost her friend and her lover. After all the years they'd spent growing up together, Mary had always thought nothing could keep them apart. She'd been wrong, and now she was terrified that she'd never really known Chase.

In the morning, she went down to work early, thankful for work to keep her mind off Chase even a little. Midmorning she looked up to see the new barista from the Lone Peak Perk standing in her doorway.

"Don't shoot me," Lucy said. "I just had a feeling you might need this." She held out the ultimate caramel frappaccino.

Mary could have hugged her. "You must be a mind reader," she said as she rose from her desk to take the container of coffee from her. "I got so busy, I actually forgot. I had no idea it was so late. I can't tell you how much I need this."

"I don't want to interrupt. I can see that you're busy," Lucy said, taking a step toward the door. "But when I realized you hadn't been in…"

"Just a minute, let me pay you."

Lucy waved her off. "My treat. My good deed for the day." She smiled her gap-toothed smile and pushed out the door.

"Thank you so much!" Mary called after her, smiling as she watched the young woman run back across the street to the coffee shop.

Hud found Chet Jensen in the barn at his father's place just down the canyon a few miles. The tall skinny cowboy was shoveling manure from the stalls. He heard him gag, and suspected the man was hungover even before he saw his face.

"Rough night?" he asked, startling the cowboy.

Chet jumped, looking sicker from the scare. "You can't just walk up on someone like that," he snapped.

"I need to talk to you," Hud said. "About Christy Shores."

"I figured." Chet leaned his pitchfork against the side of the stall. "I could use some fresh air." With that he stumbled out of the barn and into the morning sunshine.

Hud followed him to a spot behind the ranch house where a half dozen lawn chairs sat around a firepit. Chet dropped into one of the chairs. Hud took one opposite him, and pulled out his notebook and pen.

"You heard about the fight."

He nodded. "What was that about?"

"Christy." Chet scowled across at him. "You wouldn't be here unless you already knew that. Let's cut to the chase. I had nothing to do with her getting run over."

"Who did?"

He shrugged. "Not a clue. Beth Anne heard that a motor-home driver must have clipped her."

Hud shook his head. "I'm guessing it was someone local with a grudge. How long have you been involved with her?"

"It wasn't like that. I brought her back here a couple of times after we met a few weeks ago. I liked her."

"But?"

"But she liked Grady who was always throwing his money around, playing the big shot. I tried to warn her about him." He shook his head, then leaned over to take it in his hands.

"Are you saying you think Grady Birch might be responsible?"

"Beats me." Lifting his head, he said, "After we got thrown out of Charley's, I came home and went to bed."

"Did you see Grady leave?"

He nodded. "That doesn't mean he didn't come back."

"The same could be said about you."

Chet wagged his head. "Beth Anne was home. My sister knows I didn't leave. She was up until dawn making cookies for some special event she's throwing down at the flower shop. I couldn't have left without her seeing me."

"Christy have any enemies that you knew about?" he asked.

"I didn't think she'd been in town long enough to make enemies."

"But she'd been in town long enough to have the two of you fighting over her," he pointed out.

Chet met his gaze. "Grady and I would have been fighting over any woman we both thought the other wanted. It wasn't really even about her, you know what I mean?"

He did, he thought as he closed his notebook and got to his feet. "If you think of anyone who might have wanted her dead, call me."

Chapter 8

Mary was just starting across the street the next morning to get her coffee when the delivery van from the local flower shop pulled up in front of her building. It had been three days since she'd seen Chase. Both men had finally gotten the message and given her space. Not that the space had helped much except that she'd gotten a lot of work done.

She groaned as she saw Beth Anne Jensen climb out of the flower shop van. "I have something for you," the buxom blonde called cheerily.

Mary couldn't remember the last time anyone had sent her flowers. Reluctantly, she went back across the street since she could already taste her ultimate caramel frappaccino. Also, the last person she wanted to see this morning was Beth Anne. The blonde had her head stuck in the back of the van as she approached.

As her former classmate came out, she shoved cellophone wrapped vase with a red rose in it at her. "I'm sure you've already heard. Chase is back."

"I know. He came by the ranch a couple of days ago." That took some of the glee out of Beth Anne's expression.

"He's gone to work for my daddy."

Mary tried not to groan at the old news or the woman's use of "daddy" at her age. Of course, Chase had gone to work for Sherman Jensen. The Jensen Ranch was just down the road from the Cardwell spread. No wonder Chase had said he would be seeing her soon. The Jensens would be rounding up their cattle from summer range—just like everyone on Cardwell Ranch.

"Chase looks like being gone didn't hurt him none," the blonde said.

She didn't want to talk about Chase with this woman. She hadn't forgotten catching Chase and Beth Anne lip-locked before he left. Mary didn't know if she was supposed to tip the owner of the flower store or not. But if it would get Beth Anne to leave… She pulled out a five and shoved it at her. "Thanks," she said, and started to turn away.

"That's not all," the blonde said as she pocketed the five and handed her a wrapped bouquet of daisies in a white vase. "Appears you've got more than one admirer." Beth Anne raised a brow.

Mary assumed that the woman knew who had sent both sets of flowers—and had probably read the notes inside the small envelopes attached to each. But then again seeing the distinct handwriting of two men on the outside of the envelopes, maybe Beth Anne was as in the dark as Mary herself. The thought improved her day.

"Have a nice day," she sang out to Beth Anne as she headed for her office. Opening the door, she took the flowers inside, anxious to see whom they were from. She didn't want to get her hopes up. They both could be from one of the ranchers she worked for as a thank-you for the work she'd done for them.

She set down the vases on the edge of her desk and pulled out the first small envelope. Opening it, she read: "I know how you like daisies. I'm not giving up on us. Chase."

It would take more than daisies, she told herself even as her heart did a little bump against her ribs.

Shaking her head, she pulled out the other small white envelope, opened it and read: "Just wanted you to know I'm thinking of you, Dillon."

"I don't believe this," she said, and heard the front door of her building opening behind her. Spinning around, she half expected to see one or both of the men.

"Lucy," she said on a relieved breath. As touched as she was by the flowers, she wasn't up to seeing either man right now.

"Did I catch you at a bad time?" the barista asked, stopping short.

"Not at all. Your timing is perfect."

"I saw you start across the street to get your coffee and then get called back, so I thought I'd run it over to you. Your usual." She held out the cup.

"Thank you so much. I do need this, but I insist on paying you." Mary looked around for her purse. "Let me get you—"

"I put it on your account."

She stopped digging for money to look at her. "Lucy, I don't have an account."

The woman smiled that gap-toothed smile of hers that was rather infectious. "You do now. I just thought it would be easier but if I've overstepped—"

"I don't know why I hadn't thought of it, as many of these as I drink," Mary said, and raised the cup.

"I hope you don't mind. But this way, if you get too busy, just call and if we aren't busy, one of us can bring your coffee right over."

"Lucy, that's so thoughtful, but—"

"It really isn't an inconvenience. We haven't been that busy and I could use the exercise. Also it looks like you're celebrating something." She motioned to the flower delivery.

Mary laughed. "It's a long story."

"Well, I won't keep you. I better get back. It wasn't busy but it could be any minute. My shift ends soon, and I have to get back on my search for a place to live." She started to open the front door to leave.

"Lucy, wait. I have an apartment open. I haven't put up a notice that it's available. Christy was going to move in."

"The girl who died." She grimaced. "The one I replaced at Lone Peak Perk."

"Is that too weird for you?" Mary asked.

"Let me give it some thought. But could you hold on to it until later today? Thanks." And she was gone.

Mary sipped her coffee, thinking she probably shouldn't have offered the apartment without checking the young woman's references. But it was Lucy, who'd just bought her a coffee and run it across the street to her.

She turned to look at her flowers, forgetting for the

moment about anything else. What was she going to do about Chase? And Dillon?

Sitting down at her desk, she picked up her phone and called her best friend, Kara, who had moved to New York after college. But they'd managed to stay in touch by phone and Facetime. It was the kind of friendship that they could go without talking for weeks and pick up right where they'd left off.

"Chase is back," she said when her friend answered.

"In Big Sky?"

"He says he loves me and that he won't give up."

Kara took a breath and let it out slowly. "How do you feel about that?"

She sighed. "I still love him, but I've been seeing someone else. A deputy here. His name is Dillon. He's really good-looking in a kind of nothing-but-trouble kind of way."

Her friend was laughing. "When it rains it pours. Seriously? You have two handsome men who are crazy about you?"

She had to laugh. "Crazy might be the perfect word. They met the other day and sparks flew. I still love Chase, but when we broke up he didn't stay and fight for me. He just left. What's to keep him from doing it again?"

"And Dillon?"

"It's too new to say. They both sent me flowers today though."

"That's a good start," Kara said with a laugh.

"Chase sent daisies because he knows I love them."

"And Dillon?"

"A rose to let me know he was thinking about me."

"Mary! Who says you have to choose between them?"

"My father doesn't like me dating either one of them."

"Which makes you want to date them even more, knowing you."

"You *do* know me," she said, and laughed again. "How are you and your adorable husband and the kids?"

"I was going to call you. I'm pregnant again!"

"Congrats," she said, and meant it. Kara was made to be a mother.

"I have morning sickness, and I'm already starting to waddle."

Mary felt a stab of envy and said as much.

"Excuse me? If anyone is envious, it's me of you. You should see me right now. Sweats and a T-shirt with a vomit stain on it—my daughter's not mine."

She laughed. "And I'll bet you look beautiful as always."

A shriek and then loud crying could be heard in the background.

"I'll let you go," Mary said. "Congrats again."

"Same to you."

She sat for a moment, idly finishing her coffee and considering her flowers before going back to work. A while later, she picked up her phone and called Chase. "Thank you for the daisies. They're beautiful. If you have some time, I thought maybe you could stop by if you're free. Like I said, I have your package here at the office. I can tell you how to find the place."

Chase chuckled. "I know how to find you. I'll be right there."

Lucy looked out the window of the coffee shop and with a start saw Chase's truck pull up across the street.

Her heart squeezed as if crushed in a large fist. Had he seen Mary before this? Had they been meeting at night on the ranch? Jealousy made her stomach roil.

Chase had been hers. At least he had until Mary wrote him that letter. She was why he'd dumped her. To come back here to his precious cowgirl. She wasn't sure at that moment whom she hated more, him or Mary, as she watched him disappear into her office.

"Excuse me?" A woman stepped in front of her, blocking her view. It was all she could do not to reach across the counter and shove her out of the way. She wanted to see what was going on across the street. "I'd like to order."

Fortunately, she got control of herself. She needed this job to get closer to Mary and pull off her plan. If she hoped to pay back Chase, she couldn't lose her cool. She plastered a smile on her face.

"I'm sorry, what can I get you?" She hadn't even realized that her Texas accent had come back until that day when she'd finally met Mary Cardwell Savage. She'd thought she'd put Texas and her childhood behind her. But apparently all of this had brought it back—along with her accent.

As she made the woman a latte, she thought about spitting in her cup, but didn't. Instead, she let herself think about the apartment in Mary's building. Of course she was going to take it. She had already gained the woman's trust. It didn't matter that Chase was over there with Mary. Soon enough she would end their little romance.

She would just have to be careful to avoid Chase. The changes in her appearance were striking, but given what they'd shared, he would know her. He would sense her beneath her disguise. He'd feel the chemistry between them. So she needed to avoid him until she was ready to make her dramatic reveal.

Smiling to herself, she considered all the ways she could make their lives miserable, before she took care of both of them. As she'd told Christy Shores, she was lucky when it came to getting what she wanted. Hadn't she gotten this job and was about to get Christy's apartment, as well?

She wanted Chase and his precious Mary to suffer. She just had to be patient.

Chase removed his Stetson as he stepped into Mary's office. He couldn't help but admire the building and what she'd done with it. Hardwood floors shone beneath a large warm-colored rug. The walls were recycled brick, terra-cotta in color, with paintings and photographs of the area on the walls.

"Your office is beautiful," he said. "This place suits you."

Mary smiled at the compliment, but clearly she hadn't thawed much when it came to him.

"I heard you have a couple of apartments upstairs that you rent and live on the third floor," he said. "Wise investment."

That made her chuckle. "Thank you. I'm glad you approve."

"Mary, can we please stop this?" He took a step toward her, hating this impersonal wall between them. They knew each other. Intimately. They'd once been best friends—let alone lovers.

"Thank you again for the daisies." She picked up a

package from her desk and held it out to him, blocking his advance. "This is what was dropped off for you."

He chewed at the side of his cheek, his gaze on her not on the package. "Okay, if this is the way you want it. I'll wait as long as it takes." He could see that she didn't believe that. She'd lost faith in him and he couldn't blame her. For a while, he'd lost faith in himself.

"So you're working for Beth Anne's father at their ranch."

So that was it. "It's temporary. I have a job as a finish carpenter for a company that builds houses like the upscale ones here in Big Sky. It's a good job, but since it doesn't start for a week, I took what I could get in the meantime." He didn't mention that buying a new engine for his pickup had set him back some.

His gaze went to the daisies he'd had sent to her, but quickly shifted to the vase with the rose in it. "Is that from your deputy?"

Mary raised her chin. "Don't start, Chase." She was still holding the package out to him.

He took it without even bothering to look at it. He was so close now that she could smell his masculine scent mixed with the outdoors. "I can be patient, Mary," he said, his voice low, seductive. "Remember when we couldn't keep our hands off each other?" He took another step toward her, his voice dropping even more dangerously low. "I remember the taste of you, the feel of you, the way your breath quickens when you're naked in my arms and—"

His words sent an arrow of heat to her center. "Chase—"

He closed the distance, but she didn't step back as if under the cowboy's spell. With his free hand, he ran his fingertips leisurely down her cheek to the hollow of her throat toward the V of her blouse.

She shivered and instinctively she leaned her head back, remembering his lips making that same journey. Her nipples puckered, hard and aching against her bra. "Chase—" This time, she said his name more like a plea for him not to stop.

As he pulled his hand back, he smiled. "You and I will be together again come hell or high water because that's where we belong. Tell me I'm wrong."

When she said nothing, couldn't speak, he nodded, took the package and walked out, leaving her trembling with a need for him that seemed to have grown even more potent.

Chapter 9

Chase still hadn't paid any attention to the package Mary had given him until he tossed it on the seat of his pickup. The lightweight contents made a soft rustling sound, drawing his attention from thoughts of Mary for a moment.

As he climbed behind the wheel of his pickup, he considered what might be inside. It appeared to be an old shoebox that had been tied up with string. Both the box and the string were discolored, giving the impression of age. Why would someone leave him this? Mary had said the woman claimed to be a friend of his mother's.

His thoughts quickly returned to Mary as he drove back to the Jensen Ranch. He remembered the way she'd trembled under his touch. The chemistry was still there between them, stronger than ever. He'd wanted desperately to take her in his arms, to kiss her, to make love to her. If only she could remember how good they were together.

At the ranch, he took the shoebox inside the bunkhouse, where he was staying, tossing it on his bed. He told himself that he didn't care what was inside. But he couldn't help being curious. He sat down on the edge of the bed and drew the box toward him. It wasn't until then that he saw the faded lettering on the top and recognized his mother's handwriting.

For Chase. Only after I'm gone.

His heart thumped hard against his ribs. This was from his mother?

He dug out his pocketknife from his jeans pocket and with trembling fingers cut the string. He hesitated, bracing himself for what he would find inside, and lifted the lid. A musty scent rose up as the papers inside rustled softly.

Chase wasn't sure what he'd expected. Old photos? Maybe his real birth certificate with his father's name on it? A letter to him telling him the things his mother couldn't or wouldn't while she was alive?

What he saw confused him. It appeared to be pages torn from a notebook. Most were yellowed and curled. His mother's handwriting was overly loopy, youthful. Nothing like her usual very small neat writing that had always been slow with painstaking precision.

He picked up one of the pages and began to read. A curse escaped his lips as he realized what he was reading. These were diary pages. His mother had left him her diary? He'd never known her to keep one.

His gaze shot to the date on the top page. It took him

only a moment to do the math. This was written just weeks before he was conceived.

His pulse pounded. Finally he would know the truth about his father.

When her office door opened, Mary looked up, startled from her thoughts. Chase had left her shaken. She still wanted him desperately. But she was afraid, as much as she hated to admit it. She'd trusted her heart to Chase once. Did she dare do it again?

That's what she kept thinking even as she tried to get some work done. So when her door had opened, she was startled to realize how much time had gone by.

"Lucy." She'd forgotten all about her saying she might stop by later to discuss the apartment. Mary was glad for the distraction. "Come in."

The young woman took the chair she offered her on the other side of her desk. "Did you mean what you said earlier about renting me the apartment? It's just so convenient being right across the street, but I wanted to make sure you hadn't had second thoughts. After all, we just met."

Mary nodded since she'd *had* second thoughts. But as she looked into the young woman's eager face, she pushed them aside and reached into the drawer for the apartment key. "Why don't I show it to you." She rose from her desk. "We can either go up this way," she said, pointing to the back of her office, "or in from the outside entrance. Let's go this way." They went out of the back of her office to where a hallway wound around to the front stairs.

"The apartment is on the second floor," Mary told her as they climbed. "I live upstairs on the third floor.

Some people don't want to live that close to their land-lady," she said.

"I think I can handle it," Lucy said with a chuckle.

They stopped at the landing on the second floor, and Mary opened the door to the first apartment. "As you can see, it's pretty basic," she said as she pushed open the door. "Living room, kitchen, bedroom and bath." She watched Lucy take it in.

"It's perfect," the young woman said as she walked over to the window and looked out.

"There's a fire escape in the back, and a small balcony if you want to barbecue and not a bad view of Lone Peak." Mary walked to door and opened it so Lucy could see the view."

"That's perfect." She stepped past Mary out onto the small balcony to lean over the railing, before looking up. "So the fire escape goes on up to your apartment and balcony?"

"It does. I wouldn't use the fire escape except in an emergency so you will have privacy out here on your balcony."

Lucy stepped back in and closed the door. "I didn't even ask what the rent was." Mary told her. "That's really reasonable."

"I like providing housing for those working here in Big Sky. Most of the employees have to commute from the valley because there is so little affordable housing for them." She shrugged. "And it's nice to have someone else in the building at night. This area is isolated since it is mostly businesses that close by nine. The other apartment on this floor is rented to a man who travels a lot so I seldom see him."

Lucy ambled into the bedroom to pull down the Murphy bed. "This is great."

"You can use this room as an office as well as a bedroom. Since it has a closet, I call it a one bedroom."

"And it comes furnished?"

"Yes, but you can add anything you like to make it more yours."

Lucy turned to look at her. "I can really see myself living here. It's perfect. I would love it."

Mary smiled. "Then it's yours. You can move in right away if you want to."

"That's ideal because I've been staying in a motel down in the valley just hoping something opened up before I went broke."

"I'll need first and last month's rent, and a security deposit. Is that going to be a problem?"

Lucy grinned. "Fortunately, I'm not that broke yet, so no problem at all. I promise to be the perfect tenant."

Mary laughed. "I've yet to have one of those."

Back downstairs, Lucy paid in cash. Seeing her surprise, the young woman explained that she'd had the cash ready should she find a place. "They go so fast. I didn't want to miss a good opportunity. I feel as if I've hit the lottery getting first the job and now this apartment."

Mary smiled as she handed over the key. "It's nice to have you here."

"I wouldn't want to be anywhere else."

After Lucy left, Mary went back down to her office and called her mother. "I have a new tenant. It's a bit strange, but she's the barista who took Christy's place."

"That is odd. What do you know about her?"

Mary thought about it for a moment. Nothing really.

"She's nice." She told her how Lucy had run across the street to bring her coffee twice when Mary had gotten busy and forgotten.

"She sounds thoughtful."

"I like her so I hope it works out." Most of her tenants had, but there was always that one who caused problems.

"Guess who sent me flowers?" she said, changing the subject and putting her new tenant out of her mind.

Lucy couldn't believe how easy that had been. She smiled to herself as she drove back to her motel to get her things.

Mary would be living right upstairs. It would be like taking candy from a baby. She thought of the fire escape and balconies on the two levels behind the apartment. It would be so easy to climb up to Mary's on the third floor, anytime, day or night. While there was a railing around the stairs—and the balconies—still it could be dangerous, especially if Mary had been drinking.

Her thoughts turned sour though when she recalled the two sets of flowers that had been delivered this morning. Anger set off a blaze in her chest. They had to be from Chase, right? She would have loved to have seen what he'd written on the cards. Now that she would be living in the building, maybe she would get her chance.

She still felt surprised at just how easy it had been. Then again, Mary was just too sweet for words, she thought. Also too trusting. At first, she'd just wanted to meet the woman who'd taken Chase from her. At least that's what she'd told herself. Maybe she'd planned to kill her from the very beginning. Maybe it really had been in the back of her mind from the moment she decided to go to Montana and find her—find Chase.

Her feeling had been that if she couldn't have Chase, then no one else could. She'd had dreams of killing them both. Of killing Mary and making him watch, knowing there was nothing Chase could do to save her.

But in her heart of hearts, when she was being honest with herself, she knew what she wanted was for him to fall in love with her again. Otherwise, she would have no choice. It would be his own fault. He would have to die, but only after he mourned for the loss of his precious Mary. She would kill him only after she shattered his life like he'd done hers.

Living just one floor below the woman would provide the perfect opportunity to get closer to Mary—and Chase—until she was ready to end this.

It would be dangerous. She smiled to herself. There was nothing wrong with a little danger. Eventually she and Chase would cross paths. Lucy smiled in anticipation. She couldn't wait to see the look on his face when he realized she wasn't dead. Far from it. She'd never been more alive.

Chapter 10

After the first sentence, Chase couldn't believe it. The pages in the shoebox were from a diary. His mother's. His fingers trembled as he picked up another page. All these years he'd wanted answers. Was he finally going to get them?

He thumbed through the random pages, looking for names. There were none. But he did find initials. He scooped up the box and pages and sat down, leaning against the headboard as he read what was written before the initials. "I woke up this morning so excited. Today was going to be wonderful. I was going to see J.M. today. He told me to meet him in our secret spot. Maybe he's changed his mind. I can only hope."

Changed his mind about what?

Chase took out another page, but it was clear from reading it that the page wasn't the next day. He began to sort them by date. Some weren't marked except by the day of the week.

But he found one that began "Christmas Day." Whoever J.M. was, his mother had been in love with the man. And since his birthday was in September—nine months from Christmas…

The entry read: "Christmas Day! I thought I wouldn't get to see him, but he surprised me with a present—a beautiful heart-shaped locket."

Chase felt his heart clench. His mother had worn such a locket. She never took it off. It was with the few things of hers that he'd kept. But he knew there was nothing but a photo of him in the locket. On the back were the words: *To my love always.*

He picked up the phone.

Mary answered on the second ring. "Chase?"

"I don't mean to bother you. But I had to tell you. It's my mother's diary."

"What's your mother's diary?"

"In the shoebox. It's pages from my mother's diary during the time that she got pregnant with me." Silence. "I really could use your help. I think the answer is somewhere in these pages but they're all mixed up. Some have dates, some don't and—"

"Bring them over. We can go through them in my apartment."

A short time later, Mary let him into the door on the side of the building, the shoebox tucked under his arm as they climbed to the third floor.

"Do you want something to drink?" she asked as he closed the door behind them.

The apartment was done in bright cheery colors that

reminded him of Mary. "No, thanks." He felt nervous now that he was here.

She motioned to the dining-room table standing in a shaft of morning sun. Through the window, he could see Lone Peak. "Your apartment is wonderful," he said as he put the shoebox on the table and sat down.

"Thanks." Mary pulled out a chair opposite him. "May I?" she asked, and pulled the box toward her.

He nodded. "I looked at some of it, but truthfully, I didn't want to do this alone."

She took out the diary pages, treating them as if they were made of glass. "There had to be a reason her friend was told to give you this after she was gone." She picked up one page and read aloud, "'Friday, I saw him again at Buck's T-4. He didn't see me but I think he knew I was there. He kept looking around as if looking for me.'"

"She met him here in Big Sky!" Mary exclaimed as she flipped the page over. "'Saturday. I hate that we can't be together. He hates it too so that makes me feel a little better.'"

She looked up at Chase. "They were star-crossed lovers right here in Montana."

"Star-crossed lovers?" He scoffed. "From what I've read, it's clear that he was a married man." He raked a hand through his hair. "What if my father has been here in Big Sky all this time, and I never knew it?"

Mary could see how hard this was on him, just as she could tell that a part of him wasn't sure he wanted to know the truth. "Are you sure you want to find him?"

Chase had been fifteen when his mother had gotten sick the first time, and he'd come to the area to work on a neighboring ranch. Later, Mary's family had put him to work on their ranch, giving him a place to live while he and Mary finished school.

They'd both believed that he'd been sent to Montana because of one of Hud's law-enforcement connections. Her father had never spelled it out, but she now realized that both of her parents must have known Chase's mother back when she'd lived here. She must have been the one who'd asked them to look out for him.

Mary and Chase had been close from the very start. From as far back as she could remember, he'd been haunted by the fact that he didn't know who his father was. He'd been born in Arizona. He'd just assumed that was where his mother met his father. He hadn't known that there was much more of a Montana connection than either he or Mary had known. Until now.

"Truthfully? I'm not sure of anything." His gaze met hers. "Except how I feel about you."

"Chase—"

He waved a hand through the air. "Sorry. As for my…father… I have to know who he is and why he did what he did."

She nodded. "So we'll find him," she said, and picked up another page of the diary. "There has to be some reason he couldn't marry your mother."

He swore under his breath. "I told you. He was already married. It's the only thing that's ever made sense. It's why my mother refused to tell me who he is."

"Maybe she mentions his name on one of the pages," Mary suggested. "If we put them in order." She went to work, sorting through them, but quickly realized that she never mentioned him by name, only J.M.

She stopped sorting to look at him. "J.M.? He shouldn't be hard to find if he still lives here." She got up and went to a desk, returning with a laptop. "Maybe we should read through them first though. It doesn't look as if she wrote something every day." She counted the diary sheets. "There are forty-two of them with days on both sides, so eight-four days."

"About three months," Chase said. "If we knew when the affair started…" They quickly began going through the pages. "This might help," he said as he held up one of the pages.

Something in his voice caught her attention more than his words. "What is it?"

"Christmas Eve." He read what his mother had written. "'It was so romantic. I never dreamed it could be like this. But he reminded me that I didn't have much to compare it with. He said it would get better. I can't imagine.'"

Chase looked up. "I was born nine months later."

"I'm sorry," she said.

He shrugged as if it didn't matter, but it was clear that it mattered a whole lot. "I have to know who he is."

She heard the fury in his voice as he told her about the heart-shaped necklace that his mother had never taken off. "Maybe he loved her."

He scoffed at that. "If he'd loved her, he wouldn't have abandoned her. She was alone, broke and struggling to raise his child."

"Maybe the answer is in these pages, and we just missed something," Mary said after they finished going through them.

He shook his head and scooped up the diary pages, stuffing them roughly back into the shoebox and slamming down the lid.

Mary wanted to know the whole story. She looked at

the box longingly. It was clear that Chase had already made up his mind. Even after reading all the diary entries, she knew it was his mother's view of the relationship, and clearly Muriel's head had been in the stars.

"What are you going to do?" she asked, worried.

"Find him. J.M. The Big Sky area isn't that large." He stepped over to the laptop and called up local phone listings from the browser and started with the *M*s. "We can surmise from what she wrote that he's older, more experienced and married. The necklace he gave her wasn't some cheap dime-store one. He had money, probably owned a business in town."

She hesitated, worried now what he would do once he found the man in question. "I think you should let me go with you once we narrow down the list of men."

He looked at her, hope in his expression. "You would do that?"

"Of course." She picked up the phone to call her mother. Dana had known Chase's mother Muriel. That was clearly why Chase had come to live on the ranch at fifteen. "I need to know how Chase came to live with us."

She listened, and after a moment hung up and said to Chase, "Your mother worked in Meadow Village at the grocery store. She says she didn't know who Muriel was seeing, and I believe her. She would have told us if she'd known. She did say that your mother rented a place on the edge of town. So your mother could have met your father at the grocery store or on her way to work or just about anywhere around here."

Chase shook his head. "His wife probably did the grocery shopping."

"We don't know that he had a wife. We're just assuming..." But Chase wasn't listening. He was going through the phone listings.

Grady Birch had been leaving when Hud pulled into the drive in front of the cabin. For just a moment, he thought the man might make a run for it. Grady's expression had been like a deer caught in his headlights. Hud suspected the man always looked like that when he saw the law—and for good reason.

It amused the marshal that Grady pretended nonchalance, leaning against the doorframe as if he had nothing to hide. As Hud exited his patrol SUV and moved toward the man, Grady's nerves got the better of him. His elbow slid off the doorframe, throwing the man off balance. He stumbled to catch himself, looking even more agitated.

"Marshal," he said, his voice high and strained before he cleared his throat. "What brings you out this way?"

"Why don't we step into your cabin and talk?" Hud suggested.

Grady shot a look behind him through the doorway as if he wasn't sure what evidence might be lying around in there. "I'd just as soon talk out here. Unless you have a warrant. I know my rights."

"Why would I have a warrant, Mr. Birch? I just drove out here to talk to you about Christy Shores."

Grady frowned. That hadn't been what he'd expected. The man's relief showed on his ferret-thin face. Grady's relief that this was about Christy told Hud that this had been a wasted trip. The man hadn't killed the barista. Grady was more worried about being arrested for cattle rustling.

"I just have a couple of quick questions," Hud said,

hoping Grady gave him something to go on. "You dated Christy?"

"I wouldn't call it dating exactly."

"You were involved with her."

Grady shook his head. "I wouldn't say that either."

Hud sighed and shifted on his feet. "What would you say?"

"I knew who she was."

"You knew her well enough to get in a fight over her at Charley's the night she was killed."

"Let's say I had a good thing going with her, and Chet tried to horn in."

"What did Christy have to say about all this?"

Grady frowned as if he didn't understand the question. He was leaning against the doorframe again, only this time he looked a lot more comfortable.

Hud rephrased it. "What did she get out of this…relationship with you?"

"Other than the obvious?" Grady asked with a laugh. "It was a place to sleep so she didn't have to go back to her mother's in Bozeman."

"Is that where she was headed that night, to your cabin?"

Grady shook his head. "I told her it wasn't happening. I saw her making eyes at Chet. Let him put her up out at his place. I won't be used by any woman."

Hud had to bite his tongue. The way men like Grady treated women made his teeth ache. "When was the last time you saw her?"

"When Chet told her to scram and she ran into the bathroom crying."

"That was before the two of you got thrown out of the bar?" the marshal asked.

Grady nodded. "So have you found out who ran her down?"

"Not yet."

"Probably some tourist traveling through. I was in Yellowstone once, and there was this woman walking along the edge of the highway and this motor home came along. You know how those big old things have those huge side mirrors? One of them caught her in the back of the head." Grady made a disgusted sound. "Killed her deader than a doornail. Could have taken her head off if the driver had been going faster."

"Christy Shores wasn't killed by a motor home. She was murdered by someone locally."

Grady's eyes widened. "Seriously? You don't think Chet…"

"Chet has an alibi for the time of the murder. Can anyone verify that you came straight here to this cabin and didn't leave again?"

"I was alone, but I can assure you I didn't leave again."

Hud knew the value of an assurance by Grady Birch. "You wouldn't know anyone who might have wanted to harm her, do you?"

He wagged his head, still looking shocked. "Christy was all right, you know. She didn't deserve that." He sounded as if he'd just realized that if he'd brought her back to his cabin that night, she would still be alive.

Dillon was headed to Grady's when he saw the marshal's SUV coming out of the dirt road into the cabin. He waved and kept going as if headed to Bozeman, his pulse thundering in his ears. What had the marshal been doing out at the cabin? Was he investigating the cattle rustling?

He glanced in his rearview mirror. The marshal hadn't slowed or turned around as if headed back to Big Sky, and as far as Dillon could tell, Grady wasn't handcuffed in the back. He kept going until he couldn't see the patrol SUV in his rearview anymore before he pulled over, did a highway patrol turn and headed back toward the cabin.

His instincts told him not to. The marshal might circle back. Right now, he especially didn't want Hud knowing about his association with Grady Birch. But he had to find out what was going on. If he needed to skip the state, he wanted to at least get a running start.

He drove to the cabin, parking behind it. As he did, he saw Grady peer out the window. Had he thought the marshal had reason to return? The back door flew open. Grady looked pale and shaken. Dillon swore under his breath. It must be bad. But how bad?

"What—" He didn't get to finish his question before Grady began to talk, his words tumbling over each other. He caught enough of it to realize that the marshal's visit had nothing to do with cattle. Relief washed over him.

Pushing past Grady, he went into the cabin, opened the refrigerator and took the last beer. He guzzled it like a man dying of thirst. That had been too close of a call. He'd been so sure that Hud was on to them.

"Did you hear what I said?" Grady demanded. "She was *murdered*. Marshal said so himself."

Dillon couldn't care less about some girl Grady had been hanging with, and said as much.

"You really are a coldhearted bastard," Grady

snapped. "And you drank the last beer," he said as he opened the refrigerator. "How about you bring a six-pack or two out for a change? I do all the heavy lifting and you—"

"Put a sock in it or I will." He wasn't in the mood for any whining. "I have my own problems."

"The marshal sniffing around you?"

He finished the beer and tossed the can into the corner with the others piled there. "It's the marshal's daughter. Things aren't progressing like I planned."

Grady let out a disgusting sound. "I really don't care about your love life. I've never understood why you were messing with her to start with."

"Because she could be valuable, but I don't have to explain myself to you."

His partner in crime bristled. "You know I'm getting damned tired of you talking down to me. Why don't you rustle your own cattle? I'm finished."

"Where do you think you're going?" Dillon asked, noticing a flyer on the table that he hadn't seen before. With a shock, he saw that it advertised a reward from local ranchers for any information about the recent cattle rustling.

"I'm going into Charley's to have a few, maybe pick up some money shooting pool, might even find me a woman."

"You've already jeopardized the entire operation because of the last woman you brought out here."

Grady turned to look back at him. "What are you talking about?"

"Where'd you get that notice about the reward being offered by the ranchers?"

"They're all over town."

"So you just picked up one. Did the marshal see it?"

Grady colored. "No, I wouldn't let him in. I'm not a fool."

But Dillon realized that he *was* a fool, one that he could no longer afford. "I'm just saying that maybe you should lie low."

"I was headed into town when the marshal drove up. He doesn't suspect me of anything, all right? I've got cabin fever. You stay here and see how you like it." He turned to go out the door.

Dillon picked up the hatchet from the kindling pile next to the woodstove. He took two steps and hit Grady with the blunt end. The man went down like a felled pine, his face smashing into the back porch floor. When he didn't move, Dillon set about wiping any surface he had touched on his visits. He'd always been careful, he thought as he wiped the refrigerator door and the hatchet's handle.

His gaze went to the pile of beer cans in the corner and realized that his prints were all over those cans. Finding an old burlap bag, he began to pick up the cans when he saw an old fishing pole next to the door. Smiling, he knew how he could dispose of Grady's body.

Chapter 11

Dillon touched Mary's cheek, making her jump. "I didn't mean to startle you. It's just that you seemed a million miles away."

Actually only five miles away, on the ranch where Chase was working.

She couldn't quit thinking about him, which is why she hadn't wanted to go out with Dillon tonight, especially after she'd told him that she needed more time.

"I guess you forgot," he'd said. "The tickets to the concert I bought after the last time we went out? You said you loved that band, and I said I should try to get us some tickets. Well I did. For tonight."

She'd recalled the conversation. It hadn't been definite, but she hadn't been up to arguing about it. Anyway, she knew that if she stayed home, all she'd do was mope around and worry about Chase.

"You've been distracted this whole night."

"Sorry," she said. "But you're right. I have a lot on my mind. Which is why I need to call it a night."

"Anything I can help you with?" he asked.

She shook her head.

"It wouldn't be some blond cowboy named Chase Steele, would it?" There was an edge to his voice. She wasn't in the mood for his jealousy.

"Chase is a friend of mine."

"Is that all?"

She turned to look at him, not liking his tone. "I can go out with anyone I want to."

"Oh, it's like that, is it?"

She reached for her door handle, but he grabbed her arm before she could get out.

"Slow down," he said. "I was just asking." He quickly let go of her. "Like you said, you can date anyone you please. But then, so can I. What if I decided to ask out that barista friend of yours?"

"Lucy?" She was surprised he even knew about her.

"Yeah, Lucy."

If he was trying to make her jealous, he was failing badly. "Be my guest," she said, and opened her door and climbed out before he could stop her again.

She heard him get out the driver's side and come after her. "Good night Dillon," she said pointedly. But he didn't take the hint.

As she pulled out her keys to open her office door, he grabbed her and shoved her back, caging her against the side of the building.

"I won't put up with you giving me the runaround."

"Let me go," she said from between gritted teeth. Her voice sounded much stronger than she felt at that moment. Her heart was beating as if she'd just run a mile. Dillon was more than wild. She could see that he could be dangerous—more dangerous than she was interested in.

Chance had been parked down the street, waiting for Mary to return home. He needed to talk to her about earlier. Since getting the box his mother had left for him, he'd been so focused on finding his father that he wanted to apologize. She'd offered to help. He wanted to get it over with as soon as possible since he'd managed to narrow it down to three names.

It wasn't until he saw the pickup stop in front of her building that he realized she had been on a date with that deputy.

He growled under his breath. There was something about that guy that he didn't like. And it wasn't just that he was going out with Mary, he told himself.

Now he mentally kicked himself for sitting down the street watching her place. If she saw him, she'd think he was spying on her. He reached to key the ignition and leave when he saw the passenger door of the deputy's rig open. From where he sat, he couldn't miss the deputy grabbing Mary as she tried to get out. What the hell?

He was already opening his door and heading toward her building when he saw Dillon get out and go after her. He could tell by her body language that she wasn't happy. What had the deputy done to upset her?

Chase saw that Dillon had pinned her against the side of her building. Mary appeared to be trying to get her keys out and go inside.

"Let her go!" he yelled as he advanced on the man.

Both Mary and Dillon turned at the sound of his voice. Both looked surprised, then angry.

"This is none of your business," the two almost said in unison.

"Let go of her," he said again to the deputy.

Mary pushed free of Dillon's arms and, keys palmed, turned to face Chase as he approached. "What are you doing here?"

"I needed to talk to you, but I'm glad I was here to run interference for you. If he's giving you trouble—"

"I can handle this," she said.

Chase could see how upset she was at Dillon and now him. "Date's over. You should go," he said to the deputy.

Dillon started to come at him. Chase was ready, knowing he could take him in a fair fight. He just doubted the man had ever fought fair. Dillon threw the first punch and charged. Chase took only a glancing blow before he slugged the deputy square in the face, driving him back, but only for a moment.

The man charged again, leading with a right and then a quick left that caught Chase on the cheek. He hit Dillon hard in the stomach, doubling him over before shoving him back. The deputy sprawled on the ground, but was scrambling to his feet reaching for something in his boot when Chase heard Mary screaming for them to stop.

"Stop it!" Mary cried. "Both of you need to leave. Now."

Dillon slowly slide the knife back into its scabbard, but not before Chase had seen it. He realized how quickly the fight could have gotten ugly if Mary hadn't stopped it when she did.

The deputy got up from the ground, cussing and spitting out blood. His lip was cut and bleeding. Chase's jaw and cheek were tender. He suspected he'd have a black eye by morning.

The look Dillon gave him made it clear that this wasn't over. The next time they saw each other, if Mary wasn't around, they would settle things. At least now Chase knew what he would be facing. A man who carried a blade in his boot.

"Leave now," Mary repeated.

"We'll finish our discussion some other time," Dillon said to her pointedly, making Chase wish he knew what had been said before Mary had gotten upset and tried to go inside. Now, she said nothing as Dillon started toward his pickup.

"That man is dangerous, Mary. If he—"

She spun on him. "Are you spying on me, Chase?"

"No, I needed to talk to you. I was just waiting…" He knew he sounded lame. It had been weak to wait down the street for her.

She didn't cut him any slack. "I'm sure whatever you need to talk to me about can wait until tomorrow." She turned to open her door.

"I'm sorry," he said behind her, glad he'd been here, even though he'd made her angry. He hated to think what could have happened if he hadn't intervened.

Mary didn't answer as she went inside and closed the door.

As he walked back to his pickup, he knew he had only himself to blame for all of this. He'd made so many mistakes, and he could add tonight's to the list.

Still, he worried. Mary thought she could handle Dillon. But the deputy didn't seem like a man who would take no for an answer.

* * *

Torn between anger and fear, Mary closed and locked the door behind her with trembling fingers. What was wrong with her? Tears burned her eyes. She hadn't wanted to go out with Dillon tonight. So why had she let him persuade her into it?

And Chase. Parked down the street watching her, spying on her? She shook her head. If he thought he could come back after all this time and just walk in and start—

"Is everything okay?" asked a voice behind her, making her jump. "I didn't mean to startle you," Lucy said, coming up beside her in the hallway of her building.

Mary was actually glad to see Lucy. She'd had it with men tonight. She wiped her eyes, angry at herself on so many levels, but especially for shedding more tears over Chase. Her life had felt empty without him, before Dillon, but now she missed that simple world.

Even as she told herself that, she knew she was lying. Chase was back. She loved him. She wanted him. So why did she keep pushing him away?

"What was that about?" Lucy asked, wide-eyed as they both watched the two men leave, Dillon in a hail of gravel as he spun out, and Chase limping a little as he headed for his truck.

"Nothing," she said, and took a deep breath before letting it out. She was glad to have Lucy in the building tonight.

Lucy laughed. "*Nothing?* They were fighting over you. Two men were just fighting over you." She was looking at her with awe.

Mary had to smile. "It had more to do with male ego than me, trust me." She thought about saying something to Lucy about Dillon's warning to Mary that he'd ask her out, but realized it was probably a hollow threat. Anyway, she was betting that Lucy could take care of herself.

Lucy tried to keep the glee out of her voice. She'd witnessed the whole thing. Poor Chase. What struck her as ironic was that she'd had nothing to do with any of it. This was all Mary's own doing.

"Would you like to come up to my apartment for a drink? Sometimes I've found talking also helps." She shrugged.

Mary hesitated only a moment before she gave Lucy an embarrassed smile. "Do you have beer?"

Lucy laughed. "Beer, vodka, ice cream. I'm prepared for every heartbreak."

They climbed the stairs, Lucy opened the door and they entered her apartment. "I haven't done much with the space," Lucy said as she retrieved two beers from the refrigerator and handed one to Mary. "But I'm excited to pick up a few things to make it more mine. It really doesn't need anything. You've done such a good job of appointing it."

"Thank you," Mary said, taking the chair in the living room. "I'm just glad you're enjoying staying here. I'm happy to have you." Mary took a sip of her beer, looking a little uneasy now that she was here.

Lucy curled her legs under her on the couch, getting comfortable, and broke the ice, first talking about decorating and finally getting to the good part. "I had to laugh earlier. I once had two men fight over me. It was in high school at a dance. At the time I'd been mortified with embarrassment." She chuckled. "But my friends all thought it was cool."

"That was high school. It's different at this age," Mary said, and took another drink of her beer.

Lucy cocked her head at her as she licked beer foam from her lips and got up to get them another. "But I'm betting there was one of those men who you wanted to win the fight for you."

Mary looked surprised, then embarrassed.

"I wager it wasn't the deputy."

"You're right," her landlady admitted as she took the second beer. "Chase was my first love since the age of fifteen when he came to Montana to work on the ranch. We became best friends before..." Mary mugged a face. "Before we fell in love."

"So what happened to your happy ending?" Lucy asked as she took her beer back to the couch. She leaned toward Mary expectantly.

"I caught him kissing another woman. He swore the woman kissed him, but I guess I realized then that maybe what my parents had been saying was true. We were too young to be that in love. Only twenty-four. I let Chase go. He left Montana to...find himself," Mary said, and took another sip.

"*Find himself?* I'm guessing you didn't know he was lost."

Mary shook her head with a laugh. "We *were* too young to make any big decisions until we'd lived more. My father said that I had to let Chase sow some wild oats. But I didn't want him to leave."

Lucy groaned. "If he wanted to date other women, you didn't really want him to do it here, did you?"

"I wanted him to tell me that he didn't need to go

see what else was out there. That all he wanted was me. But he didn't."

"And now it's too late?"

Mary shook her head. "I still love him."

Lucy traced her fingers around the top of her beer can for a moment. "Why do you think he came back now?"

Mary shook her head. "It's my fault." She sighed. "Have you ever had a weak moment when you did something stupid?"

She laughed. "Are you kidding? Especially when it comes to men."

"I found his address online since I didn't have his cell phone number or email, and he wasn't anywhere on social media. I wrote him a letter, late at night in a nostalgic mood." Mary shook her head. "Even as I wrote it, I knew I'd never mail it."

This was news. "You didn't mail it?"

"I did put it in an envelope with his address on it. I was staying out at the ranch because my horse was due to have her colt that night. I forgot about the letter— until I realized it was gone. My aunt Stacy saw it and thought I meant to mail it, so she did it for me."

Lucy leaned back, almost too surprised to speak. "So if your aunt hadn't done that…"

Mary nodded. "None of this would have probably happened, although Chase says he was planning to come back anyway. But who knows?"

The woman had no idea, Lucy thought. "So, he's back and he's ready to settle down finally?"

"I guess."

She sipped her beer for a moment. "Is that what you want?"

"Yes, I still love him. But…"

"But there is that adorable deputy," Lucy said with a laugh. "Sounds like a problem we should all have. And it's driving Chase crazy with jealousy."

"You're right about that. He can hardly be civil to Dillon when they cross paths. He says there's something about the guy that he doesn't trust."

"Obviously, he doesn't want you dating the guy."

"I'm not going out with Dillon again, and it has nothing to do with what Chase wants. I didn't date for a long time after Chase left. I was too heartbroken. I finally felt ready to move on, and I wrote that stupid letter." She drained her beer, and Lucy got up to get her another.

"What about you?" Mary asked, seeming more comfortable now that she'd gotten that off her chest and consumed two beers.

"Me?" Lucy curled up on the couch again. "There was someone. I thought we were perfect for each other. But in the end, I was more serious than he was." She shook her head. "You know what I think is wrong with men? They don't know what they want. They want you one day, especially if there is another guy in the picture, but ultimately how can you trust them when the next minute they're waffling again? Aren't you afraid that could happen if Dillon is out of the picture?"

Mary shook her head. "I'd rather find out now than later. Trust. That is what it comes down to. Chase broke my trust when he left, when he didn't answer my letter right away or even bother to call." She seemed to hesitate. "There was this woman he was seeing."

Her ears perked up. "He told you about her?"

"He had to after I told him that she'd called me. Apparently, she'd read my letter to him. She called to tell me to leave him alone because they were engaged."

"Were they?"

"No, he says that she's delusional."

"Wow, it does sound like she was emotionally involved in a big way. He must have cared about her a little for her to react that way."

Mary shrugged. "I know he feels guilty. He certainly didn't want her to die. He admitted that he slept with her one night. But that now just the sound of her name is like fingernails on a blackboard for me. *Fiona.*" She dragged out the pronunciation of the name.

Lucy laughed. *"He even told you her name?* Men. Sometimes they aren't very smart. Now you'll always wonder about her and if there is more to the story."

Chapter 12

Mary couldn't remember the last time she'd drunk three beers. But as she'd taken the stairs to her third-floor apartment, she'd been smiling. She'd enjoyed the girl-time with Lucy. It made her realize how cut off she'd been from her friends.

A lot of them had moved away after college, and not come back except for a week at Christmas or in the summer. They'd married, had children or careers that they had to get back to. Even though they often promised to stay in touch, they hadn't. Life went on. People changed.

Mary also knew that some of them thought staying in a place where they'd grown up had a stigma attached to it as if, like Chase, they thought the grass was greener away from Big Sky, away from Montana. They went to cities where there were more opportunities. They had wanted more. Just like Chase.

They had wanted something Mary had never yearned for. Everything she needed was right here, she told herself as she drove out to the ranch. She'd wandered past the state line enough during her college days that she knew there was nothing better out there than what she had right here.

So why hadn't she been able to understand Chase's need to leave? Why had she taken it so personally? He'd wanted her to go with him, she reminded herself. But she'd had no need to search for more, not realizing that losing Chase would make her question everything she held dear.

Mary found her mother in the kitchen alone. The moment Dana saw her she said, "What's wrong?"

She and her mother had always been close. While her male siblings had left Montana, she'd been the one to stay. Probably since she'd been the one most like her mother and grandmother.

"Nothing really," she said as she poured herself a cup of coffee and dropped into a chair at the large kitchen table. Sunshine streamed in the open window along with the scent of pine and the river. "Can't I just come by to see my mother?"

Dana cocked an eyebrow at her.

She sighed and said, "It's *everything*. Chase's mother left him this shoebox with diary pages from what appears to be the time she became pregnant with him."

"About his father? That's why you called me and asked me if I knew. Isn't his name in the diary pages?"

She shook her head. "Muriel didn't mention his name, just his initials, J.M. Does that ring any bells?"

"No, I'm sorry. I didn't know Muriel well. I'd see her at the grocery store. She came out to the ranch a couple of times. We went horseback riding. Then I heard that she'd left town. Fifteen years later, she contacted me, thanked me for my kindness back when she lived in Big Sky and asked for our help with Chase."

Mary nodded. "Well, we know why she left. It appears her lover might have been married or otherwise unavailable."

"That would explain a lot," Dana said. "How is Chase taking all of this?"

Mary shook her head. "Not well. He's determined to find him. But with only the man's initials…"

"That's not much help I wouldn't think."

"I'm afraid what he'll do when he finds him," Mary said. "He has such animosity toward him."

"It's understandable. If the man knew Muriel was pregnant and didn't step up, I can see how that has hurt Chase. But is that what happened?"

"That's just it. We don't know. Either she didn't include the diary pages at the end or she never wrote down what happened. The last page we found she was going to meet him at their special place and was very nervous about telling him the news. But that she believed their love could conquer anything."

Dana shook her head. "So Chase is assuming she told him and he turned her away."

Mary nodded. "It's the obvious assumption given that his mother refused to tell him anything about his father."

Dana got up to refill her cup. When she returned to the table, she asked, "How was your date with Dillon last night?"

Mary looked away. "I'm not going out with him again."

"Did something happen?" Dana sounded alarmed,

and Mary knew if she didn't downplay it, her mother would tell her father, and who knew what he would do. He already didn't like Dillon.

"It was fine, but that's the problem. He's not Chase." Her mother was giving her the side-eye, clearly not believing any of it.

She realized that she had to give her more or her mother would worry. "Dillon doesn't like me seeing Chase."

"I see." She probably did. "So that's it?"

She nodded. "Chase isn't wild about me seeing Dillon, but he's smart enough not to try to stop me." Mary tried to laugh it all off as she got up to take her cup to the sink. "Kara says it's a terrible problem to have, two men who both want me."

"Yes," her mother said. "If Dillon gives you a hard time—"

"Do not say a word to Dad about this. You know how he is. I just don't want to go out with Dillon again. That should make Dad happy."

"Only if it is your choice."

"It is. I need to get to work."

Dana got up to hug her daughter before she left. "We just want you to be happy. Right now it doesn't sound like either man is making you so."

"His mother's diary has blindsided Chase, but it would anyone. This whole mystery about who his father is…" She glanced at the clock. "I have to get going. Remember, nothing about this to Dad."

Her mother nodded even though Mary knew there were few secrets between them.

Lucy couldn't have been more pleased with the way things had gone last night. Mary had been furious with

Chase. The cowboy had done it to himself. *Fiona* hadn't
even had a hand in it.

She was still chuckling about it this morning when
the bell over the coffee shop door jangled and she turned
to see the deputy come in.

Dillon Ramsey. She immediately picked up a vibe
from him that made her feel a kinship. They might have
more in common than Mary.

"Good morning," she said, wondering what kind of
night he'd had after everything that had happened. How
serious was he about Mary? Not that much, she thought
as he gave her the eye. He had a cut lip and bruise on his
jaw, but he didn't seem any the worse for wear.

"What can I get you?" she asked, and he turned on
a grin that told her he'd come in for more than coffee.
What was this about?

"I'd take a coffee, your choice, surprise me."

Oh, she could surprise him in ways he never dreamed
of. But she'd play along. "You got it," she said, and went
to work on his coffee while he ambled over to the window to stare across the street at Mary's building.

She made him something strong enough to take paint
off the walls, added a little sweetness and said, "I think
I have just what you need this morning."

He chuckled as he turned back to her. "I think you're
right about that." He blatantly looked her up and down.
"Go out with me."

Okay, she hadn't been expecting that. But all things
considered, the idea intrigued her. "I'm sorry, but aren't
you dating my landlady?"

"Who says I can't date you too?"

She raised an eyebrow. Clearly, he wanted to use her

to make Mary jealous. He could mess up her plans. She couldn't let him do that. Realizing he could be a problem, she recalled that Mary had plans tonight so she wouldn't be around.

"I'll tell you what. I'm working the late shift tonight. I wouldn't be free until midnight." She wrote down the number of her burner phone and handed him the slip of paper. "Why don't you give me a call sometime."

He grinned as he paid for his coffee. "I'll do that."

Lucy grinned back. "I'm looking forward to it," she said, meaning it. Dillon thought he could use her. The thought made her laugh. He seriously had no idea who he was dealing with.

Mary looked up as Chase came in the front door of her building.

He held up his hands in surrender. "I don't want to keep you from your work, but I thought maybe we could have lunch together if you don't have other plans. I really need to talk to you. Not about us. You asked for space, and I'm giving it to you. But I do need your help."

She glanced at her watch, surprised to see that it was almost noon. Which meant that all the restaurants would be packed. She said as much to him.

He grinned, which was always her undoing with him. "I packed us a picnic lunch. I know you're busy, so I thought we would just go down by the river. I'll have you back within the hour. If it won't work out, no sweat. I'll leave."

She hadn't been on a picnic in years. But more important, Chase wasn't pressuring her. There was a spot on the river on the ranch that used to be one of their favorite places. The memory of the two of them down by the river blew in like a warm summer breeze, a caress filled with an aching need.

"It's a beautiful day out. I thought you could use a little sunshine and fresh air," he said.

She glanced at the work on her desk. "It is tempting." *He* was tempting.

"I didn't just come here about lunch," he said as if confessing. "I've narrowed down the search for my father to three names." That caught her attention. "I was hoping—"

"Just give me a minute to change."

They drove the short distance to the Gallatin River and walked down to a spot with a sandy shore. A breeze whispered in the pines and off the water to keep the summer day cool.

Chase carried a picnic basket that Mary knew he'd gotten from her mother. "Was this my mother's idea?"

He laughed. "I do have a few ideas of my own." His blue gaze locked with hers, sending a delicious shiver through her. She remembered some of his ideas.

She sighed and took a step away from him. Being so close to Chase with him looking at her like that, she couldn't think straight. "It makes me nervous, the two of you with your heads together." When he said nothing, she'd looked over at him.

He grinned. She did love that grin. "Your mom and I have always gotten along great. I like her."

She eyed him for a moment and let it go. Did he think that getting closer to her mother was going to make her trust him again? "How is work going on the Jensen Ranch?"

"I've been helping with fencing so if you're asking about Beth Anne? I haven't even seen her." He shook his head. "Like I told you, it's temporary. I start as finish carpenter with Reclaimed Timber Construction next week. I'll also be moving into my own place in a few days. I was just helping out at the Jensens' ranch. Since I left, I've saved my money. I'm planning to build my own home here in the canyon." He shrugged and then must have seen her surprised expression. "Mary, I told you, I'm not leaving. I love you. I'm going to fight like hell to get you back. Whatever it takes. Even if I have to run off that deputy of yours."

"Don't talk crazy." She noticed the bruise on his cheek from last night reminding her of their fight.

"Seriously, there is something about him I don't like."

"That was obvious, but I don't want to talk about him. Especially with you."

"Not a problem," he said as he spread out a blanket in the sand and opened the picnic basket "Fresh lemonade. I made it myself."

"With my mother's help," she said as he held up the jug. She could hear the ice cubes rattling.

"I know it's your favorite," he said as he produced a plastic glass and poured her some. As he handed it to her, he smiled. "You look beautiful today, by the way."

She took the glass, her fingers brushing against his. A tingle rushed through her arm to her center in a heartbeat. She took a sip of the lemonade. "It's wonderful. Thank you."

"That's not all." He brought out fried chicken, potato salad and deviled eggs.

"If I eat all this, I won't get any work done this afternoon," she said, laughing.

"Would that be so terrible?"

She smiled at him as she leaned back on the blanket. The tops of the dark pines swayed in the clear blue overhead. The sound of the flowing clear water of the Gallatin River next to them was like a lullaby. It really was an amazing day, and it had been so long since she'd been here with Chase.

"I haven't done this since…"

"I left. I'm sorry."

"Not sorry you left," she said, hating that she'd brought it up.

"Just sorry it wasn't with you."

She nodded and sat up as he handed her a plate. "I guess we'll never agree on that."

"Maybe not. But we agree on most everything else," he said. "We want the same things."

"Do we?" she asked, meeting his gaze. Those old feelings rushed at her, making her melt inside. She loved this cowboy.

"We do. Try the chicken. I fried it myself."

She took a bite and felt her eyes widen. "It's delicious." It wasn't her mother's. "There's a spice on it I'm having trouble placing."

"It's my own recipe."

"It really is good."

"I wish you didn't sound so surprised." But he grinned as he said, "Now the potato salad."

"Equally delicious. So you cook?"

His face broke in a wide smile. "You really underestimate me. Cooking isn't that tough."

They ate to the sound of the river, the occasional birdsong and the chatter of a distant squirrel. It was so enjoyable that she hated to bring up a subject that she knew concerned him. But he'd said he needed to talk to her about the names of men he thought might be his father.

"You said you've narrowed your search to three names?" she asked.

He nodded. "J.M. I've searched phone listings. Since it was someone in the Big Sky area that helps narrow the scope."

Unless the man had just been passing through. Or if he'd left. But she didn't voice her doubts. "What is your plan? Are you going to knock on the door of the men with the initials J.M.?"

He laughed. "You have a better suggestion?"

She studied him. "You're sure you want to do this?"

Chase looked away for a moment. "I wish I could let it go. But I have to know."

"What will you do when you find him?"

He chuckled. "I have no idea."

"I don't believe that."

Chase met her gaze. "This man used my mother and when she got pregnant, he dumped her."

"That isn't what she said in her diary."

"No, she didn't spell it out, if that's what you mean. But I know how it ended. With her being penniless trying to raise me on my own. It's what killed her, working like a dog all those years. I want to look him in the face and—" His voice broke.

She moved to him. As he drew her into his arms, she rested her head against the solid rock wall of his chest. She listened to the steady beat of his heart as tears burned her eyes. She knew how important family was. She'd always known hers. She could feel the hole in his heart, and wanted more than anything to fill it. "Then let's find him."

As they started to pack up the picnic supplies, Chase took her in his arms again. "You know I've never been that good with words."

"Oh, I think you're just fine with words," she said, and laughed.

"I love you," he said simply.

She met his gaze. Those blue eyes said so much that he didn't need words to convince her of that. "I love you."

"That's enough. For now," he said, and released her. The promise in his words sent a shiver of desire racing through her. Her skin tingled from his touch as well as his words. She'd wanted this cowboy more than she wanted her next breath.

Still, she let him finish picking up the picnic supplies. He smiled at her. "Ready?"

Just about, she thought.

Lucy had been shocked when Chase had stopped by Mary's and the two had left together. She'd thought Mary was angry with him. Clearly, not enough.

Where had they been? Not far away because he'd brought her back so soon. But something was different. She could sense it, see it in the way they were with each other as he walked her to her door. They seemed closer. She tried to breathe. Her hands ached from being balled up into fists.

Watching from the window of the coffee shop, she saw Mary touch his hand. Chase immediately took hers in his large, sun-browned one. The two looked at each other as if… As if they shared a secret. Surely they weren't lovers again already. Then Chase kissed her.

Lucy brought her fist down on the counter. Cups rattled and Amy, who'd been cashing out for the day, looked over at her. "Sorry. I was trying to kill a pesky fly."

Amy didn't look convinced, but she did go back to what she was doing, leaving Lucy alone to stare out the window at the couple across the street. Chase had stepped closer. His hands were now on her shoulders. Lucy remembered his scent, his touch. He was hers. Not Mary's.

Chase leaned in and kissed her again before turning back to his pickup. It wasn't a lover's kiss. It was too quick for that. But there was no doubt that Mary was no longer angry with him. Something had changed.

She watched him drive away, telling herself to bide her time. She couldn't go off half-cocked like she had that night at the river. Timing was everything.

A customer came in. She unfisted her hands as she began to make the woman's coffee order and breathe. But she kept seeing the way Chase had kissed his cowgirl and how Mary had responded. It ate at her heart like acid, and she thought she might retch.

But she held it together as the coffee shop filled with a busload of tourists. Soon Mary would come over for her afternoon caffeine fix. Lucy touched the small white package of powder in her apron pocket. She was ready for her.

* * *

Mary tried to concentrate on her work. She had to get this report done. But her mind kept going back to Chase and the picnic and the kisses.

She touched the tip of her tongue to her lower lip and couldn't help but smile. Some things didn't change. Being in Chase's arms again, feeling his lips on hers. The short kiss was a prelude to what could come.

"Don't get ahead of yourself," she said out loud. "You're only helping him look for his father." But even as she said it, she knew today they'd crossed one of the barriers she'd erected between them.

She shook her head and went back to work, losing herself in the report until she heard her front door open. Looking up, she saw Lucy holding a cup of coffee from Lone Peak Perk.

"I hope I'm not disturbing you," she said. "When it got late, I realized you might need this." She held out the cup.

"What time is it?"

"Five thirty. I'm sorry. You probably don't want it today." She started to back out.

"No, it's just what I need if I hope to get this finished today," Mary said, rising from her desk. "I lost track of time and I had a big lunch. It's a wonder I haven't already dozed off."

Lucy smiled as she handed her the coffee. "I saw your cowboy come by and pick you up. Fun lunch?"

Mary nodded, grinning in spite of herself. "Very fun." She reached for her purse.

"I put it on your account."

She smiled. "Thank you." She took a sip. "I probably won't be able to sleep tonight from all this sugar and caffeine this late in the day, but at least I should be able to get this report done now. Thank you again. What would I do without you?"

Chapter 13

Mary thought she was going to die. She'd retched until there was nothing more inside her, and yet her stomach continued to roil.

When it had first hit, she'd rushed to the restroom at the back of her office. She'd thought it might have been the potato salad, but Chased had ice packs around everything in the basket.

Still, she couldn't imagine what else it could have been. Flu? It seemed early in the season, but it was possible.

After retching a few times, she thought it had passed. The report was almost finished. She wasn't feeling great. Maybe she should go upstairs to her apartment and lie down for a while.

But it had hit again and again. Now she sat on the cool floor of the office bathroom, wet paper towels held to her forehead, as she waited for another stomach spasm. She couldn't remember ever feeling this sick, and it scared her. She felt so weak that she didn't have the strength to get up off this floor, let alone make it up to her third-floor apartment.

She closed her eyes, debating if she could reach her desk where she'd left her cell phone. If she could call her mother...

"Mary? Mary, are you here?"

Relieved and afraid Lucy would leave before she could call her, Mary crawled over to the door to the hallway and, reaching up, her arm trembling, opened it. "Lucy." Her throat hurt. When her voice came out, the words were barely audible. "Lucy!" she called again, straining to be heard since she knew she couldn't get to her feet as weak as she was.

For a moment it seemed that Lucy hadn't heard her. Tears burned her eyes, and she had to fight breaking down and sobbing.

"Mary?"

She heard footfalls and a moment later Lucy was standing over her, looking down at her with an expression of shock.

"I'm sick."

"I can see that." Lucy leaned down. "Do you want me to call you an ambulance?"

"No, if you could just help me up to my apartment. I think it must be food poisoning."

"Oh no. What did you have for lunch?" Lucy asked as she reached down to lift her into a standing position. "You're as weak as a kitten."

Mary leaned against the wall for a moment, feeling as if she needed to catch her breath. "Chase made us a

picnic lunch. It must have been the chicken or the potato salad."

"That's awful. Here, put your arm around me. Do
you think you can walk?"

They went out the back of the office and down the
hallway to the stairs.

"Let me know if you need to rest," Lucy said as they
started up the steps.

Her stomach empty, the spasms seemed to have
stopped—at least for the moment. Having Lucy here
made her feel less scared. She was sure that she'd be
fine if she could just get to her apartment and lie down.

"I'm all right." But she was sweating profusely by
the time they'd reached her door.

"I didn't think to ask," Lucy said. "Are your keys
downstairs?"

Mary let out a groan of frustration. "On my desk."

"If you think you can stand while I run back down—"

"No, there's a spare key under the carpet on the last
stair at the top," she said. "I sometimes forget when I
just run up from the office for lunch."

"Smart."

She watched Lucy retrieve the key. "I can't tell you
how glad I was to see you."

"I saw that your lights were still on in your office,
but there was no sign of you. I thought I'd better check
to make sure everything was all right. When I found
your office door open and you weren't there…" She
opened the door and helped her inside.

"I think I want to go straight to my bedroom. I need
to lie down."

"Let me help you." Lucy got her to the bed. "Can
you undress on your own?"

"If you would just help me with my boots, I think I can manage everything else."

Lucy knelt down and pulled off her Western boots. "Here, unbutton your jeans and let me pull them off. You'll be more comfortable without them."

Mary fumbled with the buttons, realizing the woman was right. She felt so helpless, and was grateful when Lucy pulled off her jeans and helped tuck her into bed. "Thank you so much."

"I'm just glad I could help. Would you like some ginger ale? My mother always gave me that when I had a stomachache."

Mary shook her head. "I think I just need to rest."

"Okay, I'll leave you to it. I don't see your phone."

"It's downstairs on my desk too."

"I'll get it so you can call if you need anything, and I mean anything, you call me, all right? I'll be just downstairs."

Mary nodded. Suddenly she felt exhausted and just wanted to close her eyes.

"Don't worry. I'll lock your apartment door, put the key back, lock up downstairs—after I get your phone. You just rest. You look like something the cat dragged in."

Even as sick as she was, Mary had to smile because she figured that was exactly what she looked like given the way she felt.

Lucy started to step away from the bed, when Mary grabbed her hand. "Thank you again. You're a lifesaver."

"Yep, that's me."

Unable to fight it any longer, Mary closed her eyes, dropping into oblivion.

* * *

Lucy had taken her time earlier when she'd finished work. She'd casually crossed the street, whistling a tune to herself. There'd been no reason to hurry. She'd known exactly what she was going to find when she got to Mary's office.

Now as Mary closed her eyes, she stood over the woman, simply looking down into her angelic face. She didn't have to wonder what Chase saw in Mary. She was everything Lucy was not.

That was enough to make her want to take one of the pillows, force it down on Mary's face and hold it there until the life ebbed out of her.

She listened to Mary's soft breaths thinking how Mary had it all. A business, a building in a town where she was liked and respected, not to mention rentals and Chase. Lucy reminded herself that she used to have a great profession, where she was respected, where she had friends. What was missing was a man in her life. Then along came Chase.

With a curse, she shook her head and looked around the room as she fought back tears. The bedroom was done in pastel colors and small floral prints, so like Mary. She wondered what Chase thought of this room— or if he'd seen it yet. Not very manly. Nor was it her style, she thought as she left, closing the bedroom door softly behind her, and checked out the rest of the place.

She'd been sincere about Mary's decorating abilities. The woman had talent when it came to design and colors. It made her jealous as she took in the living room with its overstuffed furniture in bright cheery colors. Like the bedroom, there was a soft comfort about the room that made her want to curl up in the chair by the window and put her feet up.

But with a silent curse, she realized that what she really wanted was to be Mary Savage for a little while. To try out her life. To have it all, including Chase.

Shaking herself out of such ridiculous thinking, she left the apartment, leaving the door unlocked. As she put the spare key back, she told herself that it would come in handy in the future.

Smiling at the thought, she headed downstairs to Mary's office. It looked like any other office except for the large oak desk. The brick walls had been exposed to give the place a rustic look. The floor was bamboo, a rich color that went perfectly with the brick and the simple but obviously expensive furnishings.

She would have liked an office like this, she thought as she found Mary's cell phone on her desk and quickly pocketed it before picking up the woman's purse. It felt heavy. She heard the jingle of keys inside. Slipping the strap over her shoulder, she went to the front door and locked it.

Across the street she saw that the coffee shop was still busy and the other baristas were clearly slammed with orders. She wondered if anyone had seen her and quickly left by the back way again, turning out the lights behind her after locking the door. That's when she realized that she couldn't kill Mary here. She would be the first suspect.

Once on the stairs, out of view of anyone outside or across the street, she sat down on a step and went through Mary's purse. She found a wallet with photos of people she assumed must be relatives. Brothers and sisters? Cousins? Her parents?

Friends? She realized how little she knew about the woman.

There was eighty-two dollars in cash in the wallet, a few credit cards, some coupons... Seriously? The woman clipped coupons? Other than mints, a small hairbrush, a paperback and miscellaneous cosmetics there was nothing of interest.

She turned to Mary's cell phone.

Password protected. Swearing softly, she tried various combinations of words, letters, numbers. Nothing worked.

A thought struck her like a brick. She tried Chase. When that didn't work, she tried Chase Steele. Nope.

She had another thought, and taking the keys to the office, she went back inside. Turning on a small lamp on the desk, she quickly began a search. She found the list of passwords on a pull-out tray over the right-hand top drawer. The passwords were on an index card and taped down. Some had been scratched out and replaced.

Lucy ran her finger down until she found the word cell. Next to it was written Homeranch#1. She tried the password and the phone unlocked.

Quickly she scanned through contacts, emails and finally messages. She found a cell phone number for Chase and on impulse tried it, just needing to hear his voice.

It was no longer in service.

Surely he had a cell phone, not that she'd ever had his number. Wouldn't he have given it to Mary though?

She went through recent phone calls, and there it was. She touched the screen as she memorized the number. It began to ring. She held her breath. He would think it was Mary calling. He would call back.

Lucy quickly hit the hang-up button but not quick enough. "Hello, Mary, I was just thinking of you." She disconnected, wishing she hadn't done that. He'd sounded so happy that Mary was calling him that she felt sick to her stomach.

Just as she'd feared, he called right back. She blocked his call. He tried again. What if he decided to come check on Mary? This was the kind of mistake she couldn't make.

She answered the phone, swallowed and did her best imitation of Mary's voice, going with tired and busy. "Working. Didn't mean to call."

"Well, I'm glad you did. Don't work too late."

"Right. Talk tomorrow." She disconnected, pretty sure she'd pulled it off. He wouldn't question the difference in their voices since he'd called Mary's phone. At least she hoped she'd sounded enough like the woman. Sweet, quiet, tired, busy. When the phone didn't ring again, she told herself that she'd done it.

Hurrying back upstairs, she picked up Mary's purse from where she'd left it on the step on her way. Outside the third-floor apartment, she stopped to catch her breath. Putting Mary's cell on mute, she carefully opened the door, even though she didn't think Mary would be mobile for hours.

An eerie quiet hung in the air. She stepped in and headed for the bedroom. The door was still closed. She eased it open. The room had darkened to a shadowy black with the drapes closed. Mary lay exactly where she'd left her, breathing rhythmically.

Taking the cell phone, she stepped in just far enough to place the now turned off phone next to her bed. Then she left, easing the bedroom door closed behind her.

The apartment was deathly quiet and growing darker. It no longer felt cozy and she no longer wanted to stay. Leaving Mary's purse on the table by the door, she left, locking it behind her.

It had been an emotional day, Lucy thought. She took the stairs down to her apartment, unlocked her door and, turning on a light, stepped in. The apartment was in stark contrast to Mary's. While everything was nice, it was stark. Cold.

"That's because you're cold," she whispered as she locked the door behind her. "Anyway, it's temporary." But even as she said it, she was thinking that she should at least buy a plant.

The apartment had come furnished right down to two sets of sheets and two throw pillows that matched the couch. Suddenly Lucy hated the pillows. She tossed them into the near empty closet and closed the door. Tomorrow was her day off. After she checked on Mary, she'd go into Bozeman and do some shopping.

She needed this apartment to feel a whole lot less like Mary Savage. Now that she had Chase's cell number, it was time for her to make him pay.

Chapter 14

Lucy tapped lightly at Mary's door the next morning. Given how sick the woman had been the evening before, she thought she still might be in bed.

So she was a little surprised when Mary answered the door looking as if she'd already showered and dressed for the day.

"Oh good, you look like you're feeling better," she said.

"Much. Thank you again for yesterday."

"Just glad I could help." She started to turn away.

"Do you ride horses?" Mary asked.

Lucy stopped, taken aback by the question. She'd hoped to get close to Mary, befriend her, gain her trust and then finish this. She'd thought it would take more time. "I used to ride when I was younger."

"Would you like to come out to the ranch sometime, maybe on your day off, and go for ride?"

"I would love to." The moment she said it, she knew how dangerous it could be. Chase might show up. She'd managed not to come face-to-face with him. Even with the changes in her appearance, he could recognize her. They'd been lovers. Soul mates. He would sense who she was the moment they were in the same room.

"Good," Mary was saying. "Let's plan on it. Just let me know what day you're free. And thank you again for yesterday. I don't know what I would have done without you."

Lucy nodded, still taken aback. "I'm glad I was here." She took a step toward the door, feeling strangely uncomfortable. "Off to work," she said as she walked backward for a few steps, smiling like a fool.

Could this really be going as well as she thought it was? She couldn't believe how far she'd come from that night in Arizona when she'd gone into the river. She had Mary Savage, the woman who'd stolen Chase from her, right where she'd wanted her. So why wasn't she more euphoric about it? Her plan was working. There was no reason to be feeling the way she was, which was almost…guilty.

The thought made her laugh as she crossed the street. Guilt wasn't something she normally felt. She was enjoying herself. Maybe too much. She'd thought it would take longer, and she'd been okay with that.

As she settled into work, she realized that she would have to move up her revenge schedule. She was starting to like Mary and that was dangerous. No way could she go on a horseback ride with her, and not just because she might run into Chase. She couldn't let herself start liking Mary. If she weakened… She told herself that wouldn't happen.

But realizing this was almost over, she felt a start. She hadn't given any thought as to what she would do after she was finished here. Where would she go? What would she do? She'd been so focused on destroying Chase and his cowgirl that she hadn't thought about what to do when it was over.

That thought was nagging at her when she looked up to find Chase standing in front of her counter. Panic made her limbs go weak. He wasn't looking at her, but at the board with the day's specials hanging over her head. Could she duck in the back before he saw her? Let the other barista wait on him?

But Amy was busy with another customer. Lucy knew she couldn't hide out in the back until Chase left. All her fears rushed through her, making her skin itch. She'd come so far. She was so close to finishing this. What would she do when he recognized her?

He'd know what she was up to. He'd tell Mary. All of this would have been for nothing. Mary's father was the marshal. It wouldn't take long before he'd know about what had happened in Texas, about the suspicions that had followed her from town to town and finally to Big Sky, Montana. Once he saw through her disguise, and he would. Just like that and it would be all over. She wanted to scream.

"Good morning," he said, and finally looked at her.

"Morning." She held her breath as she met his blue eyes and gave him an embarrassed gap-toothed smile.

He smiled back, his gaze intent on her, but she realized with a start that she saw no recognition in his face. *It's me*, she wanted to say. *The love of your life. Don't tell me you don't see me, don't sense me, don't feel me standing right here in front of you.*

"I hope you can help me. I want to buy my girlfriend the kind of coffee she loves, but I forgot what it's called. She lives right across the street. I thought you might know what she orders. It's for Mary Savage."

Girlfriend? "Sorry, I'm new."

"That's all right. It was a shot in the dark anyway. Then I guess I'll take one caramel latte and a plain black coffee please."

She stared at him for a moment in disbelief. She'd been so sure he would know her—instinctively—even the way she looked now. But there was no recognition. *None.*

Fury shook her to her core. They'd made *love.* They had a connection. *How could he not know her?*

"You do have plain black coffee, don't you?" he asked when she didn't speak, didn't move.

She let out a sound that was supposed to be a chuckle and turned her back on him. Her insides trembled, a volcano of emotions bubbling up, ready to blow. She fisted her hands, wanting to launch herself across the counter and rip out his throat.

Instead, she thought of Mary and something much better. Ripping out Mary's heart, the heart he was so desperately trying to win back.

She made the latte and poured him a cup of plain black coffee. He handed her a ten and told her to keep the change.

Thanking him, she smiled at the thought of him standing over Mary Savage's grave. "You have a nice day now."

"You too," he said as he left.

She watched him go, still shocked and furious that

the fool hadn't known her. She promised herself that his nice days were about to end, and very soon.

It wasn't until he was headed across the street to Mary's office that Chase looked back at the woman working in the Lone Peak Perk. What was it about her...? He frowned until it hit him. Her voice. Even with the slight lisp and Southern drawl, the cadence of her voice was enough like Fiona's to give him the creeps.

He shuddered, wondering if he would ever be able to put the Fiona nightmare behind him. Yesterday he'd called Rick, and Patty had answered.

"I'm so sorry about what happened with you and Fiona," she'd said. "I just feel so sorry for her. I know it's no excuse, but she had a really rough childhood. Her mother remarried a man who sexually abused her. When she told her mother, the woman didn't believe her. That had to break her heart."

"Did she have anyone else?"

"No siblings or relatives she could turn to. On top of that, her stepfather had three sons."

He had sworn under his breath "So they could have been abusing her too."

"Or Fiona could have lied about all of it. When her mother, stepfather and the three sons died in a fire, I had to wonder. Fiona could have been behind it. I wouldn't put anything past her, would you?"

"Or she could have lied about the sexual abuse and then been racked with guilt when they all died."

Patty had laughed. "You really do try to see the best in people, and even after the number she pulled on you. You're a good guy, Chase. You take care of yourself."

He didn't feel like a good guy. He'd made so many

mistakes. Fiona for one. Mary for another. He couldn't do much about Fiona, but he still had a chance to right things with Mary.

Patty had put Rick on the phone. The news was the same. Fiona's body still hadn't turned up.

"Some fisherman will find her downstream. It will be gruesome. A body that's been in the water that long…"

Chase hadn't wanted to think about it.

Like now, he tried to put it behind him as he neared Mary's office door. He wanted to surprise her with coffee. He just wished the barista had known the kind of coffee she drank. Mary was helping him today with his search for a man with the initials J.M. She understood his need to find his father even though there were days when he didn't. Why couldn't he just let it go? His mother apparently had forgiven the man if not forgotten him.

For all he knew, the man could have moved away by now. Or his mother hadn't used his real initials. Or… He shook off the negative thoughts. He would be spending the day with the woman he loved. Did it really matter if they found his father today?

As Chase came in the front door of her office, Mary saw him look back toward the coffee shop and frown. "Is something wrong?" she asked.

He started as if his thoughts had been miles away. "There's a woman working over there. Lucy?"

"I know her." She took the coffee he handed her. Not her usual, but definitely something she liked.

"She just reminded me of someone I used to know—and not in a good way," he said.

"She just started working at Lone Peak Perk only a week or two ago. Why?"

He shook his head. "Just a feeling I got." He seemed to hesitate. "That dangerous woman, Fiona, who I told you about from Arizona. Lucy doesn't look anything like her, but she reminds me of her for some reason."

Mary shook her head. She really did not want to hear anything more about Fiona. "You do realize how crazy that sounds. I know Lucy. She's really sweet. I like her. I rented one of my apartments to her. I'm sure she's nothing like *your*... Fiona."

"She wasn't *my* Fiona. Look, you've never asked, but I didn't date for a long time after I left. I wasn't interested in anyone else. That wasn't why I left and you know it. If I hadn't been drinking, if I hadn't just picked up my mother's ashes the day of the barbecue at my boss's house..."

Mary stood up. "I don't need to hear this."

"Maybe you do," he said, and raked a hand through his hair as he met her gaze. "It was one drunken night. I regretted it right away. She became...obsessed, manufacturing a relationship that didn't exist. She must have stolen my extra house key and copied it. I came home several times to find her in my apartment. She knew I was in love with someone else. But that seemed to make her even more determined to change my mind." He shook his head. "She wouldn't stop. She tried to move some of her stuff into my apartment. Needless to say it got ugly. The last time I saw her..." He hesitated as if he'd never wanted to tell her the details about Fiona and she didn't want to hear them now.

But before she could stop him, he said, "She tried to kill me."

Mary gasped. "You can't be serious."

"She knew I was leaving. She said she wanted to give me a hug goodbye, but when she started to put her arms around me, I saw the knife she'd pulled from her pocket. I would have gotten to Montana weeks sooner, but she sabotaged my pickup. I had to have a new engine put in it." He shook his head. "What I'm saying is that I wouldn't put anything past her. She supposedly drowned in the Colorado River after driving her car into it. But her body was never found."

Mary couldn't believe what she was hearing.

"Lucy doesn't look anything like her except…" He glanced up at her and must have seen the shock and disbelief in her eyes. Couldn't he tell that she didn't want to know anything more about Fiona?

She shook her head, wished this wasn't making her so upset. He'd said Fiona was obsessed with him? It sounded like he was just as obsessed. "This woman really did a number on you, didn't she?"

He held up both hands in surrender. "Sorry. I thought you should know."

About a woman he'd made love to who was now dead? But certainly not forgotten. Even Lucy reminded him of her even though, as he said, she looked nothing like Fiona? Her heart pounded hard in her chest. She pushed her coffee away, feeling nauseous. "We should get going. I need to come back and work."

He nodded. She could tell that he regretted bringing up the subject. So why had he? She never wanted to hear the name Fiona again. Ever.

"I'm sorry. You're right. Forget I mentioned it. I promise not to say another word about her."

But she saw him steal a look toward the coffee shop as they were leaving. He might not mention Fiona's name again, but he was definitely still thinking about her.

Chapter 15

With Mary's mother's help, Chase had narrowed down their search to three local men—Jack Martin, Jason Morrison and Jonathan Mason. Dana had helped him weed out the ones that she knew were too young, too old or hadn't been around at the time.

His mother had been eighteen when she'd given birth to him. If her lover had been older, say twenty-five or thirty as Chase suspected, then his father would now be in his fifties.

Jack Martin owned a variety of businesses in Big Sky, including the art shop where his wife sold her pottery. A bell tinkled over the door as Mary and Chase entered. A woman passed them holding a large box as if what was inside was breakable. Chase held the door for her, before he and Mary moved deeper in the shop.

The place smelled of mulberry candles, a sickeningly

sweet fragrance that Mary had never liked. She tried not to breathe too deeply as they moved past displays of pottery toward the back counter.

Jack had begun helping out at the shop during the busiest time, summer, Mary knew. She spotted his gray head coming out of the back with a large pottery bowl, which he set on an open space on a display table. There was a young woman showing several ladies a set of pottery dishes in an adjoining room, and several visitors were looking at pottery lamps at the front of the shop.

As Mary approached, Jack turned and smiled broadly. "Afternoon, is there something I can help you with?"

Mary knew Jack from chamber of commerce meetings, but it took him a second before he said, "Mary Savage. I'm sorry, I didn't recognize you right away."

"This is my friend Chase Steele." She watched for a reaction. For all they knew, Chase's father could have kept track of his son all these years. But she saw no reaction. "Is there a private area where we could speak with you for a moment?"

Jack frowned, but nodded. "We could step into the back." He glanced around to see if there were customers who needed to be waited on. There didn't appear to be for the moment.

"We won't take much of your time," she promised.

Chase tensed next to her as if to say, if Jack Martin was his father, he'd damned sure take as much of his time as he wanted.

Mary was glad that she'd come along. She knew how important this was, and could feel how nervous Chase had become the moment they stepped into the shop.

In the back it was cool and smelled less like the burning candles. "Did you know a woman named Muriel Steele?" Chase asked the moment they reached a back storage and work area.

Jack blinked in surprised. "Who?"

"Muriel Steele," Mary said with less accusation. "It would have been close to thirty years ago."

Jack looked taken aback. "You expect me to remember that long ago? Who was this woman?"

"One you had an affair with," Chase said, making her cringe. She'd hoped he would let her handle this since he was too emotionally involved.

"That I would remember," the man snapped. "I was married to Clara thirty years ago. We just celebrated our fortieth anniversary." Jack was shaking his head. "I'm not sure what this is about or what this Muriel woman told you, but I have never cheated on my wife."

Mary believed him. She looked to Chase, whom she could tell wasn't quite as convinced.

"Would you be willing to take a DNA test to prove it?" Chase demanded.

"A DNA test? How would that prove..." Realization crossed his face. "I see." His gaze softened. "I'm sorry young man, but I'm not related to you."

"But you'd take the test," Chase pressed.

Jack grew quiet for a moment, his expression sad. "If it would help you, yes, I would."

Mary saw all the tension leave Chase's body. He looked as if the strain had left him exhausted.

"Thank you," Mary said as she heard more customers coming into the shop. "We won't keep you any longer."

"It's not him," Chase said as he climbed behind the wheel and started the pickup's engine. A floodgate of emotions warred inside him. He wasn't sure what he'd hoped for. That he could find his father that quickly and it would be over? He'd wanted to hate the man. Worse, he'd wanted to punch him. But when realization had struck Jack Martin, Chase had seen the pity in the man's eyes.

"No, it wasn't Jack," she said. "Are you up to visiting the rest of them?"

He pulled off his Stetson and raked a hand through his hair. "I'm not sure I can do this. I thought I could but..." He glanced over at her.

"It's all right."

He shook his head. For a moment, they merely sat there, each lost in their own thoughts. Then Chase smiled over at her. "Could we drive up to Mountain Village and have an early lunch and forget all this for a while? Then I promise to take you back to work. I shouldn't have dragged you into this."

She reached over and placed a hand on his arm. He felt the heat of her fingers through his Western shirt. They warmed him straight to his heart and lower. What he wanted was this woman in his arms, in his bed, in his life. He felt as if he had made so many mistakes and was still making them.

"My stomach is still a little upset. I was really sick last night." He looked at her with concern. "I'm sure it was just some twenty-four-hour flu," she said quickly.

"I hope that's all it was," he said. "I was really careful with our picnic lunch."

"And you didn't get sick, so like I said, probably just a flu bug." He must not have looked convinced. "I was just going to eat some yogurt for lunch. Maybe some other time?"

He studied her for a moment, so filled with love for this woman. "You're the best friend I've ever had."

She laughed at that, and took her hand from his arm.

"Is it any wonder that I haven't been able to stop loving you?" he asked.

Their gazes met across the narrow space between them. He could feel the heat, the chemistry. He reached over and cupped the back of her neck, pulling her into the kiss. He heard her breath catch. His pulse quickened. A shaft of desire cut through him, molten hot.

Mary leaned into him and the kiss. It felt like coming home. Chase had always been a great kisser.

As he drew back, he looked into her eyes as if the kiss had also transported him back to when they were lovers.

"You're just full of surprises today, aren't you," she said, smiling at him as she tried to catch her breath. She loved seeing Chase like this, relaxed, content, happy, a man who knew who he was and what he wanted.

The cowboy who'd left her and Montana had been antsy, filled with a need she couldn't understand. Just like he'd been only minutes ago when they'd gone looking for his father.

He needed to find him. She would help him. And then what?

"You have work to do, and I'm keeping you from it," he said. "We can have lunch another day when you feel better and aren't as busy. I've already taken up too much of your morning."

She shook her head as she met his gaze. "If I didn't have this report due—"

"You don't have to explain. You took off this morning to help me. I appreciate that." His smile filled her with joy as much as his words. "We have a lot of lunches in our future. I hope you know how serious I am about us, about our future. I'll do whatever it takes because I know you, Mary Savage. I know your heart."

She felt her eyes burn with tears at the truth in his words. "Tomorrow. Let's go talk to the other two men tomorrow morning."

"Are you sure?" Chase asked. "I don't like keeping you from your work."

She managed to nod. "I'm sure." Swallowing the lump in her throat, she reached to open her door. If she stayed out here with him a minute longer, she feared what she might say. Worse, what she might do. It would have been too easy to fall into his arms and take up where they'd left off and forget all about the report that was due.

But she climbed out of the pickup, knowing it was too soon. She had to know for sure that Chase wouldn't hurt her again. Her heart couldn't take being broken by him again.

As Chase was leaving, he glanced toward the coffee shop. Was Lucy working? He swung his pickup around and parked in front of Lone Peak Perk. Getting out, he told himself to play it cool. He had to see her again. He had to know. But just the thought that he might be right…

As he walked in, Lucy looked up. Surprise registered in those dark eyes. Nothing like Fiona's big blue ones. Still, he walked to the counter. She looked nervous. "Is it possible to get a cup of coffee in a real cup?" he asked. "Just black."

She looked less nervous, but that too could have been his imagination. He wondered what he'd been think-

ing. The woman looked nothing like Fiona and yet…
She was much skinnier, the gapped two front teeth, the
short dark hair, the brown eyes. What was it about her
that reminded him of Fiona? Mary was right. He was
obsessed with the disturbed, irrational woman.

Lucy picked up a white porcelain coffee cup and
took her time filling it with black coffee. "Can I get
you anything else?" she said with that slight lisp, slight
Southern accent. Nothing like Fiona. She flashed him
a smile, clearly flirting.

He grinned. "Maybe later." He took the coffee cup by
the handle over to an empty spot near the door. Sitting
with his back to her, he took a sip. Coffee was the last
thing he wanted right now. But he drank it as quickly
as the hot beverage allowed.

Taking advantage of a rush of people coming in for
their afternoon caffeine fix, he carefully slipped the
now empty cup under his jacket and walked out. He'd
expected to be stopped, but neither Lucy or the other
barista noticed. When he reached his pickup, he carefully set the cup on the center console and headed to
the marshal's office.

He would get Hud to run the prints because he had
to know what it was about the woman that turned his
stomach, and left him feeling like something evil had
come to Big Sky.

Lucy couldn't believe that Chase had come back into
the coffee shop. She smiled to herself as she whipped
up one of the shop's special coffees for a good-tipping
patron. As she finished the drink, she turned expecting
to see Chase's strong back at the corner table. To her
surprise, he'd left during the rush. He'd certainly fin-

ished his coffee quickly enough. She frowned as concern slithered slowly through her.

It took her a moment to realize why the hair was now standing up on the back of her neck. The table where Chase had been sitting. His empty porcelain cup wasn't where he should have left it.

She hurriedly glanced around, thinking he must have brought it back to the counter. Otherwise…

Her heart kicked up to double time. Otherwise… He wouldn't have tossed the cup in the trash and she could see from here that he hadn't put it in the tray with the few other dishes by the door.

Which left only one conclusion.

He'd taken the cup.

Why would he—

The reason struck her hard and fast. *He had recognized her.* Warring emotions washed over her. Of course he'd sensed her behind the disguise. She hadn't been wrong about that. It was that unique chemistry that they shared. But at the same time, fear numbed her, left her dumbstruck. She could hear the patron asking her a question, but nothing was registering.

Chase would go to the marshal, Mary's father, have him run the prints. Once that happened… She told herself that there was time. And, there was Deputy Dillon Ramsey.

"Miss! I need a receipt, please."

Lucy shook her head and smiled. "Sorry," she said to the woman, printed out the receipt and handed it to her. "You have a nice day now."

After his initial surprise at seeing the cowboy, Hud waved Chase into a chair across from his desk. As the young man came in, he carefully set a white porcelain coffee cup on the edge of the desk. Hud eyed it, then Chase.

"I need you to run the fingerprints on this cup."

The marshal lifted a brow. "For any particular reason?"

"I really don't want to get into it. I'm hoping I'm wrong."

Hud leaned back in his chair. "That's not enough reason to waste the county's time running fingerprints."

"If I'm right, this person could be a danger to Mary. Isn't that enough?"

Rubbing his jaw, he studied the cowboy. "You do understand that unless this person has fingerprints on file—"

"They'll be on file if I'm right."

Intrigued, Hud sighed and said, "Okay. I'll let you know, but it might take a few days."

A deputy was walking past. Hud called to him as he bagged the cup Chase had brought in. "Dillon, run the fingerprints on this cup when you have a minute. Report back to me."

"We're still on for tonight, right?" Lucy asked when Dillon called. The last thing she wanted him to do was cancel.

"You know it."

"Then I have a small favor," she said. "It's one that only you can grant." She could almost hear the man's chest puff out. "And I'll make it worth your while."

"Really?" He sounded intrigued. She reminded herself that he was only doing this to get back at Mary. The thought did nothing for her disposition, but she kept the contempt out of her voice. She needed his help.

"Really. But then maybe you don't have access to what I need down there at the marshal's office."

"Name it. I have the run of the place."

"I believe Chase Steele might have brought in a cup and asked that fingerprints be run on it?"

Dillon chuckled. "The marshal asked me to do it when I had time and report back to him."

"Have you had time?" she asked, her heart in her throat.

"I like to do whatever the marshal asks right away."

She closed her eyes and tried to breathe. Her prints were on file. Chase must have suspected as much.

"I haven't seen him though to give him the report."

Lucy took a breath and let it out slowly. "Is there any way that the report could get lost?"

He snickered. "Now you've got me curious. Why would you care about prints run on a Fiona Barkley?"

So her prints had come back that quickly? "If that report gets lost, I'd be happy to tell you when I see you. Like I said, I'll make it worth your while."

"Are we talking money?" he asked quietly. "Or something else?"

"Or both," she said, her heart pounding. "I can be quite…creative."

He laughed. "What time shall I pick you up?"

"I have a better idea. Why don't I meet you later tonight after I get off my shift? I know just the spot." She told him how to get to the secluded area up in the mountains. She'd spent her free time checking out places for when it came time to end this little charade.

Dillon thought he was going to get lucky—and use

her to bring Mary into line. She'd known men like him. He would blackmail her into the next century if she let him.

"I have to work late. Is midnight too late for you?" she asked sweetly.

"Midnight is perfect. I can't wait."

"Me either." The deputy had no idea that he'd walked right into her plot, and now he had a leading role.

Chapter 16

Later that night, as Lucy prepared for her date with Dillon, she couldn't help being excited. She'd spent too much time waiting around, not rushing her plan, being patient and pretending to be someone she wasn't.

Tonight she could let Fiona out. The thought made her laugh. Wait until Dillon met her.

She had to work only until ten, but she needed time to prepare. She knew all about forensics. While she had little faith in the local law being able to solve its way out of a paper bag, she wasn't taking any chances. Amy, who worked at the coffee shop, had seen her talking to Dillon when he'd asked her out, but as far as the other barista knew, he was just another customer visiting after buying a coffee.

If Amy had heard anything, she would have thought he had been asking her for directions. There was no law in him flirting with her, Lucy thought with a grin. That exchange would be the only connection she had to Dillon Ramsey.

At least as far as anyone knew.

She didn't drive to the meeting spot. Instead, she came in the back way. It hadn't rained in weeks, but a thunderstorm was predicted for the next morning. Any tire or foot tracks she left would be altered if not destroyed. She had worn an old pair of shoes that would be going into the river tonight. Tucked under her arm was a blanket she'd pulled out of a commercial waste bin earlier today.

The hike itself wasn't long as the crow flew, but the route wound through trees and rocks. The waning moon and all the stars in the heavens did little to light her way. She'd never known such a blackness as there was under the dense pines. That's why she was almost on top of Dillon's pickup before she knew it.

As she approached the driver's-side door, she could hear tinny sounding country music coming from his pickup's stereo. He was drumming on his steering wheel and glancing at his watch. From his expression, she could tell that he was beginning to wonder if he'd been stood up.

When she tapped on his driver's-side window, he jumped. His expression changed from surprise to relief. He motioned for her to go around to the passenger side.

She shook her head and motioned for him to get out of the truck.

He put his window down partway, letting out a nose-wrinkling gust of cheap aftershave and male sweat. "It's warmer in here."

"I'm not going to let you get cold."

Dillon gave that a moment's thought before he whirred up the window, killed the engine and music, and climbed out.

Lucy had considered the best way to do this. He had his motivation for asking her out. She had hers for being here. Everyone knew about Dillon and Chase's fight. The two couldn't stand each other. So whom would the marshal's first suspect be if anything happened to Dillon?

She tossed down the blanket she'd brought onto the bed of dried pine needles. Dillon reached for her. He would be a poor lover, one who rushed. "Not yet, baby," she said, holding him at arm's length. "Why don't you strip down, have a seat and let me get ready for you. Turn your back. I want this to be a surprise."

It was like leading a bull to the slaughterhouse.

"Well hurry, because it's cold out tonight," he said as he began to undress. She'd brought her own knife, but when she'd seen his sticking out of his boot, she'd changed her plans.

The moment he sat down, his back to her, she came up behind him, grabbed a handful of his hair and his knife, and slit his throat from ear to ear. It happened so fast that he didn't put up a fight. He gurgled, his hand going to his throat before falling to one side.

She stared down at him, hoping he'd done what he promised and lost the report on her fingerprints. Her only regret was that she hadn't gotten to see the surprise and realization on his smug face. He'd gotten what was coming to him, but she doubted he would have seen it that way.

As she wiped her prints from the knife and stepped away, she kicked pine needles onto her tracks until she was in the woods and headed for the small creek she'd had to cross to get there. She washed her hands, rinsing away his blood. She'd worn a short-sleeved shirt, and with his back to her, she hadn't gotten any of his blood on anything but her hands and wrists.

She scrubbed though, up to her elbows, the ice-cold water making her hands ache. She let them air-dry as she walked the rest of the way back to her vehicle. Once she got rid of the shoes she had on, no one would be able to put her at the murder scene.

The moment Mary saw her father's face, she knew something horrible had happened. Was it her mother? One of her brothers or someone else in the family? Chase? She rose behind her desk as her father came into her office, his Stetson in hand, his marshal face on.

"Tell me," she said on a ragged breath, her chest aching with dread. She'd seen this look before. She knew when her father had bad news to impart.

"It's Dillon Ramsey."

She frowned, thinking she'd heard him wrong. "Dillon?"

"You weren't with him last night, were you?"

"No, why?"

"He was found dead this morning."

Her first thought was a car accident. The Gallatin Canyon two-lane highway was one of the most dangerous highways in the state with all its traffic and curves through the canyon along the river.

"He was found murdered next to his truck up by Goose Creek."

She stared at him, trying to make sense of this. "How?"

He hesitated but only a moment, as if he knew the

details would get out soon enough and he wanted to be the one to tell her. "He was naked, lying on a blanket as if he'd been with someone before that. His throat had been cut."

Her stomach roiled. "Why would someone want to kill him?"

"That's what I'm trying to find out. I'm looking for a friend of his, Grady Birch. Do you know him?"

Mary shook her head. "I never met any of his friends."

Her father scratched the back of his neck for a moment. "I understand that Dillon and Chase got into a confrontation that turned physical."

"Chase? You can't think that Chase… You're wrong. Chase didn't trust him, but then neither did you."

"With good reason as it turns out. I believe that Dillon was involved in the cattle rustling along with his friend Grady Birch."

Mary had to sit back down. All of this was making her sick to her stomach. "I'd broken up with him. I had no plans to see him again. He'd threatened to ask out one of my tenants." She shook her head. "But Chase had nothing to do with this."

The marshal started for the door. "I just wanted you to hear about it from me rather than the Canyon grapevine."

She nodded and watched him leave. Dillon was dead. Murdered. She shuddered.

Grady Birch's body washed up on the rocks near Beckman's Flat later that morning. It was found by a fisherman. The body had been in the water for at least a few days. Even though the Gallatin River never got what anyone would call warm, it had been warm enough to do damage over that length of time.

Hud rubbed the back of his neck as he watched the coroner put the second body that day into a body bag. Dillon was dead; Grady had been dead even longer. What was going on?

He would have sworn that it was just the two of them in on the cattle rustling. But maybe there was someone else who didn't want to share the haul. He'd send a tech crew out to the cabin to see what prints they came up with. But something felt all wrong about this. Killers, he'd found, tended to stay with the same method and not improvise. A drowning was much different from cutting a person's throat. The drowning had been made to look like an accident. But Grady's body had been held down with rocks.

"I'll stop by later," he told the coroner as he walked to his patrol SUV. There was someone he needed to talk to.

Hud found Chase fixing fences on the Sherman Jensen ranch. He could understand why Sherman needed the help and why Chase had agreed to working for board. He was a good worker and Sherman's son was not.

Chase looked up as Hud drove in. He put down the tool he'd been using to stretch the barbed wire and took off his gloves as he walked over to the patrol SUV.

"Did you get the prints off the cup back?" Chase asked.

Hud shook his head. He'd been a little busy, but he'd check on them the first chance he got. He studied the man his daughter had been in love with as far back as he could remember. Out here in his element, Chase looked strong and capable. Hud had thought of him as a boy for so long. At twenty-four, he'd still been green behind the years. He could see something he hadn't noticed when he saw him at the marshal's office. Chase had grown into a man.

Still he found himself taking the man's measure.

"Marshal," Chase said. "If you've come out here to ask me what my intentions are toward your daughter…" He grinned.

"As a matter of fact, I would like to know, even though that's not why I'm here."

Chase pushed back his Stetson. "I'm going to marry her. With your permission, of course."

Hud chuckled. "Of course. Well, that's good to hear, as far as intentions go, but I'm here on another matter. When was the last time you saw Dillon Ramsey?"

Chase grimaced. "Did he think that's why I was in your office the other day?" He shook his head. "That I'd come there to report our fight? So he decided to tell you his side of it?"

"Actually no. But I heard about it. Heard that if Mary hadn't broken it up, it could have gotten lethal."

"Only because Dillon was going for a knife he had in his boot," Chase said.

Hud nodded. Chase had known about the man's knife. The knife Dillon had been killed with. "So the trouble between you was left unfinished." Chase didn't deny it. "That's the last time you saw him?"

Chase nodded and frowned. "Why? What did he say? I saw the way he was trying to intimidate Mary."

"Not much. Someone cut his throat last night." He saw the cowboy's shocked expression.

"What the hell?"

"Exactly. Where were you last night?"

"Here on the ranch."

"Can anyone verify that you were here the whole time?"

"You can't really believe that I—"

"Can anyone verify where you were?" Hud asked again.

Chase shook his head. "Can't you track my cell phone or something? Better yet, you know me. If I saw Dillon again, I might get in the first punch because I knew he'd fight dirty. But use a knife?" He shook his head. "Not me. That would be Dillon."

Hud tended to believe him. But he also knew about the knife Dillon kept in his boot, and he hadn't seen Chase in years. People change. "You aren't planning to leave town, are you?"

Chase groaned. "I have a carpenter job in Paradise Valley. I was leaving tomorrow to go to work. But I can give you the name of my employer. I really don't want to pass up this job."

Hud studied him for a moment. "Call me with your employer's name. I don't have to warn you not to take off, right?"

Chase smiled. "I'm not going anywhere. Like I told you, I'm marrying your daughter and staying right here."

Hud couldn't help but smile. "Does Mary know that?"

The cowboy laughed. "She knows. That doesn't mean she's said yes yet."

"Are you all right? I just heard the news about the deputy," Chase asked when he called Mary after her father left. "I'm so sorry."

"Dillon and I had broken up, but I still can't believe it. Who would want to kill him?"

"Your father thought I might," he said. "I just had a visit from him."

"What? You can't be serious."

"He'd heard about the fight Dillon and I had in front of your building," Chase said. "I thought maybe you'd mentioned it to him."

"I didn't tell him, but he can't believe that you'd kill anyone."

Chase said nothing for a moment. "The word around town according to Beth Anne is that Dillon had been with someone in the woods. A woman. You have any idea who?"

She thought of Lucy, but quickly pushed the idea away. Dillon had said he was going to ask her out, but she doubted he'd even had time to do that—if he'd been serious. Clearly, he'd been seeing someone else while he was seeing her.

"I'll understand if you don't want to go with me late to see the next man on my list," Chase said.

"No, I'm going. I'm having trouble getting any work done. I'm still in shock. I know how much finding your father means to you. Pick me up?"

"You know it. I'm going to get cleaned up. Give me thirty minutes."

"You questioned Chase about Dillon's murder?" Mary cried when he father answered the phone.

He made an impatient sound. "I'm the marshal, and I'm investigating everyone with a grudge against Dillon Ramsey."

"Chase doesn't hold grudges," she said indignantly, making Hud laugh.

"He's a man, and the woman he's in love with was seeing another man who is now dead. Also, he was in an altercation with the dead man less that forty-eight hours ago."

"How did you know about the fi—"

"I got an anonymous call."

"I didn't think anyone but me…" She thought of Lucy. No, Lucy wouldn't do that. Someone else in the area that night must have witnessed it.

"You can't possibly think that Chase would…" She shook her head adamantly. "It wasn't Chase."

"Actually, I think you're right," her father said. "I just got the coroner's report. The killer was right-handed. I noticed Chase is left-handed."

Mary felt herself relax. Not that she'd ever let herself think Chase was capable of murder, but she'd been scared that he would be a suspect because of their altercation.

As she looked up, she saw Lucy on her way to work. The woman turned as if sensing she was being watched, and waved before coming back to the front door of the office to stick her head in.

"Mary, are you all right? I just heard the news on the radio about that deputy you were seeing, the one your cowboy got into a fight with the other night."

"I know, it's terrible, isn't it?"

"You don't think Chase—"

"No." She shook her head. "My dad already talked to him. It wasn't him."

Lucy lifted a brow. "Chase sure was angry the other night."

"Yes, but the forensics proved that Chase couldn't have done it." Mary waved a hand through the air as if she couldn't talk about it, which she couldn't. "Not that I ever thought Chase could kill someone."

Lucy still didn't look convinced. "I think everyone is capable. It just has to be the right circumstances."

"You mean the wrong ones," Mary said, the conversation making her uncomfortable. She no longer wanted to think about how Dillon had died or who might have killed him.

"Yes," Lucy said, and laughed.

"Did you ever go out with Dillon?" Mary asked, and wished she hadn't at Lucy's expression.

"Seriously?" The woman laughed. "Definitely not my type. Why would you ask me that?"

"He mentioned that he might ask you out. I thought maybe—"

Lucy sighed. "Clearly, he was just trying to make you jealous. I think he came into the coffee shop once that I can remember. You really thought I was the woman who had sex with him in the woods?"

"We don't know that's what happened."

"It's what everyone in town is saying. They all think that the killer followed the deputy out to the spot where he was meeting some woman. That's why I asked about Chase. If your cowboy thought it was you on that blanket with him…"

"That's ridiculous. Anyway, it wasn't me."

"But maybe in the dark, Chase didn't know that."

"Seriously, Lucy, you don't know him. I do. Chase wouldn't hurt anyone."

"Sorry. Not something you want to dwell on at this

time of the morning. I can't believe you thought I could be the woman with him."

And yet Lucy seemed determine to believe that Chase had been the killer.

"Coming over for your coffee?" Lucy asked. "I can have it ready for you as soon as I get in."

"No, actually. I have an errand to run this morning."

Lucy frowned but then brightened. "Well, have a nice day. Maybe I'll see you later."

From the window, Mary saw her hesitate as if she wanted to talk longer before she closed the door and started across the street. She seemed to quicken her pace as Chase drove up.

Mary hurried out, locking her office door behind her before climbing into his pickup. He smiled over at her. "You okay? I saw Lucy talking to you as I drove up."

"Nothing important."

"Then let's get it over with. I never realized how… draining this could be," Chase said.

"Who's next?"

"Jason Morrison."

Morrison was a local attorney. His office was only a few doors down from Mary's. They'd called to make an appointment and were shown in a little before time.

Jason was tall and slim with an athletic build. He spent a lot of time on the slopes or mountain biking, and had stayed in good shape at fifty-five. He was a nice looking man with salt and pepper dark hair and blue eyes. When his secretary called back to say that his eleven o'clock was waiting, he said to send them on back.

Jason stood as they entered and came around his desk to shake Mary's hand and then Chase's.

Mary watched as he shook Chase's hand a little too long, his gaze locked on the younger man's.

Was it Chase's blue eyes, or did Jason see something in him he recognized?

"Please, have a seat," the attorney said, going behind his desk and sitting down. "What can I do for the two of you?"

"We're inquiring about a woman named Muriel Steele," Mary said. "We thought you might have known her twenty-seven years ago."

Jason leaned back in his chair and looked from Mary to Chase and back. "Muriel. Has it been that long ago?" He shook his head. "Yes, I knew her." He frowned. "Why are you asking?"

"I'm her son," Chase said.

Jason's gaze swung back to him. "I thought there was something about you that was familiar when we shook hands. Maybe it's the eyes. Your mother had the most lovely blue eyes."

As Chase started to rise, Mary put a hand on his thigh to keep him in his chair. "Chase is looking for his father."

"His father?" He glanced at Mary and back to Chase.

"When my mother left Big Sky, she was pregnant with me, but I suspect you already know that," Chase said through clenched teeth.

The attorney looked alarmed. "I had no idea. Wait a minute. You think I was the one who…" He held up his hands. "I knew your mother, but I was already married by then. Linda was pregnant with our daughter Becky." He was shaking his head.

"My mother left a diary," Chase said.

Jason went still. "If she said it was me…" He shook his head. "I'm sorry, but I'm not your father."

"She didn't name her married lover," Chase said. "Just his initials. J.M. Quite a coincidence you knew her and you have the exact initials."

A strange look crossed the man's face. "I'm sorry. Like I said, you have the wrong man."

"Then you wouldn't mind submitting to a DNA test," Mary said.

"I'm a lawyer. No good can come of submitting to a DNA test, not with the legal system like it is. No offense to your father the marshal, ma'am," he added quickly.

"So you're saying no?" Chase asked as he got to his feet.

Jason sighed. "I want to help you, all right? If it comes to that, I'd get a DNA test. I assume there are others you're talking to?"

"Actually, a friend of yours," Mary said. "Jonathan Mason."

Jason groaned. He looked as if he wanted to say more, but changed his mind. "My heart goes out to you. But maybe there was a reason your mother never told you who your father was."

"Other than she wanted to protect him?" Chase demanded.

Jason sighed again. "I wish I could help you. I really do. But after all this time…"

"You think I should let it go?" Chase leaned toward the man threateningly.

Jason held up his hands. "I can see your frustration."

"It's not frustration. It's anger. The man knocked up my mother, broke her heart and her spirit, and let her raise me alone. She was only seventeen when she became pregnant, had no education and no way to support herself but menial jobs. So, I'm furious with this man who fathered me."

"Then why find him? What good will it do?" the lawyer asked.

Chase leaned back some. "Because I want to look him in the eye and tell him what I think of him."

Mary rose and so did the attorney. "We'll probably be back about that DNA test," she said.

Jason nodded, but he didn't look happy about it. His gaze went to Chase and softened. "I cared about your mother, but I wasn't her lover."

"I guess we'll see," Chase said as they left.

"It's him," Chase said as they left the attorney's office. His heart was pounding. He thought about what the man had said. "It's him, I'm telling you."

"I don't know."

"He admitted knowing her. You saw the way he looked at me. He knew the moment he shook my hand. He practically admitted it."

"But he didn't admit it," Mary pointed out.

"He's a lawyer. He's too smart to admit anything."

"He admitted that he knew her, that he cared about her. Chase, I think he's telling the truth."

He stopped walking to sigh deeply. Taking off his Stetson, he raked a hand through his hair and tried to calm down. "I don't know why I'm putting myself through this. I'm twenty-eight years old. He's right. What do I hope to get out of this?"

"A father."

He let out a bark of a laugh. "That ship has sailed. I don't need a father."

"We all need family."

He shook his head. "When I find him, I want to tell him off—not bond with him. Hell, I want to punch him in his face."

At a sound behind them, they turned to see Jason hurrying toward his car.

"I think we should follow him," Mary said as they watched him speed away.

Chase nodded, his gaze and attention on the attorney. "I think you're right. He certainly took off fast enough right after we talked to him. Let's go."

They climbed into his pickup, turned around in the middle of the street and followed at a distance. "Where do you think he's going?"

"Good question. Maybe home to talk to his wife."

Mary shook her head. "He doesn't live in this direction."

"What if he is going to warn Jonathan Mason?"

"Maybe. But only if Jonathan is up at the mountain resort." Chase drove up the road toward Lone Peak.

"Maybe he's going to lunch," he suggested.

"Maybe." After a few miles, the lawyer turned into the Alpine Bar parking lot.

Jason parked, leaped out and went inside.

"He could have called someone to meet him," Chase said.

She nodded. "Let's give him a minute and go inside."

Chase pulled into the lot next to the attorney's car. It was early so there were only three cars out front. During ski season, the place would have been packed. "Recognize any of the rigs?"

She shook her head.

"Have I thanked you for doing this for me? I really do appreciate it."

She smiled over at him. "You have thanked me. I'm glad to help, you know that. But Chase—"

"I know. Try not to lose my temper."

"I don't want to have to bail you out of jail," she said, still smiling.

"But you would, wouldn't you?" He reached out and stroked her cheek, his gaze locking with hers. "I've never loved you more than I do right now, Mary Cardwell Savage." He drew back his hand. "Marry me when this is all over."

She laughed and shook her head.

"I'm serious. What is it going to take to make you realize that you're crazy about me? I want to make you Mrs. Chase Steele. We can have the big wedding I know your mother wants. But I was thinking—"

"You're stalling. Come on, let's go in," she said, and they climbed out. He caught up with her and, taking her arm, pulled her around to face him.

"For the record? I was serious about asking you to marry me. Soon." As he pushed open the door, country music from the jukebox spilled out. Chase heard a familiar song, and wished he and Mary were there to dance—not track down his no-count biological father.

He spotted Jason at the bar talking to the bartender, a gray-haired man with wire-rimmed glasses. As the door closed behind them, a man came through the back door. He caught a glimpse of a residence through the doorway and a ramp before the door closed.

The man motioned to Jason to join him at one of the tables in the back.

"Do you recognize him?" he asked Mary.

"It's Jim Harris," Mary said, and grabbed Chase's arm to stop him. "What if the initials J.M. were short for Jim? Jim Harris owns this bar. He and his wife live in a house behind it."

Chase stared at the man the attorney had joined. Blond, blue-eyed, midfifties. The scary part was that as he watched the man, he saw himself in Jim Harris's expression, in the line of his nose, the way he stroked his jaw as he listened.

Chase didn't know that he'd stopped in the middle of the room and was still staring until the man looked up. Their gazes met across the expanse of the bar.

Jim Harris froze.

Chapter 17

Chase felt as if he'd been punched in the stomach. He couldn't breathe, had no idea how he'd gotten out of the bar. He found himself standing outside, bent over, gasping for breath, Mary at his side.

The bar door opened behind him. Sucking in as much air as he could, he straightened and turned. He was a good two inches taller than his father, but the similarities were all too apparent. He stared at the man who was staring just as intensely back at him.

"I didn't know," Jim said, his voice breaking. "I had no idea."

"You didn't know my mother was pregnant? Or you didn't know you had a son?" Chase demanded, surprised he could speak.

"Neither." The man suddenly dropped to the front steps of the bar and put his head in his hands. "When

Jason told me…" He lifted his head. "I didn't believe him until I saw you."

"How was it you didn't know?" Mary asked. For a moment, Chase had forgotten she was there.

"She never told me…" Jim moaned.

"You weren't at all curious why she left?" Chase said, his voice breaking. His strength was coming back. So was his anger.

"I knew why Muriel left," the man said, meeting his gaze. "I separated from my wife when I met your mother. We fell in love. I was in the process of filing for divorce to marry Muriel when…" His voice broke and he looked away. "My wife was in a car accident. She almost died."

"And you decided not to leave her," Chase said, nodding as if he could feel his mother's pain. She'd been young and foolish, fallen for a man who was taken only to realize all his promises had come to nothing—and she was pregnant with his child. So she hadn't told him. What would have been the point since by then she knew he was staying with his wife?

The door behind Jim opened. Chase heard a creak and looked up to see a woman in a wheelchair framed in the doorway. The woman had graying hair that hung limp around her face. She stared at him for a long moment before she wheeled back and let the door close behind her. He looked at his father, who was looking at him.

"She's been in a wheelchair since the accident," Jim said quietly as he got to his feet. "I blamed myself since she had her accident after an argument we had over the bar. The bar," he said with disgust. "We both wanted the divorce. That wasn't the problem. It was the bar.

I wanted to keep it. She wanted it sold, and half the money. If only I'd let her have it…" His voice dropped off. "I wanted to be with your mother. Muriel was the love of my life. If I'd known she was pregnant…"

"But she didn't tell you after she heard about your wife's accident," Chase said more to himself than his father.

Jim nodded. "If I'd known where your mother had gone…" He didn't finish because it was clear he didn't know what he would have done.

Chase thought of how close his father had been in the years from fifteen on that he'd lived and worked on the Cardwell Ranch. All that time, his father had been not that far away. But there was no reason for their paths to cross. His father's bar was up on the mountain at the resort and Chase had lived down in the canyon.

He looked at his father and could see that the man had paid the price for all these years, just as his mother had. Jim Harris stood for a moment, his hands hanging at his sides, a broken man. "I'm sorry you didn't find a better father than me." With that he turned and went back inside.

Chase felt Mary touch his arm. "I can drive," she said, and took his pickup keys from his hand.

Hours later, she and Chase lay curled up in her apartment bed, his strong arms around her. They'd stayed up and talked until nearly daylight, and finally exhausted had climbed into her bed.

Chase had found his father. Not the man he'd thought he was going to find. Not a man he'd wanted to punch. A man who looked like him. A man who'd made mistakes, especially when it came to love.

Mary had told him what she knew about Jim and his wife, Cheryl. They'd gotten married young when Cheryl had been pregnant, but she'd lost the baby and couldn't have another. It had been a rocky marriage.

"Jim said they were separated when he met your mother, but they must have kept it quiet. She wandered down in Meadow Village and he lived up on the mountain behind the bar." She'd called her mother to ask her what she knew and Jim and Cheryl.

Dana had said she remembered that Cheryl had been staying with a sister down in Gateway near Bozeman when she'd had her accident.

"So no one knew about my mother and Jim," Chase had said.

"Apparently not. I guess they hadn't wanted it to be an issue in the divorce, especially since the bar was already one."

When it got late and they'd talked the subject nearly to death, she'd suggested they go to bed.

"Mary, I—"

"Not to make love. Sleep. I don't want you leaving after what you've been through. Also, it won't be long before morning. We both need sleep and you have to leave for you carpentry job tomorrow."

Now as they lay in bed, Chase said, "I don't want to be like him, a coward, a man who never followed his heart."

"You're not like him."

He made a groaning sound. "I have been. Out of fear. I should have stayed in Montana and fought for you. Instead, I left. I was miserable the whole time. I missed you and Montana so much. I didn't think I was good enough for you. I'm still not sure I am."

She touched her finger to his lips. "That's ridiculous and all behind us."

"Is it? Because I still feel like you don't trust me," Chase whispered in the dark room as he pulled her closer. "What is it going to take to make you trust me again?"

Lucy lay in bed listening to the noises coming from upstairs. She hadn't been able to sleep since she'd heard Mary come in with Chase. They'd gone right upstairs. She had heard them moving around and the low murmur of voices, but she hadn't been able to tell what was going on until minutes ago when they'd gone into the bedroom. It was right over her own.

Not that she could hear what they were doing. The building was solid enough that she'd had to strain to hear anything at all. But she'd heard enough to know that they were still in the bedroom. Both of them. She knew exactly what they were doing, and it was driving her mad.

Getting up, she went into the living room, got herself a stiff drink and sprawled on the couch. She had hoped that Mary wouldn't fall for him again. What was wrong with the woman? How could she trust a man like that? Lucy fumed and consumed another couple of shots until she'd fallen asleep on the couch only to be awakened by movement upstairs later in the morning.

She sat up and listened. Chase's boots on the stairs. Mary's steps right behind him. Lucy listened to them descend the stairs as she fought the urge to charge out into the hall and attack them both with her bare hands. Mary was a fool.

She cracked her door open to listen and heard them

talking about Chase leaving the area for a carpenter job he was taking. Leaving? She tiptoed to the top of the stairs, keeping to the shadows. They had stopped on the main floor landing.

"I don't like leaving you," he said. "But I'll be back every weekend. This job will only last about six weeks, and then my boss said we have work around Big Sky so I'll see you every night. That's if you want to see me."

Lucy couldn't hear what Mary said, but she could hear the rustle of clothing. Had Mary stepped into his arms? Were they kissing? She felt her blood boil.

"You'll be careful?" Chase said.

"Please, don't start that again."

Lucy heard the tension in her voice and moved down a few steps so she could hear better.

"I'm sorry, but there is still something about Lucy that bothers me," Chase said. "Doesn't it seem strange that three people have died since she came to town?"

"You can't believe that she had anything to do with that."

"Lucy just walks into the job at the coffee shop after the last new hire gets run down on the road? Then she moves into the same apartment Christy Shores was going to rent before she was murdered? A coincidence?"

"Big Sky is a small place, so not that much of a co-incidence since I live across the street from the coffee shop and had an apartment for rent."

"And didn't you tell me that Dillon was going to ask Lucy out?"

She rolled her eyes. "And that was reason enough to kill him? She said he hadn't and she wouldn't have gone out with him if he had."

Chase shrugged. "It's…creepy."

"What's creepy is that she reminds you of an old girlfriend."

"Fiona wasn't my girlfriend. But Lucy definitely reminds me of her. Fiona went after what she wanted at all costs and the consequences be damned."

"I really don't want to talk about this."

"I just want you to be careful, that's all. Don't put so much trust in her. Promise?"

"I promise. I don't want to argue with you right before you leave me."

Lucy could hear the two of them smooching again.

"I'll be back Friday night. I'd love to take you to dinner."

"I'd love that."

Lucy pressed herself against the wall as the door opened and light raced up the stairs toward her. She stayed where she was and tried to catch her breath. Chase suspected she was Fiona. So far he hadn't convinced Mary. Nor had the marshal gotten her prints off the cup and found out she was Fiona Barkley. The deputy had done his job. She almost felt bad about killing him.

But it was only a matter of time before Mary started getting suspicious.

After hearing her go into her office, Lucy inched her way back to her apartment. She wanted to scream, to destroy the apartment, anything to rid herself of the fury boiling up inside her. She'd tried to be patient, but the more she was around Mary, the more she hated seeing her with Chase.

She clenched her fists. Mary had said she wasn't sure about the two of them. Liar. But Lucy knew Chase was to blame. He'd somehow tricked his way into Mary's bed. Chase was the one chasing the cowgirl.

She'd come here planning to kill them both. It wasn't Mary's fault that Chase went around breaking women's hearts. But even as she thought it, she knew that Mary had disappointed her by falling for Chase all over again.

Not that it mattered, she thought as she calmly walked into the kitchen, opened the top drawer and took out the knife she'd planned to use on the deputy. She stared at it, telling herself it was time to end this and move on. And there was only one way to finish it.

"It's my day off," Lucy announced as she came out of her apartment as Mary was headed downstairs a few days later.

Mary couldn't help but look confused as she took in Lucy's Western attire and tried to make sense of the words. She knew that she'd been avoiding her tenant since their conversation about Dillon and Chase and felt guilty for it.

"Oh no, I'm sorry," Lucy said quickly. "You forgot. That's all right." She started to turn back toward her apartment.

"Horseback riding." Mary racked her brain, trying to remember if they'd made a definite date to go.

"You said on my day off. I thought I'd mentioned that I would be off today. Don't worry about it. I'm sure we can go some other time."

"No," Mary said quickly. "I did forget, but it will only take me a moment to change." She was thinking about what work she'd promised to do today, but she could get it done this afternoon or even work late if she had to. She didn't want to disappoint Lucy. The woman had looked so excited when she'd first mentioned it.

The more Chase had said Lucy reminded him of the woman he'd known in Arizona, the more Mary had defended her. If she never heard the name Fiona again, she'd be ecstatic.

And yet she found herself pulling away from Lucy, questioning the small things, like how close they'd become so quickly. Also she'd always tried to keep tenants as just that and not friends. More than anything, it was Chase's concern that had her trying to put distance between her and Lucy. Mary didn't want the woman always reminding him of Fiona.

So the last thing she wanted to do today was go horseback riding with the woman. But it had been her idea, and she had invited her. If anything, she prided herself on keeping her word. After this though, she would put more distance between them.

"I'll run across the street and get us some coffee," Lucy said, all smiles. "I'm so excited. It's been so long since I've been on a horse."

Mary hurried back upstairs to change. She missed Chase. He called every night and they talked for hours. He never mentioned his father, and she didn't bring it up. But she'd felt a change in him since discovering that Jim Harris was his biological father. He seemed stronger, more confident, more sure of what he wanted. He said he didn't want to be like the man. She wasn't sure exactly what he'd meant. Jim Harris was an unhappy man who'd made bad decisions before finding himself between a rock and hard place. She wondered if Chase could ever forgive him. Or if he already had.

When she came back downstairs, dressed for horseback riding, she found Lucy sitting at her desk. Two coffees sat on the edge away from the paperwork. Mary stopped in the doorway and watched for a moment as Lucy glanced through the papers on her desk before taking the card with the daisies that Chase had sent her, reading it and putting it back. As she did, she caught one of the daisies in her fingers.

Mary watched her crush it in her hand before dropping it into the trash can. She felt a fissure of irritation that the woman had been so nosy as to read the card let alone destroy one of the daisies. It was clear that Lucy resented Chase. Was she jealous? Did she not want Mary to have any other relationships in her life?

She cleared her voice, and Lucy got up from her desk quickly.

"Sorry, I was just resting for a moment." Lucy flashed her a gap-toothed smile. "I'm on my feet all day. It will be nice to sit on the back of a horse for a while."

Hud had three unsolved murders within weeks of each other and no clues. He got up to get himself some coffee when he remembered the cup Chase had brought in to be fingerprinted.

With a curse, he recalled that he'd given the cup to Dillon. Back in his office, he called down to the lab. "Last week a cup was brought down to be fingerprinted. I haven't seen the results yet."

The lab tech asked him to hold for a moment. "I have the order right here. I did the test myself, but I don't see my report on file. You didn't get a copy?"

"No, who did you give it to?"

"Dillon Ramsey, the deputy who brought it down. He asked that I give it to him personally. I did."

Hud swore. "You don't happen to remember—"

"The prints *were* on file," the tech said. Just as Chase had thought they would be. "Give me a minute. It was an unusual name. Fiona. Fiona Barkley."

Hud wrote it down and quickly went online. Fiona Barkley had been fingerprinted several times when questioned by police, starting with a house fire when she was eleven. Her entire family died in the fire.

The marshal shook his head as he saw that she'd been questioned and fingerprinted in a half dozen other incidents involving males that she'd dated.

Where had Chase gotten this cup? He put in a call to the cowboy's number. It went straight to voice mail. He didn't leave a message. Mary had said that Chase would be home Friday night. Hud would ask him then.

As Chase took a break, he noticed that Rick had left several messages for him to call. Tired from a long day, he almost didn't call him back. He wasn't sure he could stay awake long enough to talk to both Mary and Rick, and he much preferred to talk to Mary before he fell asleep. But the last message Rick had left said it was important.

Chase figured that Fiona's body had been found, and Rick wanted him to know. So why hadn't he just left that message? The phone rang three times before Rick answered. Chase could hear a party going on in the background and almost hung up.

"Chase, I'm so glad you called back. Hold on." He waited and a few moments later, Rick came back on, the background noise much lower. "Hey, I hate to call you with bad news."

"They found her body?"

"Ah, no. Just the opposite. Some dentist down on the border recognized Fiona's photograph from a story in the newspaper about her disappearance. He contacted authorities. Chase, it looks like Fiona is alive. Not just that. She had the dentist change her appearance. Apparently, the Mexican dentist thought it was strange since she'd obviously been in some kind of accident. But he gave her a gap between her two front teeth."

Chase felt his heart stop dead. Lucy. The woman living on the floor below Mary. Lucy. The barista who Mary had befriended. He tried to take a breathe, his mind racing. Hadn't he known? He'd sensed it gut deep, as if the woman radiated evil. Why hadn't he listened to his intuition?

"I have to go." He disconnected and quickly dialed Mary's cell phone number. It went straight to voice mail. "When you get this, call me at once. It's urgent. Don't go near Lucy. I'll explain when I see you. I'm on my way to Big Sky now." He hung up and called the ranch. Mary's mother answered.

"Dana, it's Chase. Have you seen Mary?"

"No. Chase, what's wrong?"

"I'm on my way there. If you see or hear from Mary, keep her there. Don't let her near Lucy, the barista at Lone Peak Perk, okay? Tell Hud. She's not who she is pretending to be. She's come to Montana to hurt me. I'm terrified that she will hurt Mary." He hung up and ran out to his pickup. He could be home within the hour. But would that be soon enough?

Or was it already too late?

Chapter 18

"You haven't touched your coffee," Lucy said, glancing over at her as Mary drove her pickup to the ranch. Lucy had wanted to see the place and asked if they could take the back roads—unless Mary was in a hurry.

She'd taken a sip of the coffee. It had tasted bitter. Or maybe the bitter taste in her mouth had nothing to do with the coffee and more to do with what she'd seen earlier in her office—Lucy going through her things.

Now she took another sip. It wasn't just bitter. It had a distinct chalky taste—one that she remembered only too well. Even as she thought it, though, she was arguing that she was only imagining it. Otherwise, it would mean that there'd been something in the coffee that Lucy had brought her that day that had made her deathly ill—and again today.

"My stomach is a little upset," she said, putting the coffee cup back into the pickup's beverage holder.

Lucy looked away, her feelings obviously hurt. "Maybe we should do this some other day. I feel like you're not really into it."

"No, I asked you and this is the first day you've had off," Mary said, hating that she'd apparently forgotten. Worse, hating that she'd let Chase's suspicions about Lucy get to her. Not that the woman hadn't raised more suspicions by her actions earlier.

Lucy turned away as if watching the scenery out the window. Mary pretended to take a sip of her coffee, telling herself that after today, she would distance herself from the woman and the coffee shop—at least for a while. It wasn't good to get too involved with a tenant, maybe especially this one.

Even the little bit of the coffee on the tip of her tongue had that chalky taste and made her want to gag. She looked over at Lucy as she settled her cup back into the pickup's beverage holder. She'd taken the long way to the ranch for Lucy but now she regretted it, just wanting to get this trip over with.

As she slowed for a gate blocking the road, she asked, "Lucy, would you mind getting the gate?"

Without a word, the woman climbed out as soon as Mary stopped the vehicle. Easing open her door, Mary poured half of the coffee onto the ground and quietly closed her door again. Lucy pushed the gate back and stepped aside as Mary drove through and then waited for her to close it.

Would she notice the spot on the ground where the coffee had been dumped? She hoped not. She also hoped that she was wrong about the chalky taste and what might have caused it. She didn't want to be wrong about

Lucy, she thought as she watched the young woman close the gate and climb back in the truck.

Mary saw her glance at the half-empty coffee cup. Did she believe that Mary had drunk it?

Looking away again, Lucy asked, "How much farther to where you keep the horses?"

"Just over the next hill." Mary had called ahead and asked one of the wranglers to saddle up her horse and a gentle one for Lucy. As they topped the hill, she could see two horses waiting for them tied up next to the barn. She tried to breathe a sigh of relief. Maybe Lucy had gotten up on the wrong side of the bed this morning. Or maybe she had drugged Mary's coffee and was angry that she hadn't drunk it.

"Is everything all right?" Lucy asked. "You seem upset with me."

Mary shot her a look. "I'm sorry. I just feel bad that I forgot about our horseback ride today. That's all."

"Not just your upset stomach?" the woman asked pointedly.

"That too, but I'm feeling better. There is no place I like better than the back of a horse."

Lucy said no more as Mary parked behind the bar and they got out. She helped the woman into the saddle. After she swung up onto her mount, they headed off on a trail that would take them to the top of the mountain. Mary was already planning on cutting the horseback ride short as she led the way up the trail.

"I'm out of sorts this morning too," Lucy said behind her. "I haven't slept well worrying about you."

Mary turned in her saddle to look back at her. "Worrying about *me*?"

"I probably shouldn't say anything, but there is something about Chase that bothers me."

She wanted to laugh out loud. Or at least say, *There's something about you that bothers him*. Instead, she said, "There is nothing to worry about."

"You just seem to be falling back into his arms so quickly. I heard him up in your apartment. He didn't leave until the next morning."

Mary felt a sliver of anger ripple through her. Chase was right about one thing. Lucy had become too involved in her life. "Lucy, that is none of your business."

"I'm sorry, I thought we were friends. You told me that night in my apartment all about him and the deputy."

"Yes." That, she saw now had been a mistake. "Then you know I never stopped loving him."

"But he stopped loving you."

She brought her horse up short as the trail widened, and Lucy rode up beside her. "Lucy—"

"You're the one who told me about this Fiona woman he had the affair with," she said, cutting Mary off.

"It was *one* night."

Lucy shrugged. "Or so he says. You said this woman called you. Said they were engaged. Why would she do that if they'd only had one date?"

Had Mary told her about that? She couldn't remember.

Lucy must have seen the steam coming out of her ears. "Don't get angry. I'm only saying this because you need someone who doesn't have a dog in the fight to tell you the truth."

She had to bite her tongue not to say that they didn't have that kind of friendship. "I appreciate your concern. But I know what I'm doing."

"It's just that he hurt you. I don't want to see him do it again."

"We probably shouldn't talk about this," Mary said, and spurred her horse forward. The sooner they got to the top of the mountain and finished this ride, the better. Chase was right. Somehow Lucy had wormed her way deep into Mary's life. Too deep for the short time they had known each other.

Lucy was jealous of her being with Chase, she realized. Had he sensed that? Is that why he didn't like Lucy? Why she reminded him of Fiona?

They rode in silence as the trail narrowed again, and Lucy was forced to fall in behind her. When they finally reached the top of the mountain, Mary felt as if she could breathe again. She blamed herself. Lucy had been kind to her. Lucy had managed to somehow always be there when needed. Mary had let her get too close, and now it was going to be awkward having her for a tenant directly below her apartment.

She just had to make it clear that her love life was none of Lucy's business. When they rode back to town, she'd talk to her.

Hud listened to his wife's frantic call. He thought of the cup that Chase had brought him wanting the fingerprints checked. "Lucy? You're sure that's what he said?"

"She's a barista at a coffee shop across the street from Mary's building and one of her tenants." He thought of the plain white cup.

"Chase sounded terrified. He's on his way here. I tried to call Mary before I called you. Her phone went straight to voice mail. I'm scared."

"Okay, don't worry," Hud said. "I'll find this Lucy

woman and see what's going on. If you see Mary, call me. Keep her there until I get to the bottom of this."

He disconnected, fear making his heart pound, and headed for his patrol SUV. The town of Big Sky had spread out some since the early days when few would have called it a real town. Still, it didn't take him but a few minutes to get to the coffee shop. As he walked in, he looked about for a barista with the name tag Lucy. There was an Amy and a Faith, but no Lucy.

"Excuse me," he said to the one called Amy. "Is Lucy working today?"

"Day off," she called over her shoulder as she continued to make a coffee that required a lot of noise.

"Do you know where she might have gone?" A headshake. He looked to the other barista. Faith shook her head as well and shrugged.

Dana had said that Lucy rented an apartment across the street. He headed over to Mary's building. With his master key, he opened the door and started up the stairs. An eerie quiet settled over him as he reached the second floor. He knocked at the first door. No answer. He tried the other one. No answer.

He was thinking about busting down the doors when the second one opened. A young man peered out. "I was looking for Lucy," he said.

"Lucy? The woman who is renting the apartment next door? I haven't met her but I overheard her and Mary talking about going horseback riding."

"Do you know where?"

"On Mary's family ranch, I would assume."

Lucy had gone horseback riding with Mary? He quickly called the ranch as he took the stairs three at a time down to his patrol SUV. "Dana," he said when she answered, "a tenant in the building said that Lucy and Mary went horseback riding. You're sure they aren't there?"

"I don't see her rig parked by the barn unless..." He could hear Dana leaving the house and running toward the barn. "She parked in back. They must have come in the back way," she said, out of breath. "Oh, Hud, they're up in the mountains somewhere alone." He heard the sound of a vehicle come roaring up.

"Who is that?" he demanded.

"Chase."

The marshal swore. "Tell him to wait until I get there. Don't let him go off half-cocked." But even as he said the words, he knew nothing was going to stop Chase. "I'm on my way." The moment he disconnected, he raced toward his patrol SUV.

Hud swore as he climbed behind the wheel, started the engine and headed for the ranch. It didn't take much to put the coffee cup and the barista named Lucy together with an apparently disturbed woman named Fiona Barkley who had a lot of priors in her past. His dead deputy had seen the report and kept the results to himself. He had the tie-in with Dillon and the barista, he thought his stomach roiling. His daughter was on a horseback ride with a killer.

Lucy gritted her teeth as she watched Mary ride to the edge of the mountain and dismount. As she stared at her back, there was nothing more Lucy could say. She could tell that Mary was angry with her. Angry at a friend who was just trying to help her. Mary thought she knew Chase better than her.

Lucy wanted to laugh at that. She knew the cowboy

better than Mary assumed. Maybe it was time to enlighten her. Look how easily Chase had cast her aside. How he'd gotten that irritated look whenever he saw her after that first night. He'd wanted her to go away. He'd gotten what he wanted from her and no longer needed her.

Instead, he thought he needed Mary. Sweet, precious Mary. She glared at the woman's back as she rode toward her, reined in and dismounted. She told herself that she'd tried to save Mary. It was Mary's own fault if she wouldn't listen. Now the cowgirl would need to die. It would have to look like an accident. Earlier, she'd thought about pulling the pocketknife she'd brought and jamming it into the side of her horse.

But she'd realized that Mary had been raised on horses. She probably wouldn't get bucked off when the horse reared or even when it galloped down the narrow trail in pain.

No, it had been a chance she couldn't take. But one way or another Mary wasn't getting off this mountain alive, she thought as she stepped over to stand beside her.

The view was just as Mary had said it was. They stood on a precipice overlooking a dozen mountains that stretched far into the horizon.

Below them was the canyon with its green-tone river snaking through the pines and canyon walls. It would have been so easy to push Mary off and watch her tumble down the mountain. But there was always the chance that the fall wouldn't kill her.

Lucy reached into her pocket and fingered the gun as she said, "I slept with Chase in Arizona."

Chapter 19

Chase roared up in his pickup and leaped out as Dana ran toward him.

"The wrangler had horses saddled for them. He said they headed up the road into the mountains," she told him as he rushed toward her. He could see that she'd been saddling horses. "Hud wants you to wait for him. If this woman is as dangerous as you say she is—"

"I'm the one she wants. Not Mary. If I wait, it might be too late." He swung up into the horse she'd finished saddling and spurred it forward. Dana grabbed the reins to stop him.

"I know I can't talk you out of going. Here, take this." She handed him the pistol he knew she kept in the barn. "It's loaded and ready to fire. Be careful." Her voice broke. "Help Mary."

He rode off up the road headed for the mountaintop.

He knew where Mary would take Lucy. It was her favorite spot—and the most dangerous.

As he rode at a full-out gallop, he thought of his misgivings about Lucy. Fiona must have loved the fact that she'd fooled him. That she'd fooled them all, especially trusting Mary. The woman had known exactly how to worm her way into Mary's life, how to get her claws into her and make her believe that she was her friend.

What Fiona didn't know how to do was let go.

He took the trail, riding fast and hard, staying low in the saddle to avoid the pine tree limbs. His heart was in his throat, his fear for Mary a thunderous beat in his chest and his abhorrence for Fiona a bitter taste in his mouth. He prayed as he rode that he would reach them in time. That the woman Fiona had become would spare Mary who'd done nothing to her.

But he had little hope. He knew Fiona. She had come all the way to Montana to extract her vengeance. She'd become another person, Lucy, taking her time, playing Mary. Did she know that they were on to her? That's what frightened him the most. If she thought that Mary was turning against her or that the authorities knew…

Mary turned to the woman in surprise, telling herself she must have heard wrong. "What did you just say?"

"I slept with Chase before you sent the letter."

She stared at the woman even as her heart began to pound. "What are you talking about?"

"I'm Fiona."

Mary took a step back as the woman she'd known as Lucy pulled a gun and pointed it at her heart.

Lucy laughed. "Surprise! I read your pathetic letter, and I hated you for taking him from me. You're the reason Chase broke up with me. Instead, the accident helped me become Lucy. You liked Lucy, didn't you? We could have been such good friends. But then Chase showed up—just as I knew he would."

Mary's mind was reeling. This was Lucy. And yet as she stared at her, she knew this was the woman who Chase said had tried to kill him before he left Arizona. The woman he'd said was delusional.

"You think you know him so well." Lucy shook her head. "I was in love with him. He and I were so good together. You don't want to believe that, do you? Well, it's true. There was something between us, something real and amazing, but then you wrote that letter." Lucy's face twisted in disgust. "You ruined my life. You ruined Chase's."

Mary was shaking her head, still having trouble believing this was happening. Chase had tried to warn her, but she'd thought she knew Lucy. She'd really thought she was a friend.

Until she'd taken a sip of the coffee this morning and tasted that horribly familiar chalky taste. "You drugged me."

Lucy shrugged. "You shouldn't have poured out your coffee this morning. That was really rude. I was nice enough to get it for you."

"You wanted to make me sick again?"

"I was being kind," Lucy said, looking confused. "This would have been so much easier if you'd been sick. Now, it's going to get messy." She jabbed the gun at her. "If you had just stayed mad at Chase, this wouldn't be happening either."

Mary didn't know what to say or do. She'd never

dealt with someone this unbalanced. "You want to make him suffer. Is that what this is about?"

Lucy smiled her gap-toothed smile. "For starters."

"You want him to fall in love with you again." She saw at once that was exactly what Lucy wanted. "But if you hurt me, that won't happen."

"It won't happen anyway and we both know it. Because of you." The woman sounded close to tears. "I could have made him happy. Before the letter came from you, he needed me. I could tell. He would have fallen in love with me."

Mary doubted that, but she kept the thought to herself. "If you hurt me, you will lose any chance you have for happiness."

Lucy laughed, sounding more like the woman she'd thought she knew. "Women like me don't find happiness. That's what my mother used to say. But then she let my stepfather and brothers physically and sexually abuse me."

Mary felt her heart go out to the woman despite the situation. "I'm so sorry. That's horrible. You deserved so much better."

Lucy laughed. "I took care of all of them, sending them to hell on earth, and for a while, I was happy, now that I think about it."

"Lucy—"

"Call me Fiona. I know how much you hate hearing that name. Fiona. Fiona. Fiona." She let out a high-pitched laugh that drowned out birdsong but not the thunder of hooves as a horse and rider came barreling across the mountaintop.

Chase reined in his horse as all his fears were realized. The women had been standing at the edge of the mountaintop, Fiona holding a gun pointed at Mary's heart. But when they'd heard him coming, Fiona had grabbed Mary and pressed the muzzle of the weapon to her rival's throat.

"Nice you could join us," Fiona said as he slowly dismounted. "I wondered how long it would take before you realized who I was."

"I sensed it the first time I saw you," he said as he walked toward the pair, his gaze on Fiona and the gun. He couldn't bear to look into Mary's eyes. Fear and disgust. This was all his fault. He'd brought Fiona into their lives. Whatever happened, it was on him.

"I knew it was you," he said, and she smiled.

"It's the chemistry between us. When you pretended not to know me, well, that hurt, Chase. After everything we meant to each other…"

"Exactly," he said. "That's why you need to let Mary go. This is between you and me, Fiona."

Her face clouded. "Please, you think I don't know that you came riding up like that to save her?"

"Maybe I came to save you."

Fiona laughed, a harsh bitter sound. "Save me from what?"

"Yourself. Have any of the men you've known tried to save you, Fiona?" The question seemed to catch her off guard. "Did any of them care what happened to you?"

She met his gaze. "Don't pretend you care."

"I'm not pretending. I never wanted to hurt you. When I heard they found your car in the river, I was devastated. I didn't want things to end that way for you." He saw her weaken a little and took a step toward her and Mary.

"But you don't love me."

That was true and he knew better than to lie. "No. I'd already given away my heart when I met you. It wasn't fair, but it's the truth."

"But you picked me up at that party and brought me back to your place."

He shook his head as he took another step closer. "Rick asked you to drive me home because I'd had too much to drink."

She stared at him as if she'd told herself the story so many times, she didn't remember the truth. "But we made love."

"Did we? I remember you pulling off my boots and jeans right before I passed out."

Fiona let out a nervous laugh. "We woke up in the same bed."

"We did," he agreed as he stepped even closer. "But I suspect that's all that happened that night."

She swallowed and shook her head, tears welling in her eyes. "I liked you. I thought you and I—"

"But you knew better once I told you that I was in love with someone else."

"Still, if you had given us a chance." Fiona made a pleading sound.

"Let Mary go. She had nothing to do with what happened between us."

Fiona seemed to realize how close he was to the two of them. She started to take a step back, dragging Mary along with her. The earth crumbled under her feet and she began to fall.

Chase could see that she planned to take Mary with her. He dived for the gun, for Mary, praying Fiona didn't pull the trigger as she fell. He caught Mary with one hand and reached for the gun barrel with the other.

The report of the handgun filled the air as he yanked Mary forward, breaking Fiona's hold on her. But Mary still teetered on the sheer edge of the cliff as he felt a searing pain in his shoulder. His momentum had carried him forward. He shoved Mary toward the safety of the mountain top as was propelled over the edge of the drop-off.

He felt a hand grab his sleeve. He looked up to see Mary, clinging to him, determined not to let him fall.

Below him, he saw Fiona tumbling down the mountainside over boulders. Her body crashed into a tree trunk, but kept falling until it finally landed in a pile of huge rocks at the bottom.

As Mary helped pull him back up to safety, he saw that Fiona wasn't moving, her body a rag doll finally at rest. Behind them he heard horses. Pulling Mary to him, he buried his face in her neck, ignoring the pain in his shoulder as he breathed in the scent of her.

"He's shot," Chase heard Dana cry before everything went black.

Chapter 20

Chase opened his eyes to see Mary sitting next to his hospital bed as the horror of what had happened came racing back. "Are you—"

"I'm fine," she said quickly, and rose to reach for his hand. "How are you?"

He glanced down at the bandage on his shoulder. "Apparently, I'm going to live. How long have I been out?"

"Not long. You were rushed into surgery to remove the bullet. Fortunately, it didn't hit anything vital."

He stared into her beautiful blue eyes. "I was so worried about you. I'm so sorry."

She shook her head. "I should have listened to you."

Chase laughed. "I wouldn't make a habit of that."

"I'm serious. You tried to warn me."

He sobered. "This is all my fault."

"You didn't make her do the things she did." Her voice broke. Tears filled her eyes. "I thought we were both going to die. You saved my life."

"You saved mine," he said, and squeezed her hand. "Once I'm out of this bed—"

"Slow down, cowboy," the doctor said as he came into the room. "It will be a while before you get out of that bed."

"I need to get well soon, Doc. I'm going to marry this woman."

Mary laughed. "I think he's delirious," she joked, her cheeks flushed.

"I've never been more serious," he called after her as the doctor shooed her from the room. "I love that woman. I've always loved Mary Cardwell Savage," he called before the door closed. He was smiling as he lay back, even though the effort of sitting up had left him in pain. "I need to get well, Doc. I have to buy a ring."

Hud leaned back in his office chair and read the note Fiona-Lucy had left in her apartment. That the woman had lived just a floor below his daughter still made his heart race with terror.

By the time, you find this, I will probably be dead. Or with luck, long gone. Probably dead because I'm tired of living this life. Anyway, I have no-where to go. I came here to make Chase Steele pay for breaking my heart. Sometimes I can see that it wasn't him that made me do the things I've done. That it started long before him. It's the story of my life. It's the people who have hurt me. It's the desperation I feel to be like other people, happy, content, loved.

But there is an anger in me that takes over the rest of the time. I want to hurt people the way I've been hurt and much worse. I killed my mother, stepfather and stepbrothers in a fire. Since then, I've hurt other people who hurt me—and some who didn't. Some, like Deputy Dillon Ramsey, deserved to die. Christy Shores, not so much.

Today, I will kill a woman who doesn't deserve it in order to hurt a man who I could have loved if only he had loved me. He will die too. If not today, then soon. And then… I have no idea. I just know that I'm tired. I can't keep doing this.

Then again, I might feel differently tomorrow.

Hud carefully put the letter back into the evidence bag and sealed it. Fiona was gone. She'd died of her injuries after falling off the mountain. Because she had no family, her body would be cremated. Chase had suggested that her ashes be sent back to Arizona to her friend, Patty, the one person who'd stuck by her.

Two of his murders had been solved by the letter. The third, Grady Birch, was also about to be put to rest. A witness with a cabin not far from where Grady's body was found had come forward. He'd seen a man dragging what he now suspected was a body down to the river. That man had been Deputy Dillon Ramsey, who the witness identified after Dillon's photo had run in the newspaper following his murder.

According to the law, everything would soon be neatly tied up, Hud thought as he put away the evidence bag. But crimes left scars. He could only hope that his daughter would be able to overcome hers. He had a feeling that Chase would be able to help her move on. He wouldn't mind a wedding out at the ranch. It had been a while, and he was thinking how much his wife loved weddings—and family—when his phone rang. It was Dana.

"I just got the oddest call from our son Hank," his wife said without preamble. "He says he's coming home for a visit and that he's bringing someone with him. A woman."

Hud could hear the joy in Dana's voice. "I told you that it would just take time, didn't I? This is great news."

"I never thought he'd get over Naomi," she said, but quickly brightened again. "I can't wait to meet this woman and see our son. It's been too long."

He couldn't have agreed more. "How's Mary?"

"She's picking up Chase at the hospital. Given the big smile on her face when she left the ranch, I'd say she's going to be just fine. How do you feel about a wedding or two in our future?"

He chuckled. "You just read my mind, but don't go counting your chickens before they hatch. Let's take it one at a time." But he found himself smiling as he hung up. Hank was coming home. He'd missed his son more than he could even tell Dana. He just hoped Hank really was moving on.

Chase couldn't wait to see Mary. He was champing at the bit to get out of the hospital. He'd called a local jewelry store and had someone bring up a tray of engagement rings for him to choose one. He refused to put it off until he was released. The velvet box was in his pocket. Now he was only waiting for the nurse to wheel him down to the first floor—and Mary—since it was hospital policy, he'd been told.

Earlier, his father had stopped by. Chase had been glad to see him. Like his father, he'd made mistakes. They were both human. He'd been angry with a man who hadn't even known he existed. But he could understand why his mother had kept the truth from not only him, but also Jim Harris.

He didn't know what kind of relationship they could have, but he no longer felt as if there was a hole in his heart where a father should have been. Everyone said Jim was a good man who'd had some bad luck in his life. Chase couldn't hold that against him.

When his hospital room door opened, he heard the creak of the wheelchair and practically leaped off the bed in his excitement. He and Mary had been apart for far too long. He didn't want to spend another minute away from her. What they had was too special to let it go. He would never take their love for each for granted again.

To his surprise, it wasn't the nurse who brought in the wheelchair. "Mary?"

She looked different today. He was trying to put his finger on what it was when she grinned and shoved the wheelchair to one side as she approached.

Mary couldn't explain the way she felt. But she was emboldened by everything that had happened. When Chase had first come back, she'd told herself that she couldn't trust him after he'd left Montana. But in her heart, she'd known better. Still, she'd pushed him away, letting her pride keep her from the man she loved.

Instead, she'd trusted Lucy. The red flags had been

there, but she'd ignored them because she'd wanted to like her. She'd missed her friends who had moved away. She'd been vulnerable, and she'd let a psychopath into her life.

But now she was tired of being a victim, of not going after what she wanted. What she wanted was Chase.

She stepped to him, grabbed the collar of his Western shirt and pulled him into a searing kiss. She heard his intake of breath. The kiss had taken him by surprise. But also his shoulder was still healing.

"Oh, I'm so sorry," she said, drawing back, her face heating with embarrassment.

"I'm not," he said as he pulled her to him with his good arm and kissed her. When she drew back he started to say something, but she hushed him with a finger across his lips. "I have to know, Chase Steele. Are you going to be mine or not?"

He let out a bark of a laugh. "I've always been yours, Mary Savage."

She sighed and said, "Right answer."

His grin went straight to her heart. He pulled her close again and this time his kiss was fireworks. She melted into his arms. "Welcome home, Chase."

* * * * *

Nicole Helm grew up with her nose in a book and the dream of one day becoming a writer. Luckily, after a few failed career choices, she gets to follow that dream—writing down-to-earth contemporary romance and romantic suspense. From farmers to cowboys, Midwest to *the* West, Nicole writes stories about people finding themselves and finding love in the process. She lives in Missouri with her husband and two sons and dreams of someday owning a barn.

Books by Nicole Helm

Harlequin Intrigue

A Badlands Cops Novel

South Dakota Showdown
Covert Complication
Backcountry Escape
Isolated Threat
Badlands Beware
Close Range Christmas

Carsons & Delaneys

Wyoming Cowboy Justice
Wyoming Cowboy Protection
Wyoming Christmas Ransom

Stone Cold Texas Ranger
Stone Cold Undercover Agent
Stone Cold Christmas Ranger

Visit the Author Profile page at Harlequin.com for more titles.

STONE COLD
TEXAS RANGER

Nicole Helm

To all the episodes of *20/20* and *Dateline* I watched with my grandma. They might have given me nightmares, but they also gave me a ton of great book ideas.

Chapter 1

Vaughn Cooper was not an easy man to like. There was a time when he'd been quicker with a smile or a joke, but twelve years in law enforcement and three years in the Unsolved Crimes Investigation Unit of the Texas Rangers had worn off any charm he'd been born with.

He was not a man who believed in the necessity of small talk, politeness or pretending a situation was anything other than what it was.

He was most definitely not a man who believed in *hypnotism*, even if the woman currently putting their witness under acted both confident and capable.

He didn't trust it, her or what she did, and he was more than marginally irritated that the witness seemed to immediately react. No more fidgeting, no more yelling that he didn't know anything. After Natalie Torres's ministrations, the man was still and pleasant.

Vaughn didn't believe it for a second.

"I told you," Bennet Stevens said, giving him a nudge. Bennet had been his partner for the past two years, and Vaughn liked him. Some days. This was not one of those days.

"It's not real. He's acting." Vaughn made no effort to lower his voice. It was purposeful, and he watched carefully for any sign of reaction from the supposedly hypnotized witness.

He didn't catch any, but he could all but feel Ms. Torres's angry gaze on him. He didn't care if she was angry. All he cared about was getting to the bottom of this case before another woman disappeared.

He wasn't sure his weary conscience could take another thing piled on top of the overflowing heap.

"How are you today, Mr. Herman?" Ms. Torres asked in that light, airy voice she'd hypnotized the man with. Vaughn rolled his eyes. That anyone would fall for this was beyond him. They were police officers. They dealt in evidence and reality, not *hypnotism*.

"Been better," the witness grumbled.

"I see," she continued, that easy, calming tone to her voice never changing. "Can you tell us a little bit about your problems?"

"Nah."

"You know, you're safe here, Mr. Herman. You can speak freely. This is a safe place where you can unburden yourself."

Vaughn tried to tamp down his edgy impatience. He couldn't get over them wasting their time doing this, but it hadn't been his call. This had come from above him, and he had no choice but to follow through.

"Yeah?"

The hypnotist inclined her head toward Vaughn and Bennet. It was the agreed upon sign that they would now take over the questioning.

"It's not a bad gig," Herman said, his hands linked together on the table in front of him. No questions needed.

Yeah, Vaughn didn't believe a second of this.

"Don't have to get my hands too dirty. Paid cash. My old lady's got cancer. Goes a long way, you know?"

"Rough," Bennet said, doing a far better job than Vaughn of infusing some sympathy into his tone. "What kind of jobs you running?"

"Mostly just messages, you know. I don't even gotta be the muscle. Just deliver the information. It's a sweet deal. But…"

"But what?"

Vaughn could feel the hypnotist's eyes on him. Something about her. Something about *this*. It was all off. He wasn't even being paranoid like Bennet too often accused him of. The witness was too easy, and the woman was too jumpy.

"But… Man, I don't like this, though. I got a daughter of my own. I never wanted to get involved with this part."

"What part's that?"

"The girls. He keeps the girls."

Vaughn tensed, and he noticed the hypnotist did, as well.

"Who keeps them?"

Vaughn and Bennet whirled to face Ms. Torres. She wasn't supposed to ask questions. Not after she gave them the signal. Not about the case.

"What the hell do you think—"

"The Stallion," Herman muttered. "But I can't cross The Stallion."

Vaughn immediately looked at Bennet. He gave his partner an imperceptible nod, then Bennet slipped out of the room.

The Stallion. An idiotic name for the head of an organized crime group that had been stealthily wreaking havoc across Texas for ten years. Vaughn had no less than four cases he knew connected to the bastard or his drug-running cronies, but this one...

"What do you know about The Stallion?" Vaughn asked evenly, though frustration pounded in his bloodstream. Still, hypnotism or no hypnotism, he wasn't the type of ranger who let that show.

"You don't cross him. You don't cross him and live."

Vaughn opened his mouth to ask the next question, but the damn hypnotist beat him to it.

"What about the girls?" she demanded, leaning closer. "What do you know about the girls? Where are they?"

Vaughn was so taken aback by her complete disregard for the rules, by her fervent demand, he couldn't say anything at first. But it was only a split second of shock, then he edged his way between Ms. Torres and her line of sight to the witness.

"Get him out," he ordered.

Big brown eyes blinked up at him. "What?"

"If this is hypnotism, unhypnotize him." Vaughn bent over and leaned his mouth close enough to her ear so he could whisper without the witness overhearing. "You are putting my case at risk, and I will not have it. Take him out now, or I'll kick you out."

She didn't waver, and she certainly didn't turn to

Herman and take him out. "I'm getting answers," she replied through gritted teeth. Her eyes blazed with righteous fury.

It was no match for his own. Vaughn inclined his head toward Herman, who was shaking his head back and forth. Not offering *any* answers to her too direct line of questioning.

"Mr. Herman—"

Vaughn nudged her chair back with his knee. "Take him out, or I'll arrest you for interfering in a criminal investigation."

Her eyes glittered with that fury, her hands clenched into fists, but when he rested his hand on the handcuffs latched to his utility belt, she closed her eyes.

"Fine, but you need to move."

When she opened her eyes, he saw a weary resignation in her slumped posture, a kind of sorrow in her expression Vaughn didn't understand—didn't want to. Any more than he wanted to figure out what scent she was wearing, because when he was this close to her, it was almost distracting.

Almost.

"If you say one word to him that isn't pulling him out of the hypnotism, you will be arrested. Do you understand?"

"I thought you didn't believe in it?" she snapped.

"I don't, but I'm not going to have you claiming I didn't let you do your job. Take him out. Then you will be talking to my supervisor. Got it?"

She sneered at him, like many a criminal he'd arrested or threatened in his career. He wasn't sure she was a criminal, but he wasn't affected at all by her anger.

She'd ruined the lead. The Stallion wasn't nearly enough to go on, and she'd stepped in with her own reckless, desperate questions, invalidating the whole interrogation.

She was going to pay for this.

Natalie sat in the waiting area of the Unsolved Crimes office. She wanted to fume and rage and pace, but she didn't have time to indulge in pointless anger. Not when she had information to find.

Who was The Stallion? Could this all possibly be related to her sister? She'd waited three years for this. Three years of dealing with sneering Texas Rangers hating that their higher-ups involved her in their investigations. Three years of hoping against hope that the next case she'd be brought in on would be Gabby's.

Just because the witness had talked about missing girls didn't mean it was her sister's case. As a hypnotist, she was never given any case details, legally bound to secrecy regarding anything she did hear simply by being in the room.

She'd lost her cool. She knew she wasn't supposed to jump in like that, but the interrogators had been asking the wrong questions. They'd been taking too much time. She needed to know. She needed…

She needed not to cry. So, she took a deep breath in, and slowly let it out. She focused on the little window with the blinds closed. Inside, three officers were talking. Probably about her. One definitely complaining about her.

She was angry with herself for breaking rules she knew Texas Rangers weren't going to bend, but she'd rather channel that anger onto Ranger Jerk.

Immature, yes, but the immature nicknames she gave each ranger who gave her a hard time entertained her when she wanted to tell them off.

The problem with Ranger Jerk was she could nearly forget what a jerk he was when he looked like…*that*. He was so tall and broad shouldered, and when he was always crossing his arms over his chest in a threatening manner, it was obvious he had *muscles* underneath the crisp white dress shirt he wore.

Like, the kind of muscles that could probably bench-press *her*. Not that she'd imagined that in those first few minutes of meeting him. Those were flights of fancy she did *not* allow herself. Not on the job.

Then there was his face, which wasn't at all fair. She'd nearly been tongue-tied when he'd greeted her. His darkish blond hair was buzzed short, and his blue eyes were downright mesmerizing. Some light shade that was nearly gray, and she'd spent seconds trying to decide what to call that color.

Until he'd insulted her without a qualm. Because his good looks were only *one* problem with him. Only the tip of the iceberg of problems.

The door opened, and she forced herself to look calm and placid. She was a calm, still lake. No breeze rippled her waters. She reflected nothing but a peaceful and reflective surface.

But maybe a sea monster lurked deep and would leap out of the water and eat all of them in one giant gulp.

Yeah, her imagination had always gotten her into trouble.

"Ms. Torres. Come inside, please."

She held no ill will against Captain Dean. He was one of the few rangers who respected and believed in what she did. He was, more often than not, the one who called her in to help with a case.

But she *had* crossed a line she knew she wasn't supposed to cross, and she was going to have to deal with the consequences—which would gall. For one, because it meant Ranger Jerk got what he wanted. But more important, because she might have finally had some insight into her sister's case, and been too impetuous to make the most of it.

"Have a seat."

She slid into the chair opposite Captain Dean's desk. The two rangers she'd been in the interrogation room with stood on either side.

They were impressive, the three of them. Strong, in control, looking perfectly pressed in what constituted as the Texas Ranger uniform: khakis, a dress shirt and a tie, Ranger badge and belt buckle, topped off with cowboy boots. The only thing the men weren't wearing inside the office were the white cowboy hats.

She wanted to sneer at Ranger Cooper's smug blue eyes, but she didn't. She smiled sweetly instead.

"You breached our contract, Ms. Torres. You know that."

"Yes, sir."

"Your job is not to question witnesses. It's only to put them under hypnosis, should they agree, to calm them and allow us to ask questions."

"I know, sir. I'm sorry for…stepping out of line." She offered both the men who'd been in the room with her the best apologetic smile she could muster. "I got a little carried away. I can promise you, it won't happen again."

"I'm afraid we can't risk second chances at this juncture. Not in this department, not in the Texas Rangers.

I'm sorry, Natalie. You've been an asset. But this was unconscionable, and you will not be asked back."

She sat frozen, completely ice from the inside out. *Not be asked back.* But she'd helped solve cases. For years. She'd received a commendation even! And he was…

"Cooper, see her out?"

Ranger Jerk nodded toward the door. "After you."

She swallowed over the lump in her throat. All her chances. All the times she'd been so close to seeing something of Gabby's case. All the *possibility*, and she'd ruined it.

No, *he'd* ruined it for her. *He* had. She stood on shaky legs, clutching her phone and her purse.

"I am sorry."

She didn't look back at Captain Dean, or Ranger Stevens. She didn't want to see the pitying, apologetic looks on their faces. Just like all those other policemen who'd come up with nothing—*nothing* when it came to Gabby's disappearance.

Apologies didn't mean a thing when her sister was gone. Eight years. And Natalie was the only one who held out any hope, and now her hope was…

Well, it had just gotten kicked in the teeth.

She managed to walk stiffly to the door and stepped out, the Jerk of the Manor still behind her. Too close behind her and crowding her out and away.

"I'll see you all the way out of the building, Ms. Torres," he said, sounding so smug and superior.

She walked down the hall, still a little shaken. But shaken had no hold on her anger. She glared at the man striding next to her. "You got me fired, you lousy son of a—"

"I'd reconsider your line of thought and blame, Ms. Torres." He continued to look ahead, not an ounce of emotion showing on his face. "You got yourself fired. Now, stay out of this case. If I catch a whiff of you being involved in it anywhere, I will not hesitate to find out every last thing about you and connect you to whatever dirty deeds you're hiding."

"I am not hiding any dirty deeds." Which was the God's honest truth. She hadn't stepped out of line in eight years. Or ever, really, but especially since Gabby had disappeared.

His eyes met hers, a cold, cold stormy blue. "We'll see."

She shivered involuntarily, because that look made her feel like she *had* done something wrong, which was so absurd.

Even more absurd was the idea of her staying out of the case. She'd take what little information she'd gathered and follow it to the ends of the earth.

Because she refused to believe her sister was dead. A body had never been found, and that Herman man had said…he'd said *he keeps the girls*. Not kept. Not got rid of. *Keeps*.

Maybe Gabby wasn't one of those girls, but it was possible. More than that, she thought. The Texas Rangers might be a mostly good bunch, but they had rules and regulations to follow. Natalie Torres did not.

God help the man who tried to stop her.

Chapter 2

The phone ringing and vibrating on his nightstand jerked Vaughn out of a deep sleep. He cursed and answered it blearily. Phone calls in the middle of the night were never good, but they always had to be answered.

Much to his ex-wife's constant complaints throughout the duration of their marriage.

"Cooper," he grumbled into the speaker.

"You're going to need to get out here."

He recognized his captain's voice immediately. "Text the address."

"Yup."

Vaughn rubbed his hands over his face, then went straight to his closet where a row of work clothes hung, always a few pressed and ready to go. He never liked to be caught without clean and ironed clothes on the ready, even in the middle of the night. He looked at the clock as he dressed. Three fifteen.

He strode through his house, gave the coffeemaker a wistful glance. Even though he always kept it ready to go, he didn't have time to sit around waiting for it to brew. Not at three fifteen.

With a stretch and a groan, he strapped on his gun and tried not to wonder if he was getting too old for this. Thirty-four was hardly too old. He had a lot of years to go before he could take a pension, but more…

He had a lot of cases to solve before his conscience would let him leave. So, he needed to get at it.

He got in his car, and when his phone chimed, he clicked the address Captain Dean had texted and started the GPS directions. It took about fifteen minutes to arrive at his destination, a small neighborhood a little outside the city that he knew was mainly rental houses. Single-storied brick buildings, a few split-levels. Modest homes at best, flat out run-down at worst.

Fire trucks and police vehicles were parked around a burned-out and drowned shell of a house. Though it still smoked, the house had obviously been ravaged by the fire hours earlier.

Vaughn stopped at the barricade, flashed his badge to the officer guarding the perimeter and then went in search of Captain Dean. When he found him, he was with Bennet. Vaughn's uneasy dread grew.

"What've we got?"

"This is the hypnotist's house," Bennet said gravely.

The dread in Vaughn's gut hardened to a rock. The house was completely destroyed, which meant—

"She's fine. She wasn't home, which is lucky for her, because someone was. Herman."

"Dead?"

Captain Dean nodded. "He didn't start and botch the

fire, either, at least from what information I've been able to gather. We'll have to wait to go over everything with the fire investigator once she's done, but I think it got back to somebody Herman squealed. Body was dumped."

"The hypnotist? Where was she?"

"With her mom," Bennet offered, "who works at a gas station down on Clark. We've got guys going over surveillance, but so far she's on the tape almost the entire night. She came home just after some neighbors called 9-1-1. She's innocent."

Innocent? Maybe of this, but Natalie Torres was hardly innocent. The day was full of far too much weirdness for her to be *innocent*. "You sure about that?"

"Cooper," the captain intoned, censure in that one word. "Do you know the kinds of background checks we did on her when she got a contract with us? I know you don't agree with it, but using a hypnotist to aid in witness questioning isn't some random or careless decision. We have to jump through a lot of hoops to make it legal. She's clean. Now she's in danger."

Vaughn wasn't certain he believed the first, but he knew the latter was fact.

"Ideas, gentlemen?"

"Well, she'll need protection." Bennet rubbed a hand over his jaw. "I'd say that's on us, and it'll make certain nothing dirty's going down."

"This is escalating." Captain Dean shook his head gravely. "If it goes much further, it becomes less our business and more current crime's business. We should be working with Homicide now. Cooper? What are you thinking?"

Vaughn didn't answer right away. He caught a

glimpse of Ms. Torres standing next to a fireman. She had a blanket wrapped around her, and she was looking at her burned-to-ash house with tears streaming down her cheeks.

He looked away. "We've got to get her out of here." He didn't particularly like the idea that came to him, but he didn't have to like it. Bottom line, everyone else trusted this woman way too much, so if she was going to come under their protection, it needed to be *his* protection, so he could keep an eye on her.

It couldn't be anywhere near here. "My suggestion? Stevens works with Homicide, then maybe you put Griffen on it too. I take the woman up to the cabin in Guadalupe. I go over things there, keep her safe and make sure she's got nothing to do with it."

"That's gonna necessitate a lot of paperwork," Captain Dean grumbled.

"She can't stay in Austin. We've got to get her out of here. We all know it."

The captain sighed. "I'll call the necessary people. I can't argue with this being the best option. But, you know who *is* going to argue?" He pointed at Ms. Torres.

Vaughn looked at her again. She wasn't crying anymore. No, that angry expression that she'd leveled at him earlier today had taken over her face. He didn't have to be close to remember what it looked like.

Big dark eyes as shiny as the dark curls she'd pulled back from her face. The snarly curve to those sensuous lips and—

No, there was no *and*. Not when it came to this woman.

"She'll agree," Vaughn reassured the captain. He'd make sure of it.

* * *

When Ranger Jerk stepped next to her, Natalie didn't bother to hide her utter disgust. "Well, thanks for getting to my house after it burned down. Add that to me losing my favorite job—also your fault. Would you like to, oh, I don't know…" She wanted to say something scathing about what else he could do to ruin her life, but…

Everything she had was gone. Her house, every belonging, every memento. Worst of all, years' worth of research and information she'd gathered on Gabby's case. All gone. Everything she owned and loved gone except for her car and what she'd had in it.

She tried to breathe through a sob, but she choked on it. The tears and the emotion and the enormity of it all caught in her throat, and she had to cover her mouth with her hand to keep from crying out.

She'd been here for hours, and she couldn't wrap her head around it. She hadn't even been able to text her mom the full details because she just…

How had this happened? Why had this happened?

She sensed him move, and she hoped against hope he was walking away. That he wouldn't say a word and make this whole nightmare worse. All of this was terrible, and she didn't want Ranger Jerk rubbing it in or—worse—feeling sorry for her.

But he didn't disappear. She didn't hear retreating footsteps as tears clouded her vision. No, he moved closer. She hadn't thought much about this guy having any sort of conscience or empathy in him, but he put a big hand on her back, warm and steady.

She swallowed, wiping at the tears. It wasn't an overly familiar touch. Just his palm and fingers lightly flush with her upper back, but it was strong. It had a remarkable effect. A strange thread of calm wound through her pain.

"This is shocking and painful," he said in a low, re-assuring voice. "There's no point in trying to be hard. No one should have to go through this."

She sniffled, blinking the last of the tears out of her eyes. Oh, there'd be more to come, but for now she could swallow them down, blink them back. She stared at him, trying to work through the fact he'd spoken so nicely to her. He *touched* her. "Are you comforting me?"

He grimaced. "Is that considered comfort? That's terrible comfort."

She laughed through another sob. "Oh, God, and now you're being funny." Obviously she was a little deliri-ous, because she was starting to wonder if Ranger Jerk wasn't so terrible after all.

Then she looked back at her house. Gone. All of it *gone*. There were rangers and police and firemen and all number of official-looking people striding about, talking in low voices. Around her house. Gone. All of it gone.

Ranger Jerk could be reassuring, he could even be funny, but he couldn't deny what was in front of them. "This was on purpose," she said, her voice sounding flat and hopeless even in her own ears.

He didn't respond, but when she finally glanced at him, he nodded. His gaze was on the house too, that square jaw tensed tight enough to probably crack metal between his teeth. He made an impressive profile in the flashing lights and dark night. All angles and shadows, but there was a determination in his glare at the ruins of her house—something she'd never seen in all those other officers she'd talked to today, or eight years ago.

Confidence. Certainty. A blazing determination to right this wrong—something she recognized because it matched her own.

It bolstered her somehow. "That's why *you're* here. It's about this morning." She watched him, and finally those cool gray-blue eyes turned to her.

"Yes, that's why I'm here," he replied, his voice still low, still matter-of-fact.

Natalie had spent the past eight years learning how to deal with fear. The constancy of it, the lack of rationale behind it. But this was a new kind, and she didn't know how to suppress the shudder that went through her body.

"We're going to protect you, Ms. Torres. This is directly related to the case we brought you in on, and as long as you agree to a few things, we can keep you safe. I promise you that."

It was an odd thing to feel some ounce of comfort from those words. Because she didn't know him, and she really didn't trust him. But somehow, she did trust *that*. He was a jerk, yes, but he was a by-the-book jerk.

"What things do I need to agree to?" she asked. How much longer would her legs keep her up? She was exhausted. She'd come home after dropping her mom off at her apartment to find the neighbors in the streets and fire trucks blocking her driveway, and her house covered in either arcs of water or licks of flame.

Then, she'd been whisked behind one of the big police SUVs, made not to look at her house burning to ash in front of her, while officer after officer asked her question after question.

Oh, how she wanted to sleep. To curl up right on the

ground and wake up and find this was all some kind of nightmare.

But she'd wanted that and never got it too often to even indulge in the fantasy anymore. "Ranger J—" Oh, right, she shouldn't be calling him that out loud. "Ranger Cooper, what do I need to agree to?"

He raised an eyebrow at her misstep, but he couldn't possibly guess what she'd meant to call him just from a misplaced *j*-sound.

He pushed his hands into the pockets of his pants, looking so pressed and polished she wondered if he might be part robot.

It wasn't a particularly angry movement, sliding his hands easily into the folds of the fabric, and yet she thought the fact he would move or fidget in any way spoke to something. Something unpleasant.

"You're going to have to come with me," he finally said, his tone flat and his face expressionless.

"Go with you where?"

He let out a sigh, and she got the sinking suspicion he didn't like what was coming next any more than she was going to.

"You need to get out of Austin. There isn't time to mess around. Herman is dead. You're in *imminent* danger. You agree to come with me, the fewer questions asked the better, and trust that I will keep you safe."

"Herman is… How? When? Wh—"

"It isn't important," he said tonelessly, all that compassion she thought she'd caught a glimpse of clearly dead. "What's important is your safety."

"But I… I didn't do anything."

"You were there when Herman talked. That's enough."

She tried to process all this. "Doesn't that put you in danger too? And Ranger Stevens?"

He shrugged. "That's part and parcel with the job. We're trained to deal with danger. You, ma'am, are not."

She wanted to bristle at that. Oh, she knew plenty about danger, but no, she wasn't a ranger, or even a police officer. She didn't carry a weapon, and as much as she'd lived with all the possibilities of the horrors of human nature haunting her for eight years, she didn't know how to fight it.

She only knew how to dissect it. How to want to find the truth in it. She needed…help. She needed to take it if only because losing her would likely kill her grandmother and mother like losing Gabby had likely killed Dad.

Natalie swallowed at the panic in her throat. "My family? Are they safe? It's only my mother and my grandmother, but…"

"We'll talk with different agencies to keep them protected, as well. For the time being, it doesn't look like they'd be in any danger, but we'll keep our eye on the situation."

She nodded, trying to breathe. Mom would hate that, just as she hated all police. She'd hate it as much as she hated Natalie working for the Texas Rangers, but Natalie couldn't quite agree with Mom's hate.

Oh, she'd hated any and all law enforcement for a while, but she'd tirelessly tried to find her own answers, and she knew how frustrating it could be. She also knew men like Ranger Cooper, as off-putting and as much of a jerk as he was, took their jobs seriously. They tried, and when they failed, it affected them.

She'd seen sorrow and guilt in too many officers' eyes to count.

"I'll go with you," she said, her voice a ragged, abused thing.

His eyes widened, and he turned fully to her. "You will?" He didn't bother to hide his surprise.

She was a little surprised herself, but it would get her the thing she wanted more than anything else in the world. Information. "I will come with you and follow whatever your office suggests in order to keep me safe. On one condition."

The surprise easily morphed into his normal scowl of disdain. "You're being protected, Ms. Torres. You don't get to have conditions."

"I want to know about the case. I want to know what I'm running from."

"That's confidential."

"You're taking me 'away from Austin' to protect me. I don't even know you."

He gave her a once-over, and she at once knew he didn't trust her. While she was sure he was the kind of man who would protect her anyway, his distrust grated. So, she held her ground, emotionally wrung out and exhausted. She stood there and accepted his distrustful perusal.

"I'll see what information I'm allowed to divulge to you, but you're going to have to come down to the office right now to get everything squared away. We'll be leaving the minute we have it all figured out with legal."

"Will we?"

"You don't have to do it my way, Ms. Torres, but I can guarantee you no one's way is better than mine."

She wouldn't take that guarantee for a million dollars, but she'd take a chance. A chance for information. If she was going to lose everything, she was darn well going to get closer to finding Gabby out of it.

"All right, Ranger Cooper. We'll do it your way." For now.

Chapter 3

Vaughn was exhausted, but he swallowed the yawn and focused on the long, winding road ahead of him.

Natalie dozed in the passenger seat, making only the random soft sleeping noise. Vaughn didn't look—not once—he focused.

The midday sun reflected against the road, creating the illusion of a sparkling ribbon of moving water. They still had another three hours to go to get to the mountains and his little cabin. Which meant he'd spent the past *four* hours talking himself out of all his second thoughts.

It was the only way to keep *her* safe and *him* certain she was innocent. She'd agreed to everything without so much as a peep. He didn't know if he distrusted that or if she was just too devastated and exhausted to mount any kind of argument.

She stirred, and he checked his rearview mirror again. The white sedan was still following them. There was enough space between their cars; he'd thought he was simply being paranoid for noticing.

That had been two hours ago. Two hours of that car following him at the same exact distance.

He cursed.

"What?" Natalie mumbled, straightening in the seat. "You're not going to run out of gas, are you?" She rubbed her eyes, back arching as she stretched and moved her neck from side to side.

With more force than he cared to admit, he looked away from her and directly at the road. "No. Listen to me. Do not look back. Do not move. We're being tailed."

"What?"

She started to whip her head toward the back—obnoxious woman—but he reached over with one hand and squeezed her thigh.

She screeched and slapped his hand. "Don't touch me."

He removed his hand, gripped the wheel with both now. Tried to erase any…reaction from touching her like that. It had only been a diversionary tactic. "Then do as you're told and don't look back."

Her shoulders went rigid and she stared straight ahead, eyes wide, breathing uneven. "You really think…"

"I could be wrong. I'd rather be safe and wrong than wrong and sorry." He looked at the mile marker, tried to focus on what was around them, where they could lose the tail. What it would mean if they couldn't.

Natalie grasped her knees, obviously panicking. As much as he knew he could figure this out, he understood that she was lost. Fire burning all of her possessions and sleepless nights on the road with a near stranger weren't exactly calming events.

"It'll be fine," he said, mustering all of his compassion—what little of that was left. "I've dodged better tails than this."

"Have you?"

"Do you know a Texas Ranger has to have eight years of police work with a major crimes division before they're even qualified to apply?"

Natalie huffed out an obviously unimpressed breath. "So you had to write speeding tickets for eight years? Didn't mean you had to dodge people following you."

Vaughn didn't bother responding. Speeding tickets? Not for a long, long time. But he wasn't going to tell her about the undercover operations he'd worked, the homicides he'd solved. He wasn't going to waste precious brain space proving to her that he was the best man to keep her safe.

Maybe when they got to the cabin he could just give her Jenny's number and his ex-wife could fill Ms. Torres in on all the ways he'd put himself in danger during his years as a police officer.

Frustrated with *that* line of thought, he jerked the wheel to get off the highway and onto an out-of-the-way exit at the last second.

Unfortunately, the white sedan did the same.

"We're going to stop at the first gas station we find. We're both going to get out, go inside and pretend to look for snacks. I'm going to talk to the attendant. You will stand in the candy aisle and wait for my sign."

"What's your sign?" she said after a gulp.

"You'll know it when you see it."

"But…"

"No buts. We have to play some things by ear." Like what the purpose of an hours-long tail was. If it was to take them out, Vaughn had to believe they would have already attempted something. The hanging back and just following pointed more to an information-grabbing tail.

It took a few miles, but a little town with a gas station finally appeared on the horizon. Vaughn kept his speed steady as he drove toward it, worked to keep himself calm as he pulled into a parking spot.

"We get out. We act normal. You watch me, and you follow absolutely any and all orders I give you. Got it?"

Natalie blinked at the gas station in front of them, and he could tell she wanted to argue, but the woman apparently had *some* sense because she finally nodded.

Vaughn got out of the car first, and Natalie followed. She didn't exactly look *calm*, but she didn't bolt or run. She met him at the front of the car.

Vaughn didn't like it, but they had to look at least a little casual. Maybe these guys knew exactly who they were, but playing a part gave him a better shot of putting doubts in their heads.

So, he linked fingers with Ms. Torres and walked like any two involved people might into the building. Her hand was clammy, and he gave it a little reassuring squeeze. He leaned close to her ear, hoping the two men outside were paying attention to the intimate move.

"Go along with anything I do or say," he said, low enough so that the cashier couldn't hear.

She didn't say anything or nod, but she didn't argue with him, either. In fact, she held tightly on to his hand.

When he took a deep breath, all he could smell was the smoke that must still be in her hair from early this morning, but underneath there was some hint of something sweet.

Lack of sleep was making him delirious. "Go find a snack, honey," he said, doing his best to infect some ease into his exaggerated drawl. With only a little wobble, she let go of his hand and walked toward the candy aisle.

Casually Vaughn sauntered to the counter. He glanced at the scratch-off tickets displayed, then glanced out the doors where the white sedan was parked, one of the men filling it up.

Vaughn flicked his glance to the bored-looking cashier. "Ma'am," he said with a nod. He slid his badge across the counter to where the cashier could see it. She didn't flinch or even act impressed or moved. She popped her gum at him.

He wouldn't be deterred. "I need you to call the local police department. I need you to give them the following license plate number, description and my DSN."

She didn't make a move to get a pen or paper. Vaughn glanced out of the corner of his eye to where the white sedan and two men in big coats and big hats stood. One eyeing his truck, the other eyeing the store and Natalie.

Vaughn flicked his jacket out of the way so the cashier could also see his gun. "This is official police business. Call the local police department and give them the following information." He inclined his head to the pen that was settled on top of the cash register keyboard. "Now."

The woman swallowed this time, and she grabbed the pen.

Vaughn looked back at Natalie who was shaking in

the candy aisle. He rattled off the information to the cashier.

He kept tabs on the men outside who were obviously keeping tabs on him. "Make the call now. Whatever you do, don't tell those men out there. Got it?"

The now-nervous cashier gave a little nod and picked up the phone on the counter next to the cash register.

As he moved away from the counter, one of the men started walking toward the door. Still, Vaughn didn't panic. He'd been in a lot stickier situations than this, no matter what Ms. Hypnotist thought of his past experience.

He approached Natalie, watching to make sure the cashier got the information to the local police before the man entered the door.

It was a close call, but the cashier had some survival instincts herself and she hung up just as the man walked inside.

Vaughn took Natalie's arm. "Let's go to the bathroom."

She arched a brow, all holier-than-thou, even though terror was clearly lurking in the depths of those big dark eyes. "Together?"

"Yes, ma'am." He nodded toward the back of the store where the bathroom sign was. "Move. And whatever you do, don't look behind us."

She started to walk toward the bathroom, still shaking, still braving it out. He'd give her credit for that.

Later.

"You know, every time you tell me not to do something, I only want to do it more?"

"Okay, don't look straight ahead. Don't step into the

women's bathroom, and certainly don't let me follow you inside."

Surprisingly, she did exactly what he wanted her to do.

Natalie couldn't stop shaking. She knew it showed weakness, and she tried to be stronger than that. For Gabby. For the hope that Gabby was still alive to be found.

But, she was so scared she wanted to cry. Someone was following them. Ranger Cooper seemed more than capable, but that didn't make it any less scary. It didn't erase her house being gone, and it most certainly didn't erase the fact someone was apparently *following* them.

Ranger Cooper immediately locked the door behind them as they stepped into the women's restroom. He was a blur, moving about the small room and the even smaller stalls, and she had no idea what he was looking for.

So, she simply stood in the center trying to find her own center. Trying to focus on what she was doing this for. On who she was doing this for. She'd pursued details of Gabby's case with a dogged tenacity that had alienated every friend, significant other and her own grandmother. Even Mom was close to losing any and all patience with her.

But how could they give up? How could *she* give up? Maybe she'd never anticipated this kind of danger, but that didn't mean she was going to shake apart and hide away. Gabby was somewhere out there.

She had to be. *He keeps the girls.* Maybe it wasn't Gabby's case, but maybe it *was*. She needed information, which meant she needed Ranger Cooper.

After a full sweep of the bathroom, he pulled his phone out of his pocket and typed something into it. Natalie simply watched him because she didn't know what else to do. She counted each time his blunt, long finger touched the screen to keep herself from panicking.

When he glanced up from his phone, those steely blue eyes meeting hers with a blank kind of certainty, she thought she might panic anyway.

"We can't waste much more time," he said, his voice as low and gravelly as she'd ever heard it. Surely he was exhausted. Even Texas Rangers got tired. Even Texas Rangers were human and mortal.

She'd really prefer to think of him as superhuman, and he made it almost seem possible when he flipped back his coat and pulled the weapon at his hip from its holster.

"If it gets back to whoever sent them they're being detained, we'll just get another tail."

Natalie subdued the shaking, jittering fear in her limbs and focused on what had gotten her here. Questions. Information. "But how can we get past them? Won't they just report back to… Do you know who it is? Is this about The Stallion? I couldn't find any information on what exactly that is. A man? A gang?"

Ranger Cooper took a menacing step toward her, reminding her of that moment in the interrogation room when he'd stepped between her and Mr. Herman.

Dead Mr. Herman.

She closed her eyes and tried to focus on how much she'd hated him then. Hated him for getting in her way.

"Do not ask questions, Ms. Torres. The less you know, the better. For your own good. Now…" He curled those long fingers around the grips of his gun. "Listen to me carefully. Do everything I say to the letter. For your own good. Let me repeat that," he said, as if talking to a small child.

"For your own good, you will do as I say. Stay behind me. Listen to me and only me. Whatever you do, don't make a sound. If we can get a little bit of a head start, we're golden. Got it?"

She couldn't speak. Every muscle in her body was seized too tightly to allow her to speak, or nod.

"Torres." It was whispered, but it was a harsh bark. "Got it?"

She managed a squeaky yes, and as he unlocked the door, she stayed behind him. As much as she didn't like him, in this moment, she would have pressed herself to his back if he'd asked her to.

He might be a jerk, but he seemed to know what he was doing. Right now, with two bulky men speaking to two decidedly not bulky local police officers in front of the cash register, she pretty much *had* to trust Ranger Cooper would get them out of this.

She met gazes with one of the bulky men, and though he had his hat low on his head, she could feel the cold, black gaze.

"Behind me, Torres," Ranger Cooper whispered with enough authority to have her feet moving faster.

One of the bulky men tried to sidestep one of the local officers, but the local officer didn't back off.

"Move again, sir, and I will pull my weapon on you."

"We ain't done anything wrong, boy."

Ranger Cooper grabbed her arm. "Move," he instructed, and she realized belatedly she'd all but stopped. But she was being propelled out the door, a skirmish breaking out behind them. "Get in the car. Now. Fast."

On shaky legs, she did as she was told, but managed to glance back in time to see Ranger Cooper shoving a broom through the handles of the door. Which caused the men inside to push against the police officers even harder, even getting past one to get to the door.

Natalie got into the truck's passenger seat, her breath coming in little puffs. That broom handle wouldn't hold them in for very long. If only because there had to be another exit, and it already looked as though the officers inside were losing the battle.

But Ranger Cooper wasn't getting in the truck. She tried to breathe deeply, but a little whimpering sound came out instead.

"Get it together. Get it together," she whispered to herself, craning her neck to see where Ranger Cooper had gone.

She watched as he casually walked over to a white sedan, weapon held to his side where only someone really paying attention could see. Then he held the muzzle of the gun to the front tire and pulled the trigger.

Even knowing it was coming, Natalie jumped when the shot rang out. Ranger Cooper was back in the truck in the blink of an eye, and Natalie glanced at the store where the two men had disappeared from the windowed doors. No doubt looking for another exit.

"That'll buy us some time," Ranger Cooper muttered, zooming out of the parking lot without so much as buckling his seat belt.

"What about those police officers? The cashier?"

He merely nodded into the distance. "Hear that?"

She didn't at first, but after a few seconds she could make out sirens.

"Backup," he said, his eyes focused on the road, his hands tight on the wheel. "Since the guys fought back, they can arrest them. But that doesn't mean there aren't more tails on us. We have to be vigilant. I want you to keep your eyes peeled. Anything seems suspicious, you mention it. I don't care how silly it sounds. We can't be too careful now."

Natalie gripped the handle of the door with one hand, pressed the other, in a fist, to her stomach.

She was in so far over her head she almost laughed. She knew Ranger Cooper wouldn't appreciate that, and she was a little afraid if she started laughing, it'd turn into crying soon enough.

She was too tough for that. Too determined. No more crying. No more shaking. No more panic. If they had bad guys to face down, she was at least going to pull her weight.

Because if she did, if they could get through all this, Gabby might be on the other side. Everything she'd been working for over the past eight years.

Yeah, no more panic. She had a sister to save.

Chapter 4

Vaughn didn't know if he trusted how relatively easy it had been to fool the tail. Or the fact another hadn't taken its place. All in all, he didn't understand what that tail had been trying to accomplish, and without knowing…

Frustrated, he scanned the road again. The Guadalupe Mountains loomed in the distance of an arid landscape. The hardscrabble desert stretched out for miles, the craggy, spindly peaks of the Guadalupes offering the only respite to endless flat.

The cabin was still forty-five minutes away, and they were the only car on this old desert highway. If he had a tail, it was a much better one.

He flicked a glance at Torres. Thinking about her as a last name helped things. He could think of her as a partner, as just a *person* he had to work with. Not a complicated mystery of a woman.

The only problem was, he didn't trust her as far as he could throw her, and that was the key to any partnership.

She sat in the passenger seat, her eyes still too big, her hands still clenched too tight. Her olive skin tone had paled considerably, but she'd gotten control of her shaking.

"You did good," he found himself saying, out of nowhere. She *had* done good for a civilian, but he had no idea why he was praising her. What the hell was the point of that?

"I just did what you told me to do."

"Exactly."

She rolled her eyes and shook her head. "You really are a piece of work, Ranger Cooper."

"Not everyone could have gotten through that, Ms. Torres. Some people freeze, some people cry, some people…" Why was he explaining this to her? If she didn't want to believe she'd done a good thing, what did he care? But his mouth just kept *going.* "There's a lot of pressure when you're under a threat, and the smartest thing you can do is listen to the person who has the coolest head. You did that. You made good choices and had good instincts."

"Well, thank you." She blew out a breath, and he noted that the hands she'd had in fists loosened incrementally.

"I wish I didn't know just *how* much I can stand up in the face of a threat," she muttered.

"Unfortunately, that was only the beginning."

"You're a constant comfort, Ranger Cooper."

She fell silent for a few moments, and he thought maybe they could make it all the way to the cabin without having any more of the discussion, certainly not any more of him telling her she'd done well. But she began to fidget. The kind of fidgeting that would lead to questioning.

It appeared that whatever nerves or fear that had kept Ms. Torres from interrogating him about what was going on had been eradicated or managed.

"Who's after us? And why? What do I have to do with any of this?" she asked, thankfully sounding more exasperated than scared.

Scared tended to pull at that do-gooder center of him. He tried to focus on *cases* rather than people. But he could get irritated with exasperation. Why couldn't she just trust him to keep her safe and leave it at that?

But he knew that she wouldn't, and he had been given permission to share certain details with her.

Considering he still didn't trust this woman, he wasn't about to give her really important details.

He focused on the road, the flat, unending desert ahead of him. "You were in the interrogation room when Herman talked."

"He didn't even say anything that was any kind of in-crimination. Certainly nothing that I would understand to be able to tell anyone. And I *ruined* your interroga-tion. They should be sending me flowers, not…fire."

The corner of his lip twitched as if…as if he wanted to smile. Which was very…strange. But the fact she owned up to ruining the interrogation, while also mak-ing a little bit of a joke in what had to be a very scary situation for her, he appreciated that. He almost admired it. God knew he didn't make light of much of anything.

"In all likelihood, they don't know what exactly was said," Vaughn told her. *Nothing* about his tone was self-deprecating or light, which he never would have noticed if not for her. "All it took was the knowledge that he was interrogated, and that we started looking into the name he mentioned. When you're mixed up in organized crime, that's enough to get you killed."

She pressed her lips together as if a wave of emotion had swept over her. Her eyes even looked a little shiny. When she spoke, there was a slight tremor to her voice. "I just keep thinking about how he said he had a daughter, and his wife had cancer, and he's just...dead."

"He worked for a man who has likely killed more people than we'll ever know about. Herman knew what he was getting himself into and the risks he was taking. Even if he wasn't the muscle, and even if he had a family, he made bad choices that he knew very well had chances of getting him killed."

"So you're saying he deserved to die?" Natalie asked in that same tremulous voice.

It had been a long time since someone had made him feel bad about the callousness he had to employ, *had* to build to endure a career in law enforcement, and especially unsolved crimes. He didn't care for the way she did it so easily. Just a question and a tremor.

But this was *reality*, and clearly Torres didn't have a clue about that. "It's not my place to determine whether he deserved anything. I'm putting forth the reality of the situation."

"I don't understand why they burned down my house, why they *killed* a man, just because he mentioned a name and you started asking questions. How is that worth following us across Texas? I mean, if they were going to kill us, wouldn't they have already done it?"

"Yes."

She waited, and he could feel her gaze on him, but he didn't have anything else to say to that.

"Yes? That's it? You're just going to agree with me, and that's it?"

"Well, honestly, they probably did try to kill you with that fire. You were lucky you weren't home. What more of an explanation would you like?"

"One that makes sense!"

He could tell by the way she quieted after her little outburst that she hadn't meant to let that emotion show. Especially when the next words she spoke were lower, calmer.

"I want to know why this is happening. I want to understand why I'm in more danger than you or Ranger Stevens. Why my house was burned down, not yours."

"I can't speculate on why they burned your house down. The reason that Stevens and I aren't in as much danger is because we're police officers. We're trained to look for danger, and quite frankly going after us is a lot worse for them than going after you. Anyone hurts a member of law enforcement, the police aren't going to rest until they find him."

"But if you go after a civilian, it's fine?" she demanded incredulously.

She gave him *such* a headache. He took a deep breath, because he wasn't going to snap at her for deliberately misinterpreting his words. He wasn't going to yell at her for not getting it. She wasn't an officer; she couldn't understand.

"We're family, Ms. Torres," he said evenly and calmly, never taking his eyes off the road. "It's like if a stranger is gunned down in the street or your sister is gunned down in the street, which one are you going to avenge a little bit harder?"

Something in what he'd said seemed to impact her a little more than it should have. She paled further and looked down at her lap. He wasn't sure if she was more scared now, or if she was upset by something.

"I'm going to keep you safe, Ms. Torres," he assured her, because as much as he avoided those soft, comforting feelings almost all of the time, that was his duty. He would do it, no matter what.

"Why?" she asked in a small voice. "I'm not law enforcement. I'm not your family. Why should I feel like you're going to keep me safe?"

"Because you came under my protection, and I don't take that lightly."

"I can't understand what they think I can do," she said, her voice going quieter with each sentence, her face turning toward the window as if she wanted to hide from him.

He was fine with that. He'd be even finer if he could stop answering her questions. "The thing about crime and criminals is that they don't often follow rational trains of thought like we do. Their motivations and morals are skewed."

"That almost sounds philosophical, Ranger Cooper."

"It's just the truth. It's easier to accept the truth and figure out what you can do about it than to wish it was different or understandable."

"But…what am I supposed to do? How am I supposed to… I have other jobs, and a family, and… It's all hitting me how much I'm los—"

"You're saving your life. Period. You won't have a job or a family to go back to if you're dead."

"Again, such a comfort."

"At this point, it's more important that we are honest than it is that I comfort you. Right now you're safe because you're with me. That's the only reason. I need you to not forget that."

"I don't expect you to allow me to forget it," she returned, reminding him of that hallway when she'd blamed him for getting her removed from the Rangers. Though it was frustrating that it was geared at *him*, her anger would serve them well. It would keep her moving, it would keep her brave.

"It's best if you don't. For the both of us. You're not the only one in danger here, you're just the only one who doesn't know what to do about it."

"What about Ranger Stevens?"

"Ranger Stevens can keep himself out of danger. All I need you to do is worry about listening to me. If you do that, everything will be fine."

"How do you know?"

"Because I give everything to my job. There is nothing about what I do that I take lightly."

So everyone had always told him. Too serious. Too dedicated. Too wrapped up in a career that didn't give him time for much of anything else.

But people didn't understand that it gave him everything. A sense of usefulness, a sense of order in a chaotic world. It gave him the ability to face any challenge that was laid before him.

Maybe it gives you a way to keep everyone at a safe distance. It irritated him that those words came into his head, even more irritating that they were in his ex-wife's voice. He hadn't thought about Jenny in over a year. Why had the past two days brought back some of that old bitterness?

But he didn't have time to figure it out. He had to get to the cabin, and he had to solve this case.

Personal problems always came after the job, and if the job never ended… Well, so be it.

No matter how exhausted she was, all Natalie could do was watch as the desert gave way to mountain. They began to drive up…and up. There were signs for Guadalupe Mountains National Park, but they didn't drive into it. Instead, Ranger Cooper took winding roads that seemed to weave around the mountains and the park markers.

There weren't houses or other cars on the road. There was nothing. Nothing except rock and the low-lying green brush that was only broken up by the random cactus.

He turned onto a very bumpy dirt road that curved and twisted up a rolling swell of land covered in green brush. After she didn't know how long, a building finally came into view.

Nestled into that sloping green swell of land, with the impressive almost square jut of the mountains behind it, was a little postage stamp of a cabin made almost entirely of stone. It looked ancient, almost part of the landscape.

And it was very, very small. She was going to stay here in this isolated, tiny cabin with this man who rubbed her all kinds of the wrong way.

"What is this place?" she asked, the nerves making her almost as shaky as she'd been earlier.

"It's my private family cabin."

"You have a family?" She couldn't picture him with loved ones, a wife and kids. It bothered her on some odd level.

He slid her a glance as he pulled the truck around to the back of the cabin and parked. "I did come from a mother and a father, not just sprung from the ground fully made."

"The second scenario seems much more plausible," she retorted, realizing too late that she needed to rein in all her snark.

She thought for one tiny glimmer of a second his mouth might have curved into some approximation of a smile.

Apparently she was becoming delusional. *But he doesn't have a wife or kids.* Really, really delusional.

"My sister stays here quite frequently as well, so hopefully you should be able to find some things of hers you can use."

"Oh, I wouldn't feel right about—"

"You don't have a choice, Ms. Torres. You don't have *anything.* And before you repeat it for a third time, yes, I realize I am of literally no comfort to you."

"Well, at least I don't have to say it for a third time."

He let out a hefty sigh and then got out of his truck. She followed suit, stepping into the warm afternoon sun. The air had a certain…she couldn't put her finger on a word for it. It didn't feel as heavy as the air in Austin. There was a clarity to it. A purity. She couldn't see another living soul, possibly another living thing. All that existed around her was this vast, arid landscape.

And a very unfortunately sexy Texas Ranger who appeared to be exploring the perimeter of his family cabin.

Even after being up since whatever time he had got

up to go to her burned-out house, after all the time getting everything squared away to secret her out of Austin, after the incident at the gas station and driving across Texas, he was unwrinkled and fresh. All she felt was dirty and grimy and disgusting. She *smelled*, and she was afraid to even glance at what the desert air had done to her hair.

She stood next to the truck, waiting for her orders. Because God knew Ranger Cooper would have orders for her.

He disappeared around the corner of the cabin, and Natalie leaned against the truck and looked up at the hazy blue sky. She let the sun soak into her skin.

For the first time since before the fire, she had a moment to breathe and really think. All of this open space made her think about Gabby. How long she'd been gone, where she was… Did she still get to see things like this?

Natalie tried to fight the thoughts and tears, but she was exhausted. They trickled over her eyelashes and down her cheeks. She tried to wipe them away, but they kept falling.

She'd worked relentlessly and tirelessly for eight years to try to find Gabby, and she thought she'd been close. A hint. *He keeps the girls.* But now she was far away from Austin, and she was with this man who couldn't pull a punch to save his life.

The hope she had doggedly held on to for eight years was seriously and utterly shaken.

What could she do here? What could she do when her whole life right now was just staying alive? People were after her, and she didn't even know why.

Why was she crying now, though? She was finally safe. She knew Ranger Cooper would do his duty. He didn't seem like the type of man who could do anything but.

Why was it now that she felt like she was falling apart?

"Everything looks good out here. I'm going to check the inside, but I need you to follow me."

No please, no warmth, just an order. She kept her face turned to the sky, trying to wipe away all traces of the tears before she faced him. She took a deep breath and let it out.

She'd had a little breakdown, and now it was over. She'd let some air out of the pressure in her chest, and now she could move forward. She just needed a goal.

She glanced at Ranger Cooper, who was standing at the door, all stiff, gruff policeman.

She needed more information. That was the goal. Information was the goal. She couldn't lose sight of that even though he was so bad at giving it.

She began to walk toward him, wondering what made anyone in his family think this was a good place for a little getaway cabin. It was rocky and sharp and dry. If you looked closely at all, everything seemed so ugly.

But when you looked away from the ground, and took in the home and the full extent of the landscape, there was something truly awe inspiring about it. It was big and vast, this world they lived in. She never had that feeling in the middle of Austin.

She walked over to the porch. It was hard to follow orders and listen to what someone else told her to do. She wasn't used to that. She had been such a strong force in her life for the past few years. She had made all the choices, asked all the questions, sought all the answers. She'd even alienated her grandmother in her quest to find Gabby, so sitting back and doing what someone else told her to do was…hard. It went against everything she had put her whole life into.

But she knew that knee-jerk reaction didn't have a place here. Not when she was with a Texas Ranger who obviously knew way more than she did about safety and criminals.

She was going to have to bury the instinct to argue with him, and it was going to be as big of a challenge as trusting him would be.

"The chances of anyone having breached the cabin are extremely low," he said, opening the door and analyzing the frame as though it might grow weapons and attack them. "But when you're dealing with criminals of this magnitude, you can't be too careful. Which means I can't leave you outside. I can't let you out of my sight. So, I'm going to go inside and make sure there's nothing off. I need you to follow right behind me, carefully mirroring my every step. Can you do that?"

"Can I walk behind you and do what you do?"

"Yes, that is the question."

She gritted her teeth. He didn't think she could walk? He didn't think she could do anything, did he? He thought she was some flighty, foolish *hypnotist* who couldn't follow easy orders.

Arrogant jerk of a man. "Yes, I can do that," she said through those gritted teeth.

"Excellent. Let's go."

He stepped over the threshold, immediately turning toward the left. She followed him, and since her job was to follow exactly in his footsteps, she watched him. That ease of movement he had about him, the surety in the way he strode into the cabin looking for whatever he was looking for.

He was all packed muscle, but there was something like grace in his movements. It was mesmerizing, and she had no problem following him around the inside of the stone cabin.

They did an entire tour of the kitchen and living area, which were both open, and then down a very narrow hallway that led to two bedrooms and a bathroom. All the rooms were small, and the stone that composed the outside of the cabin were used for the inside walls and floor as well.

It wasn't cozy exactly. It was beautiful, but it wasn't the sort of log mountain cabin she had in her head. There weren't warm colorful blankets or cute artwork on the walls. It was all very gray and minimalist.

"You have something against color?" she asked, forgetting to keep her thoughts to herself.

He glanced over his shoulder at her, and the question was kind of funny in light of the way his blue eyes looked even grayer here. It was like even the color of his body didn't dare shine in this space.

"If you're looking for color…" He opened the door to the last bedroom and stepped inside, doing his little police thing where he looked at every corner and around every lamp and out every window.

But Natalie didn't follow him this time. Where the rest of the cabin was stone and stark and sort of reflective of the outside landscape, this room was a riot and explosion of color. It was glitter and fringe.

"What on earth is all this?"

"This is my sister's room. Which means that, right now, it is your room, and you can feel free to use anything that's in here." He opened the closet and rifled through it. She still had no idea what exactly he was looking for, but she knew if she asked he would only give her some irritating half answer.

"I feel really strange about using your sister's things."

"Trust me, my sister has nothing but things, and when I explain to her why someone used them, she will be more than fine with it. As I reminded you earlier, you don't have a choice."

"Because I have nothing. Yes, let's keep talking about that."

He gave her a cursory once-over, just like he'd given the cabin. She wouldn't be surprised if he checked her pulse and teeth or frisked her for a wire.

She tried not to think too hard about the little shiver that ran through her at the thought of his hands on her. Those big hands that had covered so much space on her back when he'd placed them there in comfort after her house had been decimated.

She swallowed and looked away.

"Sleep." He barked the order, then walked right past her without a second glance or word. The door closed with a soft click, and she could only gape at the rough-hewn wood.

He was ordering her to *sleep*? The absolute gall of the man. How dare he tell her what she needed? She had half a mind to march right out of the room and tell him she was *fine*.

But, God, she was tired. So, for today, he'd get his way. *And probably for tomorrow and the next day and the next, because he is in charge here, remember?*

She sighed at that depressing thought and crawled into bed, hopeful to sleep all the tears away.

Chapter 5

Vaughn stared at his laptop screen and tried not to doze off. He would need to wake up Torres soon, if only so he could sleep. The tail had left him jumpy, and he didn't want both of them asleep at the same time at any point.

Unfortunately he was tired enough that the words of his files were simply jumbled letters. It was beyond frustrating he couldn't concentrate. Had he gone soft? He hadn't had a stakeout or any sort of challenging hard-on-the-body thing in a while. Had he lost his touch?

He scrubbed his hands over his face. This was ridiculous. He was fine. There was only so much the human body could handle and still be expected to concentrate on complex facts. Complex facts that had been hard enough to work out when he was well rested and well fed.

At the thought of food, his stomach grumbled. If he

couldn't sleep, then he could at least eat. If he made something, then Natalie could eat when she woke up.

There wouldn't be anything fresh in the pantry, but they always kept a few extras on hand just in case. The nearest store was over an hour away, and while that was pretty damn inconvenient a lot of the time, between Vaughn's desire for complete off-the-grid privacy when he wasn't working and his sister's need for a secret spot, it worked.

He and Lucy had handled their father's fame in completely opposite ways. Lucy had embraced it. She'd followed it, becoming almost as famous a country singer as their father had been. She used the cabin only when she needed a quick, quiet, away-from-publicity break, which was rare.

Vaughn had hated the spotlight. Always. Like his mother, he hadn't been able to stand the fishbowl existence.

So he'd found a way to have almost no recognition whatsoever. He'd gotten a strange enjoyment out of going undercover back in the day, knowing no one knew who he was related to.

"You are one screwy piece of work, Cooper," he muttered, grabbing two cans of soup out of the pantry and digging up the can opener.

"Do you always talk to yourself?"

His hand flew to the butt of his weapon before he even thought about it. Before he recognized the voice, before he had a chance to smooth out the movement so Natalie wouldn't know what he had meant to do.

Quickly he put his hands back to work opening the soup, and he purposefully didn't look at her because he didn't want to see that familiar look on her face. Jenny would cry for days after he had moments like that one, wondering why he couldn't ever shut it off, that natural reaction.

Why the hell couldn't he keep his mind off his past? Dad, Jenny. Why was it in his head, mucking things up when he had to be completely clearheaded and one hundred percent in the game right now?

"I'm heating some soup if you'd like some," he offered, ignoring her previous question.

"Have you been awake this whole time?"

"Someone needs to remain vigilant."

"You can't stay awake forever."

"No, I can't. Which means at some point, I'll have to trust you enough to take over the lookout position."

He finally happened to glance at her, and she had her lips pressed together in a disapproving line. As though she was surprised to hear that he didn't trust her. He'd been nothing but clear on that front. She shouldn't be surprised.

"The only option for beverage is water, and you're going to have to learn to live on the nonperishable staples in the pantry. I don't think it's safe to go to town, and certainly not worth it unless we absolutely have to."

She finally walked from the little opening of the hallway toward the table that acted as the eating area.

She had visible bags under her dark eyes, and her hair was a tangled, curly mass. The smell of smoke drifted toward him even when they were yards apart.

"The soup will keep if you want to take a shower."

"I don't suppose there's a washer and dryer around here, is there?"

"Actually, there is in the hall closet. As isolated as this cabin is, my sister isn't one to do without the modern conveniences of life. We've got a good generator and plenty of appliances."

She glanced at him then, some unreadable expression on her face. She scratched a fingernail across the corner of the old wooden table that had belonged to his grandparents decades ago. Lucy might be all up in the modern conveniences, but she had a sentimental streak that ran much deeper than his.

"Are you close with your sister?"

There was something in the way that she asked the question… Something that gave him the feeling he got when things on a case weren't fitting together the way he thought they should.

There was something this woman was hiding. Even if she had nothing to do with The Stallion or Herman, there was something going on here. He needed to figure it out.

"Well, our careers make it pretty hard for us to spend time together, but we like each other well enough. Do you have a sister?"

Her downturned gaze flicked to his and then quickly back to the table again. There was something there. Definitely.

"We were very close growing up. But…"

"But what?"

"She's…" Natalie swallowed. "Gone."

And he was an ass. Her sister had died, and he was suspicious of this woman, who probably still had painful feelings over it. "I'm sorry," he offered, surprised at how genuine it sounded coming out of him.

She glanced at him again, this time those dark eyes stayed on his a little longer. That full mouth nearly curved. "Thank you," she said. "You know, not many people just say I'm sorry. They always have to add on and make it worse."

"It may shock you to know that I'm not much of a 'add more to it' kinda guy."

This time, she didn't just smile, she laughed. The smile did something to her face, seemed to lighten that heavy sadness that had waved off her. She was pretty; it couldn't be ignored.

She's more than pretty.

But that would *have* to be ignored. He had no business thinking of her as anything other than a civilian under his protection. He shouldn't notice that she was pretty, or the curve of her hips, or the way her smile changed the light in her eyes. He shouldn't and couldn't notice these things. Not and do what he needed to do.

"So, Ranger Cooper, tell me about your cooking skills," she said, moving toward the kitchen.

"Well, first let's not set any expectations here. I have reheating skills, and that's about it. Lucky for you, there is no chance of doing anything other than reheating for the next couple days."

"Well, whatever it is, it smells delicious. I'm starving. But I do want to take a shower."

"Everything should be in the bathroom. If you don't find it in the shower, there should be a container under the sink with things like soap. As for towels, I packed a few. I'll grab you one from my bag."

She nodded without a word, and he left the soup on low heat so he could fetch her towel.

It was strange to have another presence in the cabin with him. He only ever came here alone, unless it was Christmas, and then sometimes he and Lucy would come up here with Mom.

He'd always felt like there was plenty of room when they were here. It was a small place, but Lucy had her room and he had his. If Mom came, he never minded sleeping on the couch.

Ms. Torres seemed to take up a lot of space.

Something about the way she moved, the way she smelled underneath that smoke. There was... Something there. He couldn't put a finger on it.

Perhaps that was the thing that made her feel like such a larger presence. Because he couldn't get a handle on her, he couldn't figure out what made her tick.

But he would.

He strode into his room and grabbed the duffel bag he had packed in haste. He jerked the zipper and then stopped as she stepped into the room with him.

He had meant for her to wait in the living room, or at least out in the hall, but here she was—in his space. There was something about it that set him on edge. There was something about *her* that set him on edge.

"How come the only color is in your sister's room?"

"I don't know," he returned with a grunt.

"You seem like the kind of guy who knows everything."

"I know important things. However, I don't give a damn about interior design."

She leaned against the door frame. "Well, it's a lovely place."

"It's something."

"Do you ever get lonely out here?"

The last thing he needed to think about right now was how lonely he was and for how long. He jerked the first towel his hand touched out of the bag and tossed it at her. She caught it, albeit clumsily.

She cocked her head at him. She seemed to be forever doing that, and he couldn't help but wonder if this was some sort of hypnotist trick. Cock her head, look as though she knew exactly what was going on in his mind even though there was no way that she possibly could.

"Thanks. I'll go take a shower, and then you can get some sleep. That is, if you trust me enough?"

She said it sarcastically, because she probably knew he didn't have a choice. At this point, if he didn't purposefully and decisively take a nap, he was going to keel over and fall asleep against his will. "Trust is a two-way street, Ms. Torres."

"Natalie. Please call me Natalie. I am so tired of hearing you drawl *Ms.* in that condescending Texas Ranger tone."

"Fine. Natalie." Something about saying her full name aloud with her big dark eyes on him shimmered through him. He was tired of this weird feeling. Tired of not knowing what it was that she did to him. There was some gut *itch* there, but he couldn't figure out what it was. And that, on top of all the other things he didn't know right now, was just about enough to make him snap.

A weaker man would. But he was not a weaker man.

"I'll trust you when I absolutely have to."

"So, not at all."

"Trust is a commodity not easily imparted. If you're looking for a friend to build trust with, you shouldn't have gotten messed up in the Unsolved Crimes Investigation Unit."

"Ah, you're back to your charming self. I'll take that as my cue to go."

"Don't use all of the hot water," he called after her,

not sure why he let her get to him. She was goading him. He *knew* she was, and yet he couldn't seem to let it go.

Natalie stood in the warm pulse of the shower that was shockingly luxurious. This cabin got stranger and stranger. Parts of it were stunning in their understated elegance. This, what appeared to be, all glass and marble shower, the fancy pristinely white sink and floor. It was gorgeous.

But then other parts of the home were rough-hewn and distressed. She kind of liked that, actually. It was the strangest thing. It appealed to her, those disparate parts.

But it hardly mattered if the decor interested her. All that really mattered was that she stop sniping at Ranger Cooper and start getting to the bottom of this mystery.

He just made it so easy to snipe.

She turned off the water and toweled herself dry. She had picked out a pair of sweatpants and a T-shirt from the closet in "her" room. It felt so completely wrong to wear someone else's clothes, somehow especially since they were his sister's clothes, when all of this… hiding out was due to *her* sister. The sister Ranger Cooper didn't know might be connected to this case. She didn't think.

Maybe he'd figured it out and was pretending like he hadn't, and she was an idiot for thinking otherwise. Or maybe the "girls" Herman said The Stallion kept didn't have anything to do with her sister.

She let out a gusty sigh. Right now she was too hungry to think about anything other than the fragrant soup that had been warming on the stove when she'd left the kitchen. It wasn't gourmet or anything, but she hadn't eaten since... She actually wasn't sure when she'd last eaten. Between the fire and the paperwork and the nervousness and fear during the drive, she probably hadn't eaten more than a few bites of food.

She hurriedly got dressed and pulled her hair back with a band she'd found in a little plastic bin under the sink. It would be a curly mess later, but she was sure this was the place where what little vanity she had left had come to die.

She had none of her normal hair products. No makeup. None of the clothes that fit her properly. While she had lost her job as a hypnotist with the Texas Rangers, thank you Ranger Jerk, it still felt like Cooper was more of a colleague than anything else. She wanted to dress professionally and be taken seriously and...

And she had to put her hair back into a crazy ponytail, and wear someone else's very nearly gaudy and way-too-tight sweats.

"Just what you should be concerned about, Natalie, how you look," she muttered to herself. She was hopeless. That was all there was to it.

She stepped out into the hall, her feet propelling her forward only because she could smell that soup in the distance.

Ranger Cooper was sitting at the table, spooning soup into his mouth as he stared moodily at a laptop screen.

He flicked a glance at her and then pointed toward the stove. "Help yourself." She gave him a little nod, and then did just that. He'd set out a bowl for her, and she ladled soup into it.

She heard a choking sound and looked back to find him nearly red and coughing.

"Are you okay?"

"Fine," he said, his voice nothing more than a scrape.

He wasn't the type of man to errantly choke on his soup. "What happened? Did you find something?" He had been staring at the laptop screen, but then there were windows in the kitchen too. "Did you see someone out a window?" She whipped her head around, looking for some clue as to what he'd choked over.

"No. No, none of that."

"Then what?"

"It was nothing," he replied, his voice returning to normal, his attention returning to his computer.

"Ranger Cooper, honestly, don't be—"

"It's the back of your...pants," he ground out.

"Well, they're not *my* pants," she muttered in return. She tried to look over her shoulder, searching for what he saw, but she didn't see anything except pink on the backs of her legs.

"It, uh, says something."

"It says what?" she demanded, flinging her arms in the air. "Do you have to be so infuriatingly vague?"

"Trust me, you don't want to know."

"Ranger Cooper, I swear to all that is—"

"It says Ride..." He cleared his throat. "Ride Me, Cowboy."

She blinked at him. "Ride..." She blinked again, a hot flush infusing her face. "I... I'm going to go change." She hurried out of the room and inspected every piece of clothing in the closet before choosing plain green sweatpants. She didn't quite love the too-tight fit, but that was far less...embarrassing than Ride Me, Cowboy being printed on any part of her clothing. Most especially her butt.

Wait. Why had Ranger Cooper been looking at her butt? He was probably just inspecting her for signs of weapons or something. There was no way that man checked out *anyone* in the course of his oh-so-important duty.

Only the desperate hunger situation coaxed her to return to the kitchen, otherwise she might have happily holed up in the strange little color burst of a room and never forced herself to have to look Ranger Cooper in the eye again.

Ride Me, Cowboy.

She shuddered, then took a deep breath before she stepped foot into the hallway again. She was just going to have to accept that her face was probably going to be beet red for the next…eight million hours.

There are more important things to think about than a little silly embarrassment over pants that aren't even yours.

Which was a very sensible thought all in all, but it changed absolutely nothing. She was embarrassed. She was… Well, trying very, very hard not to think about riding of any kind.

She placed her palm to her burning cheek and inwardly scolded herself as she haltingly forced herself back to the kitchen.

Ranger Cooper's gaze remained steady on the laptop, but unlike the first time she'd stepped into the open front area, he was aware she was there. He didn't move, he didn't look at her, but she *knew* he was aware of her. So much different than that moment she'd caught him lost in his thoughts.

And wondered a little too hard what those thoughts might be.

"What do you know about The Stallion?" Ranger Cooper asked in that maddeningly professional tone. As if nothing had happened a short while ago, as if this was some sort of interrogation, not him protecting her. Or whatever it was he was really up to.

"I don't know what that is. A person?" Based on what Herman said, she assumed it was, but she really didn't know. It was imperative Ranger Cooper give her a hint, but she had to play that carefully. No jumping into an interrogation mode of her own.

"Yes, a person."

She finished ladling her soup and grabbed the spoon that Cooper had left out for her. She could stand here and eat it over the kitchen counter, and she'd probably be more comfortable doing that, but she didn't want to give him that kind of power over her. She wouldn't stand to eat just because she didn't want to face him.

She walked over to the table, set down her food and then slid into the seat directly across from him. His eyes remained on the laptop.

She didn't say anything because that was the technique he always used. Give her absolutely no information, even when she asked a direct question. Say only what he wanted to, and when.

So, she ate, saying nothing else, and it about killed her. She hated the silence that settled over them like an oppressive weight. She hated not peppering him with constant questions, she hated not being able to just dive in and figure out what the heck was going on.

But she didn't trust herself not to reach across the table and pummel him if he gave her another nonanswer.

"Why did you question Herman?" Ranger Cooper

said at last. "According to Captain Dean you always follow the rules. Never once stepped out of line. What was going on in the interrogation room that caused you to ask questions?"

Natalie didn't tense. She'd spent enough time around cops to know how to keep herself immobile and unreadable. She kept her gaze level, and when his gray-blue eyes met hers, she tried not to shudder. She tried not to feel the guilt that was washing through her. She tried to ignore all of the emotions threatening to take over, and most of all, she tried to lie.

"As a woman, I find cases about kidnappings very disconcerting." She never once looked away, because she knew that would give her away more than anything else. She stared straight into his eyes and willed him to believe her words.

"That wasn't your first kidnapping case," he said, all calm, emotionless delivery.

She swallowed before she could will away the nervous response. She had worked a kidnapping case before, but just one. It had been the abduction of a little boy in the middle of a custody battle. It had been nothing like her sister's case, and she'd known that from the beginning. "He was a small boy. I couldn't see myself as a victim."

"Herman said he keeps *girls*. Last time I checked, you were a woman."

Natalie's pulse started thundering in her wrist and in her neck, panic fluttering through her. "Obviously you've never been a young woman in a rough part of town," she returned, proud of how steady her voice sounded.

He held her gaze, but he didn't say anything. He simply looked at her as though if he looked long enough, he could unravel all her secrets.

She almost believed he could.

"What do you know about The Stallion, Ms. Torres? I won't ask again."

"Good. Because I don't know anything about him. I don't even know *what* he is. So, please, don't ask me again, because this is the truth. I have no clue." She managed to swallow down the "trust me, I wish I knew more." But only just.

"Lies could get us killed at this point. Remember that."

It struck her hard, because he was right. Some lies could get them killed in this situation, but not her lies. All she was doing was not explaining why she'd been superinterested in this case.

Her interest in the girls had nothing to do with why her house had been burned down, and had nothing to do with why she was stuck in this little place in the middle of nowhere with this Texas Ranger.

Her lie was personal, but it was…incidental almost. She didn't know anything about The Stallion or what he might be into that would make him the kind of man to kill people and burn down houses.

She reached across the table, not sure why it seemed necessary to touch him, but she thought she could get her truth across if there was some sort of connection. She touched her fingertips to the back of his hand and looked him in the eye.

"I have no intention of getting us killed. I have no intention of lying to you. All I want is to be able to go back to my life." She slid her fingers off his hand, and something shimmered to life inside of her. She didn't understand that odd feeling, and why she felt off-kilter and short of breath. Why the warmth of his hand seemed to stay in her fingertips.

So, she looked down at her soup as she said, "And if we're going to discuss honesty, why don't you tell me what you know about why we're being chased? Because I think it's a whole heck of a lot more complicated than you're letting on."

She brought a spoonful of soup to her mouth and then slid a glance at him. He had narrowed his eyes, and he was still studying her, that intensity never leaving his face.

And Natalie wondered just how long she could keep her secret…

Chapter 6

Vaughn still didn't trust Ms. Torres. There was something she was hiding, he was sure of it. Despite his absolute certainty though, he found himself inclined to believe she didn't know anything about The Stallion. She wasn't scared enough. If she knew what that man was capable of, she'd be petrified.

"There's nothing about this case that seems to directly apply to you. The Stallion is the head of an organized crime ring that deals mostly in drugs. Human and sex trafficking is also a possibility."

He noted the way she paled. It could be that fear he thought she needed, but he tended to think that the mention of trafficking didn't make people pale unless they had some sort of personal stake in the matter.

He could question her again. He could keep interrogating her until she finally gave in and told him her secret.

And he would. Yes, he would, but first he needed to finish his soup and get a few hours of sleep. That was just common sense, not caring about her feelings. He certainly didn't care about those.

"We have at least four unsolved cases we think might be connected to The Stallion and his cronies. Not to even begin to mention the current cases. Getting Herman on the leash and willing to talk was a huge breakthrough in our cases. And then you ruined my interrogation."

"You were asking the wrong questions."

"I know what the right questions are. I've been doing this for too long to ask the wrong questions. You were taking too direct an approach, and it wasn't even your job to approach anything." He gritted his teeth to stop from talking. He wasn't going to let her rile him up with her ridiculous accusations.

He finished his soup and then closed out all the files he didn't want her to have access to. He set his computer up so he'd be able to track whatever she did try to look up while he was asleep.

He didn't consider it underhanded, he considered it necessary.

"I'm going to sleep. Obviously you can make yourself comfortable, but keep all doors locked, all windows covered. You hear a noise, see anything suspicious, *anything*, you come get me immediately."

"What if someone blasts through the window and I have nothing to protect myself with?"

She made a good point, but it wasn't a particularly comfortable one. Did he trust her enough to *arm* her while he slept? "What are your qualifications?"

Her eyebrows drew together. "My…what?"

"Do you have a permit? Training?"

"Well, no."

"Have you ever used a gun before?"

"Well…" She sighed at his raised eyebrow. "No."

Vaughn resisted rolling his eyes. Barely. "We'll see about training you, but in the meantime, don't touch a firearm. If someone comes blasting in here, they'll have you disarmed before you even figure out how to aim and pull the trigger."

She scowled, but she didn't argue. He'd count that as a win.

"If you see something suspicious, come get me. Otherwise, stay out of trouble."

Her full lips remained pressed together. The lips were distracting, but not as distracting as how…form-fitting his sister's clothes were on this woman. And thank goodness they were his *sister's* clothes and he could keep any wayward thoughts at bay with that reminder.

He turned abruptly and headed for his room. It didn't make sense to sit here sniping with her when he needed to catch a few hours' sleep. He didn't bother with a shower; he'd deal with that later. For now, he went straight to his bed and slid under the covers.

He was exhausted enough that his eyelids immediately closed, but he didn't drift off right away. No matter how exhausted he was, there was too much on his mind.

Unfortunately, a large portion of that was Natalie Torres. He still hadn't had a chance to dig deeper into her background beyond the file the department had kept on her while she'd been employed with them.

No criminal record. Hell, not even a speeding ticket. She'd lived at the same address for the entirety of her employment, and none of her other jobs struck him as peculiar or suspicious.

It was simply *her* that was both peculiar and suspicious. The way she'd jumped in and questioned Herman after years of following the rules. The way she'd paled when he mentioned trafficking.

The way she chewed on her bottom lip when she was thinking, leaving it wet and…

He groaned and rolled face-first into his pillow. He'd never been… He punched at the pillow, irritated with the truth. No matter how suspicious he found Ms. Torres, he was *physically* attracted to her.

Which didn't matter, of course, it was just increasingly obnoxious that the woman he didn't want to be attracted to was the one he was stuck in an isolated cabin with. For who knew how long.

But, he couldn't think like that. He had to focus on one thing at a time. If he got too worked up about what *could* happen, he'd miss something about what *was* happening, and that could get somebody killed.

He hadn't let it happen yet. He wasn't about to let it happen now. That was how he had to think. He had to be certain that he could solve this case before any more people got hurt. But he needed to get in a couple hours' sleep so he could focus on the files and find the connection he was missing.

He needed to figure out what Ms. Torres's connection was. Because she had to have one. Maybe it wasn't with The Stallion, but she was involved with *something*. He was sure of it.

And when Vaughn Cooper was sure of something, God help the person on the other side.

Natalie glanced at the hallway Ranger Cooper had disappeared down at least twenty minutes ago. Surely he was asleep. She'd been afraid to move the entire time he'd been gone, afraid that he would somehow read her thoughts and her plan and come rushing back out and take the computer with him.

But he'd left it. Ranger Cooper wasn't a stupid man. She didn't think he'd actually have anything on that computer she could access that would give her answers, but if he had the internet, or even a basic case write-up of something, she might be able to find the information she needed to make the connection. A connection between her sister and this Stallion person.

A clue. A hint. Something, something to help her figure out how to proceed.

Natalie stood, and her heart was nearly beating out of her chest. She had to get a handle on her nerves at being caught. What did it matter? He knew what she was doing. He *had* to know this was what she was going to do. Getting caught was the least of her worries.

Her heartbeat didn't seem to listen. It continued to beat guiltily in her chest, but she had do something. She took her bowl to the kitchen and rinsed it out. She waited after each movement to see if she could hear Ranger Cooper moving around or coming back out to the hallway. But the cabin was eerily silent.

Now her heart was overbeating for a completely different reason. The fact someone could be out there. Someone could be out there and watching her and just…

She squeezed her eyes shut and shook her head. She

couldn't think like that. She could only think about survival. Thinking about who or what was after her and why...

She had to push it away, just like the knowledge her house was gone, that her sister could be dead, that her family could be in danger. She had to push it all aside and focus on what she could do.

She walked out of the kitchen and headed for the table and the open computer. She put her hand on the touchpad, and the computer sprang to life. No password to enter. No apparent security practices in place. Just an open, easily accessible computer. She glanced back down the hallway with narrowed eyes.

There was no way he would leave his computer completely unattended. Even if nothing was on here. There was something to this. Some kind of setup. Or maybe he was simply trying to prove she was underhanded.

It was insulting. He thought she was *this* dumb. For some reason that made her want to do it all the more. To do everything he thought she would do. Because it didn't seem to matter what she did, he was going to think she was hiding something. She might as well get something out of it.

It was possible her sister had been taken by The Stallion. But it was also possible her sister was taken by some other lunatic, and Natalie would never find her. But Natalie was never going to know if she didn't take this chance—regardless of what Ranger Cooper thought.

So, she pulled up the web browser and tested the availability of the internet. She cursed when she couldn't find anything. No wireless, and he didn't appear to have any kind of hot spot. So what had he been reading so intently all through lunch?

She skimmed the names of the folders on his desktop. The one on the very top was named CASE FILES.

"Oh, you really think I am just such an idiot, don't you?" she muttered, more and more insulted.

She opened the folder anyway. Maybe this was all information he didn't mind her having, but that didn't mean it wasn't worth having. It would still be more than she knew. She would take this opportunity, no matter how he used it against her in the future.

When the folder opened, there were a variety of documents inside. They didn't appear to be official police documents. They weren't reports or labeled in the way she knew cases and information at the precinct was labeled. These had to be his personal notes.

Even better.

Each file name included the words "The Stallion" plus a number code of some sort. Either his own or one outside of police work.

She began to read them in order, getting lost in the twists and turns of all the possible cases they thought The Stallion might be involved in.

It was a lot of drugs. Things she didn't know anything about. She couldn't imagine her sister had been wrapped up in drugs. Surely Natalie would've noticed that. They had been too close for Natalie to have not known or suspected that.

When Natalie got to the suspected instances of human trafficking, her blood ran cold. A lot of it was mixed up with immigration issues, but the thing that hit her hard and left her reeling was a mention of the Corlico Plant.

Her father had worked there for twenty years. He'd only stopped when Gabby had disappeared from the parking lot, waiting for him to get off his shift.

He'd never been able to go back.

And here it was, in the cases tied to The Stallion. Natalie shivered, reading quicker through the notes.

Apparently the Rangers suspected the factory of being some sort of drop-off point, or transfer station based on one raid they'd conducted, but the two women who had been freed hadn't been able to give any information that gave the Rangers further leads.

Between Herman saying he kept the girls, and this connection, Natalie was more and more convinced The Stallion was keeping Gabby. That he *had* her.

She was alive.

It was strange that the rush of tears overtook her, considering how often and how much she'd cried over Gabby. How many moments of hope she'd had that had been dashed time and time again over the course of eight years. Yet this new little tiny trickle of a lead felt like a revelation.

She'd always been certain Gabby was still alive. Her certainty had been something of a crutch, really. But there'd always been that little question in the back of her mind. What if Mom and Grandma were right? What if Gabby was dead, and Natalie had wasted her life chasing nothing?

But it wasn't nothing. This was the biggest lead she'd ever had. It wasn't proof, and maybe it was even grasping at straws, but it was something. Something had to mean everything right now. On the run, in this tiny cabin with a man she didn't understand—and was afraid she was a little too interested in understanding—she finally had a sliver of hope.

She would hold on to that for all she was worth.

She kept scanning the documents, eager to find a connection between the Corlico Plant and The Stallion.

An eerie sound pierced the air. Natalie froze. She didn't know how to describe the sound, and she had even less of a clue where it might have come from. She didn't move a muscle and strained to hear something else. Something that might identify it as harmless.

What on earth would be harmless in the middle of nowhere? Again her heart pounded so loudly she could barely hear anything, and knowing she needed to hear made it even worse. She breathed slowly and evenly, trying desperately to listen carefully. She didn't want to wake up Ranger Cooper for something stupid.

A noise in the middle of nowhere isn't stupid. It was actually probably pretty damn important. Looking a little stupid was better than being dead.

Carefully, she stood. Her legs were shaky, but she tried to walk as quietly as possible, still straining to hear something, anything, to give her a clue as to what the sound might have been.

She inched her way toward the hallway, eyes trained on the door and the windows. She didn't know whether she was expecting someone to burst through one, or one of those red dots from a laser sight to show up on her chest.

The sound didn't repeat, and she slowly moved down the hallway. Just as she reached Ranger Cooper's door, she heard it again.

It was oddly high-pitched, but not quite mechanical. Where she had originally planned to be very careful and quiet, gently waking up Ranger Cooper, the sound repeating caused Natalie to move forward clumsily and jerkily, swinging open his door with no finesse it all.

He was bolting up in the bed before the door even banged against the wall. His hand immediately closed over his weapon, which had been placed on a night-stand next to his bed.

It was the second time he'd almost pulled his weapon on her in the course of not very many hours, but she was glad he had such quick reflexes. It was oddly com-forting to know he would immediately grab for his gun and try to protect them both. Considering he had never actually done anything with the gun, just placed his hand on it both times, she still felt safe in his presence.

He flung off the covers, getting out of the bed in one quick, graceful movement. He was wearing ath-letic shorts and a T-shirt, and perhaps a little bit later she'd have more time to appreciate just how sculpted his muscles were, but for right now she had her life to save.

"What's happening?" he asked, his hands clutching the gun at his side, looking like a man ready to fight.

"I…heard a noise," Natalie said, feeling foolish and scared and just damn lost.

He didn't balk, he didn't question her. He simply nodded.

Chapter 7

Vaughn tried to loosen his grip on the gun. Natalie had shocked him the hell out of sleep, and the adrenaline was still pounding through him.

He glanced at Natalie's pale face. "Tell me what you heard," he ordered gruffly, shoving his feet into his boots.

"I... I don't even know. It was kind of high-pitched, but... It didn't sound like anything I'd ever heard before."

He gave a sharp nod, not bothering to pull the laces tight. "Where did it come from?" He stepped out into the hall and motioned her to follow.

"I'm not sure. It was so sudden and out of nowhere. But, it'd had to have come from closer to the front of the cabin, I think, or it would have been more muffled."

Again, he nodded. He listened for any noise aside

from the sounds of their feet on the stone floor. Nothing. "I want you to stay in the hallway while I check the windows and doors." He stopped his progress and turned to face her. "You will stay right here no matter what. Understand?"

She scrunched her nose, but she didn't argue with him. She nodded, lips clamped together as though she didn't trust herself to speak.

She was smart, he'd give her that. He entered the living area, starting at the window closest to him. As stealthily as possible, he raised the curtain, surveyed what he could and then moved to the next window— each time all he saw was rocks and dusk.

He made it to the kitchen window and still nothing. They'd have to go outside. He debated making her stay inside while he searched, but it would be more dangerous to separate. Especially separating the unarmed civilian from the man trained to handle a weapon.

"I'm not seeing anything," he said gruffly, turning to find her exactly where he'd left her in the hall.

"I swear I heard something," she said, her eyes still round, her fingers clenched into fists.

"I believe you," he returned, barely paying attention as he tried to formulate a plan on how to investigate the perimeter without getting either one of them killed.

"You *do*?"

He glanced back at the note of incredulousness in her voice, focusing more on her than his plans for the first time. "Is there a reason I shouldn't?"

"No, I just…" She shook her head, looking completely baffled. "I'm…not used to people believing me. Especially *you*."

Those last two words shouldn't have an impact on him. What did it matter if he hadn't believed her all this time? They were here, weren't they? He was keeping her safe. Yet he felt that *especially you* like a sharp pain.

But he didn't have time to dwell on that or figure it out. Quite frankly he wouldn't want to even if he did.

"We're going to have to search the perimeter together. We're going to do the same thing we did when we got here. You're going to follow me closely. Listen to whatever I say. And hopefully we'll find the source of the noise and it's nothing."

"And if it's something?"

"There are too many possibilities for us to sit here and go over all of them. You're just going to have to follow my lead, and everything will be fine."

"Is the unwavering confidence real, or do you say those sorts of things so I'll go along with whatever you say?"

Oddly, he wanted to smile. Because it was a good question—a fair one, and the dry way she delivered it. Because he appreciated her backbone. Unfortunately, now was not the time for good or fair questions. So he simply said, "Both" and then started walking toward the door.

She followed him as she had when they'd first arrived. Though her antagonism and questioning tended to grate on his nerves, he would have to give her credit for following directions when it was required.

She wanted to fight him, it was obvious, but she didn't. He admired both. Someone who didn't get a little bent out of shape about being told what to do was too much of a pushover to be of any real help. But someone who could make the choice to listen even if they didn't want to, that was a person with sense.

You're seriously having these thoughts about that woman?

He opened the door, forcing himself to focus on the task ahead and nothing else. He used the door as a shield and scanned the front yard. Since the house was nestled into one of the swells of land that wasn't rocky mountain, the land in front of the house stretched far and wide. There'd be no place to hide within shooting range, and as he scanned the land around them, he didn't see anything that might be people or the evidence of them.

The problem was going to be the back of the house. There was a small yard between the desert and the building, and walking back there would prove even trickier without having any kind of cover.

A piercing howl of a coyote echoed in the quickly cooling desert air. He always liked listening to them, but his sister had said they were as creepy as hell.

Apparently Ms. Torres agreed with his sister because her hand clamped around his arm. "That's it. That's the sound," she said, her voice little more than a squeaky whisper.

Vaughn immediately relaxed. Dropping his gun to his side, he turned to face her. Her long and slender fingers still curled around his forearm. He glanced at her hand momentarily, not sure why such a simple touch was dancing over him like…like anticipation.

There was nothing to anticipate here. So that feeling needed to go.

"Why'd you put your gun down? What is it?" She

looked at him with those wide, scared eyes, and he couldn't help but smile. She blinked, clearly confused.

"It's coyotes. We have them here, and they occasionally get close to the house and do the howling. But it's just an animal. Nothing to be afraid of."

She looked horrified, and for a second he thought he was going to have to give a lecture about how coyotes weren't dangerous and there were far bigger things to worry about, but her hand dropped and she closed her eyes. Not fear etching over her face, but a pink-tinged embarrassment.

"I feel like such an idiot. Coyotes. That's it?"

"You've never heard a coyote before?"

She heaved a sigh. "I've only ever lived in Houston and Austin. In the city. Animal noises are not my expertise. It didn't sound…howly." She shook her head, disgusted. With herself, he imagined.

"Sometimes they'll sound like a big group howl, sometimes it's not quite so delineated, but it's definitely coyote."

"I'm so sorry," she said, all too sincerely, all too… worked up for an honest mistake. It made him itchy and uncomfortable, and irritably needing to soothe it away.

"There's nothing to be sorry about. It was an honest mistake. Unless you're apologizing for something else?"

Her mouth firmed. "No, I'm not apologizing for anything else. I… You…" Her eyebrows drew together, and those dark eyes studied him, some emotion he couldn't recognize in their depths. "But it was an animal, and nothing, and… You aren't mad that I woke you up and got you into police mode when it was nothing?"

"Of course not. You heard an unknown noise and

you reacted exactly as you should have. Exactly as I *told* you to. Why on earth would I be mad?"

"I don't understand you at all, Ranger Cooper. All the things I expect you to be hard on me about, you're not, but the things I don't expect you to be hard on me about, you are."

"Then maybe you shouldn't expect either."

She laughed at that. A bright, loud laugh, and it was a shock how much the sound of someone else's laughter surprised him. When was the last time he'd heard anyone laugh? Sarcastic laughter, sure. All the time at work. But he had been so focused on getting somewhere in the cases connected to The Stallion there hadn't been any banter at work, he hadn't had any kind of social life and he hadn't relaxed at all.

It was only now, here, in the middle of the desert and mountains, with this strange woman's laughter ringing in his ears that he realized any of that. A very uncomfortable and unsettling realization prompted by a very uncomfortable and unsettling woman.

Maybe that was appropriate, all in all.

"You should call me Vaughn." He had no idea where that instruction came from. Why on earth would she call him Vaughn? He should be nothing to her but Ranger Cooper.

And yet something about that smile and laugh made him… Well, stupid apparently. "Let's head back inside."

"Your name is Vaughn?"

"No, I'm lying," he grumbled.

She laughed again as they stepped inside, and he found himself smiling. The last thing he should be feeling now was any kind of lightness, and yet that little exchange had done exactly that—lightened him. It had to be the sleep exhaustion.

"That's a very unconventional name for a very conventional man."

"How do you know I'm conventional?"

"Oh, please. You can't possibly *not* be conventional. You showed up at that fire at three thirty in the morning all neat and unwrinkled. You don't believe in hypnotism. You were nothing but..." She pulled her shoulders up to her ears and pretended to tense all over. "Like a tight ball of contained, by-the-book energy. Everything about you is conventional."

"Ms. Torres, trust me when I say that you do not know everything about me."

Her eyes met his, and he recognized that little weird energy that passed between them. He wished he didn't, but there was no denying the flirtatious undertone to all of this. He should stop it immediately.

But she held his gaze and she smiled. "Natalie. You should call me Natalie, remember?"

That uncomfortable and unwelcome attraction dug deeper into his gut. The kind of deeper that led a man to make foolish mistakes and stupid decisions. The kind he knew better than to indulge in.

But it was also the kind that tended to override that knowledge.

Natalie's breathing became shallow for a whole different reason than it had the past few days. Looking at Vaughn, because he said she should call him Vaughn, and knowing they were doing a very weird, and very nearly flirting thing, yeah, it made her body respond in unwelcome ways.

She was too warm, and a little shaky. Not the kind Vaughn could see, but the kind that was internal. The kind that messed with her equilibrium.

She should really look away from that ice-blue gaze, but she simply stared. She really should stop. Any minute now.

"You know, not believing in hypnotism isn't exactly unconventional. It's just common sense."

Well, the man sure knew how to kill a moment. She walked farther into the living room and decided to take a seat on the comfy-looking couch. Men like him never could accept there might be a softer way about getting information than torture or the like.

"What exactly do you think hypnotism is, fun? Magic?"

"That's the point. It's not magic. It's not real."

"That's because you have the wrong perception of what hypnotism is. It's not about magic. It's not about getting someone to do something against their will. It's about giving the person being hypnotized a safe place to express something that's hard for them to express. It's about finding a center, finding calm. It's not tricks. It's not getting someone to bark like a dog on stage. It's showing someone who has every reason to be afraid of talking a calmness inside themselves that can allow them to give information they, deep down, *want* to give."

She knew she was lecturing, but he was always ordering her about, so maybe turnaround was fair play. "You can't make someone do something under hypnotism that they don't want to do. The thing is, they *want* to do this. They just have a mental block. Calming their breathing and giving them that safe place gives them the tools to get over that block. It's not magic. It's not supposed to be magic. It's a tool."

He was silent for a few moments, and she thought maybe she'd surprised him with her answer. When people actually sat down to listen to how she explained hypnotism and why it worked in terms of witnesses, they tended to understand. Even if they didn't necessarily believe in it, they at least understood that no one thought this was some magical cure. *Most* people sneered at it a lot less once she explained. She had a sneaking suspicion that Vaughn was not one of those "most people."

"If they want to give us the answers, then what's the point of you? Why don't they just, you know, give us the answers?"

"Let's use Herman as an example," she replied, relaxing into the couch, crossing her arms over her chest, refusing to back down to his disdain. "He knew that he was going to die. He knew that talking to you was going to get him killed. But let's start at the beginning? How did you get Herman to come in?"

Vaughn narrowed his eyes at her and stood there for a few minutes of ticking silence. As though he wasn't quite sure that she was worthy of the information. It made her want to smack him.

"He was pulled over. Since he had warrants, he was brought in."

"And then you and Ranger Stevens decided to question him because…?"

"Because he was connected to a case that we believe has to do with The Stallion."

"So, here is this man who has a family, daughters and a sick wife. He's scared of his boss, but he also knows that his boss is doing something incredibly wrong. So his conscience is telling him to talk to the police, his common sense and survival instinct are telling him not to talk to you. When you're in that kind of moral dilemma—where you want to save yourself, but you want to save others too—it's hard to make a choice. It's especially hard to make a choice that you know will put you in even more danger than you're already in. Having something to blame your answers on is freeing. It takes the personal responsibility off you, and then you can unburden yourself the way you really want to. I would bet money that if you somehow got The Stallion into one of your interrogation rooms and I tried to hypnotize him, it wouldn't work. It only works on people who are conflicted. A part of themselves actually *does* want to talk, or they don't."

"Did it ever occur to you to tell people this before you walk into an interrogation room?"

"Did it ever occur to you to trust the order of your superior who clearly did trust me and believed that what I was doing was useful?"

"The minute I start believing someone just because he's my superior is the minute I become a subpar police officer."

"Conventional."

She thought for a second that he was going to smile. His surprisingly full, nearly carnal lips almost curved before he stopped them and pressed them into a line.

"Have you changed your mind about hypnotism?"

"No."

"Do you want me to hypnotize you?"

"No." Again that little quirk like he might smile, or even laugh.

"I bet you have some juicy secrets you're just dying to tell me."

"There will be no secret sharing, Ms. Torres."

"What else are we going to entertain ourselves with for the next few days?"

"We could discuss whatever it was that you looked up on my computer." This time he did smile, but it wasn't a particularly nice one. It was sharp edges and a little bit of smug self-satisfaction.

Ugh. Why did he still have to be hot even when he was being smugly self-satisfied?

None of that. None. Of. That. "I just checked to see if you had Wi-Fi," she returned, smiling as saccharine as she could manage.

"All the way out here you thought I might have Wi-Fi?"

"You never know."

"Why don't you be straight with me, Natalie."

"How about I start when you start." Some of that flirtatious ease from earlier was cooling considerably degree by degree.

"I've been nothing but straight with you."

"No, you've been vague at best. Considering I'm mixed up in all of this, I really think that I deserve to know what all of this is."

"I can't put my investigation at risk," he returned, back to the implacable Texas Ranger.

"You have me in the middle of nowhere under lock and key. What risk is being posed?"

"I still don't know you. I don't know who you're connected to. I don't know what happens when you're cleared to go home. If you want to take that personally, that's your prerogative, but that's certainly not how it's meant. I don't know you, and until I do, until I know what you're after and what your connection is, there is nothing I can do to trust you. Not and do my job."

She shifted on the couch and looked away from him, because as true as it was, it was somehow still irritating. She totally understood what he was saying. It made nothing but sense, and that she was oddly hurt he couldn't trust her was ridiculous.

"I may have found a connection…" She swallowed. If she told him, he might trust her. For some strange reason, she really did want him to, but if she told him, was she putting herself at risk of never being able to touch one of these cases again? If he knew she was connected to this one little case, would he keep everything from her because her sister was involved? Or would he maybe have some compassion because he had a sister of his own?

Would it be worth suffering through having no answers to get a little bit of the possibility of a new answer? She didn't know, and she found the more she sat there and he stood there—an unmoving mountain of a man—the less she knew.

She stared into those gray-blue eyes, searching for some hint that there might be warmth or that compassion might be a word in his dictionary. There was absolutely nothing in his face to give her the inclination, and yet she so desperately wanted it to be so.

Later she would blame it on exhaustion, not just of the day, or the week, but over the past eight years. But for right now, she opened her mouth, and the truth tumbled out.

Chapter 8

"A connection?" Everything inside Vaughn tensed as he glared at her. She might've found a connection? A connection to what? How could she have possibly found something in cases he'd pored over for years and found next to nothing except gut feelings and hunches?

"There was a case in your files…" She cleared her throat, and she most assuredly did not look at him, but she also showed no remorse for going through his files. It was hard to blame her. He would have done the same thing in her situation. That's why he'd bothered to set her up; he knew she'd do it.

What he hadn't known was that she might actually offer some information. He thought he would have to drag that out of her.

She fidgeted on the couch and chewed on her all too distracting bottom lip. He could jump all over her and demand answers, which would stop the mouth distraction, but it wouldn't be the most effective route to take.

The most effective route to take with Natalie was, unfortunately, patience. To listen to what she said, to understand it. She was a hypnotist, but her fervor over the importance of hypnotism and what it offered pointed to the fact that she was conflicted herself—a moral dilemma, just as she'd said about Herman.

So, he stood, his hands clenched into fists, his muscles held tight. And he waited.

"There was a file on human trafficking. It mentioned that there was some sort of possibility of a drop-off point being at the Corlico Plant?" She looked up at him questioningly.

He hesitated for a second, but she'd already read the file, one he'd left available to her. Might as well give her the information. "Yes, we intercepted a group of people there. Based on all the information we could collect, it wasn't the first time that the trafficking went through there. But they immediately stopped since we intercepted, and we had no one to arrest, nothing to go on. We've never been able to find anything after it."

"Three years ago, right? That's when you intercepted?"

"Yes." Three years and eight months. He didn't even have to look it up. When it came to cases he thought had to do with The Stallion, he had most of the prominent details memorized.

She took a deep breath, clasped her hands together and then straightened her shoulders. She fixed him with a certain gaze, and he knew this was going to be whatever she'd been hiding.

"Eight years ago, my sister disappeared from the Corlico Plant parking lot."

She didn't have to go further. Suddenly everything came together. Why she asked Herman about the girls, why she would ruin years' worth of work with the Rangers to ask the questions that she wanted to ask instead of letting him and Stevens handle it.

She was searching for her sister.

"Unbelievable," he muttered.

She didn't even have the decency to appear shamed. She shrugged. "Do you how many years I've been waiting to have a case that might connect to Gabby? Do you know how many hours I've spent trying to figure out what happened to her? They never found a body, in all this time. No one ever found a clue that might bring her back to us. I know she's alive. I don't care if anybody believes it or not, I *know* she is."

Her eyes had filled with tears, but they didn't spill onto her cheeks. She looked straight at him, strong and determined, and so *certain* her sister was still alive. He could say a lot of things about Natalie, but she was a strong woman. Obviously stronger than he'd even seen so far.

"Something with that factory is connected. It's too big of a coincidence. She disappeared *there*. Then Herman said he keeps the girls. The human trafficking thing stops there, and that's where she disappeared— before it stopped, I might add. It was late, and she was waiting for my father to get off from his evening shift, and maybe she saw something she wasn't supposed to see, or they saw her and thought she was part of it or…"

"Natalie, that's a lot of maybes. We have to work in

fact." He tried to say it gently, but it had been a long time since he'd had to employ gentleness with someone.

"The fact is that this factory has something to do with this case. It has something to do with The Stallion. Who owns it?"

It hit him almost like a lightning bolt, painful and sharp, and he realized...

He turned to his computer and immediately pulled up the file they had on Victor Callihan. He owned the factory, and Vaughn had done extensive research into his background after the trafficking raid. He'd found nothing that might link the man to any crimes, but maybe it stood to reason to dig again, and deeper.

Callihan was a rich man. A powerful man. He'd have the means to do these things. Including keep his nose clean, even when it wasn't.

It couldn't really be that easy, could it?

Natalie was immediately behind him, looking over his shoulder at the screen. The soft swell of her breasts, accidentally he assumed, brushed his back, and he had to grit his teeth to focus on the task at hand.

"Does the name Victor Callihan mean anything to you?"

"No," she returned. "He's the owner?"

"Of the plant and the corporation that runs the plant. He's a bigwig in Austin. After the raid, we investigated him, but we didn't find anything remotely criminal. But if the plant is the common denominator, we should look into it more."

"But you don't have Wi-Fi."

"That doesn't mean I don't have wired internet." He glanced over his shoulder at her, but only came eye-level to her breasts. He quickly looked back at the computer because the last thing he was going to keep doing was noticing anything remotely sexual about her. He was too professional for that.

"First, I need to send an email to Stevens, so he can look into things from his side. He'll have access to all the Ranger files and faster internet." Vaughn tried to slide out of the chair, but again his shoulder blade kind of drifted across her breasts. Seriously. What the hell was this?

He cleared his throat and walked over to the entertainment center that held the cord he needed to hook the computer up to the internet jack. He didn't look at Natalie, and he felt like a wimpy idiot, but sometimes that was the best alternative. He certainly didn't want her to see the effect she had on him. That could lead nowhere good.

"Okay, so, what could Stevens find that might tip us off? What would we be looking for?"

"First, *you* are not looking for anything. You are an innocent bystander."

She huffed out an irritated breath. Which was better than the worried lip chewing. "I'm the one who brought this connection to your attention."

"You could have brought it to my attention a lot earlier. If you had mentioned your connection to The Stallion or this case, I—"

"I didn't know I had anything to do with The Stallion or this case. I still don't. I mean, I think it's too big of a coincidence, but that doesn't mean he has my sister. It doesn't mean…" She trailed off and looked away, and he knew that she was struggling to control her emotions.

He didn't like how easy it was to put himself in her place. Often, due to his father and sister's fame, his sister had received threatening letters or emails. Paparazzi had gotten too close, and occasionally a fan had gotten too interested. He knew what it was like to have concern for your sister's well-being.

Natalie's situation was so much worse, because for eight years now she had been in the dark. She was surviving based on faith alone. As much as Vaughn wanted to discount faith, considering you couldn't get much done with it, he couldn't ignore how admirable it was.

It was admirable that she had put herself into a position where she might find some information about her sister's case. It was admirable after all these years she believed, and she hoped. All in all, Natalie was proving to be something of an admirable woman. That was the last thing he needed right now.

"The trafficking incident was three years ago. Something could have come up in the past three years that we haven't thought to put together." She might operate on faith, but he had to operate on fact. "Knowing this little bit means that when we go back through all of that information with a fine-tooth comb. We know a little bit more about what we're looking for. And we can add the details of your sister's case with the other possible Stallion related cases. When you have a man like this, where he has his fingers in so many different things, who runs an organized crime ring, a little connection could be the connection that leads us to him."

Vaughn connected the computer to the wired internet line. She had moved away from the table, so he could sit safely at it without worrying about her body being anywhere near his.

He logged in and typed a quick email to Stevens with all the pertinent information. His instinct was to go ahead and start searching, even though Stevens would have better luck in that department. His partner would have access to all the police files at work, and faster, less frustrating internet. But when Vaughn glanced at Natalie, she was pacing the living room, wringing her hands.

He could read all sorts of emotions in her expression. It wasn't just sadness, it wasn't just fear. There was a myriad of things in there. Anger and uncertainty, hope and helplessness alike. The thing he recognized the most was that antsy kind of energy you got when you desperately wanted to fix a situation, and couldn't.

He could sit here and fool around trying to find the information he wanted, but that probably wasn't the best use of his time right now. Not if he wanted to put Natalie at ease.

Since when is putting Natalie at ease your concern?

He ignored the commentary of his brain and pushed back the chair. "I can do more searching later, but for right now we need to use what little light we have left."

She looked over at him, her eyebrows drawing together. "What do we need light for?"

"I'm going to teach you to shoot."

Natalie blinked at Vaughn. She didn't know what to say to that. It certainly wasn't what she had expected. But she hadn't known what to expect when it came to Vaughn.

She thought he'd be angrier about her not mentioning her sister's case. She thought he'd shut her down and out while he went to work trying to find information out about this Victor Callihan. She kind of wanted him to do *that*, but Vaughn didn't do anything half-assed or foolishly, so she knew there was a rhyme or a reason to him teaching her to shoot.

She couldn't decide if she wanted to know said rhyme or reason. She wasn't sure she wanted to learn to shoot. She wasn't sure what she wanted, except an hour to have a good cry.

"We don't have too much time, so I can only show you the basics, but it wouldn't hurt for you to have an idea."

"Oh. Oh. Okay." What else was there to say?

"I'll get my extra ammunition, and then we'll go outside and get started."

"And you think we'll be safe out there?" They were inside with the windows closed, and so far he'd only let her go outside as a shadow to him. But he frowned at her, as though the question were silly.

For the first time, she wondered how old he was, considering the little lines bracketing his mouth. Actually she was starting to wonder a lot of things about him. Things that she should absolutely not wonder about the man investigating a case that might have to do with her sister. Things she definitely shouldn't be wondering about the man who was keeping her safe.

"I don't suggest things that aren't safe, Ms. Torres. Remember that."

He turned and disappeared down the hallway, presumably to get that extra ammunition he spoke of. She noticed he tended to stick with "Ms. Torres" when he was irritated with her. But when he was a little soft, or a little nice, which apparently he could be—shock of all shocks—he would call her Natalie.

She *definitely* way, way too much liked the way her

first name sounded in his rough-and-tumble, no-nonsense drawl.

She really had to get herself together before she learned how to shoot a gun.

There had been a time in her life, directly after Gabby's disappearance, when she had jumped at every little thing and considered getting a gun. Even knowing her sister's disappearance was probably random, she hadn't felt safe. But in the end, the idea of carrying around a gun hadn't made her feel any safer. In fact, the idea of carrying anything that deadly when she was that jumpy only made her more nervous. So she'd never learned how to shoot and she'd never owned a gun.

But something about Vaughn was…reassuring almost. She trusted him to teach her. And teach her well. Obviously he knew what he was doing with a gun, as frequently as he reached for his.

That didn't even scare her. They were in a dangerous situation, and it had only ever felt comforting that he reached for his weapon when startled. Truth be told, nothing about Vaughn scared her. Except that nothing about him scared her. Yes, that part was a little too scary. How easily it was to trust him and listen to him and follow his orders.

She blew out a breath as he returned. He carried a box and a little black bag, and strode toward the door with his usual laser focus.

"All right. Follow me."

"Do you always express things as an order? You could ask. You could say please."

"I'm doing you a favor. I don't need to say please, and I certainly don't need to ask permission. You can follow me and learn how to shoot a gun. Or you can stay here. I really don't care which one."

She doubted that he didn't care, but she managed not to say that. Instead, she followed him outside and around the back of the house. She couldn't imagine there being much more than twenty or thirty minutes left of light, but Vaughn seemed determined to see this through.

"We're not going to worry about hitting some little target. We're just going to work with the basics of aiming and shooting."

He set the bag down and opened it, pulling out big glasses she assumed were safety related. He handed her the glasses and two little orange foam things. When she looked at them skeptically, he sighed.

"They're earplugs. You pinch the end, and you put it in your ear. It'll keep the gun noise from bothering you."

"Right."

"Now, I'm going to explain everything before we put in the earplugs, and then I'll position you the way you need to be standing and holding the gun. Understood?"

"Aye, aye, Captain," she said sarcastically, because if she was sarcastic she wouldn't overthink the phrase "position you."

He rolled his eyes, clearly not amused by her. But that was okay, because she was amused enough for both of them.

Vaughn pulled his weapon from the holster at his hip. He began to explain the different components to her, the sights, the trigger. What kind of kick to expect and how to aim. She couldn't begin to understand all the jargon or keep up with the different things. He went too fast.

"Are you following along?"

She hated to admit it to him, and herself, but his speed wasn't the issue. Oral instruction had never been easy for her. She had to do things before she fully understood them.

"It's okay if you don't understand something. You can ask as many questions as you need to."

She hated the gentle way he said that. Hated when he was nice, because it made her feel silly or like a victim, and she didn't want to be either. She wanted to be as strong and brave as him.

"I find it easier to understand something if I'm actually in the process of doing it," she gritted, far more snappish than she needed to be.

He didn't react. He simply gestured in front of him. "All right. Stand in front of me."

She did as she was told, and stiffened perceptibly as his arms came around her sides. She had to swallow against the incomparable wave of… It wasn't just attraction, though that was the most potent thing. He was tall, a hard wall of muscle. He smelled…surprisingly good. He was warm, and she wanted to lean against him. She wanted his arms to hold her.

It's just that you're afraid and in danger. That's all. It doesn't have to mean anything.

So she would keep telling herself.

"Give me your right hand."

With another swallow, she followed his instruction. He took her hand and positioned it over the grips of the gun.

"Put your index finger here, and the rest here. Curl the thumb around." He moved her fingers exactly where he wanted them to go, and the more he did to help her put her hands in the right positions, the closer he got. The hard expanse of his chest brushed against her back.

She tried to suck in her breath and hold really still so he wasn't actually touching her. Not because it was unpleasant, but because it was all too pleasant.

The hand not holding hers on the gun slid to her hip, and she very nearly squeaked when it fastened there. That was not…casual, a hand on her hip. Her *hip*. She could feel the sheer size of his hand, the warmth of his palm. She could feel far too much, sparkling through her.

"You want to plant your feet to maximize the steadiness of your arms. So, take a step forward with your right leg." As she did as she was told, he used the hand on her hip to position her in a slightly different way than she would have on her own.

"There," he said, his voice all too close to her ear, scratchy and, like, holy moly, sexy. Why did she have to find him sexy? Why would she think he was hot right now when he was teaching her how to use a deadly weapon?

She thought she heard him swallow, but she had to convince herself she was crazy. Someone like Vaughn would never be affected by this. He probably touched women all the time, and they didn't have any affect on him whatsoever. He probably thought of her as some kind of criminal, and that perceived swallow was all in her head.

"If you have to shoot, you want to be able to get into this position. Only in the most strident of emergencies should you do anything else."

"What's considered a strident emergency?"

"If a person is in the act of physically harming you,

then you have no choice. But if there's any kind of distance between you, you want to try to get in this position. It's going to make your shots straighter and smoother. In a dangerous situation, the last thing you want to do is start shooting willy-nilly. You have to know your target, and you have to be steady."

"What if I'm shaking too hard to be steady?"

"Then you don't shoot."

"But what if someone's in danger?"

"They're going to be in more danger if you shoot when you don't have a good handle on the gun or a good stance."

"Okay. So then how do I shoot?"

He stepped closer, his body pressed to the back of hers. She knew he had to do it in order to show her how to properly shoot the gun, but that didn't mean it was easy to focus on anything but the firm warmth of a wall pressing against her. She wanted to explore it. She wanted to find out what was underneath.

Because she was ridiculous, apparently.

She took a deep breath, trying not to give away how shaky it was. But considering he was pressed against her, he had to know. He had to know that he affected her. That was so hideously embarrassing she almost couldn't concentrate.

"Now, you grip the trigger." His hand tightened on hers, guiding her index finger back to the appropriate spot.

This time when Vaughn swallowed, she had no doubt. He was affected. Granted, he was probably even more horrified by that than she was, but it was still real.

This attraction wasn't a one-sided idiotic thing. It was a two-sided idiotic thing.

"Now you're going to focus on the black spot right there on the hill. Do you see it?"

"Yes," she said, her voice giving away some of her anxiety. She hoped against all hope he thought it was anxiety over shooting a gun, not anxiety about how much her body wanted to rub against his.

"You're going to focus on the black spot. Look through the sight and clear your mind so the only thing you're thinking about is that black spot. There's nothing to be nervous about. There's nothing to be concerned about. All you're trying to do is pull the trigger while focusing on that black spot."

"Oh… Okay." Except focus sounded nearly impossible when he was all but wrapped around her. Sturdy and strong and something she absolutely had to resist.

"You can do this, Natalie," he said in her ear. "I have faith in you."

He couldn't possibly in his wildest dreams understand how much those words meant to her. How big they were even though he was someone she didn't exactly care about. Or shouldn't care about.

Still, his belief, his faith, was more than the people who were supposed to love her gave her. And she understood that. Their lack of faith and belief was mixed up in grief and a terrible tragedy. But that didn't mean she didn't miss it. She understood, but that didn't mean she stopped craving some sort of support.

So when Vaughn said it, even if he was the last person in the world she should want belief from, it mattered.

He steadied her arms, he *had faith in her*. It made her feel like she could do not just *this*, but the whole thing. That together they could find the answers that had eluded her for eight years.

"Pull," he said, and she did. Because he had faith in her. Because he had given her the tools to pull the trigger.

The gun gave a surprisingly harsh kick, but she remained steady and unshaken, even as the breath whooshed out of her.

"You hit it."

She turned to face him, still kind of in the circle of his arms, their hands still on the gun. "Why do you sound surprised? You said you had faith in me."

"Faith in you to shoot the gun, not actually hit the target."

"But you were helping me."

"I didn't pull the trigger. I wasn't looking at the sights. You aimed, you pulled, I just kept your body in position. Hitting the target was all you, Natalie."

She laughed, the surprise of it all bubbling out of her. "You're screwing with me. Trying to build up my confidence."

"Trust me, if I helped, I'd let you know. It's not worth giving you confidence if you don't actually know what you're doing in the process."

She looked at the black spot and the little scarring inside it. She hadn't hit it exactly where she'd been aiming—right in the middle—but she had hit that black spot.

She looked back at Vaughn again, their gazes meeting. Their hands were still on the gun, and she was still pressed up against him. His hand was on her hip, his other arm curled around her other side. It was a very... intimate position—aside from the fact they were both still holding the gun—and yet she couldn't seem to make herself move.

She was pinned by that gray-blue gaze that seemed to have warmed up a little bit in the fading sunlight. Like something about the heavily setting dusk teased out the flashes of darker blue in his eyes.

His gaze dropped to her mouth, and her entire insides shivered and shimmered to life. As though that gaze meant something. As though he had the same thoughts she did—kissing thoughts. Maybe even naked thoughts.

He was so not going to kiss her, what was she even thinking? He didn't like her. He was the consummate professional. Mr. Conventional. Any thoughts about kissing were hers and hers alone, and so out of place it wasn't even funny.

"We should head back in now that it's just about dark."

"Right."

"You can…" He cleared his throat, his eyes *still* on her mouth.

That doesn't mean anything. Maybe you have something on your face. He's not wondering what your lips feel like on his, that's all you, sister.

"You can let go of the gun," he said, that note of gentleness she hated back in his voice as he carefully started to separate their bodies.

"Right." She dropped the weapon all too quickly, but Vaughn managed to catch the gun before it fell to the ground.

They were completely apart now, a few feet between them. Vaughn put the gun in his holster, not even needing to look at the gun to do so. Which, honestly, should ease her embarrassment. He was so in charge and in control and certain, why wouldn't she be attracted to that in a situation like this?

It was just…one of those things. Hero worship or something. Natural to find yourself wondering what a kiss would be like from the man who was dedicated to keeping you safe.

"We'll do more tomorrow. Of the…shooting. We'll shoot more tomorrow. Not… I mean." He cleared his throat. "We'll practice more *shooting* tomorrow."

She stared at him, something in her chest loosening. He had *stuttered*. Ranger Vaughn Cooper had just stuttered at her.

He was walking toward the house now, and she followed, but she couldn't quite stop the smile from spreading across her face.

Maybe just *maybe*, she wasn't as out of her mind as she thought.

Chapter 9

After two days of practice, Natalie had become proficient with his Glock. She had a natural talent, and she impressed him every day.

Vaughn tried not to think too much about that. Because the more he was impressed by her, the more he felt a certain affinity toward her, and that just wouldn't do.

He'd spent half the past two days searching for information on Victor Callihan. He traded emails with Stevens about the man, but so far they were coming up empty. Clean as a whistle, an upstanding member of the community. Vaughn didn't trust it. But he couldn't deny the fact that someone else could be at the center of all this. Just because Callihan was the owner didn't mean he was the perpetrator. There were a lot of people in his corporation who could be The Stallion and thus connecting the Corlico Plant to The Stallion.

Vaughn's frustration with the case was mounting. Especially after the email from Stevens that informed him Natalie's mother's home had been burglarized while she was at work last night. Vaughn still hadn't decided whether to tell Natalie. Which was why he was currently doing as many sit-ups as he possibly could to take his mind off of the internal debate.

Natalie would be upset. She would be more scared than she already was. He wasn't sure she needed that, but he also didn't like the idea of keeping it from her. Which wasn't personal. It was his code of ethics. He didn't like keeping things from people. That was all.

Sure, that's all.

He continued to do the sit-ups, pushing harder and harder in the hopes of dulling his brain completely. He took off his shirt before switching over to push-ups.

It wasn't just trying to outexercise his thoughts. He needed to stay sharp physically as well, and the more he exerted himself, the better he slept for the short snatches he allowed himself. Which kept him better rested, all in all.

It has nothing to do with the fact that you can't seem to help fantasize about Natalie as you're drifting off.

Yeah, it had nothing to do with that.

The fact of the matter was, they couldn't stay here indefinitely. More important, he didn't *want* to stay here indefinitely. They had to get somewhere in this case so he could go back to his life, and Natalie could go back to hers—what little was left of it. But surely she wanted to rebuild. Surely she wanted to get back to normalcy. God knew he did.

He pushed up and down, and up and down, and up and down, his arms screaming, but his mind still going in circles. How did they prove there was a connection? How did they get the answers they needed? And how did he take Natalie back to Austin once their time ran out, knowing she would be in imminent danger if they didn't figure it out?

Just another case you can't solve, the obnoxious voice in his head taunted.

Did it ever occur to you that police work might not be your calling, Vaughn? I mean, really. If you need to focus your whole attention on it, and none on me, how can this be what you're good at?

He went down and stayed on the ground, more than a little irritated that Jenny's doubts were creeping into his own mind. They'd ended their marriage because he hadn't been able to give her what she wanted, but it had really ended when he hadn't wanted to fight for someone who refused to believe in his lifework. Because becoming a police officer had never been just a thing to do, or something frivolous or unimportant. It *had* been a calling. It had been something that he excelled at. Her doubts had eaten away at what little was left of the feelings between them.

"Are you asleep?"

Vaughn pushed up into a sitting position and glanced at Natalie, standing there in the opening of the hallway. She was wearing shorts today, which seemed patently unfair. Yesterday she had worn the clothes she'd been wearing the morning they left, but the day before she'd been wearing his sister's clothes again.

On the days she wore his sister's clothes, he pretty much wanted to walk around blindfolded so he didn't have to see the expanse of olive skin, or notice how the casual fabric clung to the soft curves of an all too attractive body.

Most of all, he had to work way too hard to ignore that he couldn't remember the last time he'd been so attracted to someone. And the more time they spent together, the less that was just physical.

"No. Not asleep. Just resting."

"Right. Well. I thought we could practice shooting a little bit more before you go back to sleep."

"You need to eat something. Then I thought maybe we could work on a little bit of hand-to-hand self-defense." Which was the absolute last thing he wanted to do with her—touch her. But he thought it was important. If he had to take her back to Austin without cracking this case, she needed more than a gun to protect herself. She needed every possible tool in his arsenal.

And he wanted to give it to her. He needed to make sure she was going to be safe. No matter what happened here. Even if his superiors ended up calling him back before they could figure this all out, he would consider Natalie under his protection. He wouldn't look too far into why that was. It was just his nature. He was a man of honor, and seeing things through to the end was why he was in unsolved crimes, because he didn't give up on things. He didn't walk away when things got hard.

"Hand-to-hand…self-defense?"

She sounded unsure, so as he grabbed his shirt, he tried to give her a reassuring glance, but he noticed where her eyes had drifted.

Not to his face, not to anything else in the room. She was staring at his chest, sucking her bottom lip between her teeth in a way that made him all too glad he was wearing loose-fitting sweatpants. Because no matter how hard he had to ignore that little dart of arousal that went through him, it was still *there*. Prominently.

"There are a variety ways to protect yourself," he managed to say. "I think you should know them all."

Slowly, way too slowly for his sanity and giving him way too much pleasure, her eyes drifted back up to his face. Her cheeks had tinged a little pink, and she blinked a little excessively.

She was attracted to him. Which he needed to not think about.

"So, there haven't been any breakthroughs in the case, I'm assuming?"

This was his chance to tell her about her mother's burglary. He couldn't do it. Natalie had started to relax, and she didn't seem nervous, most of the time. He didn't want to add to that. He'd tell her before they went back, but not now. Not now when she was on some kind of solid ground.

"Not so far. Callihan continues to come up clean, but we're looking more into your sister's case, and cases similar to it that are unsolved. Herman did say girls, plural."

"So, you're doing exactly what I've already been doing for the past eight years?"

He frowned at that. "You don't have the access to information that we have."

"You'd be surprised at what I found out." She laughed, but it was a kind of bitter, sad sound. And he wanted to comfort her. He could keep ignoring that want, and he would certainly keep not acting on it, but he was having a hard time denying that it existed.

"Maybe we should sit down and talk about it. You

can tell me your assumptions, and I can match them with the case details."

She looked perplexed, and she stood there quietly for a few minutes while he pulled his shirt on.

"I thought you'd be angrier that I kept my connection from you."

"Just because I'm willing to help you doesn't mean I'm not angry that you kept something from me. But I also knew you were keeping something from me, so it's not as though it was some betrayal."

"Right. You don't care about me."

It was uncomfortable how badly he wanted to argue about that, but it was best if he didn't. It was best if he pretended like he didn't care about her at all. "I care about your safety."

"Because that's your job."

"Yes." Yes, that was the care. It certainly wasn't something more foolish with some woman he'd known for only a handful of days. He was too rational and practical for all that. Attraction could bloom in an instant, *care* could not.

She didn't say anything to that, but there was something in her expression that ate at him. Something about the unfairness of this whole situation…grating. It was beyond frustrating that he was now part of a case where he was not just failing, but he had to stand in front of someone who was affected by the case, and tell her, every day, that he continued to fail at solving it. That he wasn't doing his job as well as he wanted to.

"I'm not sure what I could tell you about my sister's case that you don't already know if you've seen her file."

"Why don't you tell me about *her.*"

"It wasn't her fault. Believe me, I've been through

every police officer who wants to say that Gabby was at fault, that she had to have done something. I have had my fill of people who want to make it into something that couldn't be helped and can't be fixed. I have no interest in doing that with you."

"Look, I can't defend every police officer that ever existed. It's like every other profession—there are good ones, there are bitter ones. Compassionate ones, and ones who've been hardened and emptied or never had any compassion to begin with. But trust me when I say, I don't treat any case as a foregone conclusion. I don't assume things about any case. That's shoddy police work, and I don't engage in it, no matter how tempting a case might make it."

"I keep forgetting you're Mr. Conventional-by the Book," she said with the hint of a smile, but her sadness lingered at the edges.

"I have a sister of my own. She's done some really stupid things that I didn't approve of, but blame is different than being stupid."

Natalie looked away, shaking her head. "I don't want to talk about her. I don't…" She cleared her throat as though she was struggling with emotion, and he realized he was probably being an insensitive dick here, pressing her on something that hurt.

"I just miss her. It hurts to miss her, and it hurts to be the only one who believes that she *is* still out there."

"In my professional opinion, after listening to what Herman had to say, you have every reason to believe she's still alive."

"You don't think it's a long shot?"

He sighed, rubbing his hands over his face. He was walking into dangerous territory here. Comforting her when he didn't know anything concrete wasn't just wrong, but it was against his nature. But comforting her was exactly what he wanted to do. "I can't promise that anyone has your sister. I can't promise that she's alive, and I can't promise you anything to do with this case. But I think you have every reason to hope for all of those things. There's enough evidence to create the possibility."

Natalie visibly swallowed, still looking away from him. She wiped the tears from her cheeks with the backs of her hands, and it was only then that he realized she'd been crying. Again he marveled at her strength, and it took everything in him to fight the impulse to offer her physical comfort.

He got to his feet and crossed to his computer. "Let's make some notes. You and me together. We'll dissect the common denominators between your sister's case and the trafficking case."

"You know, I think I'd rather do the hand-to-hand combat thing," she said, her voice raspy.

"Yeah?"

"I've examined every detail of her case over and over and over. I can't imagine we'd find something that no one else has found. Not when Stevens knows and is looking into it too. Quite frankly, I can't stand sitting around not doing anything anymore. I'm so tired of being shut up in here. The only time I feel like I'm in any kind of control is when you're teaching me how to shoot. So show me some self-defense. Show me some-thing that feels like I'm doing something."

As much as it surprised him to agree with her, he completely understood. There was only so much reading and trying to tie things together you could do before you started feeling useless and worthless and *actionless*.

So, he nodded at the furniture in the way. "Let's clear out the living room."

Natalie felt edgy. It irritated her that part of it had to do with seeing Vaughn do push-ups without a shirt on. She had stood there watching him for way, way too long. Way longer than was even remotely appropriate. She hadn't just watched, she had ogled. But how could she not ogle him when he was *shirtless* doing push-ups in the living room? What was she supposed to do with that?

His arms had been mesmerizing. Just perfectly sculpted muscle vaguely glistening with sweat. She never would've considered a sweaty muscley guy a turn-on before, but holy cow.

Ho-ly. Cow. She felt jittery and off-kilter and kind of achy. Her one and only boyfriend had been so long ago, and she had barely thought about missing out on sex. It hadn't been a big hole in her life not to have it.

But watching Vaughn do push-ups sharply and clearly reminded her what was so great about it, and even though it was stupid, she had a feeling Vaughn would be better at it than Casey had been. Vaughn was so much bigger and stronger and gruffer and…

And then he'd started talking about cases and her sister, and on top of the achy, longing feeling, he brought up all her vulnerabilities. Talking about Gabby's case made her sad and lonely. She was a little too close to suggesting that there were a lot of ways to get rid of sad and lonely, and hand-to-hand combat wasn't one of them.

Instead, she needed to focus on feeling like… Like she had some kind of power. Like she could be strong enough to fight off any threat leveled at her. Because she knew they could only stay here for so long. If no one figured out who The Stallion was, or who'd burned down her house, she'd be in danger when they had to go back.

That scared her, but not as much as it should. She had the sneaking suspicion that even if she had to go back to Austin, Vaughn would keep her safe no matter what.

And you know that is a stupid thought.

"All right." Vaughn looked around the living room that he'd cleared. He did a quick tour of the space as if measuring it. Then he fisted his hands on his hips and looked at her.

His gaze did a cursory up-and-down as though he were measuring her up. It didn't feel sexual in the least, at least until his eyes lingered on her chest. She was wearing one of his sister's shirts, which was unerringly far too tight for her in that area. She didn't think he minded that. If he did mind, it was for a completely different reason than not liking it.

"So." He cleared his throat. "The most dangerous attacks are the ones you don't see coming. There's a certain mindfulness that you have to employ when you know you're walking into a dangerous situation. And—"

"And unfortunately my life is currently a dangerous situation 24/7?"

"Natalie." He crossed to her and rested his hands on her shoulders. "You are safe with me," he said, those gray-blue eyes nearly mesmerizing and the calm certainty in his voice even more reassuring. "Know that.

My job is to protect you, and you can ask my ex-wife, I take my job far too seriously."

"You have an ex-wife?"

His gaze left hers and his hands did too. "Yes," he muttered as though he hadn't meant to share that piece of information about himself.

She hated the idea of him being married before, which was stupid, but she liked that he had given her the information against his will. That meant that maybe he had these same feelings irritating the crap out of him. All this conflicted energy. All this longing she knew she couldn't indulge in.

"Come stand in the middle of the room," he ordered.

She'd gotten to the point where she knew that when he was ordering her around, it was because he was a little off-kilter himself.

She definitely liked that too. But she obeyed and came to stand in the center of the room.

"I'm going to come from behind. I'll wrap my arms around your upper body. And then I'll talk you through getting out of the hold."

"All right."

She stood there, bracing herself for his touch. He did just as he said he was going to do, his muscled arm coming around over her shoulders and keeping her arms almost completely immobile. Though his grip was tight, it wasn't at all harsh. It was gentle. And because she was all too antsy, and all too eager to lean into that grip, she sighed.

"You know I don't think a bad guy is going to hold me nicely."

"I'm not going to hurt you while I'm trying to demonstrate how to get out of a hold."

"How can I learn if there isn't some sort of reality to it?"

"First, you're going to learn the strategy. Then, we'll try with a little more reality to it. You need to learn some patience."

"You'll be shocked to know you're not the first person to tell me that."

He chuckled, and his mouth was so close to her ear that his breath tickled over the sides of her neck. They really needed to find out who The Stallion was, because she wasn't sure how much longer she was going to keep herself from throwing herself at Vaughn. She knew she shouldn't, hell, couldn't, and yet it was bubbling inside her like something beyond her ability to control.

"Okay, so the first step when someone has you in a hold like this is to catch them off guard. If they've left your legs mobile, then that's what you use. If you can get your elbow free, that's what you use. You're always going to want to use the sharpest part of your body and hit the most vulnerable part of theirs."

"So what you're saying is, I should kick him in the crotch?"

"Yes, actually, that is exactly what I'm saying."

It was her turn to laugh. "That's not exactly the type of thing I would expect you to suggest I do."

"When it comes to keeping yourself safe, you do whatever it takes. Keep in mind that I have a sister. I've taught her how to do this. I'm taking the same approach as when I taught her."

"You're taking the same approach with me that you took with your sister?"

It was too leading of a question, and she wished it back in her mouth the minute it had come out. But she didn't know how to sidestep the silence that surrounded them. She didn't know how to make it go away. Some silly part of her wanted to know, though. Did he think of her as a sister? As someone he would never think of sexually?

"The same approach…" He seemed to consider this carefully, and she had no business thinking that meant something. Of course it didn't mean anything. She was a lunatic reading into things. Per usual. Wasn't that her pattern?

"I guess not the same approach exactly," he said at last, some odd softness to his voice.

Her breath caught at the admission, and his arm around her loosened, just the tiniest bit. If she hadn't been looking for it, she might've missed it. But he had definitely given her more space.

"Vaughn…" What exactly was she going to say? *Look at me sexually! Please!* She was really losing it.

"If someone is holding you like this," he began, sounding uneven and uncertain. Who knew she could make Vaughn Cooper uncertain? It might be the high-light of her year.

"Let me restate the fact that a bad guy grabbing me by surprise would not be holding me like this."

"Would you like me to hold you rougher? Because I can certainly oblige." There was an edge to his voice, a warning, or maybe it was a promise. She couldn't decide.

Nor could she stop the little shiver that went through her. Because even though he probably didn't mean that sexually, it sure sounded sexual. She shouldn't poke at that. She shouldn't poke at him. But somehow her brain and her mouth couldn't get on the same page.

"I think you have to start over because I lost track of what you were talking about."

This time his grasp tightened instead of loosened, but she didn't think it was because he was trying to be a bad guy. In fact, she hoped for a completely different reason. No matter how much she shouldn't.

Chapter 10

Vaughn was getting in over his head. He had lost track of what the hell he was doing in the first place. But he really lost track of what the hell Natalie was doing, because this was all starting to sound way more flirtatious than it should.

He tried to focus on the task at hand. With his arms around her. Why was he standing here? Because the minute he lost track of *the reason*, was the minute he started making mistakes. And he couldn't afford mistakes. No matter how good they smelled. No matter how they shivered in his arms when he said something far, far, far too suggestive.

"One of the important things to remember is that you want to stay as still as possible if someone grabs you." He forced himself to focus. To concentrate. To lecture.

She was quiet for a long humming second. "So, some

strange man grabs me from behind, and I'm supposed to be calm?"

"You're supposed to try. The more you practice this, the better off you'll be. It becomes habit. When something becomes a habit, then you can deal with things instinctually."

"So we're going to stand here with you holding me all day?"

"Well, if you'd stop talking and questioning everything I do, maybe we could get somewhere, Ms. Torres."

She chuckled at that, and he found that he wanted to laugh too. God knew why.

"You always revert to Ms. Torres when you're irritated with me."

"I'm irritated with you a lot."

"I know." But she said it cheerfully, as though it didn't bother her at all.

He sighed. Not sure why the back-and-forth banter gave him that stupidly light feeling again. The feeling he hadn't had in too many years. It revealed too much about how he'd lost himself, a fact he'd been ignoring for a while. And, more, he hated what it told him about Natalie, the effect she had on him, that it might not be some easily controllable thing.

Ha! He could control whatever he chose to. "So rule number one, what was it?"

She sighed. "Rule number one is try to stay still even though that is the opposite of any normal reaction to someone grabbing me from behind."

"Wonderful. Love the attitude," he muttered, trying to shift behind her without…rubbing. "Rule number two is, you want to analyze the situation as best as your mind allows. You want to try to figure out where the weakness is. You want to know what parts of your body have the freedom to move and inflict the most amount of damage. Obviously, if they've grabbed you from behind, you can't utilize your sight. So, unless they're armed, you want to lean back against them and try to discern the areas that are going to be vulnerable."

"So... You want me to lean back into you?"

Oh, hell. No. "Well, we don't necessarily have to practice that part."

"Shouldn't we practice the whole thing? You know the whole the more you practice, the more instinctual it becomes?"

She sounded far too pleased with herself, and he was quickly realizing how badly he'd lost control of this entire situation. It wasn't the fact that he'd initiated this stupid idea, the fact that however many minutes later he still had his arms around Natalie, it was the fact that she was goading him. She was... Hell, she was instigating.

Do not be charmed by that. Do not give into that.

But he must be going a little cabin crazy, because he wasn't sure how much longer he could listen to the sane, rational voice in his head. At some point, he was going to lose this battle. He was almost sure of it.

"Fine. Lean back into me." Yes, he was definitely losing this battle.

She did as he told her, and he tried to keep himself from softening too much into it. Because he wasn't a soft guy, and he prided himself on his ability to keep things *professional*.

So, he held himself tense and hard against the soft enticing curves of her body now leaning into him.

"How do I know if something is vulnerable?"

Her voice was a little ragged and a little whispery,

and he smiled at that. Because, thank God, she wasn't messing with him without having any sort of reaction of her own.

"What's your first instinct?" he asked, his nose all too close to being buried in her thick curls.

She laughed. "I'm a woman who lives in a not totally nice area, Vaughn. Trust me, my first instinct is to go for the family jewels."

"That is the correct instinct, but you have to make sure you can get a shot. If you panic, you lose the chance of hitting a really nasty blow."

"Are you suggesting I test out a really nasty blow on you?"

"No, not at all. We can practice that move without you doing any damage."

"You trust me to practice without doing any damage? Because not so long ago you didn't trust me at all."

It was said casually, but he had the feeling there was more to it. Much like the discussion about why he was protecting her and it being only because it was his job. There was something more she was looking for, and there was something more he should not in one million years give her.

"I let you fire my gun, Natalie. I trust you."

He could feel her take a deep breath, because her back shifted against his chest. This was the danger. That they affected each other, not just physically, but in the things they talked about. In the faith and the trust that they afforded each other. This was dangerous. They were already in a dangerous situation, though, and they didn't need to add any more danger to it.

"So if someone was holding me like this, I would just reach my leg back between their legs and kick, right?"

Thank God she was focusing on the task at hand. If they could both make each other do that, maybe they'd get through this. "Yes, that's part of it. But you also want to see if you can inflict damage at the same time elsewhere. So you want to get an idea if your elbows are free. The way I've got you held right now, as long as you're not wiggling and struggling, you can get in a good elbow to the gut. If you struggle, they're going to tighten their grasp or they're going to bring their other hand around and hold your arms still, as well."

He demonstrated, which was of course also a mistake, because now both of his arms were around her, and though it was from behind, he was essentially hugging her. No matter how many times he told her what she could do to inflict damage, he was still holding her in a tight embrace.

All this *sensation* waged a war on his sanity that he hadn't faced…maybe ever. It had always been so *easy* to remain in control. Except with Natalie.

"So," he said, his voice sounding rusty and ill used in his own ears. "You want to try to lift up your leg and use your elbow at the same time. I want you to practice it, and I want you to put a little force behind it, but not too much. Especially down low."

She chuckled at that, but it was also a little bit strangled. Yes, they were both affected by this. Yes, they were both stupid. And yes, they were teetering on the edge of even larger stupidity.

Somehow, none of that knowledge made him stop.

Natalie figured she was shaking apart. He had to feel that, and as embarrassing as it was, she couldn't possibly stop. He was essentially holding her. This far too attractive man who seemed to have it all together when she felt as together as a lunatic.

He was *holding* her and talking to her about fighting, but the last thing she wanted to do was fight him. She wanted to turn in the circle of his arms. She wanted to press her mouth to his. The more she thought about how much she wanted that, the harder it was to ignore. The harder it was to stop herself from doing it.

But she had to. She had to stop herself. She couldn't keep doing this either, though. She had to make a choice. Either go for it, or make sure, once and for all, her mind understood that there would be no going for it. There would be no nothing. *That* was the choice she knew she had to make.

"Practice moving your elbow and your leg at the same time," Vaughn encouraged.

She laughed again, that strangled, silly-sounding laugh. How could she get her body to move the way she wanted it to when she could barely get her brain to think the way she wanted it to?

"You know, maybe we should eat something instead of all this. Or talk about—"

"Don't be a coward."

"I'm not a coward," she said through gritted teeth. "I'm trying to make a smart choice."

She felt his exhale against the back of her neck. She didn't think a shudder went through him exactly, not the way it went through her, but there was a change in the way he held himself. She couldn't tell if it was tenser or softer; she could only tell that it was different. That this was all incredibly different. She didn't know what to do about it.

"Well, I don't plan on doing this again, so you better get your practice in."

She whirled to face him, and he either let her go, or he was surprised enough by her movement that he didn't try to stop her. "This was your idea. Why won't we do it again?" Something like panic clawed through her. That he wouldn't help, that he wouldn't give her the skills he *said* he was going to give her.

She was probably never going to *be* safe, but she at least wanted some illusion of it. The belief she could shoot a gun or fight under pressure.

"You really have to ask?" he ground out. Even though she'd whirled around, they were still close. Nearly touching, really. Something glittered in his gaze, and she didn't recognize it or understand it.

"Um, yeah! Why on earth—"

Then his mouth was on hers. Just as she'd imagined far too often. All the swirling, nonsensical thoughts and feelings in her brain stopped. All the panic faded. There was nothing except his mouth on her mouth, and his hands tangled in her hair, keeping her steady under the hot assault of his mouth. All while his hard, lean body pressed against hers.

When his tongue touched her lips, she opened them for him, greedily. She threw everything she had into that kiss. Somehow she felt braver than she had learning hand-to-hand self-defense. She felt stronger than when she was shooting his gun. The kiss was better than everything that had happened to her for far too long in her life.

He was strong, and he was sure, and she wanted all of that. All of him. She wanted the way it curled inside of her, pleasure and light, breathlessness and a kind of steadiness she didn't know existed.

"I can't be doing this." But he said it against her mouth, as though he had no intention of stopping. She didn't want to have any intention of stopping. She didn't want to stop until this aching need inside her was completely and utterly obliterated.

She wrapped her arms around his neck, arching against the hard wall that was him, and somehow *she* felt powerful and in control, even as the need and desire ping-ponged through her completely and utterly *out* of control.

No matter how wrong it was, no matter how little they should do it. It was what she wanted, and didn't she deserve a little bit of what she wanted? What she wanted without worrying about if her choices were furthering her investigations into Gabby's disappearance. Her whole life had come to center around Gabby, and this had nothing to do with it except that she and Vaughn were in the same place at the same time.

Oh, and he's trying to work to help you find your sister and keep you safe.

She wasn't sure who pulled away first. She would've expected it to be Vaughn, but the insidious voice in her head that was telling her this was a betrayal of her sister and her quest to find Gabby made her pause just as much as him coming to his senses probably caused him to pause.

"I apologize. I apologize. This has gotten out of control. It is all my fault. I'm sorry. That was…"

"Really great?" she interjected, pressing her fingers to her kiss-swollen lips. Really, *really* great. Had *anyone* ever kissed her like that? With that searing intensity she didn't think… Even if that was all it ever was, she'd never forget it.

He glanced at her then, and for the first time his eyes were very, very blue. The gray had diminished, and the blue that was left was warm, and she felt like that meant something. That it *could* mean something, anyway.

"I've never…" He cleared his throat and squared his shoulders, slowly coming back to Ranger Cooper. All business, no pleasure. All by the book, conventional, Vaughn Cooper, Texas Ranger.

What a shame.

"This was a mistake. While I freely admit that I am physically attracted to you, any involvement between us could only cause problems with this case. I know how much this case means to you. It means a lot to me as well. This has gone unsolved too long, all of it, and I need to get to a point where I'm solving things. So, this can't happen again."

She chewed on her bottom lip, trying to determine how to change his mind. Except, she knew he was right. Any kind of romantic thing between them could only get in the way of this case that was so important to both of them.

She could keep flirting with him, and pushing his buttons, and wanting more, but the bottom line was everyone involved would be hurt.

There was a selfish part of her that didn't want to care. For the first time in so long, she didn't want to *care*. It had been so long since she'd put her wants or needs ahead of someone else's, except in her want and need to find Gabby.

"Say something," Vaughn said, his voice that rough,

ragged thing that shivered across every last nerve ending in her body.

Now she knew what it felt like to have that firm, unrelenting mouth on hers. Surprisingly soft, though un-
surprisingly demanding. It felt like a reprieve from the
harsh realities of where they were and what they had to
do. The harsh reality of the possibility of this case re-
maining unsolved, and she could remain in danger, and
her questions about Gabby could never be answered.

It was silly and awful to be concerned about a kiss.
To be wrapped up in it and want more of it. Her whole
focus should be Gabby until she could find her. She
was closer than she'd ever been. To get distracted by
Vaughn now…

"I don't know what to say," she finally managed to
get out. Which was the truth. She didn't know what to
say to him when so much of what she wanted was simply to forget, to lose herself in a kiss and more, and not
think or *fear*.

At a time when they probably didn't have the luxury
of forgetting much of anything. At any point someone
could burst into this cabin and take out both of them.
They could pretend that she was learning how to shoot a
gun in self-defense all they wanted, but the bottom line
was those things only worked when you had a warning,
when you knew what was coming.

"You're just a little mixed up because I saved you,
so to speak. It's a little case of rescue wor—"

"No," she snapped, most of the *want* cooling into irritation. No surprise he could flick it off like a switch.
"I'm not stupid, and I'm not mixed up. You are the one
who kissed me. I didn't initiate that. Don't insult me
that way. I know my feelings, and I know why I kissed

you back. It has zero to do with *rescue worship*, you arrogant jerk."

"I only meant…"

"No, I don't want to know what you meant. You kissed me. Accept that. Or should I worry that you're just mesmerized by my victimhood, and you only kissed me because you can't keep your brain intact when a victim is around?"

His mouth firmed, grim and angry. Good, because she was angry too. How dare he say that? She wasn't so stupid she thought he was hot just because he'd saved her. That wasn't what was between them at all, and she wouldn't let him get away with that kind of distorted thinking.

"I just think we don't know each other that well."

Again she scoffed. "You know, I'd love an excuse for why this happened, for why I feel the way I do. But the bottom line is, we're attracted to each other. More, whether we want to admit it or not, we like each other. So stop making excuses. Let's deal with the reality of the situation. Isn't that what you told me? That we can't deal with what-ifs and maybes. We have to look at the facts."

"I can't tell you how little I like my own words being used against me," he returned, and though his voice had a cutting edge, there was the smallest hint of a smile on his lips.

"Especially when they're right?"

He smiled, one of those real, rare smiles that made her heart do acrobatics in her chest. He could stand to smile more. He could stand to laugh more.

You don't know him. Maybe he smiles and laughs all the time when you're not around.

But she really felt like she knew him, no matter how often she tried to talk herself out of that.

"Especially when they're right. So…"

"So, you kissed me." She squared her shoulders, determined to be an adult. Determined to take charge of her life in the few places she could. "We're attracted to each other, and as much as it pains me to say it, you're right. We don't have the time or the luxury of pursuing anything. So maybe it's best if we just pretend that it never happened."

"Right. Pretend it never happened. I can do that."

Except his gaze was on her mouth, and she didn't think she could do that if he…looked at her with those heated blue eyes. "Maybe you can tell me all your exwife's complaints about you so that I know what annoyances to look for when I'm overcome by attraction."

He smiled wryly. "I think somehow you'll manage, but it's mostly your average 'you care too much about your job and not enough about our marriage.'"

"Do you agree with her assessment?" Which wasn't her business, at all, and she wanted to be appalled at herself for asking personal questions. But she wanted to know, and she'd had to gain a certain comfort in quizzing people in her pursuit of information about Gabby.

He shrugged, finally looking away from her mouth. "Sometimes. I take my job very seriously. There were times I had to miss things. There were times I was in danger and she was scared, and I get why that was hard on her."

"I feel like there's a 'but' coming."

"No but. You can't… You can't have a marriage with someone who doesn't understand your passion. I'm sure it is my failing that my passion wasn't our marriage."

"I guess that's understandable."

"I take it you've never been married."

"No, not even close. The only relationship I've really had ended because he thought I spent too much time obsessing about Gabby."

"So, great, we have more things in common. That's really what we need right now."

She had to laugh at his sarcasm. She had to laugh at the circumstances. At what the hell she thought she was doing.

But she understood what it was like to lose a relationship because you were wrapped up in something else. Something bigger than you. Something that was excessively important to you that you couldn't let go of.

"Do you regret…not changing your dedication level to police work? I mean… Would you go back and do things differently?"

"I've thought about that a lot, actually. It's been three years since she said she wanted to get divorced. The thing is, I didn't… Maybe it shows how far gone I am, but I didn't think that I was that inattentive all the time. Sometimes, certain cases got under my skin a little bit extra, but I stopped going undercover for her. I stopped… Why the hell are we talking about this?"

"I had the crazy idea that it might make me not like you."

"Did it work?" he asked.

"No, I think it might've done the opposite." She wanted to step closer again, but his demeanor kept her where she was. He had made the decision this could only be a negative distraction on a very important case. She had to respect that decision. He deserved that respect.

"I should probably get my sleep in."

She smiled ruefully. "Yeah, you wouldn't want a lack of sleep to affect your decision-making skills."

He laughed at that, a little bitterly. She almost felt bad that she'd pushed him this far. "I'm sorry," she offered to his retreating back.

He stopped and turned, eyebrows drawn together. "What are you sorry for?"

"I know you kissed me and all, but I kept pushing things, and I didn't have to. It had just…been a long time since I'd wanted something solely for myself. You know?"

He swallowed, visibly, audibly. "Yeah, I know," he said, a little too meaningfully, a little too much for her to not feel as though the stopping was the mistake, not doing it in the first place.

But he turned, in that rigid, policeman way of his, and walked down the hallway.

Chapter 11

Vaughn tried to sleep, he really did. He caught bits and pieces of rest, but every time he started to doze, his mind went to that kiss. The way it had rioted through him. The way his completely irrational and stupid body had taken over.

He'd had to kiss her. It had been like there was no choice. Like his life depended on having his mouth on hers. He knew that was stupid now, but in the moment it had seemed imperative.

In the moment, he hadn't been able to think of anything else except her. The easy way she kissed him back, the way everything about her seemed to fit against him in just the right way. He'd been as lost as he'd ever been in his whole entire life.

In the aftermath, he didn't know what to do about it. Apparently run away like some immature teenager was his answer. Cowardly, all in all.

But the more he talked to her, the more he wanted to kiss her again. The more he wanted to ignore everything that his training had taught him about getting mixed up with witnesses or victims or what have you. He wanted to ignore his own personal moral code and have Natalie Torres in his damn bed.

He groaned into his pillow. He felt about as frustrated as a teenager, but with the common sense of a man to make it all that much more irritating. Never in his life had he been tempted away from following his duty to the letter. Not like this. He'd always been able to be calm and rational, even when the stray thought of being the opposite had come up. He'd never gotten overly violent with a witness or perp. He'd always been calm, rational, sensible and, yes, conventional Ranger Cooper.

Why the hell was Natalie the difference maker?

After three hours of more frustrating self talk than actual sleep, Vaughn gave up. There was no use wasting time. He could be researching Callihan. He could be looking at the case. There were a wide variety of ways to employ his mind that wasn't lying there with an ill-timed erection, trying to work out why he was so affected by a woman.

A beautiful, engaging woman who made him have the most foolish thoughts. Like, maybe she...understood. The police work being a bit of an obsession thing. She had her own obsessive situation that had ended a relationship.

He got out of his bed and looked out the window. He needed to get his bearings, and maybe looking at those mountains in the distance and remembering all he'd done to get him here could help him.

God knew he needed help.

The landscape was as barren as it had been since they'd arrived. Three days now. Three days and no one had found them or come after them. As long as this kept up, Captain Dean was going to call him home sooner rather than later. And they'd found nothing. No connections, no clues, nothing to help.

He glanced at the closet where he kept the corded phone. Since there was no cell service out here, they kept a landline open in case of emergency, but neither he nor his sister cared for people being able to call them, so they didn't keep the phones hooked up.

But sometimes a phone call was necessary.

He grabbed the phone and hooked it up to the jack in the corner of the room.

The emails from Bennet were quick and usually in list form. If he actually talked to him, he might read some frustration level in his partner's tone. And, be able to ask about the time they had left without the chance of Natalie reading the answer.

Making a phone call certainly had nothing to do with having to distract himself from the gorgeous woman in the living room of his secluded cabin. Zero connection to the fact she wanted him seemingly as much as he wanted her.

With irritated jabs, he punched in the number to the office and was patched through to Stevens.

"Still nothing," Bennet greeted him, thankfully not beating around the bush.

"I figured as much," he returned on a sigh. "How much longer are they going to let me keep her out here?"

"It'll depend on the arson inspector's report. We should be getting it today. I can call down and try to speed things up."

"Yeah, I'd like to know what time frame we're working with here."

"That bad?"

Vaughn almost let it slip that it was *terrible*. But not for the reason Bennet would think. He clamped his lips together just in time to rewire his thoughts. "I don't like that we're not getting anywhere, and we might have to bring her back in the middle of it."

"Yeah, this case…" Bennet trailed off. "Without Herman, we're screwed. We've been trying to find someone he works with, someone who'll talk. Nothing."

"Nothing on those guys from the gas station?"

"They had warrants, so they're locked up, but we had nothing on him. Not who they were working for, and not what they were trying to do to you and Ms. Torres."

"I don't like this. It's too quiet, and it's too easy." Which was as true as the fact he wasn't sure how much longer sanity was going to reign in this cabin.

"I'll call Arson, see who I can light a fire under. I'll email you the full report the minute I get it."

"Yeah. Thanks."

"In the meantime, you could relax. Laugh at my hilarious jokes. Unclench."

"When have you never known me to relax?" Vaughn returned gruffly.

"That's kind of the point. There's nothing you can do. There's nothing you can change from where you are. Your only worry right now is keeping the woman safe. Which should be easy enough in the middle of nowhere. You know I'll find any more information before you do out in the desert. So, watch a movie. Make some popcorn. Have some small talk."

"I hate small talk." Especially small talk that had

to do with his ex-wife, and any shared sucking at relationships.

"The point is, you can kill yourself over this case, or you can have some sense and save up all your frustrated anger into dedicated business for when it will actually be helpful to us. When you're back in Austin."

"As encouraging as ever, Bennet."

"I'm here for you, buddy."

Even though Bennet was suggesting he relax, when that was the last thing he could do, it was… Well, damn, it was nice to know someone cared enough to suggest it. But that didn't take away his ticking time bomb. "Be straight with me. How much time I got?"

Bennet sighed. "If they get something in the arson investigation, some kind of clue, you might have a few more days. But if there isn't a shred of evidence, and there never has been before, he's going to want you back right away."

Vaughn pinched the bridge of his nose, trying to ward off a headache, and swore.

"Relax. I'll do what I can to get you more time. The arson report comes up empty, I'll make sure it gets lost in red tape for a few days, best I can."

"Thanks."

"You really think The Stallion has something to do with Torres's missing sister?"

Vaughn blew out a breath. "I think it's more than possible. You?" Because he had to know it wasn't just his feelings for Natalie clouding that gut feeling.

"Yeah, man. I do. Herman talking about keeping the girls… I keep going back to that. Gotta be something there. Something that got Herman killed."

"Yeah. Well, I'll be waiting for an email."

"Later. Stay safe."

Vaughn turned to face the door of his room and then paced. He wouldn't tell Natalie anything until he had the arson report. Everything hinged on that, and he hated the idea that there would be nothing in it. Just like there was always nothing in all of these cases.

Maybe it was hopeless. Maybe they *should* head back. He'd find a way to keep an eye on her, but maybe, in the end, this had all been an overreaction. A mistake.

Then he heard the crash.

Natalie was brooding. She tried to talk herself out of the brood, but that never worked. Certainly not when there was emotional brooding, and sexually frustrated brooding, and her-life-was-a-mess-and-she-was-worried-about-sex brooding.

She should be looking at Vaughn's computer, poring over the trafficking case, finding commonalities. Anything but staring at the wall reliving that kiss over and over again. Because it *wasn't* going to happen again.

So, why not relive it if that's all you're going to get?

She pushed off the couch in a fit of annoyance. The few times her personal life interfered with her happiness, she'd been able to throw herself into the minutiae of Gabby's case. Whether it was because Vaughn was now hooked up in Gabby's case, or he was somehow that much more potent than all her other personal problems, nothing about drowning herself in her sister's case was appealing.

But what else was there to do in this godforsaken landscape? She was stuck in this cabin while Vaughn soundly slept in his room. Jerk.

She glared down the hallway as if she glared hard

enough, he might feel her ire. Not that it would matter.
He wasn't going to do anything about it, was he? And
neither was she, because the sleeping jerk was right. So
torturing herself over it was downright—

She heard the distant sound of...something, so in-
congruous to the quiet she'd been living in for the past
days. Though the sound immediately stopped, Natalie
knew she'd heard something, and it wasn't coyotes this
time. Whatever the sound had been, it was distinctly
mechanical. Like a car.

Before she had a chance to even think about what to
do, she was already moving toward the hallway, moving toward Vaughn. But a sudden crash caused her to
jerk in surprise so violently that she stumbled. She fell
to her hands and knees and looked back at the front of
the house where the crash had come from.

The sound repeated, and she saw the door shake just
as Vaughn entered the hallway.

"Stand up and get behind me. Now."

She scrambled to her feet and did as he ordered, the
grim set to his mouth and the icy cold in his gaze crys-
talizing the fact this wasn't a *mistake* or a random animal this time. Fear jittered through her, much like it
had in the gas station when she'd been at the mercy of
those strange men, and all she could do was shake and
listen to Vaughn.

He had his weapon drawn, and the minute she was
close enough, he jerked her behind him.

"No matter what happens, you stay behind me. Got
it?"

"But—" She could think of a hundred scenarios
where she would have to not stand behind him, but before she could voice any of them, another crash shook

the door. She had a feeling that it would only take one more harsh blow for it to open.

"What are these morons doing?" he muttered. He held his gun at shoulder level, but his other arm was extended behind him, keeping her in the box of his arm and the wall.

With absolutely no warning, he spun and shot his weapon, right over her shoulder. A thud sounded, and then a wounded grunt, and when Natalie caught up enough with the whirlwind of action and looked behind them, she saw a large man's body slumped on the floor.

"Diversion," he muttered, grabbing her arm and pulling her toward the man's body.

Vaughn kept her behind him as he approached the man who was gurgling and thrashing and reaching for a gun he'd apparently dropped. Vaughn kicked it out of his reach easily.

"Pick it up, Natalie. Train it at the front door. Anyone walks in, you shoot."

Natalie tried to agree, to nod, but she stood there shell-shocked and shaking, and—

"Natalie." This time Vaughn spared her a glance. "You can do it. You have to do it. All right?"

It steadied her. Not that she stopped shaking or stopped being afraid, but it gave her something to hold on to, something to focus on, and she managed to grab the man's gun with shaking fingers.

"Put your back to mine."

"I don't—"

"Turn around, look at the door and lean your back against mine. From here on out, you don't move unless I do. We're always touching, unless I say otherwise." He said the command low, and the man flailing about on the floor probably could have heard it, but he seemed pretty preoccupied with the bullet wound in his shoulder.

Natalie blew out a breath and did as Vaughn instructed. She pressed her back to his, absorbing the warmth and the strength, and focused on the door in the front of her. The crashing seemed to have stopped, but she held the gun up, hoping she'd be able to shoot an unfamiliar weapon. Hoping harder she wouldn't have to shoot anyone.

"Who the hell are you?" Vaughn growled.

Since Natalie was watching the door, she couldn't see what the man did in response. But it sounded like the man merely spat in response.

"You'll regret that one later."

Natalie couldn't suppress a shiver at the cold note of fury in Vaughn's voice.

Another crash sounded, and the front door shook again, but Vaughn seemed less than worried about it. She, on the other hand, was *more* than worried about it.

"What are you after?"

The man only groaned, still not saying anything.

"This is your last chance to talk. You don't talk when I ask, I don't ask. And you don't want to find out what happens then."

The man only cursed, and Vaughn remained a still, calm, rock-hard presence behind her. His warmth and his strength soothed a small portion of her concern over her too fast and hard breathing.

"Natalie, link arms with me." He held his arm back, and she did as he ordered. Then he was maneuvering her, always keeping her protected from the man on the floor.

He led her by her linked arm into his room, keeping his gun trained at the wounded man. He'd stopped writhing and was looking increasingly pale, though he kept his hand on the wound on his shoulder.

Natalie looked away.

"I need you to grab the backpack out of my closet. It's black, and it should be very heavy."

Natalie swallowed, and she didn't trust her voice. But she did what he asked. Vaughn's closet was freakishly neat and tidy, so it was easy to find the backpack.

"Is there anything you absolutely without a shadow of a doubt need from your room?"

She had so few belongings left, tears stung her eyes thinking of leaving any of it. But she also didn't want to, oh, die, so she supposed she could do without. "My ID, maybe? Unless you don't think we have—

His mouth firmed. "I don't want to leave behind anything that might give them more information on you. We're going to link arms again. We're going to get your ID. Do not look at the man on the floor. Keep looking straight ahead until we're inside, and then grab your stuff immediately. Then we'll go out the window. Or at least try."

"And if we can't?" There could be fifty men surrounding the cabin as they spoke. There could be—

"One thing at a time." He maneuvered her across the hall, his grip firm enough to help her push away the thousands of terrible outcomes.

"Go," Vaughn said gently, unlocking their arms. Because she couldn't have come up with a thought on her own to save her life, she went straight for her purse.

It was strange how unmoored and that much shakier she felt without Vaughn's arm connected to hers, but she pressed on. She grabbed her purse, and Vaughn, keeping his gun trained on the door, rummaged around in the closet and pulled out a backpack. It was pink and sparkly and utterly ridiculous.

He gave it a disgusted grunt but held it out to her. "It'll be easier to get through the mountains with your hands free instead of worrying about a purse. Shove it in there and then strap it on your back."

Again, Natalie couldn't trust her voice to actually come out of her throat, so she simply did as she was told. She shoved her purse into the outrageous backpack and then strapped it to her back. Meanwhile, Vaughn pulled on his backpack.

She looked down at her hands, the gun she held, the power she had. This was her protection. This would give her a chance. She hoped.

"You hold on to that. No matter what. If it comes down to it, you'll use it."

"What are they after?" she asked, her voice a shaky, squeak of a thing that would've embarrassed her if she'd had time for it.

He didn't bother to answer. She understood that he didn't have time to stand there and explain things to her. But she couldn't help the fact that she didn't understand anything about this. Not a thing.

"Keep your eye on the door. Keep your gun ready."

It took every ounce of focus and control to do as he said and not watch what he did. She heard the rustle of curtains, and possibly the squeak of the window. Meanwhile, all she could do was watch the door to this room, and fervently pray that no one tried to walk through it.

A shot rang out, and Natalie jerked violently. Through some lucky twist of fate, she didn't pull her own trigger.

"Follow me. Now." Vaughn's voice was terse and urgent as ever, and her feet responded to the order even if her mind whirled.

Though a million questions went through her head, she followed Vaughn out the window. It was only then that she realized there was a sound louder than the harsh flow of her breathing.

Once she was outside, she noticed there was another man slumped on the ground. But he was screaming and grabbing his leg. Vaughn paid him no attention. He was too busy scanning the surroundings.

"Stay at my back."

She was glad he kept saying it, because in her shell-shocked state she would've forgotten. She would've stood there still and silent and barely functioning. This might be the only situation in her entire life where she was *ecstatic* for someone to keep reminding her what she was supposed to do.

She stayed at Vaughn's back, mirroring his movements as he walked toward the screaming man. Vaughn spared him the most disgusted of glances, and then grabbed the large, intimidating looking gun that had fallen out of the man's reach.

"How many more of you are there?"

"Screw off."

Vaughn's mouth was a harsh, grim line. "So none. Perfect. Now, when you crawl your way back to your boss, tell him the next time someone comes after me, it better be the man himself. Because his lackeys are damn bad at this." Vaughn gave the man a swift kick in the chest so the man fell backward, screaming all over again.

Then Vaughn started walking, and Natalie had to

remind herself to follow him. It wasn't hard. Not when he exuded calm and confidence and *safety*.

He went to the front of the cabin and there was nothing that she could see, but Vaughn jerked his chin at a vehicle in the distance. "That's where they parked their car. We'll go in the opposite direction in case there are more shooters coming."

Natalie looked in the opposite direction. "But it's just...mountains."

"I hope you're ready to camp, Nat. Because God knows how long we're going to be out there."

Chapter 12

The sun was beginning to set, and Vaughn knew he needed to find a place to camp. But the adrenaline still pumped through him, and the last thing he wanted to do was stop.

He looked back at Natalie, who was…struggling. Struggling to keep up with his pace, and he thought maybe struggling to keep her composure after such a whirlwind of events. He was being an ass for not caring more about what she felt, about the toll this was taking on her.

"It's just a little bit farther. There is a series of caves up here. They'll make good shelter for the night."

"Caves?" she asked, trepidation edging her voice.

"It's perfectly safe if you know what to look for."

"What do you mean, 'if you know what to look for'?"

"Just… Trust me."

"I don't think I have a choice," she said, sounding exhausted and like she was in a little bit of shock. He couldn't blame her.

Maybe if he distracted her she might make it the last little distance they needed to travel. "You didn't happen to recognize any of those men, did you?" Because interrogating her would be distracting. He made such *excellent* comforting choices.

"No, did you?"

"No. And with no cell service, I can't call in a description to Stevens." He glanced up at the quickly fading light. It was a stunner of a sunset, pinks and oranges, a riot of colors. But how could he care about beauty when he was worried about Natalie?

Which was a problem he didn't have time to consider.

He found the entrance to a cave that looked suitable. Luckily, he'd been exploring the area around the cabin since he was a teenager. He'd been dedicated to making it a safe space for his sister, and he'd spent a considerable amount of time figuring out what that would take. Which meant he had spent some time camping in these very caves, hiking all these mountains.

Unfortunately, he didn't have the equipment he usually had, but he was a Texas Ranger. He knew how to make do.

"So you think more people are after us?"

"Two teams of two so far. I imagine if that piece of trash takes my message back to his boss, we'll see an escalation."

"Do you think he will? Do you think The Stallion would really come after us himself?"

"I don't know, but I'm tired of dealing with his lackeys." Which was an understatement. These weak attacks were practically an insult.

Though the diversion of the man trying to break in the front while another snuck in the back had almost worked. Way too close for comfort.

Natalie inhaled and exhaled, loudly. Fear and exhaustion evident in every breath she took at this point.

"Let me double-check this cave. As long as I don't see evidence of…" Noticing the wariness on her face, he didn't finish his sentence. She didn't need to know what creatures might lurk in the caves. It was best she knew as little as possible.

"Stay put for a few minutes. Keep your eyes on the horizon."

She nodded, and as he ducked into the cave, he couldn't fight the wave of admiration he felt toward her. She didn't argue with him, she didn't get too scared to move. She did what he asked, and he was able to relax enough to trust her to handle some of it.

Not everyone could do that. Hell, there were some kids who couldn't hack it in the police academy with as much poise as Natalie had showed. Even scared as she was.

He did a quick survey of the cave. They wouldn't go very far in. Just enough to have shelter from the elements. There were no signs of predatory wildlife at this particular point, and he'd have to hope that held out for the night.

He returned to Natalie at the opening of the cave, noticing the way she looked around the mountains. Wide-eyed. Awed. Afraid. He wished there was something he could do to keep her mind off of all that was going on around them.

You know what you could do.

He ruthlessly shoved that troublesome voice out of his head and focused on the task at hand.

"I don't have the gear I normally have to camp, but I have this emergency pack, and it'll get us through."

"What if someone finds us?" she asked, those wide brown eyes settling on him. He had to push away the stab of guilt, the harsh desire to comfort her at any cost, with any words, with any touch.

But it wouldn't serve either of them to lie to her. "We have three guns and a tactical advantage, and we'll be watching for them."

She nodded at that and stepped inside the cave with him. He took off his backpack and nodded at her to do the same. He started to rummage for something he could put down so she could try to rest, or maybe some food, but he noted that she was shaking.

He didn't know if it had just started or if she'd been doing it the whole time, but he found a sweatshirt from his pack and handed it to her.

She shook her head. "Unfortunately it's not cold," she said with a self-deprecating laugh. "I just…can't seem to stop."

He swallowed, because his first instinct was to pull her into a hug. Quite honestly, even if he wasn't attracted to her, that would be his instinct. As a police officer, he knew how powerful it could be to simply offer someone a shoulder or a brief, simple embrace. It could give them the courage to make it through a really tragic situation.

Which meant he had to swallow that attraction, and

act as though she were anyone else. Anyone else he would offer this to. So he stood and thrust his gun to his hip holster, where it would remain in easy reach. He took the gun she'd been carrying all this time from her shaking fingers and set it behind them. If they showed up, the shooters from the cabin would be unable to sneak around them, and the weapon would be within easy reach.

He steeled himself for what he knew would be a shock of arousal and need, and drew her into the circle of his arms.

She shook there, and he thought she might have cried. Just a little bit of a sob. Against his shoulder. It was strange to feel capable in that moment. To feel like the Ranger he'd been trained to be.

But for the first time in a long time, with Natalie in his arms, he felt in control of the situation. Because he would do anything in his power to protect her.

And that was going to be everything.

Natalie didn't love that she was crying, but it couldn't be helped. It wasn't like she was going to get any privacy to do it any time soon.

Might as well get it out now while there weren't people directly after them. Just indirectly, at some point, in the future. Probably. Did they have another few days? Or were they going have to camp in the mountains for weeks?

She couldn't bring herself to ask Vaughn any of those questions because he always answered them either far too truthfully, or not at all. So she focused on evening her breathing and getting rid of the tears, and finding that inner strength that had gotten her this far.

As she slowly calmed herself, she realized that Vaughn was rubbing his hand up and down her back. It reminded her of the night of the fire, the way he'd put that competent, strong hand on her back and it had been an odd comfort. But it hadn't been personal.

This felt *personal*. Intimate.

She wasn't crying anymore. No, she was absorbing. The strength and warmth of Vaughn, his arms around her, and the gentle, soothing motion of his hand up and down her spine.

It didn't make camping in a cave any more appealing, but it made it a little less daunting. Vaughn would keep her safe. That she knew.

She sighed, and relaxed. Into him, into the embrace. He didn't stiffen against it. Instead, he softened. Vaughn Cooper softening against her. She smiled and burrowed in deeper. Holding him closer.

"I'm going to get you out of this in one piece," he said, his voice a fierce whisper. "One way or another."

"Are you supposed to make impossible promises like that?" she asked, listening to the steady, reassuring beat of his heart.

"I shouldn't," he said, sounding a little disgusted with himself. "But you should know that I'm going to do whatever it takes. I know I can't tell you not to worry, but I can try to give you some comfort."

She looked up at him, still in the warm embrace of his arms. She smiled, and it was odd that she *could* do that in this situation, but something about his fervent need to make her feel safe, made her feel just that.

Maybe safe was an exaggeration, but she felt like there was a chance they'd survive this. A good one. Because she trusted Vaughn to do exactly as he said.

"How much distraction would it be if you kissed me?"

Some of that softness left him, a tension creeping into the set of his body. "Natalie…"

She wouldn't be so easily deterred. "I'm just saying that if you want me to feel safe, that would probably do it."

He exhaled something like a laugh.

Then he did the strangest, most unexpected thing. He actually kissed her. Lowering his mouth to hers, something gentle and sweet. The antithesis of the hot and wild thing that had passed between them earlier. This was a comfort, and that made her heart shudder with things she had no business feeling. And yet, she didn't want to stop feeling them.

She wrapped her arms around his neck, deepening the kiss, pressing herself more firmly against him.

His arm pulled her tighter to him, and one hand came up to cup her neck. The warmth of his hand there, the pressure of it, the heat of his mouth and the way his tongue traced her lips and then entered. It was soft and comforting, but it was also more. It was hot and searing. It was a revelation, because she'd never had anything like this. It was fire and sweetness, it was passion and comfort. It was everything she wanted, and all she'd had to do was ask.

She stroked her fingers over his short hair and then down his neck. She wanted to somehow know him. The shape of him. The feel of him. She wanted to understand the texture of his hair, the path of his skin. She wanted more.

That hit her. She wanted more. She wanted it all. She didn't care that they were in a *cave* somewhere. She didn't care that horrible people were after her. Because everything had been going wrong for so long that she just wanted more of this thing that didn't feel wrong.

She wanted good. She wanted Vaughn.

She trailed her hands down his chest. The soft cotton of the T-shirt he wore did nothing to hide what compact, lean muscle he was. Everything about him was hard. Strong. But she thought maybe, just maybe, there was some softness under there. In the way he wanted to protect her, in the way his mouth explored hers.

Even if there was no gentleness in him, he used his strength as a kind of softness. He was a protector, and that was his gentleness. She admired that. Deeply.

"Natalie…"

He didn't have to speak further, she could feel him pulling back, if not physically, mentally.

She clutched him tighter, not willing to let this go. She'd sacrifice her pride for this. "No, don't."

"For every minute we spend doing this, we are putting ourselves in danger. Every minute one of us isn't watching the cave entrance and paying attention to our surroundings, we are increasing the danger that we are in. Exponentially."

"I don't *care*." She knew that was stupid, but she couldn't bring herself to care. Her care was worn out and afraid and *tired*. "We're already in danger, what's a little more?"

She trailed her hand farther down his chest, across the clear indentation of his abs, doing something far bolder and more brazen than she'd ever done. Something she almost couldn't believe she was doing herself.

She placed her palm over the hard length of his erection.

He groaned, sounding tortured and desperate. She smiled, not minding making him tortured or desperate in the least.

"My job is to keep you safe. I can't... Do that..."

"Right now I want your job to be to make me forget. I want to forget I'm scared. I want to forget my life was burned to the ground. I want to forget that I'm on the run and in danger. I want to forget that my sister's missing and there has been nothing I could do about it for years upon years. Vaughn, I want to forget. Let me forget."

She traced the hard length of him, and his grip on her tightened.

"It would be a dereliction of my duty..."

"Derelict with me. Please." She stepped back from the tight embrace of his arms, and he let her. Probably thinking that that was going to be it. That she had come to her senses. But that was the absolute last thing she had come to. She pulled the T-shirt over her head and tossed it toward the backpacks on the ground.

"Natalie." His voice was all gravel, but his eyes were hot and on her.

"I want you, Vaughn. I don't care where we are, what it takes. I want this, and it's been so long since I've had anything I wanted."

She could tell he was fighting a war with his conscience, so she did her best to win it for her side. She shimmied out of the shorts she'd been wearing. Because the ground was rocky, she left her shoes on. It was probably a ridiculous sight, her in her underwear and tennis shoes. Based on Vaughn's tense reaction, she thought she was getting her point across, though.

He took a step toward her, and because she couldn't quite read his expression, whether he was going to insist she put her clothes back on or possibly do it for her, whether he was going to give in to touch her, she held out a hand to stop him.

"No, no, no. Lose your shirt and pants first."

He stood there, a solid wall of granite. The fact he was even standing there, even debating, was a triumph. It was a win.

He clenched his fingers into fists and then relaxed them, and they went to the hem of his shirt. She exhaled the breath she'd been holding. She was fairly sure that as he lifted his shirt over his head, she whimpered.

He was… Perfection. He had abs and muscles and was just this powerfully broad man whose impressive upper body narrowed to mouthwatering lean hips. She wanted to trace each cut and dip. Possibly with her tongue.

"Pants too," she said, though it was really more of a squeak than her voice.

Again there was a moment of pause. As though he couldn't believe he was doing this. But that didn't stop him. Thank goodness, it didn't stop him. He undid the button of his jeans and then the zipper and pushed them down. Underneath he wore a loose pair of black boxer shorts, but as loose as they were, she could still see the evidence of his arousal. She could see everything. And he was gorgeous and perfect and she wanted nothing more than to be underneath him. Or on top of him. Or both, alternating.

"Am I allowed to approach now?" he asked, the gravel still in his voice, but a hint of humor underneath.

She opened her mouth to say yes. In her mind she said the word regally and coolly. As though she were in control of the situation, as though she were in control of the rioting sparks inside her. In reality, nothing came out of her too-tight throat, and she just had to nod.

When Vaughn grinned at her—at *her*—nothing else mattered. Not the danger they were in, not what might happen afterward. All that mattered was him and now.

He took a step toward her, but his hands didn't reach out to touch. He stood so they were still a couple inches from being toe to toe. He looked at her, right in the eye. It felt more intimate than standing there in her underwear. The fact that he was looking at her, seemed to look *into* her. That was… Somehow huge and emotional.

"We're going to move a little deeper into the cave. That'll be a safer option. We'll have more of a warning if something happens."

"Remember when I said you were so very conventional?"

"I'm a *man*, Natalie. But I am a man determined to keep you safe, no matter what."

"Are you at least also a man determined to make love to me, not just take off his clothes?"

For the first time since this whole thing had gone wildly out of control, he didn't hesitate. "Yes. More than determined."

It was her turn to grin, and she helped him gather all of their stuff, and even though they were each holding weapons and had backpacks strapped to their bare backs, bundles of clothes in their arms, he held her hand.

He led her farther into the cave, having already pulled the flashlight out of his pack. She tried not to think too deeply about him searching every nook and cranny, and what might be hiding in any of those little places. But he found a little…corner almost, that gave them something like a wall between them and the opening of the cave.

"It'll keep us out of sight, but you're going to have to be quiet."

She giggled at that. How had they gone from running from men with guns to…quietly having sex in a cave?

"What a shame."

"The only shame is that I can't see you."

Those words clutched around her heart and her lungs. She could scarcely suck in the breath to tell him that… She didn't know what she wanted to tell him. She didn't recognize this overfull feeling in her chest. Excitement and lust or something more? She wasn't sure she wanted to delve too far into that possibility.

So she simply held her arms open for him, and he stepped inside. His mouth took hers, his body took hers, and she gave. Everything she had. In a way she never would've imagined. But knowing she had so little, and there was so much against her, it made her open up in a way she's always been scared to.

Because for the first time in her life, she really had nothing to lose. Okay, maybe her life, but she wasn't so sure she was in control of that.

This, she was in control of. Or at least partially in control of.

Vaughn's hands touched her gently and reverently, as though he was trying to find just where she like to be touched. Just where to stroke to make her forget where the hell they were.

In a cave. On the run. Giving themselves to each other. She couldn't think of anyone she'd rather give herself to, and she had the sneaking suspicion that had very little to do with the danger they were in.

Chapter 13

There was the smallest voice in the back of Vaughn's head telling him to stop this madness. But Natalie was nearly naked, all smooth skin and tantalizing curves in the not-at-all-sufficient flashlight beam. Everything about her was like a soft place to land, and the last thing he should be doing right now was landing. He should be leading and fighting and protecting.

But the driving need of his body had taken over. He wanted Natalie as his. No matter how he tried to tell himself that it was wrong, or the wrong time, or some other combination of those things, it got lost somewhere. Usually about the time he had to actually consider taking his mouth from hers, or his hands from her body. He couldn't stand the thought.

Especially when her mouth was so sweet under his, and her hands were so determined to explore him. She seemed to touch every piece of him. A finger traced the scar on his shoulder from a stab wound he'd gotten undercover. She poked her finger into the dip of his hip. But the most brain melting was the fact that she kept arching against him, a slow, sensuous rhythm that made him completely crazy. Incapable of thinking of anything else but being inside her.

He had no business thinking that or wanting that or most especially doing that. At this point, he didn't know how he'd ever stop.

He undid the snap of her bra and slowly drew the fabric down her shoulders and arms. He exhaled, surprised to find it shaky. Surprised to find how much she affected him.

"Are you cold?" he murmured as she shivered now that she was bare from the waist up.

"No," she returned.

"Are you scared?" he asked, rubbing his hands up her arms, trying to infuse some calm, some surety.

"No." This time she said it on a laugh. "It feels good. All of it." Those dark, meaningful eyes peered into his. Her smile was like the gift of sunshine after weeks of darkness. Perhaps months or years, because he had been unwittingly, unknowingly in a period of darkness. Something about Natalie lightened him, even in the middle of all this mess.

"So, I don't know how much you're going to want to hear this, but I happened to see a packet of condoms in your sister's backpack when you handed it to me. So… You know."

He squeezed his eyes shut. "Can you rephrase that in a way that I don't have to think about the fact my sister has condoms in her backpack?"

"Why? Do you think she's too young to use them?"

"No, regardless of whether she should or not, the last thing I want to consider right now is my sister having sex. Period. With anyone. Especially in the cabin that we share."

"Okay. New story—I just love carrying condoms around in my purse."

He laughed, and shook his head. "I just haven't…"

She raised her eyebrows, and he realized this was a conversation he did *not* want to get into right now. Right here. It was too close to a truth he was still trying to bottle up. The fact he hadn't slept with anyone since his ex-wife.

The fact he hadn't wanted to, that he'd thrown his life into police work just like Jenny had always accused him of.

That wanting this, Natalie, here, now, it all *meant* something.

But there was too much at stake for that meaning to be dissected in the here and now. "We'll have plenty of time to converse after. Let's not waste our present."

"Take off your underwear, and I might be inclined to agree with you." She grinned, all jokes and fun in the midst of this awful situation for her.

"Grab a condom from *your* purse. I'll lay out some blankets."

She gave a little nod and bent over the pink sparkly backpack. Vaughn focused on the tempting curve of her backside over *where* she was obtaining the condoms from. When she turned back to him, she cocked her head.

"Where are the blankets?"

"Sorry, I was distracted."

She smirked and rolled her eyes. "Then I guess turn-about is fair play. Please bend over and retrieve the blankets," she said with a regal lift of her hand.

He chuckled, but he did exactly as she asked. She made a considering sound, and he didn't waste any time retrieving the blankets. Both pieces of fabric were lightweight backpacking blankets that wouldn't do much to protect Natalie from the harsh, hard ground, but it would keep them from rolling around in rocks and dirt.

Rolling around in rocks and dirt. While armed and dangerous criminals were probably after them. "Are you sure—"

"I simply won't take no for an answer, Vaughn," she said primly. "Don't make me say it again."

He promised himself he wouldn't. He would make sure they both enjoyed this. That they would get everything they needed out of it, and when they had to face whatever they had to face tomorrow morning, they would do it together. Both having had this moment. This coming together.

He crossed to her and took her mouth. No preamble, losing some of the gentleness that had held him back earlier. He wanted. She wanted. It was time to take— and give.

She moaned against him, arching in the way that drove him crazy. He slid his fingers into her underwear, finding the soft, wet heat of her. Stroking and exploring until she wasn't just shaking in his arms, but shuddering. Panting. Desperate.

And he was desperate too.

"The ground is rough. So I'm going to lay on my back, and you're going to get on top."

"You just lay out orders everywhere you go, don't you?"

But she didn't protest when he lay down and pushed his boxers off his legs. Not a complaint, just a steady gaze at the hardest part of him illuminated only by the flashlight he'd rested on the ground. "I believe that means it's your turn to take off your underwear."

She grinned at him and shimmied out of her underwear. She knelt next to him and handed him the condom. He opened the packet and rolled it on himself, watching her as she watched him. She licked her lips and he groaned aloud.

"How on earth are we going to do this?" she asked, and though it seemed like she *attempted* to make eye contact, her gaze never made it very far.

"Just figure out however you feel comfortable."

She straddled him, that intimate place of hers not making contact with his body. She trailed her fingers down his chest and his abdomen. He could only barely make out the tight points of her dark nipples, only barely make out the seductive shape of her body.

But she was here, straddling him, those smooth legs brushing up against his sides, her scent, her warmth permeating the very air.

"Are you sure you're comfortable?" she asked before chewing on her bottom lip in that sexy and distracting way she did whenever she was worried.

"Baby, all I feel is you." Which was true. When it was all said and done, he might notice the way the rocks dug into him, but for right now, all he could see, feel, think, want was her.

She leaned over him, her breasts brushing his chest,

her lips brushing his mouth. "Then take me," she murmured.

It was his turn to take the order, and he did, sliding home on a moan, moving deep and steady, paying attention to the way her breath caught and exhaled. The pleasure and excitement coiled so deep and so hard, he wasn't sure he'd ever survive.

His hands dug into the softness of her hips, but he let her set the pace. Slow and tentative at first, and then she moved faster, everything about her softness, her breathy moans, *her* driving him closer and closer to that reckless edge.

She was beautiful, moving against him, sighing, gasping as she chased that rhythm that would lead to her release. It bloomed in him, big and hard, something more than where their bodies met.

She said his name, pulsed around him. He thought he could make out the way the flush in her cheeks had spread across her chest as she sighed out her release.

But it wasn't enough. He pushed himself into a sitting position, pulling her legs around him. Her gaze met his, glazed with pleasure.

"Again," he ordered.

And when she opened her mouth to protest, he covered it with his own.

Again. The harsh, demanding way Vaughn had said those words echoed in her head. Again? She'd just lost herself over some edge she'd never known, how could she possibly do it again?

But he was kissing her, using that harsh, steady, hot grip on her hips to pull her forward. She arched against it, against him. She loved the way her breasts scraped across his chest. She loved the way his hands were commanding and sure. She loved this. Being with him. Being filled by him. Being driven to some sort of climax that was bigger than she'd ever known.

She was starting to think it might be a dream.

But Vaughn kept moving, urging her to take more of him, and then less, over and over again in a steady, unrelenting rhythm. The blooming edge of pleasure began to build again. The heat that should've been unbearable, but she couldn't stand to lose. A fire in her veins that she didn't want to be cooled.

He broke the kiss and his mouth streaked everywhere. Her cheeks, her neck, her chest. He was everywhere, driving her into a faster and faster pace. She could feel his desperation grow, the closeness of his own release, just thinking about that, of being with him, finding that pleasure together, it pushed her over that last humbling, bright edge.

Vaughn held her there, deep and strong, his harsh groan echoing in the expanse of the cave.

She wasn't sure how long they sat there wrapped up in each other, holding on for dear life. She wasn't even sure how long the orgasm pulsed through her. She didn't care. In this dark cave with Vaughn, it didn't matter what time it was. All that mattered was that he was holding her, that he was a part of her.

"You're shaking again, and I think it's cold this time," he murmured into her ear, so gentle and sweet.

It was hard to think she could be cold, but as he grabbed a sweatshirt and pulled it over her head, she realized he was right. She was shivering with cold, *among* other things.

The sweatshirt he put on her was his, oversized and

warm, and it smelled like him. Clean and soap and Vaughn. She wanted to snuggle into that smell and him forever.

"We should get dressed."

If he hadn't kissed her forehead and her cheek and then her neck before moving, she might have been fooled by that tense note in his voice. But he was so gentle, and affectionate, and she realized that his tenseness wasn't about what had passed between them, it was just that he was coming back to the job he had before him.

He was dedicated to her safety. He was dedicated to her. She couldn't help but be warmed by that.

She rolled off him and tried not to watch with too much interest as he got rid of the condom. He handed her a pair of pants that would be too big, but they would keep her warm. The cave was much cooler than the outside air.

"You can change back into your clothes tomorrow when we set out. The sweats will be too big to move in, but the shorts and shirt won't be enough to keep you warm tonight."

"Have you always been such a good caretaker?"

"I guess it depends on who you ask."

"I'm asking you."

Those inscrutable gray-blue eyes met hers in the eerie glow of the flashlight beam. Something in his gaze shuttered, and she realized this was quite the sore spot for him. "You've done nothing but take care of me so far," she said firmly, wishing she could erase those doubts in his eyes.

"That's my job."

"It's more than that."

"Do you want to rest, or do you want to try to eat

something first? All I have are some granola bars and some jerky."

"Vaughn, I want to talk."

"We can talk about whatever you want, except about my caregiving tendencies."

She frowned at him as he got dressed. He seemed to have an endless supply of things in that black backpack of his. She sat on the blankets that he'd stretched out, dressed in his clothes, watching something like irritation make his shoulders hunch.

"So, is this the part where you're just certain that I'm going to look at you like your ex-wife looked at you?" she asked, perhaps too bluntly, but if she was going to have ill-advised sex with the man, she was going to ask him too-blunt questions.

If her life was in danger, she was going to push where she normally wouldn't. She was going to demand what it would never occur to her to demand in her real, unassuming, obsessed-with-Gabby life.

He faced her, and in the light everything about him seemed hard and unreachable. Granite she'd never be able to push through. Except she had. She *had*.

"We had sex once, Natalie. I like you, I do. But you're nothing like a wife."

It was a nasty thing to say, and it hurt even though she knew it shouldn't. She wasn't his wife, she wasn't even close to his wife. She'd be lucky if there was anything they could salvage after this whole ordeal.

But just because words were designed to hurt, no matter the truths or lack of truth behind them, didn't mean that she could let it go.

"I'm not trying to be an ass," he said on a sigh, rubbing his jaw. "But don't make me into something I'm not."

"I'm not making you into anything. I'm reflecting on what I've seen from you, and if you can't accept that part of yourself, that's fine. Don't take it out on me."

"I'm not big on sorry." He said it with such a grave finality she opened her mouth to tell him he was a jerk, but he kept going.

"But I'm sorry. Because I was feeling guilty for letting my personal feelings interfere with this case, and I took it out on you, and that's less than fair."

Her heart ached for him then, because she knew that she'd initiated this. She'd pushed for it. Not that Vaughn hadn't wanted it or hadn't enjoyed it, but it had come at a cost to him. It required him to bend that ironclad moral code he lived by, and that meant something, not easily distilled no matter how great the orgasm might have been.

It was crazy to think she might love him. She barely knew him. And yet everything in her heart said that love was what this feeling was. Love, or the seeds of it. There was so much possibility, and yet so much against them.

"Apology accepted," she said, hoping her voice sounded light rather than as ragged and rocked as she felt.

"Just like that?"

"This wasn't a mistake, but I understand why it might be hard for you to accept. But I'll never regret it. No matter what happens."

"You say that now…"

"And I'll say it always. No matter what." She stood, because she needed to somehow prove to him that she was strong. That she meant it. "That was what I needed, at that exact time I needed it. And you gave it to me. Nothing you could do could take that away. Nothing that happens changes what you gave me."

He stared at her, and she thought she saw some pain there, and she assumed it probably had to do with his marriage that had dissolved. No matter how much or how little he'd given, that relationship had clearly left scars. She wished she could sew them together, kiss them, make everything okay.

But she couldn't. And not just because they had dangerous men after them.

"Let's eat something, and then one of us can try to sleep."

He kept staring at her for a few humming seconds of silence. Then slowly, oh so painfully slowly, he crossed to her. He touched her face, his blunt fingertips tracing the lines of her cheekbones and then her jaw, then her neck. His eyes bore into hers, and her heart hammered against her chest.

She wanted to say silly things like I love you, and she knew she couldn't. She absolutely couldn't.

"For the record, I'll never regret it, either."

When he kissed her, it was gentle, and it was sweet. And Vaughn Cooper gave her something that no one else had for a very long time.

Hope.

Chapter 14

Vaughn managed a few hours of sleep, after he watched Natalie sleep for far too long. It had been tempting to lie next to her, to wake her with a kiss. So, he'd done neither. He'd stood guard the entire time she'd slept, and then he'd woken her by nudging her with his foot.

Because he was a bit of a coward, all in all.

Though his brain and body were nothing but a swirling mass of confusion he didn't have time for, exhaustion won out and he slept quick and hard.

Natalie woke him at the first sign of dawn, just as he'd instructed, and then he began to pack everything.

"Are we going back to the cabin?" she asked him, trepidation coloring her every movement.

"No. We're hiking farther."

"Until what?"

"I know the area well enough to lead us toward civilization. Somewhere our phones work and we can call for help. It's too dangerous to go back to the cabin."

"But what about your truck?"

"They slashed the tires," he returned. He hadn't wanted to tell her all the things he'd noticed as they'd escaped from the cabin. That they took care to not shoot anyone, that they'd snuck their way into a position to *take* not murder.

He supposed murder would be scarier, but the idea of Natalie being held by those men... He wasn't going to let that happen.

"When did you notice that?" she asked incredulously.

"When I kicked Worthless Number Two over, I saw the tires were flat." And that the man had been carrying handcuffs and rope. Duct tape. Vaughn swallowed at the uncomfortable ball of rage and fear in his gut.

Natalie blew out a breath. "How long will it take to get us back to civilization?"

Vaughn pulled out the map of the Guadalupe Mountains that he kept in his emergency pack. He'd studied it last night while Natalie was sleeping, but he was worried and thorough enough to look at it again.

He inclined the map so she could see too. "This is the path we're going to follow." He showed her with his finger the mountains they would have to cross to get inside the national park and finally find service or a ranger station to assist them. "I don't know exactly where we'll get cell service, so we just have to keep going until we get it. Or find someone who can help us. My hope is that they don't expect us to keep moving forward this way, and it'll give us enough of a head start that by the time they realize it, we'll be close enough to call for help."

Natalie chewed her bottom lip and studied the map.

"Do you have enough supplies to get us through all of this?"

"It'll be tight and we'll be hungry, but we'll survive."

"You don't know the meaning of sugarcoating, do you?"

"Do you want me to sugarcoat it?" Because he would, if that's what she wanted. He wasn't sure who else he'd afford that to.

She sighed again, pulling her hair back in a ponytail. It stretched the tight T-shirt across her breasts, and he had to stop himself from wondering how much he'd be able to see if they indulged in each other right now. In the pearly light of dawn easing its way into the cave. Her skin would glow, she would—

They didn't have time for that, and even if he'd lost his mind once, he couldn't do it again. At least not if it meant wasting daylight. Maybe tonight...

He shook his head and told himself to focus. "First things first, we're going to start moving toward higher ground. Hopefully that gives us a tactical advantage, and we can see if anyone's following us before they catch up."

"What do we do if they are?"

"Well, that depends on how close they are. We'll either book it, or we'll pick them off. But that's a lot of what-if, Natalie."

"You shot those other men. Do you think..." She swallowed, and he didn't know if it was her conscience or something else bothering her, but either way that was something that she was going to have to work out on her own.

Every officer who vowed to protect the innocent and took up a weapon had to come to terms with what that meant and the power it offered. They had to come to grips with what they were willing to do. He couldn't convince her of his morality or his lack of guilt, and, in the next few days should she have to use her weapon, only she could deal with the aftermath of that. He couldn't do it for her, no matter how much he'd like to.

Because if he had the choice, he would save her from every hard decision. Which was another thing in a long line of things he didn't have the time or energy to think about right now.

"It was my intention to give them non-life-threatening wounds, but without medical attention, it's hard to know if they survived, and quite frankly I can't concern myself with it. The only thing I can concern myself with right now is keeping you and me safe."

She didn't say anything for a long while, and he let her be quiet as they walked out of the cave. They would need to make it to another shelter by nightfall, and though he could read the map and do some general calculations, he couldn't be sure where they'd end up when the sun set.

So, they needed to head out and get as far as they could. He didn't think they could make it to cell service today, but if they got good enough mileage behind them, they could hopefully get there tomorrow.

They hiked in silence for most of the morning, and though Vaughn was sorry that she was obviously brooding about a difficult situation, he couldn't feel bad that there wasn't any conversation to distract him from his task at hand.

Occasionally they stopped and ate a snack and drank some water. Vaughn would consult the map, but mostly they walked. He knew she was exhausted, and probably on her last legs, but he also knew that she was strong and resilient, and that he could push her and she would survive. That was one of the things he most admired about her.

"You're holding up remarkably well, you know," he said as they sat on rocks and Natalie devoured a granola bar.

She glanced at him, the granola bar halfway to her mouth. Her gaze didn't bother to hide her surprise. "I haven't really had a choice, have I?"

"We always have a choice. One of the choices is to lie down and die, to give up. One of the choices is to think that you can't, and so then it's a self-fulfilling prophecy. You could be so busy complaining about the lot you've been given that we never got anywhere. But you've chosen to move forward. To keep fighting. Not everyone could have done that, not everyone has that kind of wherewithal. I'm not sure anyone should *have* to have that kind of wherewithal, but it's special. And you deserve to know that."

She smiled a little and looked down at her granola bar for a second before leaning over and giving him a long, gentle kiss. Her arm wound around his neck, and it took all the willpower he had not to lean into that, not to pull her into his lap. He couldn't let her distract him, but...

She pulled away, that sweet smile playing on her lips. "You know Vaughn, I like you a lot. That's not something I would have said about five days ago."

He chuckled a little at that. "Well, that's very mutual."

It was her turn to laugh, but she sobered quickly. "When we get back..." she began, emphasizing the *when* meaningfully. But her seriousness morphed into a grin. "You're going to have to let me hypnotize you."

He narrowed his eyes at her, but he couldn't help from smiling in return. "Like hell, Natalie."

"Why not? Are you afraid?"

"No. You told me that the person has to be willing. I'm never going to be willingly *relaxed*. Unless it's by things other than hypnotism."

She snorted at his joke. "Do you have secrets to hide that you're not willing to share, Ranger Cooper?"

"I don't have any secrets." Which had become true the minute they'd discussed his marriage. There was nothing about himself kept under wraps, because there wasn't much there. Work.

She might not know he was related to a few celebrities, but that wasn't *his* secret in the least.

Natalie looked down at the last bite of granola bar, something in her gaze going serious. "I guess I don't really have any more secrets from you, either." Her eyebrows had drawn together, and she didn't look at him. "Everything in my life has been Gabby for so long…"

She swallowed, and Vaughn could tell she was dealing with some big emotion, so instead of pressing or changing the subject, he gave her time to work through it.

"I want her back so much, and I just *have* to believe she's alive… But…" She shoved the granola wrapper into her backpack forcefully, irritated. "I feel terrible saying this, it feels like a betrayal, but when we make it out of here, I want a life that isn't solely focused on her." Her brown gaze met his, and he had a bad feeling he knew where this was going.

And where it couldn't *possibly* go. Because his feel-

ings for Natalie ran very deep, but he'd been here before—loving someone and knowing that her views on
the world would never allow them to make something
permanent, to make something real.

"One step at a time. Remember?"

She frowned at him as though she could read his
thoughts, as though she could read everything. He didn't
like that sensation at all. But in the end, he didn't have
to bother figuring it out because a shot rang out in the
quiet, sunny afternoon.

Immediately Vaughn had Natalie under him, protecting her body with his, scanning the horizon for where
the shot might have come from.

"Wh-where?" Natalie asked in a shaky voice.

"I don't know." Based on the sound, he didn't think
it had come from behind them. It seemed more likely
it came from higher ground. From someone who'd presumably assumed his plan all too easily. He swore vi-
ciously and tried to reach for his pack without leaving
Natalie vulnerable.

Another shot sounded, a loud crack against the quiet
desert, this one getting closer. It had to be coming from
the other side of the mountain they were climbing. They
couldn't stay put, they were too vulnerable, too exposed.
And he had no idea where to shoot toward.

"We're going to have to run from it," he said flatly,
his eyes never stopping their survey of their surroundings.

"Run for it? Run where?"

He pointed to a craggy outcropping a little ways behind them. "You run there. No matter what happens to
me, you run there and get behind those rocks."

She tried to twist under him, but he wouldn't let her.

"What do you mean no matter what happens? You can't honestly expect me to—"

"The most important thing is that you stay safe. Out of the way of a bullet. If I—"

"What about you? What about your safety?" she demanded, a slight note of hysteria in her voice.

"Natalie, listen to me," he said, his voice calm, his demeanor sure. Because not only was it his *job* to take a bullet for her if the circumstances necessitated that, but he wanted to. He'd never be able to live with himself if she ended up hurt because of an error in his judgement.

"My job is to keep you safe."

"Well, Vaughn, I want *you* to be safe too, regardless of what your job is."

He'd analyze the way those words sliced a little later. "I'll be safe. If you listen to me, we'll both be safe. We're going to make a run for it. You first. I'll follow."

"I don't like this."

"Unfortunately, Nat, it doesn't matter what you like, this is what we have to do."

She exhaled shakily, and it wasn't until she spoke that he realized it was anger not fear. "If you get shot," she said, her voice trembling with rage, "I will finish off the job myself. Do you understand me? You will not get hurt saving me."

Everything inside him vibrated with a kind of gratitude and hurt and all number of things he couldn't work out at the moment. He kissed her temple, which was the only place on her head he could reach.

"You just listen to me, and everything will be fine. I've gotten you this far, haven't I?"

"Yes, and I know you'll get me the rest of the way. We'll get each other the rest of the way."

He hated that she was worried about his safety. Her safety was of the most importance, not his. He was a man who could be replaced easily enough, but there was no one like Natalie.

But if she cared about him, and her safety depended on his, then he would keep himself safe. He would keep them both safe.

"On the count of three, we run. That's our destination. If I happen to get hit, you keep going. You can't save me if you're dead."

"And you can't save me if *you're* dead," she argued.

Another shot rang out, and Vaughn knew that one was way too close for comfort. The next one would hit, and if they weren't trying to kill them, all the more danger.

"One, two, three, go." He launched to his feet, pulling her with him, and then they ran.

Natalie ran, just as Vaughn instructed. There was a certain hysteria bubbling through her, but with a specific destination—behind that rock—she managed to focus enough to get her feet to move, as fast as they possibly could.

Another shot rang out, and Natalie jerked in fear and surprise and almost tripped at the sound, but Vaughn's steady grip on her arm propelled her forward. She tumbled behind the rock, and Vaughn was right behind her, covering her with his body again.

As glad as she was to have someone protecting her, someone like Vaughn, so sure, so capable, worried about her safety, she had fallen in love with the man, and she hated the thought that he was ready to give his life for hers.

She knew this was his job, but that didn't make it easier. Certainly not easier to know he was risking his neck for her. She didn't feel worthy of it. She didn't feel worthy of any of this.

Why were these men after *her*? All she'd done was pathetically fail at trying to find her sister for *eight* years. Failure after failure. Why on earth did they think her worthy of this kind of manhunt?

Now was not the time to worry about those questions, about her failures, but every insecurity, every pain, every hurt seemed to center inside her along with this bone-deep panic.

Vaughn made an odd grunting sound as he rolled off her. She glanced over at him, and he was trying to pull off his jacket. She didn't quite know why he was bothering with that when—

"I'm going to need your help," he said, his voice strangely strained.

"What's wrong?" she asked, despite the way her throat tightened. Something was off, something—

Then she saw it, the angry streak of red in the middle of a rip on the T-shirt fabric across his shoulder. She felt like *she'd* been shot, seeing that horrible gash and the way the blood trickled down his beautiful, strong arm. For her.

He spared her a glance. "Not going to pass out, are you?"

"No," she said firmly, though she did feel a little woozy and light-headed at the sight of him bleeding so profusely, but she wasn't going to be so weak she couldn't help him. She would find a way to push through her physical reaction and give him everything he needed.

"Tell me what you need me to do."

"Grab something out of the backpack that you can wrap tight around the wound." He had his gun pulled and was holding it with his good arm. Ready to take a shot. Ready to protect her in the middle of this barren mountainous desert. "I can do it myself if you want me to—"

"I can do it." Natalie would do whatever he asked, whatever he needed. Over and over again.

He kept his gaze trained on the area around the rock that protected them. Natalie did her best to hurry to find something she could wrap his arm with. She hoped this was at least a little bit like in the movies, because then she would at least know a little bit of what to do.

There was a T-shirt at the very bottom of his pack, and she pulled it out. Without thinking too much about it, she pulled and pulled until she ripped a good strip. She repeated the process over and over until she had several strips. While Vaughn remained the lookout, she folded the strips over the worst part of the wound and then tied the longest one around his upper arm as tight as she could manage.

He hissed out a breath, but that was the only outward sign that he hurt.

"That should hold for little bit," she said, scared and worried that she'd screwed it all up. But what could she do? All she could really do was everything he asked, hoping for the best. She had no other options here, so there wasn't even a point in worrying about what else there was. Like Vaughn kept saying, there was only now. No time to worry about later.

"On the slim chance that we have a signal, check your phone and mine."

Natalie scrambled for both, powering them on and checking their screens. But there was no service. She wanted to cry, but she blinked back the tears. Tears would get them nowhere.

A shot hadn't rung out in a while, and the longer the silence lasted, the more both their nerves seemed to stretch thin and taut.

"Pull up the texting on both phones. I want you to put in a message to this number, and hopefully if we try to send it now, it'll send the first second we have service without us having to keep checking."

Natalie furiously typed the information Vaughn gave her. She kept glancing at the T-shirt bandage, and because it was a white T-shirt, she could see the blood already seeping through. She tried not to panic at that.

"Get out the map." Though he still sounded like cool and collected Vaughn, that strain never left his voice.

He'd been shot. *Shot.* It took everything she had to pull out the map and spread it out for him. Her hands shook, but he still handed her the gun she'd dropped while trying to bandage him up, trusting her. Believing in her. She held on to that fiercely.

"Shoot at anything that moves."

She swallowed and nodded, watching the harsh surroundings and fervently hoping nothing moved.

"We don't want to retrace our steps," he muttered. "We need to keep moving forward. We've got to keep searching for cell service. We don't get out of this without help."

She wanted to make another joke about him not sugarcoating anything, but her voice didn't work anymore. Whether it was panic or fear or some combination of all of the emotions rioting through her, she couldn't push out joking words. Only desperate ones.

"Are they going to come after us?"

"They might. I didn't get a glimpse of where they were coming from. I still have no idea what the hell they're trying to prove. If they want us dead, they could have had us dead on the road before the gas station. I don't get this at all, unless they want us. Alive. Or…"

He didn't have to finish that sentence, and she knew, sugarcoating or no, he wouldn't. Because he meant *or they want you.* She could tell that bothered him more than anything. That he didn't know what they were trying to do, that she might be the target.

Natalie didn't really care what they were trying to do. As long as they were shooting at them, she wasn't a fan.

"To keep cover we're going to have to backtrack a little bit, but then we'll circle around, really try to get higher ground on the off chance there's a tower around here somewhere. If you hear the message sent notification from either phone, tell me. Otherwise we need to stay completely silent, just in case. They don't want us dead. Or at least they don't want you dead, and that's pretty damn frightening."

"But…"

For the first time his glare turned to her, rather than their surroundings or the map. "What the hell do you mean, but…"

"If they have Gabby…" She swallowed at the lump in her throat. Maybe they wanted her too. If they did…

"No. No way in hell. You're not sacrificing yourself for her right now. First of all, not on my watch. Second of all, because you just told me you want a life beyond all that."

"I didn't know how close I was."

"I'm sorry. I know she's your sister, and I know you'd do anything to find her, but it's been eight years. If she survived that, a few more days won't hurt her. You don't know what they're trying to do to you, so we're not taking that chance. Not even for your sister, Nat."

"You'd do it for your sister," she returned, quiet and sure. He'd sacrifice himself for less, she was certain.

"It would depend on the situation, and not in this one. If they had my sister, I'd do exactly what I'm doing now. Which is trying to get them. Because if we don't have them, everyone under their control is in danger."

She saw a point to that, but the idea that if they took her she might be reunited with Gabby. If they took her… Vaughn might be safe.

"Natalie, you have to trust me on this. I need you to promise me."

Natalie swallowed. She hated lying to him, but she also knew they wouldn't get anywhere if she didn't make that promise. She forced herself to look him in the eye—those gorgeous blue eyes she thought she'd never be able to read—and now she knew she'd never not be able to see what was in those depths.

He was strong and he was brave, and he knew that he could get them out of here. But he was also afraid, because whether he was going to admit it, whether he would admit it, he cared about her too. He wouldn't have slept with her in the middle of all this if care wasn't part of that. That she knew.

"All right. I promise," she said, holding on to the thought of care, of love.

Vaughn swore harshly. "Don't lie to me." He grabbed her arm and winced a little, since he'd used his bad arm.

But he didn't back down. "I don't have time to argue with you on this, but if you put yourself in danger you will answer to me. Now, let's go."

He didn't give her a chance to argue; he pushed and pulled her in the direction he wanted to go. And Natalie let him lead, let him order her around.

But she had no doubt if the situation presented itself, she'd sacrifice herself for both the people she loved.

Chapter 15

Vaughn didn't know what to do with the searing rage inside him. She was lying. How dare she lie about something so important? How could she be willing to sacrifice herself with so many unknowns and so much at stake? She didn't even know for sure if her sister was alive or with The Stallion. All they had were hunches and possibilities, and Vaughn was beyond livid that she would take such a chance with her life.

It didn't matter that he would do everything in his power to make that impossible for her, because it wasn't about him. It wasn't about what he could do. It wasn't about how well he could keep her safe. It was about the fact that she was *willing*. It was about the fact that…

She should've cared more about herself. She should've cared more about her future.

Which does not include you, so maybe calm down.

Frustrated with himself, more than frustrated with the situation, he pushed them forward at a punishing pace, doing his best to keep them behind things that would keep them out of sight and safe from bullets.

But even as they hurried and zigzagged and did their best to stay low, Vaughn could hear the sound of an engine getting closer and closer. He swore, because no matter how good he was, no matter how strong he was, no matter how smart he was, he could not outrun a vehicle. He couldn't outrun whatever was coming after them.

They'd made it around one of the craggy desert mountains, and whatever was coming for them would have to come around one of the sides. Vaughn kept his weapon drawn and his eyes alert. "We're going to find somewhere to hide you."

"But—"

"No but. You will listen to me. You will follow my directions. If I tell you to hide, you will damn well hide." He didn't have time to see how she was taking that harsh order. He didn't have time to look at her and make sure she was okay. He was a little afraid if he did take that time, he'd fall apart.

He'd been in some dangerous, uncomfortable, scary situations, and he'd never been scared that he might fall apart. It poked and ate at him. Hell, it just about killed him that she'd become that important. Which meant the only choice was to keep going.

He found a very small opening, more crevice than cave, in the base of the mountain. With less finesse than he might have had otherwise, he gave her a little push into the crevice. She fit, though barely. But it would keep her out of sight.

He looked around to make sure he couldn't see a car anywhere. He could hear that engine, so they were close, but not close enough to see him just yet.

"Stay here. No matter what. You do not come out of here until I come to get you. Someone tries to get you out, you shoot him wherever will do the most damage." He didn't even have time to ask if she understood. He gave her one meaningful look and tried not to let those big, soulful brown eyes undo him.

He didn't have time for that, or to ascertain whether she would listen to his order. He could only keep moving. Because if he stayed there and the vehicle came around one of those bends, they would know exactly where to find Natalie.

Vaughn took off running as fast as he could, ignoring the screaming pain in his shoulder. His heart was pounding and his breath was scorching his lungs, and he had the sinking suspicion it had more to do with the fact that he'd left Natalie alone than with the fact that he was running.

He slowed his pace, took a quick look at his surroundings. He could still see the crevice where he'd pushed Natalie, but he couldn't see her. He was far enough away that it would take a lot of searching for anyone to find her.

Now he had to figure out which direction he wanted to go to, and—

The sound of a gunshot made Vaughn skid to a halt. He glanced around, trying to ascertain where the sound had come from. There were little craggy outcrops all over the desert. There were cacti and other plants that a stealthy person might be able to hide behind. Vaughn searched and searched, but he didn't see anyone, or anything.

The sound of the engine had stopped, and he did his best to keep his gaze everywhere rather than always on where Natalie was. He didn't want to give it away, because who knew what these men had. They could be watching him with binoculars, they could have an army of cars. They could have anything, and he didn't know.

He couldn't think about the what-if. He had to think about the right now.

"Ranger Cooper."

Vaughn whirled to see a man walk out from behind the opposite curve of the little mountain. He appeared to be alone, but Vaughn wasn't stupid enough to think that was true. Any number of people could come pouring from the other side of the mountain. There could be an *army* of men behind the curve, and that was daunting, but it couldn't stop what Vaughn had to do.

"Mr. Callihan, I assume?"

The man laughed and spread his hands wide, though Vaughn noticed that the gun he carried was pointed directly at Vaughn's chest regardless of the gesture.

"It took you only how many years to figure that out?"

"A lot fewer years than it will take me to kill you."

The man kept walking closer and closer, and Vaughn's hands tensed on his gun. He could shoot the man and be done with it, and there was a very large part of him that wanted to. But he resisted, because his mission wasn't to kill every bad guy who roamed the earth; it was to bring them to justice.

He believed in justice, and while he believed in using his weapon with deadly force if necessary, as long as this man wasn't actively trying to kill him, or take or harm Natalie, Vaughn was having a hard time rationalizing shooting first.

Maybe some of it had to do with the fact this could potentially be the only man on earth who knew where Natalie's sister was. If Vaughn killed him without trying to retrieve more information, what might Natalie think of him? What might she lose?

It was the absolute last thing he should be concerned with, but, still, he didn't shoot.

"But you see, Ranger Cooper, I know you, and I know your type. It's why I've managed to do as much damage as I have. Because you're all so honorable, or easy to buy off."

"Try to buy me off and see what happens."

The man chuckled, all ease and…something like charm, though Vaughn wasn't at all charmed by it. Still, these were the most dangerous criminals to deal with, the ones without much at stake, except their own pride, or whatever was going on in their warped heads.

Of course he'd be charming and smooth, men like him were always charming and smooth. That was why people didn't suspect them. That was why he'd gotten this far. But also because reason and rational thinking wouldn't change their course. Nothing would. The man standing before him could do anything with zero remorse.

"But I'm not here for you," Callihan said with an elegant flick of the wrist. "I'm here for the woman. I have plans for the woman who thinks she can get her sister away from me."

Vaughn's entire body turned to ice. Even in the quiet desert, he didn't know if they were close enough for Natalie to hear that, but it was an admission. It was a certainty that Natalie's sister was with this man, and that he was after Natalie. For very specific reasons.

His finger itched to pull that trigger, to end this, now. Though they were still yards apart, Vaughn thought he saw Callihan's gaze drop to his gun.

"Lucky for me, Ranger Cooper, I don't need you. Quite frankly, wherever that woman is, I'll find her, but you'll be de—"

Vaughn pulled the trigger. The whistle of the shot, followed by the man's piercing scream, were barely heard over the beating of his heart.

He'd purposefully shot for the man's weapon-wielding arm, and as Vaughn raced toward the dropped gun, Callihan started screaming for someone in Spanish.

Even though he knew Callihan was yelling for backup, which likely meant people with even larger weapons would be coming around that bend, he raced for the gun. Even though he knew he might have signed his death warrant, there was always a chance Callihan had only a few men with him, a chance Vaughn would be able to pick them off before...

But there was *no* chance if he didn't get to Callihan's weapon first.

Vaughn was so intent on reaching the weapon, and reaching Callihan that he didn't realize there were footsteps behind him.

"If you so much as touch that gun with a fingertip, I will shoot you, and I'm not a very good shot, so if I aim for your heart, I might just hit your head."

Vaughn skidded to a stop and looked back at Natalie, who was walking steadily toward them. She had the gun he'd taken from one of the men in the cabin trained on Callihan's writhing form.

The man merely smirked, his hand still reaching for the weapon, before Vaughn could pull his weapon, Natalie shot.

"That's the problem with women," Callihan all but spat. "They can never shoot on tar—" She shot again, and this time Callihan howled.

Red bloomed at his stomach, and Natalie kept calmly walking forward, though now that she was close enough, Vaughn could see the way her arms were shaking. Callihan was screaming for someone named Rodriguez while he thrashed and moaned on the ground.

Right before Natalie and Vaughn reached Callihan's weapon, a large man stepped out from behind the curve of mountain. He was dressed all in black, had black sunglasses and black hair, with multiple guns strapped to him—all black. Everything about him was large and muscular and ominous.

"Shoot them!" Callihan screamed. "Kill them both. What are you doing?"

Vaughn didn't pull his trigger, and not just because the man didn't pull out a gun. The man was shockingly familiar. Not because he'd arrested him before, not because of anything criminal. He'd *trained* him a few years ago on undercover practices, though Vaughn couldn't come up with his name.

Callihan kept screaming at him to shoot, but the man didn't make a move to reach for a weapon. He walked calmly toward the three of them.

"Tell your woman to put down the gun," he said in Spanish, nodding toward Natalie, who was holding the gun trained on the man.

Vaughn glanced at her then, noting that everything

about her was shaking and pale and scared. But she was ready to take the shot.

"Put it down, Nat," he murmured.

"I won't let anyone kill us. Not now. Not when that man has my sister."

Callihan made a grab for his supposed henchman's leg piece, but the man easily kicked him away.

"Ma'am, I need you to put your weapon down," he said, steady and sure, making eye contact with Natalie. "I'm with the FBI. I've been working undercover for Callihan. I know where your sister is. She's…safe."

Natalie didn't just lower the gun, she dropped it. Then she sank to her knees, so Vaughn sank with her.

"Does this mean it's over?" she asked in a shaking, ragged voice.

"I think so," he said, stroking her hair. "I think so."

Natalie sat in a truck squished between Vaughn and this… FBI agent. Vaughn and the man discussed the case, the particulars of the FBI's involvement and what the agent was allowed to disclose.

Natalie knew she should be listening, but everything was just a faded buzz. She couldn't seem to stop shaking, and all she could concentrate on was the fact the man in the back had become completely silent.

She'd shot him. Right in the stomach. He hadn't shut up though, he'd gone on and on as Vaughn and the agent, Jaime Alessandro, or so he said, had done the best to bandage Callihan, while also keeping him tied up.

Callihan had shouted terrible things about what he'd done to Gabby, but before he'd really gotten going, Agent Alessandro had knocked him out. Just a quick blow to the head. Then, they'd taped his mouth shut and thrown him into the truck he'd brought out to the desert.

All Natalie could concentrate on was how she'd tried to kill a man, and failed. She should be glad that she had failed, she should be glad that she hadn't apparently hit any internal organs, and that he would probably survive. She should be glad that he would stand trial.

All she felt was regret. She wished she would've killed him. For Gabby, for Vaughn, for herself. She wished he was dead, and she didn't know how to reconcile that with who she'd thought she was.

Despite being sandwiched between these two, strong, powerful men who were fighting for what was right and good, Natalie felt alone and vulnerable and scared. Which was something she didn't understand, either. Because it was over. This hell was over and they had survived, and with very little hurt.

But Gabby had been hurt. Gabby had survived eight years of that horrible man, and Natalie didn't know how… Now that it was over, *over*, she didn't know what on earth would possibly come next.

Jaime pulled into what appeared to be the national park's ranger station. "If you stay put, I'll have them call for an ambulance, as well as call your precinct. We'll see if there's any word on the raid on Callihan's house, where your sister was."

Vaughn nodded stoically and Natalie just…stared. Word on the raid where her sister was. How was she supposed to respond to that? What was left? What was she supposed to do?

"Do you have questions about Gabby?"

She didn't glance at Vaughn, because she didn't know how to look at him. She didn't know how to look at the future. It was like dealing with all the fear and the threat had completely eradicated her ability to look beyond…anything. And now…it was all gone.

What did she do? "I don't know what to ask," she managed to say. Because she was numb and somehow still scared, and she didn't know why.

Vaughn didn't move or say anything for a long time, but eventually his hand rested on her clutched ones. He rubbed his warm strong palm over her tight, shaking hands.

It was warm, it was comfort. But when she looked up at him, his gaze was blank and straight ahead. Though he was offering her comfort, it was much more like the comfort he'd offered her that first night after the fire. There was something separate about it. Something stoic.

This wasn't the hug he'd offered her at the cabin, and that lack of…personal warmth made the frozen confusion inside her even worse. So she mimicked him. She didn't look at him anymore, she didn't move, she stared straight ahead.

When Agent Alessandro came back out, he explained that an ambulance would be waiting for them at the exit of the park, and he would have agents there who would confiscate Callihan's car. He would accompany Callihan to the hospital and keep him in FBI custody. Someone from the local police department would be there to escort Natalie and Vaughn to the airport, where the FBI would fly them back to Austin, after a medic checked Vaughn's wound.

He began to drive, explaining all sorts of things Natalie knew where important. What would be expected of her, what she would need to do and what questions she would need to answer before she was released.

But she couldn't concentrate. All she could think about was… "What about…"

"Your sister?" Agent Alessandro supplied for her.

"Yes."

"As I mentioned, the FBI is conducting raids on all of Callihan's properties while I had him…distracted, so to speak. The property your sister has been at is on that list. As I've been working my way up in his organization, I've released some of the women, but—"

She whipped her head to face him, this stranger who'd helped them. "But not my sister?"

Something in his face hardened. "She wouldn't go."

"Wouldn't go? What does that mean?"

"I'm afraid that's all I'm at liberty to say." His hands tensed and then released on the steering wheel. "But now that we have Callihan in custody, and with all of the information that I've gathered over my two years, there should be no doubt that the trafficking ring, and his entire business, will be gutted. You have my word on that Ms. Torres."

She didn't care about trafficking rings or business or anything like that, though she supposed she should. All she cared about was her sister, and why her sister could have been saved and wasn't.

Natalie pushed out a breath, doing her level best not to cry. Not yet. Not in front of Alessandro and Vaughn.

Only then did Natalie realize that Vaughn had released her hands. No comfort. No connection. Just an officer and a victim.

If she had any energy left, she might've felt bereft. She might've cried. And now… Now, all she wanted to do was go home. To be alone. To deal with the last week in the privacy of her own house…

Except she didn't have one, just a burned-out shell. She had so very little. She'd come out of this ordeal with her life, and she knew that was important.

Maybe in a few days, when the shock wore off and she saw Gabby again and held her and understood what had happened, she'd know how to feel.

Maybe it would take a few days for all the dust to settle, to hurt and grieve and *feel*. But for the time being, all she could do was feel numb.

Chapter 16

Vaughn wasn't sure he'd ever felt so numb. Not even after his undercover mission years ago. He had never in his entire career left a case feeling so completely screwed up inside.

He'd stayed with Natalie through the debriefing. They'd been with each other through their medical evaluations. And yet, they'd said almost nothing to each other. They'd offered no reassuring glances, no comforting touches. The last time he'd touched her in any sort of personal capacity had been to put his hand on hers in the car.

He'd made sure to stop in that moment, because he'd realized he couldn't do this anymore. He couldn't possibly pretend that what they'd had in the cabin was real, and he couldn't give her false hope that he could be anything other than the man that he was. His job would always come first, someone else's safety would always come before his own.

How could he possibly tie another woman to him knowing where that ended?

It took days to get everything situated, questioned, figured out. When Natalie finally got to go home, or at least to her mother's home, he hadn't gone with her. She hadn't asked him to, and he hadn't offered. They had turned into strangers, and he felt like a part of him had simply…died.

It was so melodramatic he was concerned about his mental state, but he couldn't eradicate that feeling. He felt a darkness worse than after the failure of his marriage, more than his most difficult undercover missions. He'd lost some piece of himself, and he didn't know where to go to find it.

That's a lie, you know exactly what's missing.

He ruthlessly pushed that thought away as he talked to Agent Alessandro about the release of Natalie's sister. They would be reunited today. There was no reason Vaughn should be there. At this point, the case been taken over by the FBI, he'd released all files potentially related to The Stallion over to Alessandro and he'd… been expected to move on.

So, he had no reason, no right to be there when Natalie saw her sister again. In fact, even if they hadn't left things so oddly, it wouldn't be his place to be there. She deserved a private homecoming with her sister.

"You know, if you'd like to be there, I can see if I can make arrangements."

Vaughn ignored the tightness in his throat as he responded to Jaime. "I'm not sure that would be…what they wanted."

"I can check, though, is what I'm offering."

"You'd been under for a long time, hadn't you?" Vaughn asked, changing the subject, turning it away from the numbness in his own chest.

The man on the other end of the line was silent for a while. "Yes, I had."

Jaime had been in the academy right after Vaughn had left undercover work, before he'd gotten on with the Rangers, and before Jaime would have gotten on with the FBI. Vaughn had taught a class on undercover work.

He didn't remember all the recruits, but he remembered the best ones. The ones with promise. Jaime had been one.

"Well, in all the tying up of loose ends, I don't think I thanked you. You sure made getting out of that situation a lot easier."

"I was just doing my job. You know how it goes."

"Yeah, I do." Too well. How often had he been doing his job and giving nothing else?

"I can ask if they want you to be there. Clearly…" Jaime trailed off, and Vaughn was glad for it. He wasn't looking for a heart-to-heart.

"I'm glad the case has been resolved. If there's anything else you need from me or the Rangers, you know where to—"

"You know, that class you taught back at the police academy…it stuck with me. In fact, there was something you said that I'd always repeat to myself, when I needed to remember what I was doing this all for."

Something trickled through the numbness. Not a warmth exactly, some…sense of purpose. Some sense of accomplishment.

"You gave a big lecture about not losing your hu-

manity, and being willing to bend your rigid moral ob-
ligations, without losing that human part of yourself.
That was…by far the hardest part. Because I only had
myself. At first."

"At first?"

"I guess it changes you, or should. Shifts your pri-
orities."

"What does?"

Jaime was quiet again, a long humming stretch of
seconds. "You know, finding…someone." He cleared
his throat. "I just assumed you and Ms. Torres…"

He let that linger there. *You and Ms. Torres.*

"Well, anyway, I've got plenty to do. But, if you want
me to pave the way for you, I can try."

"No. It's not my place."

"If you say so. I'll be in touch."

Vaughn hung up and scowled at the phone. Him and
Natalie. Yeah, there'd been a thing, but it had been a
thing born of fear and proximity. He'd known Jenny
since he was fourteen. They'd dated for six years before they'd gotten married.

What disaster would he cause if he tried to build
something on a few days of being in the same cabin?
No matter what pieces of themselves they'd shared, it
was based on a foundation that hadn't just crumbled,
but no longer existed.

*I guess it changes you, or should. Shifts your pri-
orities.*

It had. Profoundly. Not Jenny or his love for her, but
police work. It had altered him, and Jenny had never
been satisfied with those changes.

He thought about that time, about how it had been
easier, for both of them, to blame the job rather than

admit there was a problem deep within themselves. How it had been far easier to blame some failing inside him than change it. Easier for her to blame his failings too.

He thought about those moments in the desert when he hadn't cared about all the moral choices he'd made as a police officer. When he hadn't cared about anything but Natalie's safety.

He pushed away from his desk. This was insanity. He scrubbed his hands over his hair, ready to throw himself into another case, into anything that wouldn't involve thinking about *him*. Or most especially *her*.

A knock sounded on his office door and Captain Dean stepped in. "Cooper," he greeted with a nod.

"Captain."

"I've just talked to a supervisor from the FBI, along with the officers from the gas station incident, and the other agencies involved in The Stallion case."

"Sir?"

"Everyone has what they need from you, so you're free to go."

"Go?"

"Vaughn, don't be dense. You've been working round-the-clock for nearly a week, you have an injury."

"Doctors and psych cleared me to do desk work."

"Go home. Sleep. Recharge. That's not a suggestion, Cooper. It's common sense."

Vaughn could have argued, he could have even pushed, but for what? In one FBI raid, half his cases had been wiped out. Families were being reunited, people were getting answers.

The crimes that had been committed would leave a mark, there were still people to find, but Vaughn had what he'd been on the brink of losing his mind over. Case closure.

He still felt dark and empty.

Because things *had* shifted. Natalie had given him light for the first time in a long time. A priority that existed beyond cases and police work. Someone who understood what it was to put someone else first, and the complexity of dealing with the unsolved.

Natalie *understood*, in ways most people probably couldn't. The unknowns, the toll it took, the complex emotions.

And that…that was a foundation that existed. A foundation that was stronger than any he could build with his own two hands. Possibly…possibly even a foundation that no one else could touch.

Natalie was nothing but a bundle of nerves. Her mother sat stoically next to her in the hospital waiting room, and her grandmother was saying fervent prayers over her rosary.

The relationship between all three of them had been strained for so long, Natalie didn't know how to breach it now. For eight years she'd been certain her mother and grandmother's irritation and frustration with her obsession with Gabby's case had been a weakness.

It had been a betrayal. How dare they give up on Gabby?

But now…she realized they had all dealt with tragedy in the ways they could. They were all strong, independent women who had endured too much loss and hurt, and had dealt with it in the differing ways that suited them.

A nurse came through the door first, holding it open

for a woman. Though she was nearly unrecognizable from the young woman Natalie remembered, it was too easy to see Dad's nose and Mom's pointed chin, and Natalie's own big eyes staring right back at her.

Natalie didn't remember getting to her feet, and she barely registered Grandma's loud weeping. Everything was centered in on…something indescribable. This woman who was her sister, and yet…not.

Her skin prickled with goose bumps, and she could scarcely catch a breath. Was she moving? She wasn't sure, but somehow she was suddenly in the middle of the room with…her sister.

Taller, older, *different*. And yet *hers*. She was flesh and blood and *here*. Natalie reached out, but she wasn't sure where to touch, or how.

"Nattie."

Even Gabby's voice was different, the light in her eyes, the way her mouth moved. Natalie was rendered immobile by all of it, crushed under the reality of eight years lost. Of the grief that swelled through her over losing the sister she'd known, that nickname, and all it would take to…

Her outstretched hand finally found purchase…because Gabby had grabbed it. Squeezed it in her own. It didn't matter that she wasn't the same person she'd been all those years ago, because Natalie wasn't the same person, either.

But they were still sisters. Blood. Connected.

"Say something," Gabby whispered, barely audible over the way Mom and Grandma were openly sobbing.

"I don't know…" What to say. What to do. Even as she'd thought about this moment for *years*, actually being here… "I'm so sorr—"

But Gabby shook her head and cupped Natalie's face with her hands. "No, none of that."

Which broke Natalie's thin grip on composure, and soon she was sobbing as well, but also holding on to Gabby, tight, desperate. Gabby held back, and though she didn't make a sound, Natalie could feel tears that weren't her own soak her shoulder.

"Mama, *Abuela*," Gabby's raspy voice ordered. "Come here."

Then all four of them were standing in the middle of a hospital waiting room, holding on too tightly, struggling to breathe through tears and hugs.

Gabby shook, something echoing all the way through her body so violently, Natalie could feel it herself.

"Are you all right? Do you need a doctor? I'll go get the nu—"

But Gabby held her close. "I'm all right, baby sister. I just can't believe it's real. You're all here."

"They…told you about… Daddy?"

Gabby swallowed, her chin coming up, everything about her hardening all over again. "The Stallion made sure I knew."

"But…"

Gabby shook her head. "No. Not today. Maybe not ever."

Natalie had to swallow down the questions, the need to pressure. The need to understand. She could want all she wanted, but Gabby would have to make the choices of what she told them herself. That was her right as survivor.

"One of us needs to get it together so we can drive home," their mother said, her hand shaking as she mopped up tears. Her other hand was a death grip around Gabby's elbow.

"I'm all right," Natalie assured them. "I'll drive. Right now. We're free to go. We're... Let's get out of here. And go home."

"Home," Gabby echoed, and Natalie couldn't begin to imagine what those words elicited for her sister. She couldn't begin to imagine...

Well, there'd be therapy for all of them, there'd be healing. One step at a time. The first step was getting out of this hospital.

But as they turned to leave the waiting room, someone entered, blocking the way.

It took Natalie a moment to place him, because the last time she'd seen Agent Alessandro he'd had much longer hair, a beard. He'd looked as menacing as The Stallion, if not more so.

He'd had a haircut and a shave and today looked every inch the FBI agent in his suit and sunglasses.

Gabby stopped and everything about her stiffened. "Agent Alessandro," Gabby greeted him coolly, and despite the tear tracks on her cheeks, she was shoulders-back strong, and Natalie couldn't begin to imagine what Gabby had endured to come out of this so... self-possessed, so strong.

"Ms. Torres." There was an odd twist to the FBI agent's mouth, but his gaze moved from Gabby to her. "Ms.... Well, Natalie, I've got a message for you."

Gabby's grip tightened on her arm, but when she glanced at her sister, all Natalie saw was a blank stoicism.

"It's from the Texas Rangers Office."

It was Natalie's turn to grip, to stiffen. Because she

heard "Texas Rangers" and she thought of Vaughn, she wanted to cry all over again for different reasons.

Anger. Regret. Loss. Confusion.

Mostly anger. She didn't have *time* for anger, all she had the time and energy for was Gabby.

Agent Alessandro held out a piece of paper and Natalie frowned at it. "They couldn't have called me? Sent an email?" she muttered, and though it was more rhetorical than an actual question, she glanced up at the agent.

His gaze was on Gabby again, and she was looking firmly away. They'd obviously had some interaction when Alessandro had been undercover, and Natalie could only assume it hadn't been a positive interaction.

She glanced at the piece of paper, a handwritten note of all things. She opened it and scowled at the scrawl.

Once you've settled in with your sister, there are a few pressing questions I'll need to ask you in person for full closure in the case.
Vaughn

Everything about it made her violently angry. That he'd written a *note*. That he couldn't have called and been a man about it. That he'd dared sign his name *Vaughn* instead of Ranger Cooper when that was *clearly* all he wanted to be.

She didn't want to get settled with her sister first. She wanted all of this to be over. Now.

"Agent Alessandro, would you be able to escort Gabby and my family home while I see to this?"

His eyebrows raised. "I'd love to be of service, but I doubt your sister..."

"Oh, no, please escort us, Mr. Alessandro. *I* don't

have a problem with it in the least," Gabby replied, link-ing arms with Mama and Grandma. There was a battle light in Gabby's eyes that Natalie didn't recognize at all.

She almost stepped in, ready to put her own battle on the back burner. But Gabby's intense gaze turned to her. "Tie up loose ends, sissy. I want this over, once and for all."

"It will be," Natalie promised. It damn well would be.

Chapter 17

Vaughn paced. He hadn't expected Natalie to come right away. He figured she'd want time with Gabby, and it would give him time to set up everything. But Jaime's clipped message had said that she was on her way. And it would probably be quick, despite the fact the hospital was on the other side of Austin.

"Can't lie that I don't mind seeing you like this," Bennet said companionably as Vaughn stalked his office.

"Thanks for your support," Vaughn muttered trying to figure out what the hell was trying to claw out of his chest. He'd expected time...possibly to talk himself out of the whole thing.

"You have all my support. In fact, I'm going to be the nice guy here and tell you that a simple apology probably won't cut it."

"You don't even know what the hell is going on." But apparently he was transparent because everyone seemed to know.

"You're right, I don't. But I know you're all tied up in knots, and I'd put money on the hot little hypnotist—"

At Vaughn's death glare, Bennet didn't even have the decency to shut up. The jackass laughed.

"Yeah, you're hooked."

"Define hooked," Vaughn growled.

"Going feral any time anyone even begins to mention her was the first hint."

Vaughn wanted to argue with him just for the sake of arguing with him, but Natalie was on her way over here, and he didn't have time. "So maybe something happened," he admitted through gritted teeth.

"And you screwed it up, of course. I'm not one to tell you what to do, Vaughn," Bennet began, all ease and comfortable cheerfulness.

When Vaughn snarled, Bennet laughed.

"Okay, maybe I don't mind telling you what to do all that much, but point of fact is, if you're trying to woo a woman, especially this particular woman, you're going to have to do something that I'm not sure you have in your arsenal."

"What's that?"

"Anything remotely romantic that includes putting your heart on the line. I think you're incapable of that."

"I'm not…incapable," Vaughn grumbled, but he was a little afraid that he was. Afraid that no matter what he decided about trying to start something with Natalie, something real, something that might turn into something long-term—a *chance*. All he wanted was a damn chance.

But Bennet was still yammering on. "Since you don't have flowers, I'd figure out a romantic gesture or two."

Vaughn might have physically recoiled at the phrase *romantic gesture*.

"Probably something she'd never expect you to do, but you do because you want her."

Damn it. He *hated* that Bennet was right. Because he'd screwed this up, worse than he'd screwed up his marriage. Because the past few days of treating Natalie like a stranger at best... He'd known it was wrong. He'd felt it, in his bones, and the only thing he'd had to do to fix it was *speak*. Reach out. Put a little bit of pride on the line.

But he hadn't. So now that he was doing it, now that he was done being a little wimp, he had to not just put it all on the line, but offer it up wrapped in a damn bow.

"I need an interrogation room, and no interruptions. Can you make that happen?"

Bennet grinned, but he didn't give Vaughn any more crap. "On it. Good luck, buddy."

Yeah, luck. Strange all Vaughn could feel was an impending sense of dread.

But no matter how much dread he felt, no matter how little he knew about putting his pride or his shoddy heart on the line, he knew that the minute he saw her, that's exactly what he had to do.

Natalie burst into the Texas Rangers offices, and after jumping through all the hoops she had to jump through to get to the floor with Vaughn's office, Ranger Stevens was there to greet her. "Ms. Torres. It's good to see you under better circumstances."

"*Are* they better circumstances?" Which was flippant, because of course they were better. Her house hadn't burned down today, and she'd been reunited with her sister.

But she was angry, and she wanted to fling her anger at everyone who got in her way. Every second she was away from Gabby, she was going to be angry.

"Follow me," Ranger Stevens offered, sounding far too amused.

She followed him, pausing at the door to an interrogation room. It was the interrogation room where she'd all but signed Herman's death warrant. Where she'd set everything into motion, because she hadn't been able to keep her mouth shut.

She wasn't foolish enough to think that had put *everything* into motion. Obviously the FBI had had its own thing going on. It was happenstance she had gotten mixed up in it.

It was all *too* much, and Vaughn—the man who'd been *silent* for *days*—had the gall to send her a note— a *note*!—to answer more questions.

She ignored the part where she'd been silent too. Because she was afraid if she let go of any of her rage, she'd simply fall apart.

"He's waiting."

She scowled at Stevens, but then she entered the room on that last wave of fury.

Vaughn stood with his back to her, his palms pressed to the interrogation table. It hurt to look at him. To look at him and not touch him. It seemed that seeing Gabby this morning had broken that dam of feeling that she'd been hiding behind since she'd shot the man who'd kidnapped Gabby.

She'd been numb for days, but now, all she could do

was *feel*. All she could seem to do was hurt. She was afraid she was going to cry, but she swallowed it down as best she could.

"You summoned."

Vaughn turned, and she wasn't prepared for those gray-blue eyes, the way the sight of his body and mouth trying to curve in a smile slammed through her.

She wanted to hug him and to cry into his shoulder. She wanted *him*.

But despite that a world of emotion *seemed* to glitter blue in those smoky eyes, he merely gestured to a seat at the table. "Have a seat, Ms. Torres."

"I think you're damn lucky I've taken a vow of antiviolence, because I'd as soon shove that seat up *your* seat as sit in it."

She had clearly caught him off guard with that, and she felt a surge of victory with all that anger. Let him take a step back. She wanted him to react.

"Natalie, just sit down and—"

"Go to hell." Which was probably cruel, but she wanted to be cruel, because maybe if she was, this could be over, and she could move on. She whirled toward the door.

"I was going to let you hypnotize me."

She whirled back, somehow every sentence he uttered making the violent thing inside of her larger. "What?"

"It's supposed to be romantic," he returned, clearly irritated she wasn't falling into line.

"What the hell is romantic about me hypnotizing you? You can't tell me how you feel unless I put you under?"

"You gave me a whole lecture about people being unable to give information under hypnotism unless they want to, and I'm trying to show you how *willing* I am to—"

"Then just *say* it!"

"I love you."

They both stood in stunned silence for Natalie wasn't sure how long. She clutched her hands at her chest and tried to…process that. Meanwhile Vaughn stood stock-still, his eyes a little wide as if he was shocked by his own words.

"I don't…believe in a lot of…" Vaughn rubbed his palm across his jaw and then took a step toward her. "Natalie, I fell in love with you. Your strength, your dedication." He swore. "And I thought that'd go away, or dull, or… I don't want to *fail* someone else. I'm so sick of feeling like I failed, and I just wanted to show you that I'd do it anyway."

"Fail?" she asked incredulously.

"Try!"

"Oh." He loved her, and he wanted to try. He was trying to be…*romantic*. Vaughn Cooper. For her.

"Will you sit now?"

"No."

His eyebrows drew together, but before he could be too confused over her refusal, she found the courage to do what she'd wanted to do the moment she'd stepped in the room.

She moved into him, wrapping her arms around him, holding him through the ragged exhale he let out. "Nat—"

"I love you too," she whispered fiercely. Because that was such a better emotion to focus on than anger. *That* was what she should have taken away from this morning and being reunited with Gabby, not feeling *anything... Love.* Hope. Faith.

"I wasn't sure… I'm not sure I know how to go from the most important thing to me being your safety— and me *keeping* you safe, to you just…being safe. How does…any of this work?"

She pulled back a little and tried to smile, but a few tears slipped out instead. She could tell it bothered him, but he didn't rush to stop her. No, for all Vaughn's gruff, by-the-book protector conventions, he always seemed to give her the space she needed to work it out.

And hold her through it if she needed.

"My life is literally burned to the ground, and I have a sister who's been held prisoner for eight years finally back in it. I don't know how *any* of this works, but I just guess you…figure it out."

"Together?"

"We make a pretty good team."

He wiped away one of her tears, his rough thumb a welcome texture against her cheek, his mouth gently curved, that *love* shining so clearly in his eyes. "We do," he agreed, his voice rough and…true.

Because Vaughn didn't lie, and he didn't sugarcoat. This man, who understood obsessions and failures, violence and the absence of it. How to keep her safe, how to give her space.

They made a *wonderful* team, and Natalie was certain that's exactly what they'd continue to be.

* * * * *

Love Harlequin romance?

DISCOVER.

Be the first to find out about promotions, news and exclusive content!

f Facebook.com/HarlequinBooks

🐦 Twitter.com/HarlequinBooks

📷 Instagram.com/HarlequinBooks

𝓟 Pinterest.com/HarlequinBooks

You Tube YouTube.com/HarlequinBooks

ReaderService.com

EXPLORE.

Sign up for the Harlequin e-newsletter and download a free book from any series at
TryHarlequin.com

CONNECT.

Join our Harlequin community to share your thoughts and connect with other romance readers!
Facebook.com/groups/HarlequinConnection